ANNA'S

BOYS

BILL PEZZA

To Andy & Joyce,
With Best
Wishes.

Bill Pezza

Bloomington, IN Milton Keynes, UK

authorHOUSE®

AuthorHouse™
1663 Liberty Drive, Suite 200
Bloomington, IN 47403
www.authorhouse.com
Phone: 1-800-839-8640

AuthorHouse™ UK Ltd.
500 Avebury Boulevard
Central Milton Keynes, MK9 2BE
www.authorhouse.co.uk
Phone: 08001974150

This book is a work of fiction. People, places, events, and situations are the product of the authors imagination. Any resemblance to actual persons, living or dead, or historical events, is purely coincidental.

First published by AuthorHouse 8/11/2006

This is a revision of the edition first published 4/12/2006.

ISBN: 1-4259-3042-5 (sc)

Printed in the United States of America
Bloomington, Indiana

This book is printed on acid-free paper.

Foreword

Captain David A. Christian, U.S.A.

The Vietnam War was America's longest war, and dramatically shaped who I am, the goals I hold for my country, and the loyalty I feel for my fellow veterans. While we were fighting, people often said that they supported the soldier but not the war. While echoes of those sentiments are being repeated today, it's important to remember that we have to know where we have been to know where we are going. *Anna's Boys* reminds us of where we have been in a personal way. The nine million men who served during the Vietnam Era, the sixty thousand who died, and the three hundred thousand who were seriously wounded deserve more than just a footnote in a textbook. Today's veterans deserve more as well. President John F. Kennedy used to say, "poor is a nation that has no heroes, but beggared is a nation that has and forgets."

Bill Pezza, the author of *Anna's Boys*, likes to say that history is most effective when it presents a human face rather than an academic thesis. He believes that touching the heart can be a catalyst to stimulating the intellect, and that *feeling* history can fuel a curiosity to learn more. The characters and events in *Anna's Boys* have that effect. While readers may not agree with everything they do or say, and may have different perspectives of how national events are portrayed, one thing is clear, the message *Anna's Boys* conveys about our nation's obligation to its veterans is one that I embrace. Wars often create political divisions that may fog our view of the men and women who fight them. *Anna's Boys* reminds us that this is wrong.

One of the characters in these pages says, "The people who fight our wars endure them long after the last shots are fired." This will certainly be true of the men and women currently engaged in the Middle East. I hope this book turns its readers into advocates for them, even after the conflict comes to a close. I believe *Anna's Boys* will have that effect.

Captain David A. Christian, U.S.A., is the "youngest most decorated American Military Officer of the Vietnam War." He was awarded the Distinguished Service Cross, 2 Silver Stars, seven Purple Hearts, The Bronze Star, The Air Medal for 25 Combat assaults into "Hot Landing Zones," numerous other American and Foreign Awards for Valor and Honor and has been recommended for the Congressional Medal of Honor- twice. David is past National Commander of the Legion of Valor, America's oldest Veterans Organization. To qualify one must have either the 1st or 2nd highest medal for valor of the Unites States. David A. Christian enlisted in the Service as a Private E-1, was promoted to Sergeant at 17, 2nd Lieutenant at 18 and Captain at 20. David was a member of the elite Green Berets and led the 1 Division "LURPS" Long Range Recon Patrol and Recon 1/26 Infantry into the jungles of Vietnam. David was hospitalized for seven years as a result of wounds received in combat and became an activist fighting for Veterans Benefits from the State House to the White House and to the Halls of Congress. David has two brothers, Douglas and Daniel, who also entered the service from Bristol, Pennsylvania. All three Christian brothers are Disabled American Veterans as a result of wounds received during the Vietnam War.

Acknowledgments

Writing a book is an exciting, but lonely and difficult venture that requires considerable support. Fortunately, I was blessed with a host of friends to whom I offer heartfelt thanks. To my beautiful wife and first critic Karen, whose Saturday morning ritual was expanded from her usual coffee, toast, and cryptogram, to include a reading of my week's work. She laughed and cried at the right parts, which I took as a good sign. To fellow teachers Tim Reilly and Eve Mont, who bear no responsibility for the book's flaws but deserve significant credit for its improvement. To my good friend and highly capable colleague, Debbie Kanefsky, who provided thoughtful and insightful feedback for two years. To my special friend and former student, Matt Leskowitz, whose review and enthusiastic approval brought our teacher-student relationship full circle. To my friends and neighbors whom Karen and I recruited to read and respond: Luke and Mary Antonelli, Vincent B. Cordisco, Louis Quattrocchi, and Connie Zimmer. Their input was highly valued. To Dr. Harry "Doc Quinn" Quinlan, for his early and valuable word crafting. To Angela Zenzel, Bert Barbetta, Frank and Ellen McKee, John and Maryann Roche, and Heather Quattrocchi, all of whom tried nobly to assist this storyteller in his efforts to become a writer. Finally, I want to thank my talented cover artist, Al Feuerstein, for his skillful design.

I chose Bristol, Pennsylvania, as the backdrop for this story because it's the town I love. However, aside from the events and personalities from history who are obviously real and clearly identified, the characters and episodes in this book are purely fictional and any similarity to real persons, living or dead, is entirely coincidental.

The church in this book, St. Therese, is fictional, and is in no way intended to represent either of Bristol's fine Catholic parishes, St. Ann or St. Mark, or people, past and present, who are or were a part of them. This is also true of all of the other wonderful congregations and houses of worship in the town.

The story contains a fictional description of a football game that took place in 1965, but I should mention that in the actual game played that year Bristol defeated Morrisville 35 to 12. Ted Kowal was the coach of the Bristol Warriors. Tony Embessi threw four touchdown passes that day, three to Tommy Carpenter and one to Norman Davis. Charlie Kohler added a rushing touchdown and Joe Lelinski kicked a perfect five for five extra points. Clyde Light was a standout on defense for Bristol, while Nick Calabro and Tom Tootell played well for the Bulldogs. Although the 1965 game had a lopsided score, the fictional contest depicted in these pages is far more representative of the wonderfully balanced and intense rivalry that has existed between the schools over the years.

Jim Gafgen sculpted the Michael Dougherty statue mentioned in the introduction, and Dougherty's namesake division of the Ancient Order of Hibernians sponsored the project, while State Senator Tommy Tomlinson and State Representative Tom Corrigan spearheaded the fund raising.

Finally, although the book covers events that occurred during a charged political climate, it is intended to be apolitical, and presents central themes that all Americans can and should embrace. It is dedicated to the men and women of the armed forces and their families who bear such a heavy burden while the rest of us go peacefully about our lives.

Bill Pezza
Autumn 2006

Introduction

I was baptized Christine, but my younger brother called me Sissy when he was small, and the name stuck. Most people would tell you that my mother, Anna Francelli, had two kids: me and Johnny, but I know better. She had eight if you count my brother's six friends whom she adopted emotionally. Mom and I were always close, but I know that her world revolved around those boys, especially as events unfolded that had a profound impact upon their lives. She passed away recently with the joys and sorrows of their experiences deeply embedded in her heart.

We all grew up in Bristol, Pennsylvania, a town of ten thousand people located in Bucks County just north of Philadelphia. Bristol is a place with a past. It's got bumps and bruises, which proves it's been in the game, but it's a town with heart and character that has seen boom, bust, and resurgence in its long history. It was a great place for kids like us to grow up in the 50s and 60s, a colorful place with even more colorful inhabitants who suffered some bumps and bruises of their own. That was certainly true of my brother Johnny and his friends.

There's a Chinese proverb that says, "May you live in interesting times." Unfortunately, coming of age in Bristol when we did often became a little too interesting for us. Sometimes it felt like being in a multiple car pileup on Interstate 95. Each time you thought the worst was over, another car plowed into you from nowhere. We'd let our guard down and wham; we'd get hit again. Sometimes the hit came from life's daily problems, and sometimes it came from world events, but it always came. Of course the biggest crash of all was the Vietnam War. That one hit like a tractor-trailer, and for some it was a war that never ended.

Speaking of wars, Bristol can boast of a Congressional Medal of Honor winner. His name was Michael Dougherty and the Ancient Order of

Hibernians erected a statue in town in his honor. I'm told that he came to America from Ireland as a teenager, and one year later he found himself fighting to help Lincoln preserve the Union. The statue reminds me that Bristol has had other war heroes too, some famous and some not, even a couple I knew personally. In fact, it's had far too many heroes if you ask me because they come at a high cost.

When I think back to the boys growing up, my mind is flooded with images of the town that nurtured them. I see the huge Grundy Clock Tower, Bristol's most recognizable landmark. To many it offers silent testimony to the town's past industrial might, but to kids growing up, it was something much more. Sometimes people away from home have images they miss: the barn at the end of the road, the big oak tree with a swing, or the clapboard house with the white wicker glider on the front porch. For Bristol kids the image was always the Grundy clock.

I see water because Bristol has a river made by God and a canal dug by Irish immigrants in the early 1800s. The canal wasn't that good for swimming, but you could swim in the river, which my brother Johnny and his friends did all the time. At high tide they'd go to a spot they called Penny's, at the end of Penn Street, and swim all afternoon. Mom wouldn't have liked it if she knew because the river had dangerous currents. Johnny and his friends did it on the sneak, not out of disrespect, but because they were drawn to the adventure. In time, they'd be drawn to other, much more dangerous things.

I see proud, hard-working men like my dad, wearing blue-collar shirts and carrying lunch pails as they left for their jobs. Dad worked at the giant steel mill a few miles north of town until he left for his shift one morning and died before he got home, leaving mom to raise us alone.

So this is the town where my brother and his friends grew up, a proud, gritty, ethnically and racially mixed, blue-collar town. They loved it and soaked up every experience they could. I know because they practically lived at our house, and I watched them like a spy, listening in on their conversations and generally snooping around. I'm glad I did it because I learned a lot. And what I didn't learn at the time, I learned later from their endless stories.

I learned that Johnny and his friends were loyal, fun-loving guys, who were devoted to their country, their town, each other, and, of course, my mother Anna. They certainly weren't angels, but in many ways I think they were saints. If you knew them, you might feel the same way.

As I've grown older I've learned that the people who fight our wars endure them long after the last shots are fired. I've also learned that Bristol probably isn't much different from thousands of small towns across America, towns with guys who had the same fun, made the same sacrifices, and bore the same losses as my brother and his friends. But I only know the ones who grew up in my town and hung out at my house. They were Anna's Boys, and this is their story.

1- Frankie

Frankie Mayson had just gotten into the carpenters' union and was meeting with the business agent to review his benefits. He knew he should be happy about finally getting in, but with no one around to celebrate with, he just wasn't feeling it.

It was obvious from the agent's appearance that it had been a long time since he had done any carpentry work, or even hammered a nail. Wedged into his swivel chair, he looked almost as wide as he was tall, and the top buttons of his shirt were unfastened to accommodate his bulging neck. A half-eaten hoagie, which Frankie guessed was his mid-afternoon snack, was on the corner of his desk. The agent had reluctantly pushed it aside when Frankie arrived and glanced at it often as he completed the paperwork.

"The last piece of the package is your life insurance policy," he said. "How old are you? Twenty-five? Twenty-six?"

"I'm twenty," Frankie said. "Born December 18, 1947."

"Damn, you look a lot older. Must have started right out of high school. You're lucky. Lots of guys don't get in the union."

Frankie smiled at the comment. He rarely thought of himself as lucky any more.

"Anyway, I know you young guys don't think about stuff like life insurance, but it's important for the people you leave behind."

Frankie nodded.

The business manager looked him over. "So the guys call you Big Frankie huh? Are you healthy?"

At six-two and two hundred forty pounds Frankie was clearly overweight, but not nearly as much as the guy asking the question.

"Healthy enough," Frankie said, feeling his neck muscle twinge.

"Okay," the agent replied, sensing Frankie's discomfort.

"It doesn't matter anyway. As part of your package you get a $25,000 life insurance benefit. No medical exam required. And," he added with enthusiasm, "it doubles if you die on the job." The agent chuckled at that and leaned forward. "I got a quick story to tell ya about that." He treated himself to a bite of the hoagie, and as he chewed, he looked around as if he was about to give up a highly guarded secret. "I knew this broad once who was married to a union plumber. They were fighting all the time and probably heading for divorce. One night the guy has a heart attack at home and checks out right before her eyes."

"Must have been terrible for her," Frankie said.

"Yeah, real friggin' terrible. She dressed the poor stiff, dragged him to the car, and, at five in the morning, drove him to his job site and dumped him near the foreman's trailer."

Frankie leaned forward. "Are you serious?"

"Dead serious." The agent smirked. "She wanted the extra twenty-five grand."

Frankie shook his head. "So what happened?"

"The foreman arrived early that morning and saw her leaving. When he found the body, he called the cops. First they investigated her for murder, which scared the crap out of her. When she told them the truth, they went after her for insurance fraud, abuse of corpse and some other stuff."

Frankie waited for more, but the story was over and the agent leaned back. He eyed Frankie briefly and said, "So what's the moral here kid?"

Frankie shrugged. He didn't see one.

"The first moral is don't get married if you can help it. Broads can't be trusted. Second, if you're feeling real bad, don't call out sick. Go to work. If you're lucky, you'll die on the job and your survivors will get the extra cash." He let that sink in for a minute. When Frankie didn't respond, he asked, "Make sense?"

Frankie just wanted to finish the paperwork and leave. "Thanks for the advice," he said.

"Okay, I need to list your beneficiaries on this form, the people who get the money if you fall off a roof or something." He grabbed his pen and prepared to write.

"So, after all that, are you married?"

"No," Frankie said.

"Good, stay that way. Brothers? Sisters?"

"I'm an only child."

The business agent nodded. "Probably leave the money to your parents then?"

"My father took off when I was five. Mom passed away a couple of months ago."

"Hey, I'm sorry kid," the agent said. He looked like he meant it.

"So does that mean I don't get to name anyone?" Frankie asked.

"Hell no. You can leave it to your first grade teacher if you want to."

Frankie smiled and considered that. Sister Mary Therese had been a sweet lady, and the nuns at the convent could certainly use the money. Then he had another thought.

"How about friends? Can I leave it to friends?"

"Anybody," the guy said. "But let's do it. I'm in a hurry." He looked at the hoagie again.

"Is there a limit to the number?" Frankie asked.

The agent scanned the form. "Don't look like it. There's lots of space here. How many do you want? Remember, the more you list, the less each gets."

"Six," Frankie replied.

"Six!" the agent shot back. "Damn, we'll be here all day. We're talking money here kid. Nobody has six friends worth leaving money to."

"I do," Frankie said quietly.

"Six?"

"Yeah, six."

The agent still looked annoyed, but resigned himself to the number. "Okay, who's the first one?"

"Johnny Francelli."

"Spell it."

"F-R-A-N-C-E-L-L-I."

"Next."

"Angelo Marzo. M-A-R-Z-O."

"Damn, kid, are they all Italian?"

"No," Frankie said. "But what's the difference?"

"Never mind, keep 'em coming."

"Nick Hardings. Spell it like it sounds."

"Hardings, got it."

"Jimmy Wright. With a W."

"Damn right! Jimmy Wright." The agent chuckled as he wrote, proud of his wit again.

"Who's next?"

"Ralph McGinnis. M-C-capital G-I-N-N-I-S."

"The undertaker on Route 13?"

"Same family. Ralph's the undertaker's nephew. He's named after his uncle. Do you know him?"

"No, but I know the guy's the biggest undertaker around. He's got to have money." He studied Frankie for a minute. "Hey kid. Do you really think this McGinnis guy needs your money if you croak?"

"Put Ralph McGinnis on the list," Frankie said firmly. "He's my friend."

"Okay, it's your call. McGinnis. Got it. That's five. Who's the last one?"

"Billy Moyer."

"M-O-Y-E-R? Like the attorney in town?"

"You got it," Frankie said. "His son. Just put him on."

"That's six." The agent looked at the list and shook his head. "These guys your age, older, or what?"

"They're all my age. We graduated from Bristol High together."

The agent sat back and rubbed his eyes. "Listen kid. I don't give a rat's ass who you leave your dough to. But I gotta tell ya, you're young. Over time, guys go their separate ways. Friendships don't last. At least not this many."

"These will," Frankie said.

"You sure about that?"

"Positive."

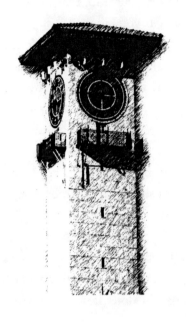

Part II
Spring 2001

2- Angelo & Nick

Angelo's Deli looked like it had closed years ago. It needed a paint job and its faded window signs advertised products that no longer existed. Things weren't much better inside, where two large refrigerated cases, one lightly stocked and the other dead and empty for years, flanked the front door. The wall behind the counter displayed an eight by ten photograph mounted with scotch tape that had yellowed and cracked with age. It showed seven teenagers dressed in tuxedoes, posing on the porch steps of a row home. The hand printed caption read: Junior Prom 1965. Above the photo was a large, dusty wall clock that had stopped running years earlier. The hardwood floors were heavily worn and had separated as they shrunk with age. Only the exposed back kitchen showed any signs of upkeep. While some people thought the place was charming, most considered it a dump. But that didn't matter to Angelo's friends who drifted in each morning.

Angelo Marzo lived in the residence attached to the store. Every morning at 6 o'clock he'd find Nick Hardings out front, standing next to his bicycle, guarding the morning deliveries of milk, bread and newspapers. Nick was in his early fifties and had been a regular for a quarter century. He had an old, burnt-orange, three-speed with pitted handlebars and rusted spokes. No one ever saw Nick actually ride it because he walked wherever he went, pushing the bike at his side. Nick's shaved head was cocked as though he had a permanent stiff neck, and he usually wore a striped blue mechanic shirt he bought at a yard sale. It had a white oval trimmed in red on the breast pocket, with the name "Ed" embroidered inside.

Nick was a pleasant looking, friendly guy who always greeted people with the current weather report. He'd say, "It's raining," if it was raining and "It's cold," if it was cold. At times he'd risk a prediction like, "It's going to rain soon," but that was rare. He preferred the sure thing of the present.

Nick's job was to bring in the deliveries while Angelo started the coffee and prepared for the day's cooking. On weekends Angelo catered events all over Bristol like baby showers, First Communion parties, and funeral receptions. During the week, he supplied lunches for office meetings and local businesses.

As usual, Nick took his seat at the single round table surrounded by folding chairs, while Angelo prepared Nick's breakfast choice of scrapple, melted cheese and chili peppers on a Kaiser roll. As Angelo cooked, Nick scanned the morning paper and began his news report. "It says here Bush is going to meet with Tony Blair again." He shook his head and added, "That's a long trip. Why can't they just e-mail?"

Angelo ignored him and hoped Jimmy would be there soon to occupy his friend.

"Don't get any stains on the paper," Angelo said, as he delivered Nick's sandwich and coffee. "I need to sell it later." Then he walked away, savoring the few minutes of silence he'd have while Nick attacked the food.

3- Jimmy

Jimmy Wright would arrive at six-thirty and take his seat at the table. Angelo would already be cooking Jimmy's breakfast choice of pepperoni, cheese, three eggs over lightly with Tabasco Sauce, and four slices of plain white bread. He had a hearty appetite for someone who weighed maybe a hundred and twenty-five pounds with rocks in his pockets. Nick would greet Jimmy with the weather report and Jimmy would always say, "I know, I was out there." The exchange drove Angelo nuts.

Jimmy was Nick's age and had taken an early retirement from the steel mill. Like Nick, he helped Angelo make deliveries and ran the lottery machine, but never on Wednesdays, when he drove Nick to Philadelphia for business.

Speaking of Philadelphia, Jimmy was an avid Phillies fan, a nut actually. On summer nights he'd sit on his porch or on Angelo's corner and listen to the ballgame on his portable radio, even when the games were televised. If anyone asked why he didn't watch the game on TV, he'd get annoyed and say he didn't like being cooped up at night. Those who knew him best understood why.

_____

It was a Phillies game that brought Jimmy the only luck he'd had in a long time. Two years earlier, in 1999, he bought tickets to a Phillies-Cubs game for him and Nick to celebrate Nick's birthday. It turned out to be a pretty good game, and they peppered each other with trivia and gorged on hot dogs as they watched.

"Okay Nick," Jimmy said between bites. "Here's one. I'm going back exactly twenty years to 1979 for this question. Who had the most wins as a Phillies' pitcher that year?"

"That's easy," Nick said immediately. "It was Steve Carlton."

Jimmy was annoyed that he got it so fast. "Doesn't count," he said. "It was way too easy."

"You asked it," Nick said.

"Doesn't matter. I didn't know how easy it was. It doesn't count."

Nick shook his head. "Fine, ask me a different one. Anything. I'm a damn baseball encyclopedia."

Jimmy thought for a minute. "Okay smart ass. Who led the team in stolen bases that same year."

"That's a tough one," Nick said, rubbing his head. He thought a little longer and then said, "I give up. Who was it?"

"I have no idea," Jimmy said.

"What do you mean you have no idea? You asked the question!"

"That's right," Jimmy said. "I ask the question and you have to answer it. It's not my fault that you don't know the answer."

"Are you crazy?" Nick protested. "You have to know the answer if you ask the question."

"No I don't. You do."

Jimmy was always a little slow, and Nick loved to humor him, but this time he was asking too much. "Okay, fine," Nick said. "I just remembered; the stolen base leader was Pete Rose."

"Wrong!" Jimmy said. "It wasn't him."

"I thought you said you have no idea?"

"I don't," Jimmy said. "But it wasn't him."

"Jimmy," Nick said, "I love ya like a brother, but you're an idiot. Let's watch the game."

Their game was interrupted during the seventh inning stretch when the grounds crew drove a new 1999 Ford pickup onto the field. The stadium erupted when it was announced that Harris Ford was donating the truck to a fan sitting in a lucky seat.

The crowd fell silent as the announcer carefully called out the section, row, and finally the seat number of the winner. Jimmy sat stunned as he heard his seat called. The guys behind him were patting him on the back, and Nick was going wild, jumping up and down, waving his arms and screaming, "It's Jimmy, it's Jimmy!" As the stadium cameras focused on the winning section, more than 35,000 fans saw the big-screen image of Nick flailing his arms while Jimmy sat in shock. Someone behind him yelled, "Stand up you smacked ass. You won!" Someone else showered him with popcorn. A plastic beer cup sailed over his head, hitting a woman three rows down. Still Jimmy just sat, staring at his ticket. Eventually, two stadium officials showed up and he was taken to an office where he signed some papers.

Then the trouble started. After the transfer paperwork was completed, the attorney for the dealership explained that Jimmy had to sign an IRS document acknowledging his responsibility to pay the gift tax on the vehicle, which amounted to almost two thousand dollars.

Jimmy flipped. "Two thousand dollars is almost all I have. What kind of gift is this?"
"It's a very generous gift, valued at over $20,000," the attorney said.
"And you're making me pay taxes on it?" Jimmy asked indignantly.
"We're not, Mr. Wright. The IRS is."
"Screw the IRS! This country owes me!" He turned to his friend. "Tell him Nick. Nothing good has ever happened to me since Vietnam. Winning the truck is good, but this stinks."
Nick got embarrassed whenever Jimmy had one of his temper episodes. Nick said to the attorney, "He's not usually like this."

"Yes I am!" Jimmy said. "Don't make excuses for me. Do you think somebody like me should have to pay taxes when he wins something?"

"Tell ya what," Nick said. "I've got some money saved. I'll pay the taxes for you and you can drive me around."

Jimmy exploded. "Like hell you will. You're the last guy who should pay it. Harris Ford should pay it. The President of the United States should pay it. Somebody who's not you or me should pay it, but not us. This prize was a nice thing and they spoiled it."

"With all due respect Mr. Wright," the attorney said, "Mr. Harris has been quite generous."

"Boy, this is really something," Jimmy said. "I come to a game to relax and have a little fun. Next thing I know you're pushing this truck on me, telling me I owe taxes, making me sign papers. I like to keep things simple. What did I do to deserve this?"

The attorney looked at Nick and Nick shrugged. Turning back to Jimmy the attorney said, "Sir, if you'd rather not have the truck..."

"Sure I want the truck. I don't want the taxes!"

The attorney had heard enough. "If you'll just sign here please, indicating your understanding of the tax liability, I'll be on my way." Jimmy gave him a hard stare and then signed. "I'll pay the damn taxes," he said, "but it ain't right."

"There's just one more thing," the attorney said. "Mr. Harris would appreciate it if you would stop by the showroom Saturday morning. He'd like to have a photo of the two of you posing with the truck. Maybe a short thank you note too. He'd like to display the photo and note in the showroom."

Jimmy looked him in the eyes. "Is the truck mine now?"

"It's all yours," the attorney said smiling.

"Everything's legal, notarized?" Jimmy asked.

"Perfectly legal," the attorney added, pleased to see Jimmy warming up to the idea.

"Good," Jimmy said, smiling now. "Go tell Mr. Harris to pound sand. He ain't gettin' no letter and I ain't posing for no photograph."

Nick remained quiet as they left the meeting. When they were alone Jimmy said,

"You mad at me?"
"Disappointed," Nick said. "You were a little rough on that guy."
"It's just that sometimes I get so mad about things, ya know?"
"I know," Nick said reassuringly. "But you have to work on being in control."
"I know," Jimmy replied. "I'm trying. I really am."

4- Nick's Letters

Events at the deli followed a predictable pattern. By eight-thirty breakfast was over and Angelo was busy preparing lunch orders. He and his wife Donna had cultivated dependable customers. Good food, prompt delivery, and reasonable prices ensured that once Angelo got someone's business, he kept it. Although Nick and Jimmy helped out, they weren't employees. Their pay was their food and a place to hang out. While Angelo cooked, Nick cleaned after him and made trips to the storage room while Jimmy stayed by the register and sold an occasional lottery ticket.

In the old days, Bristol had an abundance of small grocery stores. In fact, people often identified their neighborhood by the markets where they shopped: Bono's, Mazzanti's, Cullura's, Danis's, Morici's, Aita's, Asta's, Dugan's, Roche's, Napoli's, Accardi's, Larrisey's, Indelicato's, Franceschini's, Giantomass's, and, of course Angelo Marzo's. There were dozens of them, spread throughout town. And when Angelo's father ran the store, it was always a busy place, but that was before supermarkets put most corner grocers out of business. Now, there weren't many street customers, but Jimmy was at the counter just in case.

Angelo was proud to run one of the few stores that survived, but was sensitive about the drop-off in street trade. Once, when Jimmy playfully put a sign on the cash register that read, "Express Lane- 15 Items or Less," Angelo didn't see the humor and kicked him out for three days. It was only Nick's constant lobbying that got Jimmy back in.

At eleven-fifteen they would begin their lunchtime deliveries and return before noon. Then Nick and Jimmy would watch the mid-day news on the counter TV while Angelo served them lunch. After the news, as Angelo prepped the dinner orders, Nick would sit at the table to write his daily letter. Jimmy watched the sports channel and never bothered Nick while he wrote.

Pete the mailman would make his delivery around two o'clock and take a short break.

"Hey, there he is," Jimmy would say, when Pete arrived.
After Nick commented on the weather, the fun would begin.
During Pete's most recent visit, Jimmy started.
"Neither rain, nor snow, nor dark of night, shall keep us from our appointed rounds," Jimmy said. "Isn't that the postal slogan?"
"You ask me every day," Pete said. "It's the same answer."
"How about Pit Bulls? Do they keep you from your appointed rounds?" Nick asked.
Pete ignored him and went to the soda case.
When Pete first met Nick and Jimmy a year earlier, he thought they were trying to start trouble with their constant jabber, but Angelo assured him they were just having fun. Eventually, Pete learned to go along with their kidding.
"I bet those Pit Bulls are a bitch," Jimmy said. "Kenny Munn has a Pit Bull. Is he on your route?"
Pete scanned the few items on the Tasty Kake rack.
"You know," Nick said, "they should give you guys guns. They give them to airline pilots, why not mailmen?"
Pete pointed to the pepper spray on his belt. "I've got this. There's no need for a gun."

"That's true," Jimmy said. "You get some trigger happy mailman and there'd be dead dogs all along the route. Then you'd have pissed-off dog owners wanting revenge. Before you know it, we'd have a war, with mailmen and dog owners shooting at each other. Have to guard against trigger-happy people. No guns."

Pete checked the expiration date on a lemon pie before opening it.

Nick watched him eat for a while and said, "You should stay longer when you come Pete. Be one of the guys."

"Five minutes a day is plenty," Pete said, through a mouthful of pie.

"Now there's an idea for you guys to think about," Angelo said to Nick and Jimmy from behind the counter. "Come for five minutes a day and then get out the hell out!"

Nick ignored him and stayed focused on Pete. "We hardly know you man. Next time, stay for a while. Put your feet up and tell us about yourself."

Pete threw his empty soda can and pie wrapper in the trash and paid for the food, carefully counting the change Jimmy gave him. Then he took Angelo's mail out of his bag and placed it on the counter.

"Anything for me?" Nick asked, as he did each day. Pete shook his head. "Not today." The answer was always the same. Like every other day, Nick handed him the letter he'd just written. "Would you please see that this is mailed for me Pete? I'd appreciate it."

"Pete has to," Jimmy said. "It's an appointed round." Then he winked and said, "Have a nice afternoon Pete."

5 - Ralph the Undertaker

Ralph McGinnis was the most successful undertaker in town. Things had gone well since he took over his aging uncle's business years ago. Most of his work came from funerals held at St. Therese's church, not far from the deli. It was an old parish with an aging population, and on a good week he'd arrange as many as three burials. Ralph was a busy guy, but he'd try to stop in at the deli a couple of times a week to have a cup of coffee with the guys.

"There he is!" Jimmy said when Ralph arrived. "Welcome to Starbucks!" Ralph was the only guy in town Jimmy knew who drove a BMW. "Hey Angelo," Jimmy shouted toward the back of the store, "the yuppie's here. Is the Cafe' Mocha ready yet?"

"Make it extra hot," Nick added, "It's chilly this morning."

Ralph shook his head and smiled, "You guys are always bustin." Then he turned to Jimmy. "It's 2001, nobody says yuppies anymore."

"You drive a BMW right?"

"Sure do," Ralph replied.

"And tell the truth, you prefer that café'lattee crap to Angelo's real coffee, right?"

Ralph played along. "I enjoy a flavored coffee occasionally."

"Then you're a yuppie."

Ralph grinned. "You're hopeless Jimmy."

They had been friends since high school, and Ralph was still trying to be accepted. He was studious when they were kids, and didn't hang out at night the way the other guys did. His father drove a milk truck, but his childless uncle had big plans for young Ralph, which included college and mortuary school. In those days Bristol High had several ability tracks. Ralph and Nick were in the highest, but while Nick had natural ability and coasted through school, Ralph had to work for his grades. So on most nights when the guys hung out, Ralph was home studying. When he occasionally showed up, he never felt fully accepted. Now, thirty-five years later, he was still trying to be one of the guys.

"Hey Ralph," Nick said, "I was wondering; do you guys charge more for bad weather?"

"How do you mean?" Ralph said as he poured a coffee and winked at Angelo.

"You know, do you charge more for funerals if they're in the rain or snow? Kind of a bad weather surcharge, like maybe eleven thousand for the funeral instead of ten."

"Our funerals don't cost that much," Ralph said. "And no, we don't charge extra for bad weather."

"You should," Jimmy said. "Then you could buy another Beamer."

Angelo joined in from behind the meat counter. "Now that's dumb. How do you define bad weather? How would you bill people?"

"Easy," Nick said. "Use an index like they do for the cost of living. A person's raise may be based upon the inflation rate. Why can't a person's funeral bill be tied to the amount of rain or snow recorded that day?"

"I think he's got a point," Jimmy said. "You could make a contract listing the fees per inch. You could do the same for days that are too hot or too cold."

"That would hurt business," Ralph said, checking his watch as he played along. "People would use other funeral services."

"That's what collusion is for." Nick replied. "Get together with your competitors and jack up prices."

Angelo changed the topic. "Is there a funeral today?

"Ten o'clock," Ralph said. "I've got to get going."

"Who died?" Angelo pressed.

The funeral conversation always started with a short biography of the deceased, followed by the cause of death and then progressed to the "final judgment."

"Harry Brown," Ralph said.

"No kidding," Nick replied in a respectful tone. "Isn't that the guy who used to work at the auto body shop?"

"No," Ralph replied. "That's Harry's father. Harry worked for the electric company."

"The son died?" Nick said, somewhat surprised. "How old was he?"

"Forty-two," Ralph said. "Heart attack. It was a shock to everybody. Wife, two kids."

"I bet it was," Angelo said. "That's way too young."

"I know guys younger than that who died," Jimmy said. "Guys who were half as young." Everyone knew what he meant, but no one wanted to get into Vietnam again.

"This is different," Nick said.

"Yeah, it's different all right. "They died younger. I'd rather live to be forty-two than twenty-one. How about you?"

"It's still a damn shame," Angelo said. "I remember him now that I can place him."

"A real shame," Nick agreed.

"Are you catering the luncheon after the funeral?" Jimmy asked, trying to set Angelo off. If Angelo were cooking for a funeral reception that day, Jimmy would have known about it.

"No one asked," Angelo answered, slightly annoyed. He thought for a minute, then said,

"You know, it's coming back to me. A few years ago this guy Harry who died had a run in with Mike Hudson, from over on Pond Street. Harry accused Mike of fooling around with Harry's wife. He didn't have any real proof, but it got pretty nasty. Anyway, it blew over, but this guy Harry held a grudge. A couple of years later, Mike's kid goes out for Little League baseball, and guess which coach drafts him?"

"Oh boy, trouble coming," Jimmy said.

"You got it," Angelo continued. "Harry Brown drafts Mike's kid to be on his team."

"Bingo!" Nick said.

"The way I remember it, in the first game, Brown doesn't start Mike's kid. The kid's a good ball player, but Brown doesn't start him. He's taking things out on the kid. Mike's sitting in the stands, and he's fuming. But it gets worse. The kid hasn't played the whole game, and with each inning, Mike's closer to exploding. Now the kid's team is winning big as they take the field for the last inning and the kid still don't get in."

"Put the kid in!" Nick erupts.

"Exactly," Angelo said. "At that point the people in the stands had to hold Mike back." The next day Mike made the league put his son on a different team."

"Can you believe it?" Nick said. "What kind of a crud would do that to a kid?"

Jimmy didn't say much. He didn't like it when they criticized the dead. He thought about his own funeral and wondered if people would ask, "What kind of a crud wouldn't send a thank you note to a guy who gave him a truck?"

6- Frankie & Jane

Big Frankie Mayson lived two blocks from the store. Every morning he'd walk the kids to the Catholic School down the street and then make a short stop at the deli before work. Frankie was six-two and had ballooned to two-sixty. He was a gentle, soft-spoken man, especially with twelve-year-old Joey and ten-year-old Erin. He'd hold Erin's hand and put his arm on Joey's shoulder as they walked. Most kids their age would be embarrassed by that, especially a boy like Joey, but with Big Frankie, Joey didn't mind. Frankie loved the kids as though they were his own. Legally, they were.

Their mother, Jane, was a waitress at the new diner on Route 13 when her improbable relationship with Frankie began, and except for their ages, their courtship was a cliché. He was another lonely guy hanging out at the diner, and she was a hard-luck, single mother, working the counter. Frankie was more than twenty years older than Jane. He'd stop in for a sandwich on Wednesday nights after shooting darts at Fred's Bar and kill time at the counter, reading the sports page and nursing his food. He and Jane would exchange small talk and an occasional smile. She looked like someone who'd been worn down by life early. She had dirty blond hair and wore just a little too much make-up, but she had appealing eyes and there was an easiness about her that Frankie liked.

With no where else to go anyway, Frankie's Wednesday night visits soon grew to several nights a week.

Gradually, their chats lengthened, and she ended up sharing everything about her past. Her parents were abusive alcoholics who lost interest early. She was a poor student in high school who partied with the wrong crowd and quit school pregnant at seventeen. She had two kids by the time she was nineteen, each with a different absentee father. Over the years she had absorbed plenty of marijuana and vodka and a fair dose of physical abuse. Her parents turned her away after Erin was born, and she relied on friends to find a subsidized apartment and day-care assistance. She landed a job at Wal-Mart and swore she'd never involve herself with a man or her parents again.

It was then that she hit rock bottom. Finding it impossible to make ends meet, she began taking small things from the store. She took deodorant, lipstick, vitamins, mouthwash- all necessities that barely added up to twenty-five dollars a week, but on her budget, every dollar counted. Finally, she was caught and fired on the spot.

After a few weeks of mounting bills and free meals from neighbors, she took a friend's advice and went to see Duke White, the diner's owner and cook. She was told Duke liked giving people a second chance in life.

"I hear you had a problem," Duke said at their meeting. "Tell me everything. If I hire you and find out later that you left something out, you'll be gone."
She had nothing to lose, so she explained everything: the kids, the stealing, the drugs, her split from her parents, and her desire to make a fresh start and provide for her children.
Duke sat expressionless. When she finished he said, "I need someone to work the counter. We'll train you tomorrow and you'll start the next

day. I expect the cash register to balance. If you want to take some food home for the kids, ask me first."

Then he smiled and shook her hand. "Keep your chin up," he said. "You'll be fine here."

It was the first good thing that happened to Jane in a long time. The money still wasn't great. And the pressure of bills, long hours, and caring for the kids was overwhelming. But she was determined to try.

One night, Jane said to Frankie, "I've told you my life story, but I haven't heard much about yours. Any dark chapters in your past?" Frankie seemed like a solid guy, so she didn't expect much, but she looked like she struck a nerve. Reluctantly at first, he reached back over the decades and told her his story. It took some time, and his eyes welled as he spoke. By the time he was finished, Jane was crying. She put her hand on his and said, "I'm so sorry Frankie." Then she added, "I know how you must feel, but it's not your fault."

Frankie didn't accept that, but thought it was nice of her to say it anyway.

Their relationship began to change. Frankie felt he saw a good person trying to emerge from a troubled past. He started having feelings for her that went beyond friendship. And the more he knew about what she'd been through, the more he cared for her. Given their age difference, it seemed crazy, but that's how he felt.

He started leaving bigger tips, not big enough to make things awkward, but more than most would leave. He brought in small gifts for Joey and Erin, and in the spring he bought them baseball gloves. He picked up little things for Jane too, but was careful not to make them too personal. Because he was so genuinely kind, and the gifts were modest, Jane accepted them. In time Frankie offered to pick up the kids or drive them somewhere if Jane had a work conflict, and she gradually became dependent upon his help. The kids liked him, and that made it easier.

Frankie and Jane were experiencing something for the first time. Jane had learned to associate men with pain and disappointment, but Big Frankie was gentle and caring. As for Frankie, he had never had any close relationships with women, but Jane was becoming someone special, and so were her children.

One night the conversation turned to a movie that neither of them had seen. "I haven't been to a movie in years," Jane said lightly.

Without much thought, Frankie said, "Why don't we go?"
Jane smiled. "Are you serious?"
"Sure. We could get a sitter for the kids and go after you finish work. Maybe even stop for a drink afterwards."
She took it as a dare. They had never been alone outside of the diner before. She threw her small hand-towel at his chest playfully and said, "Let's do it!"
The night went better than either of them had expected, and several other "dates" followed. Frankie knew people were whispering about their ages, but he didn't care. She was fun and he felt good when he was with her, and Jane felt the same way about him. She told her girlfriends that he wasn't a father figure like some of them had hinted. He was just a kind, strong, gentle guy. And the kids had fully welcomed him into their lives.

Lonely people move quickly, and after less than a year, they were married. A loving wife and two adorable children had replaced Frankie's loneliness, and he never felt happier. Soon he told Jane he wanted to adopt the kids and give them his name. Then they'd be a true family. When they told the kids, Erin squeezed his neck so tightly that he couldn't breath. Joey cried and laughed at the same time.

Things were going great. As a master carpenter Frankie made good money. They were able to live comfortably, while paying their bills, including Jane's old credit card debts. They moved into the small twin home Frankie owned and every night after work, Frankie would spend a couple of hours transforming it from a bachelor pad to a warm and charming home.

7- Party at Frankie's

As Frankie patched the cracks in the walls of their home, some new ones appeared in their relationship. He had never been fond of Jane's girlfriends, who he thought were a little wild, and he'd thought her time with them would lessen as time went by, but it didn't. In fact, their weekly girls' night out had turned into two nights a week. Sometimes Jane would drink too much and snap at the kids when she got home. This eventually led to their first real argument. Others followed.

Frankie finally finished the house, and Jane suggested they have a small party to show it off. He was glad she liked the place and jumped at the idea. They invited just a few people, mostly her friends and Angelo and Donna. Nick and Jimmy always got nervous at public gatherings and declined. Frankie stocked the bar and Angelo brought his trademark Boardwalk Sausage with peppers and onions. Jane's boss Duke didn't come, but he sent a tray of his famous perogies. There were plenty of jokes and laughs, and things were going very well.

After a few beers, Angelo suggested they play some music, so he and Frankie went to the CD cabinet to pick something out. Finally, Angelo held up an oldies CD and said, "Now, here is the greatest music of all time." Soon, the Cadillacs were singing *"Gloria,"* and Frankie and Angelo were singing along in the corner, harmonizing just like they'd done in high school. Jane and Donna enjoyed watching their husbands relive their youth, especially Donna, who hadn't seen Frankie unwind like this in a long, long time. Jane was surprised at how good they were, but not Donna. She'd dated Angelo since high school and remembered their glory days, when Frankie and Angelo were part of the best a cappella group in the area. They called themselves the Tone Kings. It sounded cheesy now, but it was cool at the time. The next song was "Since I Don't Have You," by the Skyliners," and Frankie and Angelo continued their concert.

Shortly into the second song, one of Jane's friends, shouted, "Can we turn off that crap and put on some real music? Maybe something that was made in my lifetime."

They stopped singing and Frankie turned off the CD. The room grew quiet and Angelo looked like he wanted to punch the girl. Frankie looked like someone had just punched him. Jane shot a disapproving look at her friend and rushed up to her husband.
"I'm sorry Frankie," she whispered. "She's just drunk. Let's not let this ruin the party. Why don't you check on the kids and then we'll start over."
"That's ok," Frankie said. "It's no big deal."

"We'd better go anyway," Angelo said. "Six o'clock comes early."
Frankie walked them to the door, kissed Donna good-bye and went upstairs to check on the kids. On the way back he could hear laughter downstairs. When he returned to the living room, he couldn't believe what he saw. Jane and her friends were sitting in a circle on the floor, passing around a joint. The girl who had offended Frankie said, "Hey, I'm sorry big guy. I was pretty ignorant." She patted the space on the rug next to her. "Sit here and take a little hit with us," she slurred. "We'll get this party going again."
"Get out," he said quietly. They looked at him in disbelief, but didn't move. Then he shouted, "everybody get out, now!"
Jane was startled. "Frankie!" she screamed in protest, but he ignored her.
"Everybody! Get out!" He repeated. His face was red and his fists were clenched. As the guests hurried to the door, they offered quick good-

byes to Jane, who was apologizing to them and shouting at Frankie at the same time.

When they were alone, Frankie and Jane turned on each other. "I've never been so humiliated. How can you do that to my friends?" she shouted. "Besides, what's the big deal? When did you become such a stiff?"

Frankie looked shocked. "You were willing to smoke marijuana with the kids in the house? How could you do that?"

"They were asleep Frankie. It was no big deal," she sighed. "Besides, you're not my father!"

"They could have seen you with it," he said, ignoring her comment.

"They're my kids Frankie and you're more worried about it than I am. It was nothing."

Frankie couldn't believe what he'd just heard. "Your kids? I thought they were our kids," he said sadly. Then he turned and went upstairs.

The next day Jane apologized and blamed her behavior on the booze.

"When I drink I say things I don't mean," she said.

Frankie fought the urge to suggest that she drink less. Instead, he said he probably overacted and was sorry if he embarrassed her in front of her friends. Then he kissed her on the forehead and changed the subject.

Neither apology was sincere, and over the next couple of weeks it showed. Frankie was clearly hurt and Jane still seemed resentful. She became subdued, almost distant. Then one morning Frankie awakened to the smell of fried bacon and coffee brewing. When he shuffled into the kitchen, he was surprised to find four places set at the table and Jane cooking a full breakfast. "Good morning," she said cheerfully and gave him a hug and a long kiss.

Frankie noticed the kids' freshly ironed school uniforms hanging from the closet doorknob.

"What are you doing up?" he asked.

Jane usually slept in when she didn't work the breakfast shift and Frankie would wake up the kids, give them some cereal and walk them to school before work.

"I thought it might be nice if we got up earlier today and spent some quality family time before we begin our day," she said. "We have scrambled eggs, bacon, home fries, toast, cereal and coffee. Why don't you wake the kids and I'll finish getting things ready."

Frankie was elated. Jane was more animated than she'd been for weeks, and he was eager to roll with it.

The change in mood was infectious. The kids talked about school and their friends, and everyone laughed a lot. Jane mentioned she loved each of them. After the kids got ready for school, she gave them an extra long hug and said she loved them again. As Frankie led the kids out the door, she gave him a kiss too. She watched them from the doorway as they walked off. As always, Frankie held Erin's hand and rested his free arm on Joey's shoulder.

8- Jane's Letter

Life seemed better for Frankie that morning. He was working in town, and at lunchtime he decided to visit Jane on her day off. He stopped at Bristol Florist on the way home to pick up a flower arrangement. The house was empty when he got there. The breakfast dishes were gone, and so was the usual clutter in the TV room. The kitchen and bathroom smelled like they were freshly cleaned. He put the flowers in water and was ready to leave when he noticed an envelope on the kitchen table with his name on it.

Everyone knew something was wrong when Frankie walked into the deli. He looked terrible. He went straight to the back where Angelo was cooking and held out Jane's note without saying a word. His hand was shaking. Angelo eyed it like a bomb. Then he wiped his hands, unfolded the note and read.

Dear Frankie,

No one knows better than you that I can make some awfully bad decisions and I know I'm making the worst decision of my life right now. The problem is that I just can't help it.

I've never had a chance to really have fun. From the time I quit high school my back has been against the wall because of the kids. I love them more than anything, but I resent them too. I've missed so much of my life by taking care of them.

I have to live Frankie. I have to see and do things I've missed. I hope you know that I truly love you and always will, but you're too good for me. I guess a shrink would say that I'm leaving because I'm afraid to try to live a normal life, surrounded by good people. Maybe he'd be right. All I know is that I have to go.

Somehow you'll have to explain this to the kids. At least I carried them, and that should mean something. But you've given them more genuine love in this short time than I have their entire lives. I know you'll be good to them Frankie, and that somehow you'll think of something to say to them that won't hurt too much.

Love,
Jane

Angelo shook his head. "Jesus, Frankie. That's rough. Real rough," he said, handing back the letter.
"I'm not surprised she did it," Frankie said. "It hurts real bad, but like I said when we talked before, it was worth it."

Angelo thought back to when Frankie first told him he was going to marry Jane.

"Frankie, you're a brother to me," he had said, "and it's been great seeing you this happy. But she's so young. It's going to be tough to make it last. I hope you've thought this through."

He remembered Frankie's reply.

"Let me tell you about my cousin Maryann from Philly. She was a quiet girl. Didn't get out much. Didn't see many guys. She was in her thirties and still living at home. Then, all of a sudden, she starts dating some guy and she's on top of the world. Her parents are happy too. Then she finds out that the guy's married and still living with his wife. My Aunt Mary and Uncle Joe are sick over it. Maryann says she's going to break up with him, but she doesn't. It's a big family crisis. Finally, my aunt tells me that uncle Joe's a wreck. He's taking pills for his nerves. Maryann has moved into an apartment and she's still seeing the guy. My aunt's afraid Uncle Joe's gonna hurt somebody. Then she says that maybe I should talk to her.

"When I get to Maryann's, she does the talking. She tells me about her rotten past. No dates, no prom, no Valentine's, no nothing. Now she's got a guy in her life. She says when she first heard about his wife she was going to leave him. But then she thought about her old life and changed her mind. She said that she hoped he would leave his wife some day, even though she knew he wouldn't. Then she said something that really floored me. She said she'd rather be a man's second woman than no man's woman at all. 'This man has given me a life,' she said, 'filled with real people and real problems. It's not the life I wanted, but it's better than the life I had.' Then she said, 'I've been alone too long, Frankie, and I don't want to be alone anymore.'"

Frankie had looked Angelo in the eyes back then and said, "I don't want to be alone anymore either."

Angelo's thoughts returned to the present. "So now what?" he asked.

Frankie shook his head. "I take care of the kids and wait. See if she comes home."

Angelo asked his next question very carefully. "What if she doesn't come back?"

Frankie was quiet for a while before answering. "If she doesn't come back, I'll raise those kids, give 'em a good home and find a way to send them to college. They're great kids. They deserve better than they've gotten."

Part III
1957
School Days

9- Johnny and Frankie

Frankie Mayson and Johnny Francelli had an exceptional bond growing up. By the time they were eight, they had made the woods near the old Delaware Canal their special place. They went there every Saturday to climb trees and play. By children's standards the woods were vast, so they chose a large, uprooted oak by the canal as their base and called it the log. The log's first penknife carving dated back to fifth grade; it read, "Johnny F. 1957."

In the woods their imaginations flourished. They loved finding stuff near the canal like beer bottles, tires, and rusted tools, and made up stories about the people who left them. When they played army they could be Davy Crockett, Sergeant York, or any war hero they pleased. They planned attacks against unseen enemies from every era and every part of the world. They fought Russians, Germans, or Chinese communists. They were Spartans, Marines, volunteers at the Alamo, and Indian fighters. Armed with tree branches as guns, they vanquished their adversaries with amazing feats of valor, and rewarded each other with well- deserved medals.

The woods held other memories as well. It was there that Johnny and Frankie brought Patty Shenk and Allison O'Brien to the log for their first kisses. When the boys were eleven they choked on their first cigarettes there, and it was there that they stashed the *Playboy* Frankie had stolen from the barbershop. The woods added a sense of freedom from their otherwise structured world.

They were tough kids, but in the woods they could let their guards down. They shared their secrets and their fears, and nothing said in the woods was ever repeated. They used the woods to hide from trouble or to find peace when they needed to think. When Frankie was cut from the seventh grade basketball team because he was too heavy and too slow, he and Johnny escaped to the woods. Sitting on the log, Johnny assured Frankie they would become great high school football players together. They eventually did. When Johnny ran off the day he learned his father died, Frankie found him at the log and stayed with him until he was ready to go home.

As they got older, the woods served other purposes. As teenagers they and their friends drank beer there. They'd chip in and pay old Davy Nelson to deliver six packs to the log. Sometimes he'd just keep the money and not show up. Other times he produced the beer as promised. They didn't drink much, seven or eight guys sharing two six packs, but they saw it as an important step toward manhood.

It was during these parties at the log that Frankie, Johnny, Nick, Angelo and Billy Moyer learned they could sing. They sang oldies, the best songs from the best a cappella groups, and everyone said they were good. They practiced at other places too, the shower in the boys locker room, the tunnel under the railroad overpass, the street corner at Jake's Arcade, and Johnny Francelli's basement, but it was at the log where they got their start.

If the woods gave the boys a sense of freedom, Johnny's house and Mrs. Francelli gave them comfort, security, and plenty of good food. The house was a row home, like many of the houses in Bristol. There were three steps leading to a small front porch. Inside were a living room, dining room and kitchen on the first floor. The only bathroom was upstairs. The homes in the blue-collar neighborhood were small, but Johnny's father had taken down the wall between the living room and dining room, creating a sense of openness. He had also converted the basement into a recreation room. Compared to some of the other homes in town, Johnny's house was a mansion.

Johnny's mother, Anna, always loved kids, and, after her husband was killed in a terrible accident, she filled the void by surrounding herself with her children, Johnny and Sissy, and their friends. Besides having her children's companionship, she wanted to keep an eye on them while growing up. So she made it clear that their friends were always welcome. To ensure they'd come, she kept a pot of homemade meatballs on the stove, supplied plenty of chips and soda, and bought a brand new TV. The incentives worked. The place became a magnet for kids. From after school until early evening, Johnny's friends came and went. Jimmy, Nick, Angelo, and Billy Moyer were regulars, and it seemed like Frankie never left. Ralph McGinnis showed up less frequently, but Mrs. Francelli still counted him as one of her boys. She greeted the kids with a hug when they arrived and another when they left. While there, the kids would eat, watch TV, do their homework together or fool around in the basement. Some of Sissy's friends came too, but they spent most of their time upstairs in Sissy's bedroom.

Mrs. Francelli had strict rules, as the kids got older. No one was allowed in the house if she wasn't home. She warned that if she ever caught them drinking or smoking, she'd make them drink soap detergent. Cursing was not tolerated and they needed to let their parents know where they were and give them Anna's phone number. And they had to clean up after themselves. Once the rules were understood, the kids pretty much policed themselves. If someone slipped with a curse, Frankie usually cuffed him out of respect for Mrs. Franchelli.

The television was the focal point of the gatherings. As kids they watched the Mickey Mouse Club and eventually graduated to American Bandstand. When Elvis appeared on the Ed Sullivan show in 1956, Anna's boys were there. Sporting events were big too. During football season, Anna's boys cheered for the Philadelphia Eagles and played street football after the games. Anna's TV was well used.

10- JFK

Fall 1960

Anna was a political junkie who wanted to share her passion with the kids, so she carefully mixed in high interest news events with the "fun stuff" on TV. Over time, the kids welcomed the chance to view special news stories, which she carefully explained. As a result, the kids watched in awe when President Eisenhower sent the 82nd Airborne to Little Rock to integrate Central High School. Bristol was a racially mixed community, and the kids couldn't understand all of the fuss about a few black kids attending school. Like everyone else, they were worried when the Soviets launched Sputnik. They witnessed the coronation of Pope John XXIII, and appreciated the day off from St. Therese's. Living at the height of the Cold War, they had practiced air-raid drills in school, so they watched with concern as Castro's Cuba turned communist, and with fear as Nikita Khrushchev, the man with his finger on the Soviet nuclear button, banged his shoe in anger on a desk at the UN. But nothing captured their interest more than John F. Kennedy's arrival on the national stage.

During the 1960 presidential campaign, Kennedy supporters surrounded the kids. Bristol was a democratic town, and most of the people were blue-collar union members, so the kids heard plenty of positive talk about Kennedy at home. At St. Therese's, Sister Catherine and the other sisters hardly made an effort to conceal their excitement over the prospect of electing the country's first Catholic president.

Anna Francelli's enthusiasm for Kennedy exceeded Sister Catherine's. She had a virtual shrine to the candidate in her living room. There was an eight-by-ten photo of JFK above the TV and another photo of the Kennedy family next to it. There were Kennedy-Johnson election brochures on the coffee table, and the candy dish was filled with quarter-sized campaign buttons from the local election headquarters. She even had a Kennedy for President bumper sticker on the refrigerator.

When the Kennedy campaign announced a visit to the Levittown Shopping Center five miles away, Mrs. Francelli pulled some strings with her husband's former union buddies and got front row passes. Kennedy's opponent, Vice President Nixon, had visited eight days earlier, but Kennedy was the one she wanted to see. She took Johnny and Sissy with her and allowed each child to take a friend. Of course, Johnny selected Frankie. The trip proved to be the most exciting thing they had ever experienced. It was the first election in which presidential candidates had visited Bucks County in modern history, and neither boy had ever seen so many people or policemen in one place. One of the rally organizers, a man named Ding, introduced himself to Johnny as a very good friend of his father's from the old days at work. Johnny was thrilled when the man escorted them to a roped off area near the front of Pomeroy's department store, where Kennedy would speak. The boys recognized some of the dignitaries on the speaker's platform as local officials, whose pictures they had seen in the newspaper. Anna pointed out author James A. Michener, but Johnny had no idea who he was. Mrs. Francelli pointed out that the Bristol Bracken Cavaliers, a drum and bugle corps from town, was on hand to perform. On summer evenings, Anna loved to sit on her front porch and listen to the Cavaliers practice in the distance. She was pleased that they had been given the honor to be a part of the senator's visit. At one point a well-dressed woman standing nearby assured them that Kennedy would pass by right where they were standing.

After waiting for what seemed to be hours, they could hear sirens in the distance. The woman looked at Johnny and winked knowingly. The sirens were barely recognizable at first, but as they grew louder, the noise of the crowd rose as well. People were straining to see Kennedy's arrival. Then the sirens stopped and a nearby state trooper's radio crackled. The trooper relayed a message to a nervous looking man on the platform, and the man approached the bank of microphones to address the crowd. "Ladies and gentlemen, I'm told Senator Kennedy's motorcade has arrived. Let's give the next president of the United States the kind of welcome he deserves." With that, the crowd erupted in applause and a band played. Then there emerged a roar from the crowd as John Fitzgerald Kennedy and his entourage came into view. At that point, all noise was filtered out for Johnny and Frankie. The senator was walking directly toward the ropes where they waited. Mrs. Francelli put her hand to her mouth and said, "Oh my God, we're going to see him." Sissy hugged her friend in excitement and said, "Look at his hair." The two boys stood there speechless. Kennedy randomly greeted people along the rope as he slowly made his way to the speaker's platform. He shook the hands of some, then walked a few feet and paused again to shake more hands. His staff kept him moving. As he approached the boys, one of the secret service agents took Kennedy by the elbow, signaling it was time to move directly to the platform. As Kennedy turned away from the rope, Frankie shrieked, "Senator Kennedy!" Kennedy turned back toward the voice. Then he smiled and walked back to the rope. He shook Johnny's hand and put his left hand on Frankie's shoulder. "Thanks for coming boys," he said. "Our country needs young people like you to build our future." Then he smiled at the girls and Mrs. Francelli and moved away quickly.

Kennedy spoke for ten minutes that day, but in the car driving home, no one could remember anything he said; they had been too overwhelmed by his presence. The boys had heard TV commentators discuss the contrast between the elderly Eisenhower and the youthful, handsome Kennedy. But the differences were far more apparent in person. There was an energy and magnetism about Kennedy that was difficult to describe. To them, he radiated something that they hadn't experienced before. And even though they were too awestruck to remember *what* he had said, the *way* he had said it provided an inspirational experience that they wouldn't forget.

From that day on, Mrs. Francelli didn't need incentives to convince the boys to watch the news; she could hardly keep them away. The whole gang watched the televised Kennedy-Nixon debates and, of course, declared Kennedy the winner every time. They wore campaign buttons to school, which certainly endeared them to Sister Catherine, at least until the idea caught on and everyone wore them. They heard the news commentators say repeatedly that the election would be close, but they didn't believe it. Practically everyone they knew in Bristol was voting for Kennedy. On election night, Frankie slept over and they sat in stunned silence as the returns trickled in. NBC's David Brinkley said it was shaping up as one of the closest elections of the twentieth century. Mrs. Francelli did her best to explain why it would be close, but the boys didn't understand. They were emotionally invested in the campaign and wanted it to be a blowout, but in the end, they rejoiced in Kennedy's paper-thin victory.

January 20th was a school day, and Sister Catherine brought a portable TV into the classroom for the noon broadcast of the inauguration. Kennedy had invited eighty-nine year old Robert Frost to deliver a poem Frost had written for the occasion. Much of the class was surprised to learn he was alive. They had read some of his poems in class, and assumed all poets were dead. But there he was, looking two hundred years old, his white hair blowing in the bitter cold. He seemed unable to see the page, either because of his age or the glare from the sun. Eventually, he put the new poem aside and recited from memory a poem he had written about America some time before, called, "The Gift Outright." It was a poem they had read in class, and Sister Catherine was pleased that the students recognized it.

Then Chief Justice Earl Warren prepared to administer the oath to president-elect Kennedy. Johnny remembered looking at the defeated Vice President Nixon, sitting nearby on the platform, and wondering what it must have felt like to lose such a close election and have to pretend not to be bitter. He focused on Nixon's forced smile as Kennedy rose and placed his hand on the Bible. Following the oath, the class heard "Hail to the Chief" for the first time. Then Kennedy spoke. The event was magical.

The next day Mrs. Francelli had a newspaper copy of the Inaugural Address. The media had focused upon what would become his most famous line, *"Ask not what your country can do for you, ask what you can do for your country."*
But Johnny and Frankie noticed that Anna had circled a different passage. It read,
"Let every nation know, whether it wishes us well or ill, that we shall pay any price, bear any burden, meet any hardship, support any friend, oppose any foe, in order to assure the survival and the success of liberty."

11- Jake's Arcade

The gatherings at Anna's house diminished as the kids entered high school. When the boys weren't with their girlfriends, playing sports, or working part-time jobs, they were spending time at a small joint down the street called Jake's. It had some pinball machines, a jukebox, pool table, and the best cheese steaks in Bristol. The cops and everyone else in town knew that Jake was the neighborhood bookie, but shrugged it off. People wanted to play the numbers and Jake provided a service.

The boys spent what little money they had on the pinball machines, but mostly, they just hung out. Mrs. Francelli wasn't crazy about the boys hanging there, but she remembered fondly her own drugstore soda-fountain days, where she met Johnny's father, so she understood.

The kids still found time to stop in at Anna's often, even if only to say hello. On special occasions like school formals, every boy in the gang brought his date to Johnny's house first, so Anna could take pictures. On their way out each of her boys would get a big hug, but Johnny's would be the tightest and the longest. Mrs. Francelli couldn't think of a single time when Johnny had been disrespectful since the day his father died. No chore was protested and no request unfulfilled. Each time she hugged him she'd think back to the hug she gave her husband when he left for the steel mill the day he died. She remembered the strength of his arms and their brief, tender kiss. But most of all, she remembered his smile. Johnny was fifteen now and he looked more like his father every day, especially when he smiled, which was often.

12- November 22, 1963

The 1963 football game between Bristol and St. Anthony's of Trenton was scheduled for Friday, November 22, and Johnny was sky high. He, Nick and Frankie were the only sophomores starting. All week, he'd been preoccupied by thoughts of a home game under the lights, with every Bristol girl watching him play, especially Allison O'Brien. Now, in eighth period history class, his thoughts were far from Mrs. Lincoln's lesson on Andrew Jackson. Kickoff was in five hours and nothing else mattered.

Nick Hardings, who sat directly behind Johnny, leaned forward and whispered, "Big night tonight, Johnny. Real big."
"I'm ready," Johnny whispered back. "I've been ready since Monday."
"I know you are Johnny boy. I've been watching you. I see you doing good things tonight."
Mrs. Lincoln was lecturing about Old Hickory and the Battle of New Orleans, but Nick wasn't listening. He was one of the brightest students in the room, but with a football game looming, Andrew Jackson just didn't matter. He would read the chapter over the weekend and do fine on the test. He leaned forward again. "Pick off a couple of passes Johnny and you'll have ten girls waiting for you outside the locker room tonight."
"There's only one girl I want waiting, but I'll pick off the passes anyway," Johnny replied.

Then the principal came on the public address system.
"May I have your attention please?" His voice was subdued. "This is Mr. Murphy. I apologize for the interruption, but I have some very difficult news." There was a long pause before he continued. "This afternoon, President John F. Kennedy was shot while on a trip to Dallas, Texas." Mr. Murphy's voice cracked as he spoke. At first the class was too stunned to make a sound. Mrs. Lincoln gasped and leaned back to support herself on her desk.

Mr. Murphy continued. "It is my very sad and difficult duty to inform you that CBS news has just announced…" He stopped and cleared his throat. "CBS News has just announced that President John F. Kennedy died this afternoon."

There was chaos for a few seconds, followed by quiet as Mr. Murphy went on. "Vice President Lyndon Johnson will be sworn in as president shortly. We don't have much more at this time. Please observe a moment of silence for President Kennedy and his family."

There was anything but silence in the room. Some were crying openly. Mrs. Lincoln tried to comfort the students who appeared most upset. Johnny went numb. After a few seconds Mr. Murphy was back on the speaker. "We will be playing a radio broadcast through the public address system to enable you to hear additional information as it unfolds."

Questions and comments flew around the room. Some students remembered the Cuban Missile Crisis of the year before and thought the Russians were probably behind the assassination. Many wondered out loud if this would mean war. Would the Russians attack us while we were without a leader? Would we attack the Russians first? Mrs. Lincoln was in no condition to give answers. Her attempts to reassure the students were unconvincing. Some wondered about Mrs. Kennedy's well being. Someone mentioned that Caroline and John-John would be without their father.

The radio broadcast came over the intercom. Information was still sketchy and the announcer seemed to be relaying it as it was received. Johnny heard repeated references to Parkland Memorial Hospital; a guy named John Connally, who had also been shot; and the Texas School Book Depository, whatever that was. Sensing that people across the country were just tuning in, the announcer must have repeated a hundred times that Kennedy had died.

It annoyed the hell out of Johnny that they kept saying Kennedy was pronounced dead at 1:00 P.M. Central Standard Time and 2:00 P.M. Eastern Standard Time. What difference did it make what time zone he died in? In Johnny's view, the greatest president in the history of the United States was dead. Just like that. He thought back to the day he and Frankie met him at the shopping center three years earlier. It was the most exciting event in Johnny's life. He remembered the day when Sister Catherine brought the television to class so the students could witness the president's inaugural. Although Johnny remembered only a few of the words, the message was still as clear to him as the crisp January day when it was delivered. America had a new president and a new generation was emerging. The whole thing had been inspiring. Although Johnny wasn't exactly sure what he was inspired to do, the speech had instilled in him a feeling that his generation was destined to do something important for their country.

Johnny felt trapped. He had an urge to call his mother. He was never a mama's boy; it wasn't about that. But so much of his Kennedy experience had been the result of his mother's efforts, and he wanted to grieve with her and know what she was thinking. Surrounded by people he knew, he felt terribly alone. He was worried about how Sissy was reacting to the news. She had been crazy about Kennedy ever since she saw him. Then he thought of running down the hall to Frankie's English Lit class. Frankie would be good to be with. Frankie would understand what Kennedy meant to him, to both of them. They had shaken his hand for God's sake. He had spoken to them. Then he remembered Nick behind him, and felt some relief. But when he turned, he saw Nick slumped in his seat with a distant look in his eyes.

Just before the day ended at 2:25, Mr. Murphy interrupted the broadcast to announce that all after school and evening activities, including the football game with St. Anthony's, had been canceled. Students were encouraged to go straight home after school to be with their families. Within one class period, Johnny lost his president and the chance to play football. Tears streamed down his face.

Johnny's house was empty. His mother worked until four and he had no idea where Sissy was. He turned on the television. By then they were saying that the Dallas police had arrested someone they believed was involved in the shooting, but the details were still thin. A policeman had been shot in a movie theater.

Johnny went to the kitchen and opened a bottle of Coke. He felt restless. He had told Nick he'd meet him at Jake's and he knew some of the other guys would be there, but he wasn't in the mood to go. Somehow, going there now would seem disrespectful. At three forty-five it was reported that Johnson had been sworn in just minutes earlier on Air Force One. It didn't seem right using President Kennedy's plane for someone else so soon, even if Johnson was the new president. The reporter said that Mrs. Johnson and Mrs. Kennedy were present for the ceremony and that the president's coffin would be placed on the same plane to be flown back to Washington. Johnny couldn't imagine what that trip would be like for Mrs. Kennedy.

He started pacing. Events were unfolding around him and he felt isolated. Just then the phone rang and he answered it.
"Hi Johnny," the voice said. "It's Jill."
Johnny rolled his eyes. Jill Smith had been chasing him for a long time. She was good looking and he liked her okay, but she didn't seem to get it that Allison O'Brien was his girl.
"I'm calling to see how your are. Isn't this awful? I don't know what to do."
"It's terrible," Johnny agreed.
"I just can't believe it. I keep hoping that someone will say it was all a big mistake."
"I know what you mean," Johnny said distantly. He thought about Coach Lukins, who was always saying that football was a game of inches. Inches matter, coach always said. Why couldn't the shooter have missed by a couple of inches? Why couldn't the news report have been

that someone shot at the president in Dallas today, but the president escaped injury?

"Why would anyone do this?" Jill asked. "Who is this man Oswald they're talking about on television? He looks so weird."

Johnny looked at the screen and saw a man wearing a white undershirt being led down a hallway through a crowd of police and reporters.

"I don't know Jill. I'm just seeing it now. Is he the person they think killed the president?"

"That's what they're saying," she said.

Johnny looked at the screen again. He wondered how such a creepy, insignificant looking person could strike down the most powerful man in the world and cause such sorrow.

"And did you hear that they're going to make Johnson the president?" Jill asked.

"They already did," he replied. "He was sworn in a little while ago."

"But why him?" She asked.

What kind of a question was that? Johnny thought. Obviously Civics wasn't Jill's specialty. "He was the vice president," Johnny replied flatly.

"Who cares?" she said defiantly. "They should keep Johnson as vice president and let the president's brother Bobby be president."

Johnny needed the conversation to end. "They can't," he said patiently. "The law says the vice president becomes president."

Jill didn't budge. "That's a stupid law."

Johnny didn't respond. He didn't want to be rude, but he was trying to think of a way to get off the phone.

Jill filled the silence. "Have you ever seen Johnson's ears?" she asked.

He had, but he didn't see the relevance. "Yes, why?"

"Did you ever notice how big they are?"

Again he chose not to participate.

"Kennedy was so handsome and young-looking," Jill said. "Johnson looks like," she paused to search for the right word. "I don't know what Johnson looks like. But I know this, things will never be the same again."

"I think you're right," Johnny said, as he turned up the volume to the television.

Sissy and Mrs. Francelli looked devastated when they got home. The three of them hugged and exchanged stories about where they were when the news broke. Then they sat together and watched the images unfold.

The events of the next three days became seared into the psyche of the nation. The worst part of Friday night was the coverage of Air Force One landing in the early evening darkness at Andrews Air Force Base in Washington. They watched the president's coffin being taken from the plane and saw Jackie walk from the plane to the hearse, escorted by Bobby Kennedy. She was still wearing the same blood-splattered suit she had on when the president was shot. In news footage from earlier that day she had looked radiant. At times the crowds that lined the motorcade route in Dallas seemed to be reacting to her as much as they reacted to the president. Now she looked so fragile. Her expression was trance-like. The contrast was incredibly painful to watch and Sissy and her mother cried, while Johnny sat there feeling numb.

President and Mrs. Johnson stepped off the plane and went directly to a bank of microphones.

This is a sad time for all people, Johnson said. *We have suffered a loss that cannot be weighed. For me it is a deep personal tragedy. I know the world shares the sorrow that Mrs. Kennedy and her family bear.* Then he looked directly into the cameras and added, *I will do my best. That is all I can do. I ask for your help and God's.*

Johnny felt torn. He hated the fact that Kennedy's charismatic and vibrant leadership would be replaced by this older man who seemed to lack any of Kennedy's qualities. But he couldn't help feeling sorry for him. "I will do my best, that is all I can do," Johnson had said. It wasn't exactly on a level with Kennedy's Inaugural Address, but it was real. Johnny thought back to his conversation with Jill. Things certainly would be different.

The news coverage continued all day Saturday. There were memorial services across the country and around the world. Former Presidents Eisenhower and Truman spoke about the strength of democracy and the continuity of government. Congressional leaders promised a spirit of legislative bipartisanship. Foreign Heads of State streamed in to the capital to pay their respects. Prominent artists, writers and educators offered poignant memories of the slain president who had done so much for the arts. As information about the funeral arrangements was released, people developed an overwhelming sense of history.

Frankie showed up looking pretty bad and joined the family in front of the TV. After hearing more about Oswald, the boys decided to go to Jake's.

When they got to the arcade, most of the guys were there. Nick and Jimmy were shooting a quiet game of pool. Angelo was eating a cheese steak at the counter and watching the television broadcast with Jake. Nick greeted them first. "Hey, where have you guys been?"
"Didn't feel much like coming out last night," Johnny said.
"Me neither," Frankie added.
"I know what you mean," Nick replied.
"Can't stay in the house though," Jimmy said. "My mother has been crying all day."
"Stella's the same way," Jake called from the counter. "I can't get her to shake it." Stella was Jake's wife. They had an apartment in the rear of the arcade.

"I feel like we should be doing something for the Kennedys," Nick said. "But I don't know what."

"There's the son of a bitch!" Angelo interjected, wiping some grease from his mouth.

Oswald was on the TV screen again. It was the same crowded scene in the police station that Johnny had seen at least a dozen times.

"I bet those cops are beating the crap out of him," Angelo said.

"I hope they are," Jimmy said.

"Maybe some serious shots to the head with a thick phone book," Nick added.

"Do you think they'll do that?" Frankie asked innocently.

"Are you kidding?" Angelo said through a mouth full of cheese steak. "Forget about the president for a minute. The crazy bastard killed a cop. Officer Tippet or something like that. I guarantee you he's getting the crap kicked out of him in the back room."

"No way," Frankie said. "The FBI is there. They won't let that happen."

Angelo looked at Frankie like he was a child. "The guy killed the president! All bets are off. Trust me; they're bouncing him around pretty good."

"Like I said before," Jimmy added. "I hope so."

Jake jumped in. "You wait a while," he said. "I'm telling ya, that guy that killed the president works for the mafia. You'll see. It's going to come out."

"Where did you get that idea?" Nick asked.

"This is Bobby Kennedy's fault," Jake said. "Ever since he's been attorney general, he's been bustin' the chops of the racketeers, the big guys. I think they had enough of him and took out his brother."

Jake had a way of relating almost anything to organized crime. But he did have some credentials. Word was that he rented his pinball machines from vendors who were connected, and everyone knew Jake used the arcade as a front to book numbers and horse bets. Once a month a carload of nasty looking thugs from Trenton visited the store and Jake kicked all the young guys out. Angelo said the visits were to collect a piece of Jake's action. But in spite of his credentials, no one in the arcade was buying Jake's theory.

Johnny and Frankie ordered sodas and sat at the counter. The network was showing highlights of Kennedy's presidency. They showed him giving a commencement address at American University, and said he spoke eloquently about peace in a nuclear age. Next came a clip of Kennedy's speech at the Berlin Wall.

"I was in Berlin after the war," Jake said. "It was a mess. We bombed the hell out of it; then we rebuilt it. Now, the goddamned communists put up the Berlin Wall. It was like putting a whole city in prison. You guys should hear this," he said, turning up the volume. Kennedy was speaking to thousands of people.

"There are many people in the world who really don't understand, or say they don't know what is the great issue between the Free World and the Communist world." He paused for emphasis and then said emphatically, *"Let them come to Berlin."* The crowd loved it and cheered wildly. *"There are some who say that communism is the wave of the future."* This time he added even more defiantly, *"Let them come to Berlin."* By now the crowd was caught up in the refrain and erupted into a continuous cheer. Kennedy raised his voice to be heard above them. *"And there are some who say in Europe and elsewhere we can work with the Communists. Let them come to Berlin."* The scene was electric. A sea of free people living in a walled off city were embracing a foreign leader in a way that hadn't been seen before. Kennedy allowed the noise to subside before continuing. *"And there are even a few who say that it's true that communism is an evil system, but it permits us to make economic progress."* This time he said in German, *"Laßt sie nach Berlin kommen. Let them come to Berlin!"* With that, the cheers grew to a sustained roar. *"Freedom has many difficulties and democracy is not perfect,"* Kennedy continued *"but we have never had to put a wall up to keep our people in…"*

The most inspirational moment came when he said that there was no prouder boast a person in the modern world could make than to say that he was a citizen of Berlin. Again the crowd went wild, chanting, "Ken-na-de, Ken-na-de." It gave Johnny chills.

"You have to admit," Jake said when it was over. "The guy had something. He really did." No one disagreed.

The broadcast turned to the funeral arrangements. Kennedy's casket would be at the White House for private viewing by family members and dignitaries. Around 1 o'clock on Sunday there would be a solemn procession of the president's casket from the White House to the Capitol Rotunda where it would lie in state for public viewing. The funeral would be Monday morning at St. Matthew's Cathedral.

"We should go," Jimmy said quietly.

"Go where?" Angelo said

"To see it," Jimmy replied.

"See what? Angelo said. "What the hell are you talking about?"

"We should go to Washington to see the president's casket!" Jimmy said boldly. "Everybody is doing something. We should too," he added.

Jimmy was a follower, never much of an idea man, and the other guys were surprised that he was offering one.

"No way," Nick said, the city will be packed.

"Who cares?" Jimmy said.

"Never happen," Johnny said. "My mom would never let me go."

"Neither would my parents," Nick said.

Angelo liked the idea. "So we don't tell them," he said, still chewing the last bite of his sandwich.

"Are you serious?" Frankie asked. "We just go to Washington and not tell anyone?"

"You can tell whoever you want, if you're allowed to go," Angelo said. "But if I tell my parents they'll say no. So if we go, I'm not telling them."

"If we go? You're talking like it's going to happen," Johnny said.

"Why not?" Angelo asked. "I think Jimmy has a great idea. We're all feeling like crap, let's do something to show our respect."

Jimmy looked proud. The other guys were quiet for a few seconds, considering the idea.

Frankie broke the silence. "It's too far away."

"It's a three hour drive!" Angelo said. "We went there for our eighth grade class trip. It's no big deal."

"So how do we get there?" Nick asked. "Train, bus?"

"I don't know," Angelo said. "I don't know the schedules, or even if they run on Sundays. I don't know how much it costs either."

Jimmy was excited. It seemed like the idea was catching on. "How much could a train be?" he asked.

"A round trip ticket to Washington for all of us? Forget it. It will cost plenty," Nick said. "None of us has that kind of money."

"I wish someone could drive," Jimmy said.

"Me too." Nick added, sounding now like he would go if they could figure out a way. But no one owned a car and only Nick had gotten his license yet. His parents rarely let him use the car for anything.

"We could chip in for gas money, " Jimmy continued.

Jake moved away from the counter. Over the years he had learned when it was better not to hear some of the things the guys were plotting.

They were quiet again, still thinking.

Finally, Frankie said, "I would go Jimmy if we had a way to get there."

"Me too," Nick said. "I definitely would."

"Then let's figure it out," Angelo said. "There's got to be a way."

"There is." Johnny said. "I think I know someone who can take us."

"You can't ask your mom," Frankie said. "If she says no our parents will find out and we'll be stuck."

"I wasn't planning on asking my mom. Plan on going Sunday after church."

Ten o'clock Mass at St. Therese's was filled, as churches always are in times of tragedy.

It was at times like these when Father Creeden felt most inadequate. He knew that the assassination would send people searching for answers, and he had none. It was difficult enough helping grieving families at a time of loss. Ever since the news broke, he wondered how he would approach a tragedy of this magnitude. So he did what he always did when he lacked confidence. He prayed.

Following the Gospel, Father Creeden paused to scan the people in front of him. He smiled before speaking. For many, it was the first time they saw someone smile in two days.

"Given the circumstances, I've decided to make President Kennedy's passing the subject of my homily," he began. "Before I do, I want to say that I won't be speaking of him as a Catholic president, although he certainly was our beloved first Catholic president who broke that all important barrier of prejudice. And I won't be speaking of him as a democrat, although he certainly was a democrat, beloved in this working class town of democrats. And I won't be speaking of him as a flawless person, because, like all of us, he was flawed. I will be speaking of him as a person who had the potential to unite and uplift all of us, regardless of our political or religious persuasion. So I ask this morning that you join with me in remembering John Kennedy as someone who transcended political labels and whose death teaches us some important lessons."

He took a deep breath and continued. "As we gather today during this time of profound sadness, we are filled with questions. Why did this happen? Why was a man so full of life taken so suddenly? Why must this good nation be subjected to such pain? Unfortunately, I don't have the answers to these questions. No one does. But I do know this. There is tremendous redemptive power in tragedy. I know that suffering makes us stronger. I know that heartbreaks such as this cause us to reflect upon the importance of life, to examine ourselves. I know that when parents see the president's beautiful young children, suddenly left fatherless, it should cause them to reflect upon their relationship with their own children. I know that when married couples witness Jackie Kennedy's grief, it should cause them to reflect upon their relationship and take nothing for granted. We should use this tragedy as a stark reminder that each day is precious. If we do this, then something good will have come from this tragedy."

Father paused and smiled again before continuing.

"As true as these words are, you've heard them before. They relate to the untimely death of anyone, but the death of President Kennedy has much broader implications. It is a loss of national and international importance. So I understand why a woman stopped me yesterday and said, 'Father, why did God take such a wonderful gift from us?' It's a question I know many of you share. But I prefer to look at things differently. I'd like to think of John Fitzgerald Kennedy as a gift that God gave us, not a gift that he took away. John Kennedy was a man who spoke eloquently of peace abroad and social justice at home. To the millions of struggling people living under communist oppression behind the iron curtain, John Kennedy was a gift of hope. For millions of our fellow black Americans, John Kennedy was a gift of promise, and to all of mankind living under the fear of imminent nuclear disaster, John Kennedy was a gift of reason. And most important perhaps, to a new generation of young people, John Kennedy was a gift of inspiration."

Father took a deep breath. "So now I have a question for you. Who are we to expect this gift to last forever? How many times did we need to hear President Kennedy's call before we answered it? John Kennedy was a realist who understood the dangers and complexities of politics and diplomacy. So he moved slowly in educating us and cautiously in dealing with his adversaries. But at the same time he extended a bold challenge to each of us to be better, better as a nation and better as a people. What hurts so much is that he inspired so many to follow his lead, and now our leader is gone." He paused for emphasis. "What will we do now?"

"I don't profess to know God's plan in all of this, but perhaps John Kennedy's death, after such a short time with us, will cause each of us to focus more upon the things he stood for, things people of all political persuasions can adhere to. Perhaps his parting will anger us enough to say that we will not let the principles he stood for die. Perhaps his passing will motivate our youth to take up the torch he spoke of in his inaugural address.

"John Kennedy was a beacon of light shinning in a dark, troubled world. That light need not be extinguished by his death. Whether the light of John Kennedy's dream for a better future will continue to glow depends upon how you and I choose to live our lives. To be right with God, it is imperative that we be right with each other. We can begin today. We can search for a way to serve, to do something good and just.

He paused to allow the congregation to reflect. Then he smiled once more and said, "May God bless John Fitzgerald Kennedy and his family. And may God help us to carry on his work for a more peaceful and just world without him."

Mrs. Francelli hosted a card and dinner get together for her girlfriends every Sunday afternoon that ran well into the evening. She thought about canceling it because of the President, but she and her friends decided they'd rather be together for emotional support than sulk alone at home. They might do a bit less card playing and a bit more wine tasting this time, but they were going to be together. So she began her preparations as soon as she and the kids returned from church.

Johnny explained that he planned to spend the day with Frankie and that they would eat together. He said he'd be home by his ten o'clock curfew. He hated to deceive his mother and took some small comfort in the fact that everything he said was true. But he felt guilty for not mentioning that he and Frankie would be spending their time in Washington, not Bristol. But it was something he felt he had to do. They kissed good-bye and he left.

When Johnny arrived at Jake's, Angelo, Nick, and Jimmy were waiting for him. Frankie arrived soon after.

"Okay," Johnny said as they gathered around the pool table. "Let's empty our pockets and see what we have."

"Are you sure she's coming?" Angelo said.

"Positive," Johnny replied. "But she won't do it unless she's sure we have enough money for gas and food. She's afraid of getting stranded someplace in Maryland. So let's see it."

The five of them put their money on the pool table. Johnny counted thirty-seven dollars.

Jimmy looked concerned. "Do we have enough money or don't we?" he asked.

"I think so," Angelo said. "I've asked around. We'll need a tank of gas each way. I figure it's eight or nine bucks each time we fill it up, so twenty bucks should do it. That leaves seventeen dollars to eat with."

"Ten for me," Frankie joked, rubbing his stomach.

"What about the map?" Johnny asked.

"I have it right here," Nick said and unfolded it on the table. "Jake and I were looking at it before you came. We go right down Route 1 until we hit Route 95. Piece of cake."

Jake appeared and handed a bag to Angelo. "Here're some hoagies, chips and soda," he said. "They're on me. I'm not crazy about you guys taking off like this. You should tell your parents." Then he added, "But I wish I was going with you. Be careful and don't do anything stupid."

The boys were touched. "Thanks, Jake," Angelo said. Then he added, "Jake, if anyone asks..."

"I know," Jake interrupted. "I won't say nothin', but you guys better not get me in trouble."

"No sweat, Jake." Angelo said. He looked at his watch. "Three hours to get down, an hour there, an hour to eat, three hours to come back. We'll be home by eight-thirty. That's if our ride ever comes."

"She'll be here," Johnny said.

Sissy arrived right on time and beeped the horn. The boys said good-bye again to Jake, went outside, and piled in to the Chevy Bel Air.

When Johnny first said he could get his sister to drive them in the family car, no one thought it would happen. Sissy was a senior and a good driver, but she was pretty straight, and they couldn't imagine her sneaking off with her mother's car. But Johnny knew how she felt about Kennedy. As soon as Johnny asked her, he could tell she wanted to go, but was afraid. It took some convincing that they could pull it off, and when their mom said that she was going ahead with her Sunday card party, that sealed it. This was one day when Johnny was glad that almost no one in Bristol had a driveway. Their mom wouldn't notice the car was gone from their crowded street.

Jake waved good-bye to the kids and went back to the counter to turn on the television. In a minute he couldn't believe what he was seeing. *"I repeat,"* the announcer said. *"Lee Harvey Oswald, the accused assassin, has been shot while being transported by Dallas police from the Dallas City Jail. As many of you saw live here on NBC, Oswald was in the lower level of the police station and was flanked by police officials when an assailant stepped out of the crowd and shot him. We have unconfirmed reports that Oswald is dead. We will replay the scene for you now."*
Jake watched in disbelief as Oswald appeared on the screen. He was handcuffed and escorted by men in suits and cowboy hats. A short, stocky man simply stepped forward and shot him at point blank range. The guards wrestled the gun from the assailant as Oswald grimaced and fell to the floor. It was the most incredible thing Jake had ever seen on television.
The announcer continued. *"We have just learned that the assailant's name is Jack Ruby. He was distraught over the assassination and told police he didn't want Mrs. Kennedy to go through the pain of a long trial for Oswald."*
The announcer looked at the camera and shook his head slightly. *"Once again, we have confirmed reports. Lee Harvey Oswald, President Kennedy's accused assassin, is dead."*

Jake went in to the apartment to find Stella.

13- The Rotunda

Anna was awakened at 6:00 AM on Monday by a phone call from Frankie's mother.

"Anna, this is Kathy Mayson. I'm terribly sorry to disturb you at this hour, but I'm so worried. Frankie didn't come home last night. I went to bed early, but when I checked in on his room this morning, his bed hadn't been slept in. Have you seen him?"

Anna was still not fully awake. The wine had flowed more freely the night before, and she had slept deeply. Anna knew that Frankie's mother had been ill for some time and didn't want her to be upset.

"That's ok, Kathy," she said. "He and Johnny were together yesterday, and I went to bed before they got home. Maybe he just decided to sleep here last night although it was a school night. Let me go check for you." She was back in a minute. "Kathy, they're not upstairs. I bet they fell asleep in the basement watching TV. Let me check and I'll call you back."

She walked down the basement steps, confident that she'd find them asleep on the couch and easy chair. She didn't. Worried now, she went quickly back upstairs to see if Sissy had seen the boys the night before. It was almost time to wake her for school anyway. When she discovered that Sissy's room was empty too, her concern turned to fear. Kathy Mayson had been battling diabetes for a long time, and Anna didn't want to frighten her. Still, when she called Frankie's mother back, she sounded shaken.

"Kathy, they're not here, and Sissy is gone too."

"Oh, my God," Mrs. Mayson said. "Where could they be?"

Anna struggled to stay calm. "I don't know, but I'm sure they're fine, or we would have heard something." She thought for a moment. "Why don't you start calling some of the other boys to see what they know? I'll try calling some of Sissy's friends."

"What about the police?" Kathy asked. "Maybe we should call them." Anna resisted. "Let's wait. I'm sure they slept at one of the boys' houses."

"Sissy too?" Mrs. Mayson asked. Anna didn't have an answer.

She dressed quickly, her mind racing with frightening possibilities. She needed to think and decided some caffeine would help. As she fumbled with the coffee pot, she noticed the hook where she kept her extra set of car keys. The keys were gone.

She raced to the front door and remembered that Sissy had parked down the street after church. She ran to the sidewalk and looked. The car was gone.

Anna called one of her card party friends who was a nurse and asked her to check with the Lower Bucks Hospital emergency room. She waited ten agonizing minutes for her reply. No teenagers had been brought to the emergency room all night. She called the families of two of Sissy's closest friends. Neither had seen her nor knew where she might be. Frankie's mother called back to say that she had called the other parents. Angelo, Jimmy, and Nick were missing too. Anna said she'd call her right back and got off the phone. She felt as if she would faint. Where were they? And why in the world would Sissy be with them? At six-thirty she was about to call the police when the phone rang. It was Sissy.

"Mom, please don't hate me!"

"Sissy," Anna screamed into the phone. "My God. Where are you? Are you all right? Is Johnny with you?"

"Yes, Mom, Johnny's right here. We're both all right." Sissy was crying. "We're sorry, Mom. We're really sorry."

Anna tried to compose herself, but was crying too. For a moment it was five years earlier, when the policeman had called to say that her husband had been in an accident. He didn't tell her Jack was dead, but she knew. Even when he told her they were sending a car to take her to the hospital, she sensed that he was already gone. She had been fighting off the memory of that phone call all morning, but it had been crushing her with fear. She had steeled herself for the worst, and now that she knew they were safe, her defenses crumbled.

"Are you sure you're all right?" Then she added with more of an edge, "Don't lie to me!"

"Mom, I'll never mislead you again. We're fine. I swear!"

"Put Johnny on the phone. I want to hear his voice."

There was a pause and then Johnny came on the line.

"Hi, Mom," he said sheepishly. She didn't respond, but he could tell that she was crying. "Mom, I want you to know that this was all my fault, not Sissy's."

"Johnny, where in the world are you?"

"We're at a rest stop in Maryland," he said painfully.

"Maryland!" she exploded. "What in God's name are you doing in Maryland?"

"We drove to Washington yesterday afternoon to see President Kennedy's casket. We thought we would…"

Anna cut him off. "You drove to Washington without telling anyone? Are you crazy?" she shrieked. "What were you thinking?"

"We didn't mean to…"

"Is Frankie with you?"

Johnny wished that he were dead. He swallowed hard before answering. "Yes, Frankie's here. So are Nick, Jimmy, and Angelo. We all wanted to see the President. I'm really, really sorry, Mom."

Anna was speechless. Her children had stolen her car and took four of their friends to Washington.

"Put your sister on the phone," she said tersely.

When Sissy came on, Anna's voice was cold. "Do you have enough gas?" she asked.

"Yes," Sissy said. "We're starving, but we're not going to eat in case we need the money to fill the tank again."

Good, Anna thought. As long as they're okay, I'm glad they're hungry.

Then she said firmly. "Sissy, come straight home. Take your time. Don't speed, but come straight home. Are you awake enough to drive?"

"Yes, I think so," she said. "We slept for about two hours in the car."

The comment raised more questions than Anna wanted to ask right then.

"If you find yourself feeling too tired, I want you to pull over at a rest stop and sleep. Do you hear me?"

"Yes, Mom."

"Promise me you'll do that."

"I promise."

"Get back to Bristol. Drop off the boys and get home! Tell the boys that Frankie's mother and I will call the other parents."

"Okay, I will, but they're calling them too." She paused a minute and said, "I love you, Mom."

Anna forced herself to wait before replying. "I love you too," she said, but her words didn't sound endearing. "Now get home!"

When they arrived two hours later, they expected a tirade, but they didn't get one. Instead, Anna pulled them both to her and held them for a long time. She looked terrible. Her eyes were red and swollen and her hair hadn't been combed. She led them to the couch and motioned for them to sit. She still hadn't spoken and neither had they.

Finally, she composed herself, swallowed hard, and said firmly, "I want you to tell me everything you did from the time you left Bristol until this moment. Everything!"

Johnny went first. He told her about the planning and the early part of the trip when things were going smoothly. Then he said, "We were driving to Washington and missed a turn on the Washington Beltway.

We saw it on the map, but we missed it. From that point on we got totally lost, and we got to Washington two hours later than we planned. By then Sissy was crying pretty bad and we had to drive around for a long time looking for a parking space."

"We looked for a spot for almost an hour," Sissy said. She looked as though she would cry again, and Johnny put his arm around her before continuing.

"Finally, a nice cop told us to park at the Union Station a few blocks away from the Capitol. After we parked we started to walk to where President Kennedy was. They called it the Rotunda. It's that big dome you see all the time on television. Anyway, by then it was six-thirty, three hours later than we thought we'd be there."

Sissy took over. "We were walking on this street called Louisiana Avenue, and I started to calm down. That's when we really felt that we were in Washington and we started soaking up the buildings around us."

"I wish you could have seen it, Mom," Johnny said. "The city was beautiful at night with the monuments fully lit. The Washington Monument was ahead to our right. The Lincoln Memorial was farther away and the Capitol Rotunda was to our left."

They told her how their attention was drawn to the dome which, fully illuminated, projected strength and stability. They said that looking at the dome was like looking at American history. Everything they knew about America's past seemed to be embodied in that image. They were drawn to it, but approached it with conflicted feelings of excitement and sadness. They were struck by the silence of the city and its eerie peacefulness.

"You should have seen it, Mom," Johnny said. "We were walking in the dark and there were thousands of people walking with us. Hardly anyone was talking or if they were, they were being real quiet."

They described the sense of sameness they felt with the other strangers. Everyone had traveled some distance to get there. Everyone was drawn to the same place for the same purpose. Everyone there had felt compelled to come. They said it was like they knew and shared the thoughts of every stranger in the crowd.

They told Anna that the streams of people blended into a river of bodies waiting on line to enter the Capitol. The kids weren't nearly as close to the Capitol as they thought they would be, and they knew the wait would be long.

"A National Park Service guard said the line was over a mile long and the wait to enter the Rotunda would be at least four hours," Sissy said. "That's when I started to cry again."

Johnny tightened his grip on his sister. "It was my fault, Mom. I talked her into it, and I really felt bad when she got so upset."

"That's okay. I wanted to be there," Sissy said.

The kids explained that it was already approaching eight o'clock. They had planned to be half way home by then. They decided to stay, not in disregard for the worry they knew it would eventually cause, but because they had no choice. Sissy was in no condition to drive right away after what she had been through. But they said they stayed for another reason too. They couldn't leave because they had become part of something they knew they'd never experience again.

They told her about the nice people in front of them in line, a couple in their fifties from West Virginia. The man's name was Stanley, and he was a coal miner. They never got his wife's name. Stanley said he had seen Kennedy in person during the West Virginia Primary of 1960, when Kennedy was running against Senator Hubert Humphrey.

Johnny said he told Stanley and his wife about the time they saw Kennedy at the Levittown Shopping Center.

"They were really nice people," Sissy said. "We got along real good."

Anna sat stone-faced but took in every word. Worries about her children had always occupied most of her time, especially after her husband's death. Would they have financial security and fulfilling careers? Would they find someone to love? Would they be blessed with healthy children? But she also worried about whether or not they would remain an important part of each other's lives. Anna and her husband came from small families and had no siblings, so her kids lacked the network of aunts, uncles and cousins that other families enjoyed. She wanted them to build a closeness that would bond their future families for life. She hoped that they would live near each other, that they would drive each other's kids to school or baseball practice, that their families would rent shore cottages together or plan family trips. She hoped Johnny and his eventual brother-in-law would go fishing together or to the Phillies' game. She hoped Sissy and Johnny's wife would bond like sisters. These were the things she wanted.

Now, she took comfort in what she was hearing. As angry and terrified as Anna had been, she felt that she was witnessing something that could have lasting significance in their lives. More than experiencing history, they were building the type of bond that she had hoped for. So she listened as her children continued to talk.

Johnny told her about Sam and Louise, the black couple from Baltimore who were behind them in line. The couple had been to the city just three months earlier for the March on Washington and Martin Luther King's "I Have a Dream" speech." Louise proudly told the kids that President Kennedy had invited Dr. King to the White House after the speech, after which he proposed a strong civil rights bill to Congress. Kennedy was a friend of Black America, and Sam's eyes revealed his fear that King's dream may have died with Oswald's bullet.

The kids said that when Nick asked Sam and Louise if they had met King, Sam pointed to the Lincoln Memorial on the far end of the reflecting pool. Its lights were barely visible in the distance. Sam explained that King had spoken from that spot and the closest they could get was about a quarter mile away. Sam had told them that there were hundreds of thousands of people there that day, and it was the proudest day of their lives. Sam and Louise said they had a son in college who wanted to join the Freedom Riders down south a couple of years ago, but they wouldn't let him because they were too afraid. The kids had no idea what Freedom Riders were, but they listened politely.

"The line was moving really slowly," Johnny said. "And the park rangers announced that they were shortening the time people could spend in the Rotunda. They said they would keep the Rotunda open all night if they had to, but they would have to cut it off in the morning because the casket had to be moved for the funeral mass at St. Matthew's Cathedral at ten."

"I was afraid we wouldn't get in," Sissy said.

They described how cold it got as the November night wore on. They hadn't dressed warmly enough, and by eleven o'clock Sissy was shivering. Frankie offered her his jacket, but then, Louise took a small blanket out of her bag and draped it over Sissy's shoulders without asking. Nick talked to the couple from West Virginia so much that they gave him chocolate bars for everyone. They told Anna that, while they were in line, there was no cutting up or joking around. Angelo, who usually complained about everything, didn't, and no one picked on Jimmy.

They told Anna how slowly the time passed. They were cold; their legs ached, and they were hungry. At midnight Nick estimated they'd make it inside by about one-thirty. Sissy wanted to cry again, but didn't.

They said they reached the bottom of the capitol steps a little after one o'clock and found new energy. The excitement grew as the guards gave instructions about moving through the Rotunda. They would make a half circle through the round room and exit through the back. They were to follow the directions of the park rangers and keep moving at a steady pace. They were not to touch the velvet ropes that surrounded the coffin, and no photographs were allowed.

"By the last half hour my heart was pounding," Sissy said. "No one spoke, because no one knew what to say."

"We finally got into the Rotunda at exactly 1:20 in the morning," Johnny said.

They said it was the most magnificent room they had ever seen. Their eyes were immediately drawn to the ceiling, which was so high that they couldn't see the apex without arching their backs. It followed the shape of the outside dome they had been looking at for hours. Near the top it flattened out to a large circle with a celestial painting. Ringing the base of the dome were countless arched windows. They said that as their eyes dropped further, they noticed the large paintings depicting events from American history. Sissy recognized one of the signing of the Declaration of Independence and another from the Revolutionary War. They explained that as they took a few more steps into the room they saw the flag draped coffin of the President. It rested on a box draped in black fabric with black tassels. It was surrounded by eight members of the honor guard, each wearing the uniform of his branch of service.

"The men in the honor guard were as still as the statues in the room," Johnny said. He said that their shoes glistened, their buttons shined, and their uniforms were stiff and creased. The only sounds in the room came from the people's sobs and the shuffling of shoes on the marble floor. Both were amplified as they echoed through the cavernous room.

They said it was all over in less than ten minutes. Their journey had started thirteen hours earlier. At that point they just wanted to sit on the Capitol steps and rest, but the rangers kept them moving. At the bottom of the steps, they exchanged hugs with Stanley and his wife and Sam and Louise, strangers from West Virginia and Baltimore whom they would never see again but would remember for a lifetime.

Walking back they passed the people still waiting in line, and felt fortunate to have made it through. They considered calling home, but decided to spare Anna the worry by letting her sleep. Besides, they still thought they could make it home before she got up. When they arrived at the car at two o'clock, Sissy was too exhausted to drive, so they used the train station rest rooms again, drank from the water fountain and fell asleep in the car.

They slept until almost five, when they got directions from a policeman and began their drive home. They drove for an hour and a half when they finally called her at six-thirty from the rest stop in Maryland. That was everything.

They ended their story by telling Anna how sorry they were for betraying her trust. It was the last thing in the world they wanted to do. They said that they would accept any punishment she gave them, and that no punishment could match how terrible they felt for doing this to her. Then they slumped back on the couch exhausted.

Anna sat in silence for a long time, reflecting on what she had just heard. Tears started streaming down her face. When the kids saw this they cried too. Then she surprised them. "I'm so glad you went," she said, fighting back the tears. "I really am. I know that if you would have asked me if you could go, I would have said no. If you would have asked me to drive you I know that I wouldn't have. But now that you went, I'm really glad you did. In fact, I'm proud of you. I was hurt and angry, and I guess I'm still a little of both, but mostly, I'm proud."

She smiled. "I'll figure out how to punish you later. I don't think we're the most popular family with your friends' parents at this time, and we'll have to deal with that. You will obviously miss school today, and we'll have to deal with that. But for right now, I have some French Toast and sausage warming in the oven for you. Let's get you some food and then get you some sleep."

As Johnny rested in his bed, he thought about the things he wanted to say to his mother but was too self-conscious to share. Something had happened to him in Washington. Ideas swirled through his head, and he felt differently about things. He wanted to tell her how he felt about his country, how connected he felt to Washington, how he admired the men in the honor guard. He wondered how they were selected. He wondered if he could ever become one. Being in the honor guard would be a thrill, but maybe it wouldn't be enough. He thought about what it must be like to have a statue erected in one's honor, like those of the great men on display in the Rotunda. Having been in such a great building, that had seen so many great men in history, having been there during such an important time, paying his respects to a fallen President, all of that caused him to want to do something for his country. He wanted to serve somehow. It was confusing, but in a strange way, he felt he was destined to do something good. He was sure of it. Those were his thoughts as he drifted off to sleep.

14- Allison O'Brien

October 1964

Allison O'Brien was a goddess, and Johnny had worshipped her ever since their first kiss at the log in fifth grade. Now, as she stood at the front of the room in Mr. Rush's eleventh grade American Government class, she never looked better. Over the years, Johnny enjoyed seeing her evolve from a cute tomboy, who enjoyed running through the woods and climbing trees, to the beautiful creature he was watching now. Her ash blond hair fell to just above her shoulders. Her eyes were clear and blue, and her smile was bright, even radiant. It was torture having a class together because each time he saw her his knees grew weak.

He remembered the previous spring. By then their relationship had matured, and they were serious about each other. In Johnny's eyes she had become the perfect girl. She was bright, funny, pretty, and athletic. Unlike other girls her age, she enjoyed pick-up games with Johnny and the guys more than caring for her make-up or hair. But she still looked better after a touch football game than most girls looked at the prom.

Johnny didn't own a car, but it didn't matter. They did everything together that spring. They played catch, took long bike rides, went miniature golfing, shared pizzas, and did their homework at the public library. Sometimes they'd just walked around town, usually ending up at the gazebo in the park, where they would spend some quiet time together in the shadows. She was a nice girl, who made sure that their intimate time was short and modest, but offered just the right amount of affection. To sixteen-year-old Johnny, the girl was perfect.

On nice evenings, after a pizza or miniature golf, Johnny and Allison would sit on the steps of her front porch and play a game they made up. They would count the cars that drove by on her street, keeping track of the number of Fords and Chevys. Allison always chose Fords, because her dad owned a dealership. The object of the game was to see which of them would have ten cars of their model pass by first. The number was usually balanced and the game was fun. Johnny loved the fact that he was with a girl who actually recognized car models. When the mood was right, they could play for hours, laughing and talking until her parents called her in. Johnny felt that if he could have fun doing something as stupid as counting cars with Allison, then she was probably the girl he would marry some day.

Unfortunately, Allison's attraction to Johnny vanished suddenly during the summer before eleventh grade. It all started when her father decided he would take the family to Cape Cod for the summer. The news crushed Allison, and both she and Johnny were miserable over the prospect of a three-month separation. She pleaded with her parents to allow her to stay home with her aunt, but her parents held firm. They told her it would be a wonderful experience. And besides, they were growing uneasy about the time she and Johnny were spending together. Johnny was a nice boy, they said, but it was time she learned about other opportunities available to her. They assured her that there were plenty of boys at Cape Cod, and she would certainly find some to occupy her time. She was going, they concluded, and there would be no more discussion.

The night before she left, she and Johnny walked to the gazebo where she made a solemn pledge to write every day and date no one while she was gone. He, of course, made the same promises. But a summer is a long time in a teenager's life and, in spite of their best intentions, things didn't work out. After a couple of weeks Allison's postcards became less frequent, and by mid July they stopped coming. Johnny eventually gave up writing as well. Still, Allison was the only girl he truly cared about, and he would just have to straighten things out when school started. In the meantime, he spent more time with the guys, and in late July he met a girl at the church carnival who filled the void for the two weeks until his summer football practice started.

Johnny returned to school ready to patch things up, only to find that the fun-loving girl he once knew had turned prissy and aloof. Without explanation or apology, she ignored Johnny and his friends and spent her time with what Jimmy later called the smart, rich kids.

And she wasn't just acting differently; she looked different too. While most of the students at Bristol adopted the casual style of the sixties, she dressed each day as though she were meeting her mother for lunch at Wanamaker's Tea Room. She wore plaid skirts of modest length, starched blouses that did little to accentuate her blossoming figure, and liked having a sweater draped over her shoulders with the arms tied loosely around her neck. Her hair and make-up looked like she just left an expensive salon. She looked great, but she wasn't the Allison that Johnny knew.

He finally confronted her in the hallway, hoping to talk things out.

"Hi, Allison," he said cheerfully. "That is you, isn't it?" When she kept walking he realized that sarcasm might be a bad idea. So he walked with her and tried again.

"Okay, Allison. I don't know what's going on here, but can we talk for a minute?"

She finally stopped. "Hello, Johnny," she said grudgingly. "I'm sorry, but I can't talk. I'm on my way to meet some people in the library."

Probably your prissy-ass new friends, Johnny thought.

"I just need a minute," he said. "How was Cape Cod?"

She rolled her eyes. "Look, Johnny, we had some fun together when we were kids. We're older now and things are different."

"Kids?" Johnny said. "It was three months ago!" He thought of skipping the dialogue and just asking her if she wanted to go to the gazebo that night, but she didn't give him the chance.

"Good bye, Johnny," she said over her shoulder as she walked away, faster this time.

He gave chase again and grabbed her elbow to make her stop.

"Are you okay?" he asked. "What's happened to you?"

"Would you please let go of my arm?" she said firmly.

"Sure," he said, relaxing his grip. "Would you please stop running away?"

She looked at her watch impatiently.

"I asked you a question. Are you all right?"

"I'm perfectly fine," she said. "Why wouldn't I be?"

"Well, for starters, you look like you're trying to disguise your identity. What's with the outfit?"

"I don't need your insults," she said.

With that she started walking again, speed walking actually.

Johnny knew he looked silly chasing after her, but he didn't care.

"Don't make me tackle you again, Allison," he said, as he raced to catch up. Once, during one of their pick-up football games, he had forgotten she was a girl and actually tackled her. The guys had to stop the game for five minutes as the two of them rolled on the ground laughing. Now, he ran a couple of steps to get in front of her and blocked her path.

"Damn it, Allison," he said, trying to smile, "Will you please knock it off? I just want to talk."

She stopped walking but didn't say anything. For a minute he thought he detected a slight smile, a glimpse of the old Allison. But she recovered quickly.

Johnny eyed her up and down. "I didn't mean to be sarcastic. You look great," he said. "It's just that you look so different."

"People change," she said authoritatively. "They mature."

"Yeah. I guess they do," he said, eying her blouse briefly before diverting his eyes back up to hers.

"That's a beautiful tan you have," he said, changing the subject.

"Thank you," she said, still without a hint of friendliness in her voice.

"A beautiful tan," he repeated. "You look like the Coppertone girl, without the dog tugging at your pants."

She smiled briefly before catching herself.

Johnny turned serious. "Okay, Allison, tell me what I did wrong. A couple of months ago we were both ready to jump in front of a train rather than be apart. Now, you look right through me."

"You didn't do anything wrong," she said, softening a little. "We had a great time together. But things are different now."

"In what way? Don't you think we should at least talk about it?"

"My parents thought it would be best if we made a clean break."

"Your parents? Your parents weren't dating me, you were," he said, his voice rising.

"I know. But I agree with them and so does Drake."

Johnny looked bewildered. "Drake! Who the hell is Drake?"

"He's the boy I'm dating now."

Johnny felt like he'd been punched hard in the stomach.

"You're dating a guy named Drake! That sounds like a goddamned explorer or something."

Allison ignored the sarcasm. "We dated most of the summer," she said defiantly. "His family owns a boat. He taught me to sail. We sailed almost every day. We even won a prize at the yacht club regatta."

Johnny didn't know what a regatta was, but it sounded like the cheese his mother put in her lasagna.

"His father is a judge," she continued. "He named his boat 'Lady Justice.'"

"Sounds like he did a better job naming his boat than naming his kid," Johnny replied.

"Drake is his mother's maiden name. It's not uncommon for some families to do that."

Johnny thought for a minute.

"My mother's maiden name is Limongelli. I guess she did me a favor."

"Look, Johnny. You wanted to talk and we did. Now I have to go."

"Wait," he said, stepping in front of her again. "Where does this guy Sir Francis live?"

"His name is Drake," she said with a hint of anger. "He lives just outside of Providence and attends a private high school there. Last year he was on the rowing team and played lacrosse. My parents said I can visit him during the school year to see some of his games and his rowing events."

"No one plays lacrosse," Johnny said.

"Not true Johnny. It's very common in the prep school leagues."

"Of course," Johnny replied. "The prep school leagues, what was I thinking?"

Johnny struggled to drop the sarcasm. He needed to take one final shot at getting her back.

"Allison," he said softly. "We both know how great we were together. You have to admit that. It was really something special. I'd like to try it again. I can't believe you can be happy with this guy you're describing."

"Believe it Johnny," she said stiffly. "There's a different world outside of Bristol, and I'm going to be part of it." She stepped around him and left.

That was it. Johnny's emotions were swirling. He was crushed. He prayed that none of his friends would ever find out that he'd been dumped for a guy named Drake. As he watched her walk away, he chided himself for noticing how good she looked from behind. Somehow, she'd become bad news, and to survive, he would have to wipe Lady Justice from his mind.

That was two months earlier. Slowly the glamour of Cape Cod wore off as she got back into her normal surroundings. Within a few weeks Allison grew tired of her long distance relationship with Drake and broke it off. She came back to earth, and started wearing normal clothes again and mixing with her old friends. She even sent hints through friends that she was interested in getting back with Johnny, but difficult as it was, he wouldn't bite. As far as he was concerned, the whole episode had been a valuable lesson. If a girl as wonderful as Allison could turn so quickly, how could he trust her or any other girl in the future? She'd hurt him badly and he wasn't about to let it happen again. He doubted that he'd ever find another girl as beautiful or as much fun as Allison, but he wasn't going to go through that pain again. So he adopted a new policy. He'd date a girl a few times and move on. There were plenty of girls out there, and he'd be fine without Allison. He still loved and hated her; actually, he was still crazy about her, but he summoned all the strength he had to resist. Seeing her in the front of the room now was an exceptionally hard test.

Allison was an excellent student and was in all of the honors classes, well out of view from Johnny. The only exception was social studies. The school chose social studies classes for their great social experiment of mixing ability levels. In the class, Allison was the cream of a very mixed academic crop.

Fridays were student presentation days. Each student was assigned to make a five-minute report on a current issue. Mr. Rush announced Allison as the next speaker, as though this would be a special treat for everyone. It was unclear whether the treat would be the quality of the presentation or the appeal of the presenter. Either way, Allison stood at the front of the room exuding confidence and smiling broadly. She had placed two large white poster boards on the chalk ledge and awaited her cue from Mr. Rush.

"Allison will be reporting on some of the major issues surrounding the presidential election coming up in a little over a week," Mr. Rush said, as if Walter Cronkite himself was about to give the report. "I expect all of you to take copious notes."

He always used the term, "copious notes." Johnny didn't know what it meant, but he was pretty sure it didn't mean to doodle, which was his favorite classroom pastime.

Allison smiled broadly. "Thank you, Mr. Rush," she said with her trademark perkiness.

"As Mr. Rush said, my report is on the upcoming presidential election of 1964. As you know, the democratic candidate is Lyndon B. Johnson. The republican candidate is Barry Goldwater."

She turned around the first of the white poster boards to reveal large photos of the two candidates that she had cut out of *Life* magazine. "Johnson is the incumbent," she continued, "which means he is the person currently in office. He's the president."

"Good word," Mr. Rush called out. "Make sure you get that down. Incumbent."

Allison smiled proudly and continued. "Barry Goldwater is a United States Senator from Arizona."

The class wrote feverishly.

"On issues at home, President Johnson is a liberal and Senator Goldwater is a conservative," she said.

"Correct," Mr. Rush called out to reinforce the point.

"I've chosen to focus on two major issues in the campaign. The first is President Johnson's Great Society program."

"Good choice," Rush said, and the class continued to write.

She was reading from her note cards now. "In May of this year President Johnson proposed the Great Society, which is a series of federal programs to give aid to the poorest areas of the country. There is a component for the cities and one for our poor rural areas. The program is very ambitious and expensive." She paused to allow the students to record every word. "It has been praised by urban leaders and legislators from poor rural areas like Appalachia."

"Great information," Mr. Rush said. "Who are its critics?"

It was like the two of them had rehearsed the exchange. Allison smiled broadly and continued.

"A leading critic of the program is Senator Goldwater himself. Goldwater feels the program is much too expensive and places too much of a burden on the taxpayer. As a conservative, he favors less involvement by the federal government in economic matters, not more."

Mr. Rush was ecstatic. "Now this is what a good report sounds like," he said. "Would you please repeat your reference to the conservative philosophy so that the class can get it down?"

As she did, Johnny thought about what a great boost she could provide to his grades if they were still a couple.

Allison glanced at the poster boards on the chalk ledge and realized she hadn't turned around the second poster yet.

"I'm sorry," she said as she turned the board. "I should have flipped this poster earlier."

Across the top she had stenciled the title, "1964 Campaign Issues." Listed below were two items. The first read, "Johnson's Great Society," and the second read, "Vietnam."

"This takes us to my second issue of the campaign, the debate over America's role in Vietnam."

Johnny decided that regardless of how smart she was, someone had to have helped her with this report. It was too smooth. Maybe her old man the car dealer hired someone.

Allison checked her note card briefly before continuing. "As you know, the United States is in Vietnam to help the South Vietnamese people stop the spread of communism." She glanced at the card again. "We currently have about twenty-thousand advisors there."

Nick was in the class. He was a strong student who knew Mr. Rush liked it when students asked questions during oral reports. So he managed to come up with at least one each Friday, and now was the time to make his move. He put is hand up high.

Allison noticed it and called on him reluctantly.

"Allison, I don't understand. Why do we have twenty thousand advisors in Vietnam? It seems like two or three would be enough. Who are they advising?"

Allison looked at her cards, but the answer wasn't there.

"The Vietnamese," she finally said, without conviction. Her beaming smile was gone.

Nick had never forgiven her for breaking his friend's heart, so he enjoyed seeing her squirm. Johnny enjoyed it a little, but felt sorry for her at the same time.

It was time for Mr. Rush to intervene.

"Good question Nick. They are not advisors in the traditional sense of the word. We call them that because they are there to train the Vietnamese army on military tactics and how to use the weapons we are giving them. They are not supposed to fight unless they are attacked. They are also there to protect our airfields and planes." He paused to see if there were any other questions. There were none, so he nodded to Allison to continue.

"There's a lot of debate about how active our troops should be in Vietnam. Senator Goldwater is a hawk on the war."

"Great term!" Mr. Rush called out. "And what does that mean?"

Allison had regained her confidence. She knew this was in her notes. "A hawk is someone who wants to take a more aggressive posture in Vietnam," she read.

"Excellent," Rush bellowed. "Please continue."

"Goldwater has been critical of the Johnson administration, saying it isn't doing enough to protect our troops or the South Vietnamese people who are fighting for their freedom."

"Yes," Mr. Rush said. "And how does Johnson respond?"

"Well, my Dad said..." she caught herself, but the damage was already done.

"Bingo!" Johnny said under his breath.

Allison looked embarrassed, but recovered quickly. "As far as I can tell, President Johnson has to convince the voters that he will defend Vietnam from communism, without scaring the voters into thinking we're going to get involved in a big war after the election."

"Excellent analysis," Mr. Rush said, coming to her aid again.

"Give her dad an A," Johnny muttered softly.

Allison's confidence was back. "I have a quote from President Johnson I can read to the class if you like."

"Please do," Rush said.

Allison searched for the card. "Here it is," she said and cleared her throat. She was rounding third base, and she hoped that reading the quote would take her home.

"Just a couple of days ago, on October 21, 1964, President Johnson said, 'We are not about to send American boys nine or ten thousand miles away from home to do what Asian boys ought to be doing for themselves.'" She looked up from the card and said, "That seems to clear things up about what Johnson feels our role in Vietnam should be." She took a breath and said, "That's the end of my report. Thank you for listening."

"That was an outstanding job," Mr. Rush said, and the class applauded politely.

She turned to collect her posters and take her seat, with home plate just inches away, when Nick hollered out, "Can I ask another question?"

Allison stopped and exhaled deeply and the class stopped clapping.

"Of course, Nick. What is it?" Mr. Rush said.

He directed the question to Allison. "I don't really know where Vietnam is. Can you tell me?"

Allison's expression revealed that she couldn't. She stalled for a minute and then said weakly, "It's in Asia."

"I think you're right," Nick said. "But can you be more specific? I mean, Asia is a big place." The question sounded sincere, but Johnny knew that Nick couldn't have cared less about where Vietnam was. It wasn't the end of the world if Allison didn't know either. But Johnny knew she liked to be academically perfect, and it was killing her that she didn't know. He felt a little sorry for her again.

"I think it might be near India," she said hopefully, looking like she might cry at any moment.

It was time for Mr. Rush to come to her rescue again.

"It's okay, Allison," he said, as he stood and walked to the front of the room. I don't think most Americans know where Vietnam is located. You can take your seat, and thanks again for a very good report."

Allison noticed the shift in terminology from outstanding to very good. As she walked to her seat, she looked at Nick as if she wanted to scratch his eyes out.

Mr. Rush pulled down a large map of East Asia that hung in the front of the room and turned to the class. He pointed to an area south of China, labeled French Indochina. "This is an old map," he explained. "It dates back more than a decade, before the French left the region. But within this area labeled French Indochina, there are several modern day countries, including Laos, Cambodia, and this easternmost country called Vietnam."

He turned to Nick. "So the answer to your question is that Vietnam is located in Southeast Asia, just south of China."

"Thanks, Mr. Rush," Nick said. "Can I ask one more question?"

"Fire away," Mr. Rush said.

"You said earlier that most Americans probably couldn't find Vietnam on a map. If we have twenty thousand soldiers there, don't you think we should know where it is?"

"Yes, Nick," Mr. Rush replied. "I certainly do."

15- Wedding

Spring 1965

The boys loved crashing wedding receptions. In a town where there was little to do, it was great fun eating and drinking as uninvited guests at the wedding of strangers. There was an element of excitement too. If caught, they could be beaten by a drunken brother of the bride, tossed out by angry cousins, or cursed by outraged grandmothers. All of which made it enticing for them.

By the spring of 1965, the boys had elevated their wedding crashing to an art form. Any covert mission requires a well-selected target and good field intelligence. The boys were careful about both. They avoided the elaborate affairs held at exclusive ballrooms. Those receptions were expensive with elaborate cocktail hours and lavish sit-down dinners with assigned seating. The father of the bride paid big bucks for those parties and would be keenly aware of who was invited and who wasn't. So instead, the boys targeted simple, blue-collar weddings held in firehouses or fraternal lodges. These were the weddings where people sat on wooden folding chairs at long, rectangular tables, otherwise used for bingo. The food at these affairs was usually arranged buffet style and included stacks of roast beef or ham sandwiches, accompanied by large bowls of potato salad and cole slaw. The bar was usually limited to half-kegs of beer and birch beer. The bar also provided plenty of ice and mixers for guests who brought a bottle of hard stuff from home. Drinking age rules didn't apply at weddings in the 60's. Anyone tall enough to reach the bartender's tip jar was considered old enough to drink.

The boys had a network of sources to help them pick their targets. Billy Moyer's mom worked part time at a flower shop, and she'd bring home order lists with references like, "Wedding/Farber-Atkins/Moose Lodge/ Sat. April 24/Head table arrangement." Billy would casually review the lists and record the information. The key was in the names of the wedding couple. The boys obviously had to select weddings of strangers, where each family would believe that the boys were part of the other family's guest list. Angelo served as another source of information. His father sometimes received orders for pounds of roast beef and dozens of rolls to be delivered to one of the halls. Big Frankie was a source too. He landed a part time job unloading kegs on Saturday deliveries for the local beer distributor. All of this information was carefully collected and studied to determine when and where the gang would strike.

Wedding commandos required proper attire, and the boys had mastered this element as well. Once an invasion was planned, the boys would meet at Jake's Arcade at seven on Saturday night, wearing dress shirts, jackets, and ties. Properly dressed, they could easily mingle with the guests.

Johnny's natural leadership abilities usually provided the motivation to pull off the adventure, and now, on a beautiful Saturday afternoon in early May, the boys were meeting at Jake's to plan that night's escapade and Johnny was in charge.

"Remember, we're gonna drink their beer and eat their food, but this isn't about that. This is about adventure. This is about having guts. This is about staying cool under pressure. We're going to walk in there with all of the confidence in the world, blend in, laugh, talk, eat, drink, maybe even dance a little if you meet a lady. We'll party for as long as we can, and when we've had enough or when things start getting hot, we'll leave just as smoothly as we went in. Long after we're gone someone will ask, 'Hey, who were those guys?' and no one will know. It'll be great. Isn't that right, Jimmy?"

Jimmy was always the nervous one, deathly afraid of getting caught. He could be counted on to try to talk the guys out of it. It was a ritual they had come to enjoy. In the end, Jimmy's protests never mattered, because he could be talked into anything.

"I don't think we should do it this time," he said.

Johnny laughed and plunged into the game. "Why not, Jimmy boy?" He asked as he squeezed his friend's shoulder. "Are you afraid you'll be caught in the closet with a bridesmaid?"

Everyone laughed and Angelo joined in. "Can you see Jimmy and the maid of honor playing kissy-face in the closet when grandma walks in? Could be embarrassing."

Jimmy waited while everyone had an extra long chuckle. Even Jake had a good laugh behind the counter.

"I don't think we should go tonight because the groom is a cop!" he finally said. "Billy told you himself. The name of the couple on the flower list was Corporal John Bowers and Sally Ann Myers. I'm telling ya; we shouldn't go."

Johnny winked at the group. "For God's sake, Jimmy. What do you think he's gonna do, pull handcuffs out of his tuxedo and arrest us? He'll be busy having a good time. This is no big deal. We're not robbing a bank. We're just having some good clean fun. No harm done. Besides, we're not going to get caught."

"What about two months ago when we all had to run out of the wedding at the club on Wood Street? That was close," Jimmy said.

"That was because of dumb ass Ralph," Angelo said. "He went to the bathroom and panicked when somebody used the urinal next to him. Instead of keeping his mouth shut, the simple bastard said he was the groom's half-brother! When the guy said he was the groom's uncle, Ralph took off. When we saw Ralph running from the bathroom, we knew it was time to bolt. We left with time to spare. No harm done. Besides, it was exciting."

Jimmy was softening up. "Is Ralph coming tonight?"

"No," Angelo said. "He probably has to help his uncle stuff one of the stiffs at the funeral home."

Johnny motioned to Nick, who moved toward the pool table where Billy and Angelo were having a game.

"Jimmy, Nick has something to show you that will make you feel better about tonight."

Nick reached under the pool table and pulled out two beautifully wrapped packages. One was about the size of a shoebox and was wrapped in silver paper with white ribbon. The other was slightly larger and was wrapped in blue and silver.

"What are they?" Jimmy asked.

"Wedding gifts for tonight!" Nick said triumphantly.

Jimmy looked pleasantly surprised.

"No kidding," he said. "What did you get them?"

The boys laughed so hard that they couldn't answer.

Now Jimmy was losing his patience. "What's in the boxes?" He shouted above the laughter.

"The boxes are empty!" Nick said. "They're our ticket in tonight. We'll walk in with these under our arms, make sure everyone sees them, take our time placing them on the gift table, and we'll own the place. The bride's family will think we're guests of the groom and the groom's family will think we belong to the bride. We'll party all night."

Jimmy smiled. He liked it. "Who wrapped the boxes?"

"I wrapped one and Frankie wrapped the other," Nick said.

"And they're empty?" Jimmy repeated.

"Yes," Nick said.

Frankie moved closer. "Mine isn't empty," he said. Everyone looked at him.

"What do you mean?" Nick asked shaking the box. "It feels empty."

Frankie looked embarrassed. "I put a note in my box before I wrapped it."

"A note!" Nick said in disbelief. "What does it say?"

"It says, 'I hope you have a happy life together.'"

Johnny put one arm around Frankie's shoulder and gave him a playful punch in the stomach. "You big softy," Johnny said. "You're the nicest guy I know." In fact, Frankie was the nicest guy any of them knew.

"Nice touch," Nick said. "Can you picture it? The bride and groom will open their gifts after the reception and find one empty box and one with a note. Years after they forget the fine bowl their Aunt Ethel gave them, they'll still wonder who gave them the boxes."

"Okay guys. Seven o'clock tonight," Johnny said. "Still coming, Jimmy?"

"I'll be there," Jimmy said.

There was never any doubt.

They met at Jake's at seven and actually looked good in their jackets and ties. There were five of them, which was pushing it. A larger group would have made them far too noticeable, but they were confident they could pull it off with five.

Nick and Frankie brought along the wrapped gifts. Acting on a last minute idea, Johnny brought along a white envelope with the words *Corporal and Mrs. John Bowers* written across the front.

"What's that?" Frankie asked.

"I've decided to give cash instead of a gift. You know how people are with gifts; they just want to return them," Johnny said proudly. Then he reached inside his jacket pocket and produced another envelope.

"Here, Jimmy. I brought one for you too," he said. "Just keep it visible when we walk in. It's your ticket to a good night."

Jimmy asked, "Is there money in it?"

Everyone had another good laugh.

As they got closer, Johnny said, "Okay, let's do some goal setting. Our record stay at a reception is fifty-two minutes."

"Yeah, but that was an Irish wedding," Angelo said. "Everyone was drunk before the reception even started. Nobody was in any shape to notice us."

"Watch it when you talk about my people," Nick joked. "That's an unfair stereotype and I'm deeply offended."

"Stereotype! Isn't that the wedding where the bride threw up?" Frankie asked. "It's pretty easy to go unnoticed when the newlywed is upchucking on her beautiful white dress."

"Classy broad," Johnny added. "Can you imagine having your family and all of your relatives at the wedding when your new wife gets plastered and blows lunch all over herself?"

"What about the first time the newlyweds go to the groom's house for Thanksgiving?" Jimmy added. "Her in-laws might put a tarp under her chair to protect the carpet."

Johnny was happy to see that Jimmy was loosening up. "Back to goal-setting. What should we shoot for tonight?"

"I'm feeling pretty good," Angelo said. "Real confident. Too bad Billy isn't here, we could shoot for the ultimate goal."

The ultimate goal was to have the Tone Kings sing, Johnny, Angelo, Frankie, and Billy Moyer, sing at the reception. Everyone loved it when they sang at school, so they shared a vision of crashing a wedding some day, befriending the disk jockey, and using his microphone to sing "In the Still of the Night" while the bride and groom danced.

But girls came first with Billy, and he opted for a date with his latest squeeze instead of a night with the boys. The group had a pact not to perform unless all five were present. And as for Jimmy, he just couldn't sing.

Much to Jimmy's relief, the boys eventually agreed that a half-hour visit, accompanied by at least a pitcher of beer and a sandwich would be a success. Anything more would be great.

When they reached the last block, Johnny reminded everyone to say as little as possible and follow his lead. Johnny was by far the smoothest talker in the group, and no one had any problem letting him do the talking.

As they approached, there was an elderly woman in front of them taking the steps slowly. She held a shopping bag in one had and grasped the railing with the other. The bag obviously contained her present. Johnny rushed up to help her. Taking her by the arm, he said, "Excuse me miss, can I help you."

The woman was slightly winded and welcomed the offer.

"Thank you, young man. If you could just carry this until I'm up the steps, " she said, handing him the bag.

"It's my pleasure. Be careful now," he said, as he took her arm with his free hand.

At the top of the steps the woman reached for the bag, but Johnny pretended not to notice. Instead, he turned and said, "Frankie, can you get the door for us?"

"Oh, you're so kind," she said while stepping inside, still holding Johnny's arm.

"I'm a widow and I drove here myself from Bensalem. I'm a little tired. My sister offered me a ride, but I didn't want to be a bother. I guess I should have accepted." Then she smiled. She seemed like a nice lady. "Anyway," she added, "I wouldn't miss my nephew's wedding for anything."

"Is Corporal Bowers your nephew?" Johnny asked.

"Yes, he is," she replied. "And I'm so proud of him."

"That's how we feel about Sally Ann," Johnny said.

Jimmy looked like he was going to faint. Nick savored the opportunity to watch a master at work. Frankie was alert for any other assignments Johnny might throw his way, and Angelo just wanted a pitcher of beer.

"Are you related?" she asked.

Johnny pretended to be distracted and said, "I'll be happy to take your bag to the gift table for you if you like." He still didn't know which side of the room her relatives were sitting on, and he was stalling for time.

Just then, Johnny noticed an older man, with a drink in his hand and a cigar stub in his mouth, smiling as he made his way to them. "Alice," he said, giving her a hug. "It's good to see you. Josephine and I have a table right over there." He pointed to the right side of the room, and Johnny could see another elderly woman wave to his new friend.

Alice waved back and said to Johnny, "This is my cousin Bob. Bob, these nice boys helped me in."

Johnny stuck out his hand and said, "It's nice to meet you sir."

Bob shook his hand quickly. He was preoccupied with getting Alice settled.

"This is Alice's bag. Do you want us to take it to the gift table for her," Johnny asked, doing his best Boy Scout impersonation.

"Yeah. Do that," Bob said, speaking through the cigar stub.

"Thank you so much," Alice said.

"You're welcome." Then Johnny added with a wink, "I hope you'll save me a dance for later."

By the time Bob led her away Alice looked as though she was considering putting Johnny in her will.

"Just don't wind up with her in the coat closet," Angelo whispered as they moved deeper into the room.

"Have a little respect," Johnny said. "She's somebody's grandmother."

The exchange with Alice was priceless. To anyone who might have been wondering who the boys were, it was clear they knew someone and belonged.

"Okay, let's drop this stuff off and get settled," Johnny said.

They took a slow, deliberate walk to the table to deposit their gifts, exchanging pleasant nods with guests whose eyes met theirs. The room was about three-quarters filled and had about a hundred and fifty people. Big crowds were good; they made it easier to disappear.

The table was already stacked high with gifts of assorted sizes. It also had a white birdcage, decorated with silver ribbon. The cage was filled with gift envelopes.

Johnny removed Alice's gift from the bag and glanced over to where she was sitting. She was watching just as he knew she would be. Older people didn't part with their money easily. He smiled and raised the box slightly for her to see. Reassured, she smiled back and waved. He placed the box in a prominent place, and she looked pleased. Frankie and Nick put their boxes on the table as well.

Sliding his envelope into the birdcage, Johnny said, "I bet they return half of the stuff on this table. I'm telling ya, money is the way to go. Right Jimmy?"

"Exactly," Jimmy said, depositing his gift next. "Give the young couple starting out in life some cash so they can buy what they really need."

"I'm sorry," Nick said. "But I think money is too impersonal. The right gift will be treasured for years to come."

"Can we cut the crap and get some beer?" Angelo said.

The bar was close to the gift table, and they moved to it. Jimmy was sweating a little so Johnny decided to keep him occupied. "So, Jimmy, are you going to hang in there with the Phillies after they broke your heart last year?" Johnny asked loud enough for everyone to hear.

"You're damned right I am." Jimmy said. "I'm loyal."

"After the September they had? Blowing a six and a half game lead with just twelve games left? Losing ten games in a row? I don't know if I can do it," Frankie said.

"That's what's wrong with people; no one is loyal. Those guys battled for us all year. They played their butts off. Things just went bad at the end. It just wasn't meant to be. But I can't turn my back on them after all the thrills they gave me from April to August. I don't forget what people do for me."

A guest in front of them in line turned around and said, "Those guys are paid to win. When they don't win they deserve to take some heat."

Jimmy was about to jump all over him when the bartender said, "Next."

Frankie smiled at the guy and said, "That's you."

The guy turned and ordered his beer.

When it was their turn, Angelo unfolded three one-dollar bills and placed them on the bar. It was important that the tip be more generous than most, but not so big that it aroused suspicion. The boys agreed beforehand that three bucks would be just right.

"We'll need two pitchers and five glasses," Angelo said.

The bartended eyed him briefly, then pocketed the money and reached for a pitcher.

Aside from Angelo, the boys didn't really drink much. Four of them would split the one pitcher and Angelo would drain most of the second one by himself, depending upon how long they stayed.

The hard part was over. They'd been served! They found an empty table near the back, helped themselves to some sandwiches, and settled in to enjoy the show. So far the night was a home run.

The DJ introduced himself to the crowd as Skip Evans and promised everyone a fabulous time. Then came the boys' favorite part of the night, the introduction of the bridal party. They were great people watchers and nothing matched the awkward procession of barely acquainted couples who had to enter the hall arm in arm to the hoots and cheers of the adoring crowd. The boys liked to rate the girls as they were introduced.

With the theme from "Zorba the Greek" playing in the background, Skip introduced the parents of the bride. His enthusiasm made it clear that he knew who was paying him at the end of the night. Then came the bridal party. Fortunately, there was no flower girl or ring barer in the party. The boys had little patience for the shy little kids who picked their noses as the crowd oohed and aahed.

Skip introduced the first couple and Jimmy whispered "three" as soon as he saw the girl. "Like hell," Angelo said. "Two at best, and only if I'm real, real lonely."
The next girl wasn't much of an improvement and Nick said, "Are we allowed to use negative numbers?"
Frankie was annoyed. "This isn't right. You guys shouldn't do this. Maybe she's a nice person."
"Thank God we have Frankie as our conscience," Johnny said. "You're a good man Frankie."
"He's a big pussy," Angelo said. "Lighten up."
Everyone at the table knew that Frankie could crush Angelo or just about anybody else if he wanted to, but he was so good-natured that it wasn't possible.
As expected, Frankie shrugged off the insult.
"I just don't think it's right to make fun of how people look," he said.

Just then Skip announced the next couple, Jason Waller and Susan Dompter, or something like that.

Susan was so heavy that her dress was a different design from the rest of the party. It was the same color, but significantly different.

"Jesus," Jimmy said. "What's going on tonight?"

Susan was one of those overweight people who was completely at peace with herself. She was beaming as she entered the room. Her escort looked like someone who wanted to kill whoever made the wedding pairings. His facial expression said, "I'm only with her for another ten minutes."

Even Frankie had to allow himself a snicker.

Angelo said, "At least the beer is cold," as he poured himself another.

Skip was still generating energy at the microphone.

"And now," Skip said. "It is my privilege to introduce the best man, Sergeant Paul Becker and maid of honor, sister of the bride, Miss Amy Myers.

Finally there was some visual relief. Amy was cute and perky and the table was divided between sevens and eights. But it wasn't Amy who held the boys' attention, it was Sergeant Becker, who looked like he just stepped out of an army-recruiting poster. Instead of a tuxedo, Becker wore the dress uniform of the United States Army. He had a buzz haircut, and his uniform did little to conceal a muscular body. He had a strong angular face and stood perfectly erect. The stripes on his sleeve and the ribbons on his chest completed the picture. No one wanted to be tossed out of the wedding reception by him.

After Amy and the Sergeant were positioned, Skip gathered himself for the big moment. Sounding like a circus ringmaster, he boomed, "Ladies and gentleman, for the first time ever as husband and wife, please join me in welcoming Corporal and Mrs. John Bowers."

The crowd cheered, clapped, and called out their names as they passed. The couple looked great. Sally Ann was even cuter than her sister. She was slender, had a beautiful smile and was obviously in love. John looked good too. He certainly wasn't the physical specimen Sergeant Becker was, but he was obviously fit and pleasant looking. They made a great couple.

Everyone remained standing as Skip explained that the couple would now dance its first dance as husband and wife. They had selected "Chapel of Love" by the Dixie Cups. The crowd seemed genuinely happy as the bride and groom danced and the music filled the room.

It was weird, but Johnny and the rest of the boys actually found themselves happy for the total strangers dancing in front of them. Nick even wished he had brought a real gift.

As the dance continued Sally Ann's expression changed. There was some sadness mixed in with her joy. She seemed to hold John tighter and buried her head on his shoulder. When the dance finished, she smiled brightly in response to the guests' applause, but there were tears in her eyes. Even Angelo, the hard-ass, was touched.

Members of the wedding party took their places at the head table as Skip continued the show. "Ladies and gentleman, please remain standing as our best man, Sergeant Paul Becker, offers a toast to our happy couple."

Sergeant Becker took the microphone. "Good evening," He said. His voice was strong and deep. "I know most of you don't know me. In fact, I've only known John for the last year and a half. That's when we first met at Fort Dix, New Jersey. We've been assigned there training recruits. I know a year and a half isn't a long time to build a best-man type friendship, but when you bunk with someone, share the same mess table, and lift your share of beers together, you can get to know someone pretty good. And I want all of you to know that I've grown to love John like a brother. And Sally Ann, although you and I have spent just a few hours together, I feel like I know everything about you. John has kept me up well into the night on more than one occasion, telling me about his love for you and the dreams you share. You are all he talks about."

Sally Ann was smiling, but tears were streaming down her pretty face freely now. She snuggled closer to her husband as Becker continued.

"Now if you watch the news, you know that last month President Johnson ordered 40,000 additional troops to Vietnam."

The crowd was so quiet that Johnny could hear the compressor on the ice machine humming.

"This is a big deal," Becker said. "Up until now, our military presence there has been solely advisory. Now, we're going as combat units. We're going to help those people over there defend themselves against those communist invaders."

The crowd clapped. Some people leaned closer to people at their table to whisper questions. Many wondered where Vietnam was.

Becker lightened the mood a little. "Now some of you from out of town may be wondering why this wedding was arranged so quickly. Well, let me assure you, it's not what you think. Sally Ann is a nice girl and John is a soldier gentleman." Everyone laughed politely.

"The fact is, John and I and the rest of our unit are shipping out to Vietnam on Wednesday. We're going to a place called Cam Ron Bay where we will be assigned for at least a year. These two people are in love, and they wanted to get married before John leaves. That's why we're here."

"Okay, enough of the explanation," Becker said. "It's time for the toast." He raised his glass and turned to Sally Ann and John. "I know it's difficult now, but I want you two to look into the future and know that everyone here wishes you a long and happy life together, with plenty of kids that John has told me you both want. Then he turned to the crowd and said, "I expect every person in this room to give Sally Ann all of the support she needs while John is gone." Turning back to the bride, he said, "And Sally Ann, I promise you that John will come home safely if I have to carry him all the way back myself." Then he raised his glass high and said, "To John and Sally Ann."

The guests echoed somberly, "To John and Sally Ann" and took a sip of their drinks.

As Skip put on some music, Sally Ann stood suddenly and ran from the room crying, followed by every girl at the head table.

The boys looked at each other. They were obviously moved by what had just taken place.

"I think I just lost the mood to party," Johnny said. "What time is it?"

Frankie checked his watch, "It's eight twenty-two."

"Well, that's a record," Johnny said. "Let's go home."

16- Thanksgiving

November 1965

The Thanksgiving Day game between the Bristol Warriors and the Morrisville Bulldogs was one of the oldest rivalries in the state. Sportswriters showered the public with every cliché their editor would allow like, "team records don't count on Thanksgiving Day," and "mediocre teams can make their season with a win." *County Times* reporter, Willard Bracey, did an annual article on the game's greatest upsets. Over the past forty-five years, the underdog had won almost half the time. Eleven times the favored team lost the championship on Thanksgiving Day, and in seven of those games an undefeated team lost its dream of a perfect season. Championships were won and lost on the big day, and individual legends were born.

The game was a family event since many of the spectators had participated in some way in past contests. Bracey wrote moving stories about players whose fathers once played in the game. Women shared in the glory. Many had been cheerleaders, band or color guard members, or wore the sequined outfits of the renowned Bristol Baton Team.

Nowhere was Warriors' pride more evident than in the Boosters club. The boosters ran the snack bar, sold the programs, lined the field, worked the sideline chains, and collected tickets at the gate. Although the "gritty little blue-collar town" as Bracey called it, had seen better economic times, the boosters raised thousands of dollars for scoreboards, uniforms, and team jackets.

The boosters sponsored the pre-game father-son breakfast in the school cafeteria and an army of mothers prepared the meal. Comments were strictly limited to a prayer by the clergy, a short introduction of the guest speaker by Coach Lukins, and the featured speech by a past hero of the big game. The speaker could be counted on to deliver a moving account of a game when Bristol overcame impossible odds to win a stunning victory. The speaker would reluctantly share details of his personal exploits, as well as an account of the life-long rewards the game bestowed and the unbreakable bond he still shared with his teammates. Near the end, the hero would assert his belief that this year's team was poised to earn its rightful place in Bristol's rich football history, and that some young athlete, sitting with his dad that morning, would claim his spot in the Bristol High School Hall of Fame.

Pausing for dramatic effect, he would close by asking, "Who will be that player today?" Then he'd pan the audience slowly, extending the challenge to each boy whose eyes met his. The silence would hang over the room as hearts pounded, adrenalin flowed, and fathers and sons dreamed of imminent glory. Coach Lukins always allowed the emotion to build before setting off a thunderous release of cheers from the audience. Amid shouts and whistles, fathers and sons embraced, and teammates shared looks of fierce determination and unshakeable brotherhood. Then, Coach Lukins would shout, "Suit up," and the boys would make their way to the locker room. For those fleeting moments, it was the most powerful bonding experience a father and son could have.

Frankie's father ran off when he was six, so neither he nor Johnny had a father present at the breakfast. Frankie invited his uncle Vince, who had tried to fill in over the years, and Johnny invited his neighbor, Mr. Forney. Both were good guys, but the morning was still a difficult reminder of the void in the boys' lives. With their fathers gone, they had learned long ago to rely on each other and their mothers for emotional support.

As they put on their pads, they talked about their meeting at the log the day Frankie was cut from the seventh grade basketball team, when Johnny had assured Frankie that he would be a football star some day. They'd had lots of glory since then, especially Frankie.

Frankie was five feet eleven and weighed two-twenty when he showed up for summer practice as a freshman. He was soft, slow, and timid, but Coach Lukins loved his size and was determined to make him a player. The coach was tough on everyone, but especially Frankie. He dubbed him "Big Frankie" and rode him so much that the kid wanted to quit. Coach's favorite phrases were, "Come on, Frankie, move your big ass," and "Damn it, Frankie, hit somebody!" Frankie hated the abuse, but the encouragement of Assistant Coach Tom D'Pinto, kept him going. D'Pinto liked Frankie and worked with him. They worked on quickness off the ball, foot speed, staying low, and using hands. The two coaches played good cop, bad cop. The more Lukins belittled Frankie, the more D'Pinto gave him support. When Lukins called him "lard ass," or "blubber gut," or "Francis," Coach D'Pinto would whisper, "Keep working, Frankie, your time will come." Johnny reinforced the message in the locker room.

Gradually, Frankie's time did come. He grew three inches. He practiced hard, hit the weights, trimmed down and improved his speed, strength, and skills. But the most notable change was in his mental toughness. His mild manner in school was replaced with fierce aggression on the field. By the middle of the first season, Frankie had exacted revenge on all the teammates who had laughed during Lukins' insults. One by one they felt the blow of his forearm, or the force of his helmet in their ribs. D'Pinto smiled at his protégé, and Lukins, ever the drill sergeant, still rode him hard, but became more selective in his insults.

The improvement continued. He and Johnny lifted weights and ran in the off-season. When Frankie returned for his sophomore year, the fat had turned to muscle, and his agility had improved. By the second game, he was a two-way starter. He made all league as a junior, and by his senior year he was regarded as one of the best small school lineman in southeastern Pennsylvania.

Johnny was a small, quick running back. He scored nine touchdowns his senior year and gained over eleven hundred total yards. The crowd knew that at crucial parts of the game, Coach Lukins would find a way to get Johnny the ball.

This Thanksgiving Day game would not be for a championship. Bristol had a great season and boasted a 7-2 record going into the final game. But Morrisville was undefeated and had clinched the league championship the week before. So this game was for pride only, and the football that would be placed in the trophy case of the winner.

Morrisville was strong in every phase of the game, but especially their defense, and while the Bristol players and fans dreamed of an upset, few objective observers thought it was likely. The Bristol Warriors had plenty of heart, but the Bulldogs had heart, talent, and an undefeated season to protect.

Once the game started, it was clear that Morrisville's hype was well deserved. Their defense smothered the Bristol offense. Quarterback Nick Hardings was under relentless pressure each time he attempted to throw, and the running game was ineffective. Bristol's most valuable player in the first half was Angelo Marzo, their punter, whose booming kicks kept Morrisville out of good field position. Fortunately, this was Bristol's day to play great defense too. Frankie made big plays all morning. That, plus some lucky breaks, kept Bristol in the game.

The Bulldogs had completely dominated the half, but at halftime there was no score. WBCB radio broadcasted the game locally, and Bracey gave the halftime analysis. "There are several things keeping Bristol in this game: good defense, great punting, and some lucky calls from the officials. But there is something else. Bristol's quarterback, Nick Hardings is doing a fantastic job protecting the football. He's been sacked six times and taken monstrous hits running the option, but each time, he's held on to the football. That has allowed Bristol to punt the ball away and give their defense a chance."

Buzz Baker, the play- by- play announcer agreed. "Not only that, Walter, he's been an inspiration to his teammates. He just keeps picking himself up and encouraging his team. There's no finger pointing, no complaints about missed blocks. He's really showing some leadership out there. I just don't know how much longer this can go on."

"We've seen Hardings play well all year, but this is by far his most courageous effort," Bracey said.

Morrisville kicked off to begin the second half and Johnny returned the kick to the Bristol thirty-five yard line. On the play, Angelo Marzo leveled the Morrisville kicker with a clean hit, just as Coach Lukins had taught him, and the kicker limped off of the field with an injured ankle.

The teams began exchanging punts again until early in the fourth quarter, when Morrisville's Dawkins found a hole, and raced untouched sixty-four yards for a touchdown. This time there were no flags.

Morrisville's kicker limped from the bench to take the field for the extra point. Letting him kick was a mistake. He kicked the ball into his center's back, and Morrisville led by only six.

On the ensuing kickoff, Morrisville was forced to use their back-up kicker. He dropped the ball to the thirty-two yard line. Billy Moyer fielded it on the run and returned it twenty-three yards to the Morrisville forty-five yard line. It was Bristol's deepest penetration of the day. On first down, Bristol ran a flea flicker, and Nick lofted the ball to Jimmy Wright, who was racing down the sideline.
Scott Robinson, Morrisville's all-state safety, moved toward Jimmy and the incoming pass and got there a split second after Jimmy reached for the ball. The Bristol crowd cringed as Robinson delivered a devastating hit. But somehow, Jimmy held on and the referee signaled a catch. Bristol had a first down on the Morrisville four-yard line. The crowd went wild.

Nick coolly broke his team from the huddle. Bristol lined up with three wide receivers, and Morrisville scurried to cover them as the ball was snapped. Nick dropped back to pass against a ferocious pass rush. As Morrisville penetrated the perimeter, he stepped up, tucked the ball and raced straight up the middle on a quarterback draw. He went into the end zone untouched.

Not everyone in Bristol was at the game. Grandmothers were home basting turkeys; young mothers were caring for their infants; some elderly were housebound. Public servants had to work. But *everyone* at home or work was listening on the radio. *Everyone* heard Buzz Baker scream, "Touchdown Bristol!" over and over. Mothers shrieked, babies cried, grandmothers dropped their spoons, and nurses hugged. All of

Bristol was ecstatic. Then, the jubilation changed to unbearable tension, as Bristol prepared to kick the extra point. The Bristol kicker hit the ball perfectly and Bristol led 7-6 with three and a half minutes left in the game.

Morrisville responded like the champions they were. Morrisville's Dawkins simply refused to go down easily, moving the ball methodically down the field. Bristol was hitting as hard as they had all game, but Morrisville was like a wounded animal that refused to die. Finally, the Bulldogs faced a fourth and six at the Bristol twenty-four yard line. There was one minute left. The game would ride on this play, and everyone in the stadium expected Dawkins to get the ball. But on the play, Morrisville used some razzle-dazzle of its own. Their quarterback pitched the ball to Dawkins, who started running left. The defensive backs rotated to his side, and Johnny and the linebacker converged on him, but no one saw the quarterback slip out of the backfield to the right. Dawkins stopped and lofted a pass across the field to the quarterback who had no one within ten yards of him. He caught the ball at the five-yard line and trotted into the end zone.

Mitch Bloom, who had been operating the Bristol scoreboard for twenty years, searched the field for penalty flags, but there were none. He searched again before reluctantly changing the score. It read Morrisville 12 Bristol 7. The Morrisville Bulldogs were just forty-six seconds away from a perfect season.

This time Morrisville decided to run the ball instead of trying to kick the extra point. The home crowd couldn't have cared less. The jubilation that existed just minutes earlier had given way to stunned disbelief. The band was silent, the cheerleaders were sobbing, and some fans began to leave to get a jump on traffic. After all, it was Thanksgiving, and there was still plenty to do at home.

Coach Lukins saw every game as an opportunity to build character. He never tolerated self- pity, and he coached every game one play at the time. So, when Morrisville called time to avoid a celebration penalty, Coach Lukins called his defense to the sidelines and met them part way. Some were crying, all were dejected.

"Get your heads up," he said. "This is a great football game and everyone in those stands is proud of you. You can cry later during dinner or in bed tonight. I don't give a damn. But right now, your job is to pull yourselves together, show your pride, and stop them on this extra point." Later, some kids said that Lukins seemed to be fighting back tears of his own, something he would never admit.
"I'm proud of you," he added. "Now go kick some ass on this play."

Morrisville lined up, but their thoughts were already on the victory dance that night. The play was a sweep to Dawkins, which surprised no one. Frankie forced the play wide, and Dawkins was buried by the swarming Bristol defense. Morrisville led 12-7.

There were forty-six seconds left in the game, and Bristol took its last time out before the kickoff. Again Coach Lukins huddled the team around him.
"No time for speeches. Their kicker is hurt, so they'll probably try a squib kick. I want the deep men up. If they kick it to a lineman, flip it to a deep guy. Everybody else, knock somebody down! We're out of time outs, so line up quickly after the kickoff. Remember to use the sidelines to stop the clock." Then he smiled. "What the hell, boys, we've got forty-six seconds left. Let's use 'em"

Morrisville's replacement kicker was told to "top" the ball to one of Bristol's linemen. But inexperienced athletes don't always do what they're told. The kicker made contact lower than he meant to, and lifted the ball in a short arc.

Billy Moyer fielded it again on the dead run and again put on a burst of speed up the middle. The Morrisville players were caught off guard by the quick return, and Moyer was by most of them before they could recover. For a moment it looked like Moyer would score, but Robinson, Morrisville's all state safety, converged on him. With less than forty seconds left in his high school football career, Billy Moyer was hit harder then he had ever been hit before, but he held on to the football. As he was swarmed by his teammates, he saw that he was standing on Morrisville's twenty-five yard line.

Mrs. Francelli never missed Johnny's home games, but she rarely watched him play. The hitting was just too much for her. So, she worked in the snack bar, where the game was nearby, but out of her vision. When the announcer said Morrisville scored the go-ahead touchdown, she was heartbroken for her son and all of the boys she had known since grade school. But she was also relieved that in another minute or so, her son's playing days would be over, and he would no longer be at risk. As some Bristol fans began to make an early exit, she finished wiping down the counter with the other volunteers. In the background she heard the announcer say that Morrisville would be kicking off.

Seconds later there was pandemonium as the Bristol stands erupted. Fans making their way to the exits started running back to the field. Someone nearby yelled, "Damn, he almost broke the kickoff!" The band started playing the fight song. Instinctively, Mrs. Francelli tossed aside the cleaning towel and followed the crowd to the fence surrounding the field.

With no time outs left and the ball on the twenty-five yard line, everyone, including Morrisville's ferocious pass rushers, knew Bristol would have to pass. Running would take too much time.

Nick listened carefully as Coach Lukins gave his instructions. Nick was a natural leader, and Lukins had taught him that a team takes the personality of its quarterback. If he was poised and confident, they would be too.

In the huddle the players were sky high, chattering and pumping each other up until Nick said, "Shut up and listen." Everyone did. "Ok," he said. "We're running a pro-left, 28 counter pitch. Johnny, don't forget to use the sideline to stop the clock." Then he added with a smile, "Frankie, coach said to move your fat ass."

It was a running play. In an obvious passing situation like this, Morrisville would attack the passer without much concern for the run. Lukins was gambling to use Johnny's speed to get outside, gain some yardage, get out of bounds to stop the clock, and have time to throw a shorter pass on the next, and probably last, play. If it didn't work, he'd be crucified in town, but it was his team and his call.

Bristol lined up in the passing formation, and Morrisville prepared to blitz. Bristol was going to fake right and quick pitch left. With the defensive backs moving in the wrong direction, and the defensive line penetrating to rush the passer, Johnny might get some decent running room outside.

Frankie, at left tackle, would loop out into the flat to block the outside linebacker. Frankie had to be quick to get out in front of the ball carrier, and Coach Lukins was sure he would be.

The play began perfectly. The receivers drew their defenders. Frankie got a good first step and got out in front of Johnny, who received the pitch cleanly. Jim McDougal, the Morrisville linebacker Frankie was supposed to block, tried to change direction, but slipped and fell.

The next day in Mickey's Barber Shop, they talked about the play. "The paper said that kid McDougal fell," Mickey said to everyone in the shop, "but I think he just didn't want any part of Big Frankie. The kid just bailed out. You could see it. I've been cutting Frankie's hair since he was in first grade. I love the kid." Then he added chuckling, "I'm sure the kid stole a Playboy from the shop when he was ten. He thinks I don't know it, but I'm gonna tell him next time he comes in. Maybe I'll get him to sign me a new one."

With McDougal on the ground, Frankie turned up field to find another target, while Billy Moyer put a beautiful block on the other safety. Now the only person between Frankie and the goal line was Scott Robinson, who was recovering from the fake and closing in.

Johnny was running the play exactly as taught. He gained depth in the backfield to let Frankie get out in front of him. The only way Robinson could get to Johnny was by going through Frankie. Frankie's massive frame was moving at full speed, and Robinson was breathing fire and moving on a path to meet him. The collision occurred at the seven-yard line.

Just before impact, Frankie dipped and exploded up and out. The crowd gasped as Robinson was knocked backward and fell in a heap. Frankie kept his feet, and had to jump over Robinson as he continued on.

Frankie Mayson and Johnny Francelli crossed the goal line the same way they did everything in life- together.

The next day, the front page of the *County-Times* featured a picture of Big Frankie holding Johnny off the ground in a bear hug as Johnny held the ball high. Above them the headline read:
Bristol Upsets Morrisville 13-12.

17- **Graduation**

Summer 1966

High school graduation was bittersweet. The "freedom" the boys longed for during most of their senior year soon proved far less appealing than they had imagined. For Johnny, Frankie, and Jimmy, college wasn't an option. They were average students at best, and, even if they did qualify academically, financial aid was scarce. Like many kids in the modest income town, they simply couldn't afford to go. Angelo was bright enough to go, but it was always clear that he would be needed to run the family deli that would be his someday.

Some entered the job market right away. Jimmy took a job at the steel mill where Johnny's father worked before he died. It was difficult and dangerous work, but he was grateful to earn a steady wage. Frankie's uncle helped him land an apprenticeship in the carpenter's union. If he stuck with it, he'd have a valuable skill and a solid income for the rest of his life. As expected, Angelo worked in the store.

Johnny wanted to work in the mill like his father, but Mrs. Francelli wouldn't hear of it. He had some other possibilities to work as a laborer, one in a garment factory and the other in a lumberyard, but she rejected them too. She wanted more for her son. The jobs paid decent money, but not enough to give him the life she dreamed of. She knew too many stories of boys who took low-level jobs and enjoyed having money in their pockets as young men, only to realize later that they were stuck in dead-end positions. One of their neighbors was working hard to get Johnny into the electrician's union, which would be a great opportunity for him, but openings were tight and it would take some time. While they waited, Mrs. Francelli allowed Johnny to take a job delivering flowers for the Livingni Flower Shop in town. It would give him just enough money to get by, but certainly not enough to make him complacent.

She wanted him to set goals, to see the big picture. She also made him promise to take some courses at the new community college.

Nick loved growing up in Bristol, but he wanted to get away, to see other parts of the country and gain new experiences. He had solid academic ability and would have been a strong college candidate, but there was no way his family could afford fulltime tuition. So his father encouraged him to talk with the local army recruiter. After a series of tests, the recruiter told Nick that he could qualify for any number of opportunities in the army. He also explained the GI benefits that would pay for his college after discharge. To a bored eighteen year old looking for adventure, this sounded good, so he signed up to leave in the fall.

Not everyone had limited options after high school. Billy Moyer was an outstanding student and the pride of Bristol High. He played sports, was a leader in student government, got straight A's, and still found the time to hang with the guys. He wanted a career in politics or law, and everyone knew he would be successful. Washington had enthralled him ever since his eighth grade class trip there. So he applied to and was accepted as a Political Science major at Georgetown University. Georgetown was expensive, but Billy's father was the most prominent attorney in town, and money wasn't an issue.

Thanks to his rich uncle, Ralph McGinnis was also college bound. With good grades and strong SAT scores, he was easily accepted at Penn State University. Ralph's family had always dreamed that he would attend college, but became even more adamant about it as Vietnam draft quotas increased. In 1966 college students were deferred from the draft, and Ralph's parents wanted to make sure he never went to Vietnam. In fact, Ralph told his friends that if the United States ever eliminated college draft deferments, his uncle would pay to send him to McGill University in Montreal. At the time, this seemed pretty drastic, but no one really gave it much thought.

The boys made the graduation party circuit that summer. Almost every proud family hosted one for their graduate, and the invitations ran well into July.

The parties became a problem for Johnny because Allison was at most of them.

On one occasion, Johnny brought another girl, and Allison left in tears. He felt a strong urge to run after her, but he didn't. At the next party, Allison retaliated with a date of her own, someone he'd never seen before. Johnny put on a great show, pretending not to care. He told jokes, laughed a lot, and flirted with every willing girl, but the hurt was there all over again. Knowing Allison was dating other guys was hard enough; actually seeing her with someone else was far worse.

Once, Frankie said, "Why don't you stop this game-playing and just go out with her? You know it's what you're both dying to do."

"No way," Johnny said. "It would be good for a while, but then she'd just burn me again."

"Just give it a try," Frankie persisted.

Johnny gave him a hard stare. "Have you ever had the crap beat out of you, Frankie?"

"Not really," Frankie said.

"Well I have," Johnny admitted. "By her, and it's never gonna happen again."

"If you ask me, it seems like you're still getting beaten up, every time you see her."

"I'm taking a few punches maybe, but there aren't any knockdowns like before."

"Do you know that girls are afraid to go out with you?" Frankie asked. "Everybody knows that you're still crazy about her. They see it when you're with another girl and you're stealing looks at Allison across the room. Pretty soon you're gonna be shut out."

"There are plenty of girls, Frankie. I'll handle it."

"But there's only one Allison, and I think she's changed. So she dumped you once for a while. Big deal. She's grown up and obviously cares for you. Give it another shot."

Johnny got quiet for a minute. When he spoke, there was no hint of the self-assured Johnny that everyone knew.

"Okay, big guy, do you want to know the truth?"

"It's about time," Frankie said.

"The truth is that she's too good for me. Really. She's too damn beautiful and too smart. She has too much money and too good of a future. She's going away to school, and I'm not. She's gonna have an army of guys following her wherever she goes, guys with brains and money and goddamned sailboats. Even if she really believes I'm the guy for her now, that will change; I'm sure of it. And it won't be her fault. When she broke up with me the first time, she said there was another world out there besides Bristol, and she was going to soak it up. She was right. So I'm not gonna go through that again. I'll never feel the same for another girl the way I feel about Allison, but we're not going to end up together, so there's no use in starting over."

"I think you're wrong, but it's your life I guess," Frankie said, and dropped it.

The boys also resumed their cherished visits to the beach. Bristol was located on the Delaware River, just over the bridge from New Jersey and only an hour and a half away from the Jersey shore. Their favorite spot was Seaside. It wasn't as swanky as some of the other towns, but it had a boardwalk loaded with arcades and places to eat. It catered to a younger crowd, and the boys could rent a room overnight for four bucks each.

But Seaside's most important attribute was its girls. There were tanned, bikini-clad girls on the beach, smiling girls on the boardwalk, cheering girls on motel balconies, and girls in convertibles cruising the main drag. There were girls in the ice cream shops and girls in the pizza parlors. It was impossible not to meet girls at Seaside. And best of all, they were friendly and always looking for a good party. In fact, the boys declared Seaside a snob-free community. Even Frankie, who was usually unlucky in romance, found an occasional girl.

They weren't sure why the girls were so friendly, but there were many theories. Frankie swore it was the salt air. Johnny said it was his charm and good looks. Nick said it was the work of a benevolent God. Whatever the reason was, Billy showed off his Georgetown potential by calling it the greatest concentration of feminine splendor and affability ever assembled. Jimmy didn't know what any of that meant, but he knew it was something good, so he agreed.

The boys rarely told the truth when they met girls. They changed their names, inflated their ages, placed themselves in colleges, and even created majors. They were future engineers, journalists, attorneys, or whatever struck them at the moment. They fibbed about the things they owned. They'd claim to have a motorcycle at home or a rare old sports car undergoing restoration. Knowing girls liked adventure, they made up exciting stories about sailing, surfing or backpacking in Europe. Sometimes they'd pretend to be tough guys, who had brushes with the law. It was clear that no one was looking for lasting relationships at Seaside, so as long as the stories could be sustained for a night or a weekend, they didn't matter. The girls either believed them or enjoyed their storytelling so much that they didn't care. Ironically, the only story any girls absolutely refused to accept was when Johnny and Frankie would tell them they once met President Kennedy. They eventually had to drop it to preserve their credibility.

The stories worked well with the girls, but their singing worked even better. On nights when the mood was right and their confidence was high, they'd pick a spot on the boardwalk and sing. They'd start with the Drifter's "Under the Boardwalk," then go to the Duprees with "You Belong to Me." Next, they'd slide into songs by the Skyliners, the Capris, or whatever else moved them. Soon clusters of adoring, friendly girls would surround them. There was no better memory than the time they spent at Seaside on weekends in the summer of 1966.

18- Pizza at Frankie's

August 1966

Frankie had tickets for the Phillies game and picked up Johnny at one o'clock, but before leaving town, he drove to his house and parked.

"What's up?" Johnny asked.

"I forgot the tickets. Come in and I'll show you my new stereo."

"How's your mom?" Johnny asked as they got out of the car.

"She's not doing well. Her diabetes is way out of line. She's away this weekend visiting my aunt in Delaware."

"So Frankie has the house all to himself," Johnny kidded. "You should plan a big party."

"Actually, I planned small one," Frankie said, as they entered the house.

"Really?" Johnny said.

"Yeah. There's been a change in plans. I'm taking Angelo to the game, and you're staying here."

Johnny looked puzzled.

"There's pizza in the kitchen and plenty to drink in the fridge. I won't be home until late tonight, so lock up when you leave."

Johnny laughed. "What are you talking about?"

Frankie patted him on the back and whispered, "Please don't blow this," before tuning to leave.

Just then Johnny's jaw dropped as Allison appeared in the kitchen doorway.

"Hi Johnny," she said, sounding terrified.

At first Johnny couldn't speak. He heard the door close behind him. With effort, he managed to say "Hi." He wasn't sure if he wanted to kill Frankie or thank him.

"Please don't be mad," she said.

"Not mad," he mumbled softly, without taking his eyes off her.

"This was my idea. I just asked Frankie to help."

"Good ol' Frankie," he replied.

She wore jeans with an oversized sweatshirt, and her straight blond hair fell to her shoulders. Simple beauty, Johnny thought. It was the way he always liked her best, and she knew it.

He hadn't moved yet, and his heart raced as she crossed the room toward him.

She tried smiling to mask her fear, but it wasn't working. She never looked more vulnerable, Johnny thought, or beautiful. When she stopped they were face to face.

"I've been thinking for a long time about what I would say to you," she said. "And I still don't know."

He hadn't seen her eyes this close in a long time. They sparkled.

She gently wrapped her arms around his neck and pulled him closer. Then, without speaking, she kissed him, a warm, tender kiss that didn't end. Reluctantly, he allowed his arms to wrap around her, lightly at first, and then tighter, until he became a willing partner. The moment turned into two, then ten, and more. Then they lost all sense of time.

It was dusk before they found their way to the food in Frankie's kitchen. The pizza was from Cesare's and was their favorite. It reminded Johnny of his football days before their breakup. After night games, everyone would head to Cesare's for pizza and sodas. Allison would wait for him outside the locker room on Garfield Street so they could walk to the joint together.

The locker room was a central part of Johnny's world, and he remembered it all, the laughing and towel snapping, the blaring music, the hoots and catcalls of teammates, the smell of sweat, athletic tape, and analgesic balm, the camaraderie of combat and victory. It was a world Johnny loved, but outside was a world he loved even more, Allison's world. He'd do some brief celebrating with the guys, shower quickly, and hurry to meet her, anxious to replace his boisterous teammates with the soft embrace and sweet smell of his girl.

With the game's adrenalin wearing off, the soreness from countless hits would set in, that and tremendous fatigue. "Don't leave anything on the field," Coach Lukins used to say. Johnny never did. On the field he was alert, coiled, ready to explode. By the time he reached Allison, he was spent. He'd walk gingerly, feeling every muscle. She'd be waiting in the same spot each week, smiling in her red and gray cheerleading uniform, her cheeks just slightly red from the crisp, fall air. They'd hug, and he'd be engulfed by a wonderful tranquility. In her arms his soreness and fatigue felt good, an affirmation that he had given his all. Her touch would soothe him, and the pain would slowly drain from his body.

Together they'd walk to Cesare's. His arm on her shoulder, hers around his waist. For the next few blocks, she was his strength. She knew football, and she'd talk quietly about the game, recounting every play he made, while he listened in silence. He knew that when they reached Cesare's, friends would be competing for their attention, so he savored their time together. Johnny Francelli and Allison O'Brien, walking alone on Wilson Avenue after a victory. The world was a perfect place.

"So what now?" Allison said, snapping Johnny back to the present.
"That's a good question," he replied. "What now?"
She reached across the table and put her hand on his. "Now we plan our future," she said smiling.
Johnny didn't respond and his expression wasn't what Allison expected.
"What's wrong?" she asked, removing her hand.
"Nothing," Johnny said, unconvincingly.
"Are you sorry I came today?"
Johnny forced a smile and shook his head. "I couldn't be happier. This was one of the best days of my life," he said.

"I thought so too," she said. "But it doesn't seem that way now."

Johnny looked at her. "I'm afraid," he confessed. "Very afraid."

She made a nervous laugh. "Johnny Francelli's afraid, of what?

"Of us," he said quietly.

She leaned back in her chair. "What's there to be afraid of? We'll be together, like we always knew we would be."

"Not always," Johnny replied, regretting the comment as soon as he made it.

"What's that mean?" she said, her tone changing.

"Forget it," he said, knowing that she wouldn't.

"You're still hung up about Cape Cod, aren't you?"

"No," Johnny lied slightly. "It's not the past I'm worried about. Like I said, it's the future."

"It's our future," she said. "We decide what it is."

When Johnny didn't respond, she went to the refrigerator and opened a coke. She took a sip and banged the bottle on the counter a little louder than she had intended.

"This is all about pride," she said. "I made a mistake once, and you won't forgive me."

"That's not true," Johnny said. "It's not about pride; it's about insecurity. Mine."

Allison rolled her eyes. "About what?"

Johnny hesitated. "That it will happen again."

"Great!" she exploded. "So it's about trust. Allison O'Brien can't be trusted. She cheated on her boyfriend when she was sixteen, so she can never be trusted. That's entirely fair. Maybe you should be a judge, the famous hanging judge, Johnny Francelli. Make just one mistake and you're dead meat!"

Johnny ignored the sarcasm. "It's about reality. You're going to Boston College in two weeks. I'll be stuck here, working and going to the community college. You're gonna meet hundreds of people and have tons of guys chasing you. Guys from a different background."

"Don't start with that again," she said.

"It's true. And nothing against your parents, but they're not sending you to BC so you can come home to Johnny."

"I'll make my own decisions."

"I believe you will," Johnny said, "but I'm not sure what they will be."

"My God!" she thundered. "Doesn't coming here today tell you something about my decision?"

He thought briefly before responding. "Allison, I have no doubt that you want to get back together and believe we can. I want the same thing. But I'm not sure you realize what it will be like when you're away."

"I know what it can be like," she said defiantly. "We'll write. We'll call. You'll visit once in a while. I'll come home once in a while. We'll have summers. That's what we'll do. It can work!"

"For four years?"

"Yes!" She said with exaggerated conviction. "For four years."

"And you won't see anyone? No dates, no parties?"

"Exactly," she insisted.

Johnny shook his head. "I'm sorry Allison, but I'm not even sure you believe that. I don't think you're lying, but I just don't think you realize what you're saying. I'm not even sure that would be fair to you."

"Why don't I decide that?" she said.

Impulsively, she took another sip. She wanted time to think. Her bitterness was obvious when she spoke.

"Maybe it's you who wants to date other people. Maybe that's it."

"That's not it," Johnny said.

Allison ignored him. "Fine," she said. "You win. We'll write, call, visit each other, and in between we'll see other people, if that's what you want. Are you happy now?"

"No I'm not, because that's not what I want." Johnny said. "I can't do that, maybe with other girls, but not with someone like you who I care about. I can't share you. I can't visit you on one weekend, knowing the guy next to me in the student cafeteria might be going out with you the next."

Allison looked stung. "Did you say 'care about?' That's an interesting choice of words. How about love? Does that word work for you?" She looked him in the eyes. "Do you love me, Johnny?"

Johnny paused again. "More than you can imagine."

"But," she added sadly.

Johnny nodded. "But I'm not convinced you love me, and I need that. I was hurt awfully bad before. I'm afraid to let myself go again. I'm afraid I'll get whacked even harder."

"Damn you!" She said. "So this is about pride and punishment and trust, and everything else I said before."

"I told you. It's about fear. I just can't go though that kind of pain again."

"So we're finished then," she said, through a mixture of anger and tears. "I love you, but you don't believe it. I'm willing to not see anyone else, but you don't believe it. I see us together forever, but you don't believe it. Who do you think you are?"

"You're making it sound different than it is." Johnny said.

"It sounds pretty lousy to me," she said, brushing past him as she started for the front room.

"I have a different idea," he called after her.

She stopped and turned. Tears were streaming down her face now. "And what's that?"

"You go to school and do your thing. We don't pretend we're a couple. We don't call or write, or anything else that complicates things. See how things unfold in Boston. If you still want me after some time with the BC crowd, you'll know it, and I'll know then that we have something that's real. Until then, I won't expect anything so I won't be disappointed."

She wiped her eyes. She had dreamed of this meeting for months. Now she was wondering how such a good day could have turned so bad.

"And how long does this little experiment last?" she said.

"I don't know," Johnny said. "I need to know you really want me."

"How long?" she shouted.

"A year, maybe two. When the time's right, we'll either know that it's over, or that we really have something."

"I think what I have is a guy with a far bigger ego than I realized," she said bitterly. "Someone who still wants to punish his old girlfriend."

"That's not true Allison. You mean everything to me. I'm pretty sure I love you, but I can't be positive until I know that you can be true to one person."

She laughed sarcastically. "Know what Johnny? You don't want this. I tried my best, but it wasn't good enough. So you can shove your little test."

He started to speak, but she wouldn't let him.

"Screw you, Johnny. You won't be hearing from me anymore."

"Allison wait," Johnny said as she headed for the door. "It's not like what you're saying."

"Clean up Frankie's kitchen," she called over her shoulder, just before she slammed the door behind her.

Part IV
Scattered

19- Saying Good-Bye

September 1966

As the summer of '66 came to a close, the boys grew more and more subdued. Most of them had been together since first grade, and it was difficult knowing they were going their separate ways. Billy Moyer left first in late August for freshman orientation at Georgetown. The night before he left, they gathered at the log to reminisce and share a few beers. They joked about school memories, the wedding crashes, their football exploits and their trips to the shore. They toasted the breakup of the Tone Kings and talked about what might have been. In the end there were strong embraces, stifled tears, and vows to remain close forever.

Ralph was next. He had to be at Penn State by the day after Labor Day and when it came time to go, he seemed shaken. He was obviously apprehensive about leaving home. The boys had always considered Ralph a "part-timer" because he spent more time with his books than with them at Jake's, the log, or at Johnny's house. They had also teased him a lot about working with the "stiffs" at his uncle's funeral home. But he was a good guy, and it was sad to say good-bye.

Nick was scheduled to leave for the army in mid September and was pretty cool about it, but Jimmy was a wreck. The two had been best friends from the first day they met. Nick was Jimmy's protector in the early grades at St. Therese's, always coming to his defense when other kids made fun of his limitations. Jimmy loved him like a brother and didn't know how he'd get by without him. The night before Nick left, he, Jimmy, Frankie, Angelo and Johnny met at Johnny's house to say their good-byes. To lighten things up they began recounting the closing minutes of the Thanksgiving Day game with Morrisville the year before. After basking in their glory for a while, Nick said, "Jimmy, I never told you this before, but remember when you made that big catch and held on to the ball after that kid hit you so hard?"

"Does he remember?" Johnny kidded. "He won't let us forget."

"Right, Mr. Touchdown," Jimmy replied. "And what about that?" He said, pointing to the photo on the wall of Frankie holding Johnny up in the end zone.

"That's my mom's picture, not mine." Johnny said.

"Yeah, sure," Jimmy said.

"Anyway," Nick interjected. "I never told you this before, but after that kid hit you and you came back to the huddle, you had snot dripping from your nose. I'd heard the expression before, but I'd never actually seen someone have the snot knocked out of him."

The guys roared with laughter. Even Jimmy had to smile.

"There I am," Nick continued. There's a minute left in the game. I'm trying to keep my head and figure out what play Coach Lukins wants me to run, and I look at Jimmy and he's got snot running down to his mouth. I almost barfed right through my face mask."

When the laughter finally died down, Jimmy said, "Yeah, but I held on to the ball."

"You sure did, Jimmy," Nick said, putting his hand on Jimmy's shoulder. "You won that game for us."

Jimmy let that sink in for a few seconds, and then he said quietly, "Johnny scored the winning touchdown."

"That's true," Johnny said. "But if you didn't make that catch, the game would have been over a lot sooner."

"I was just lucky," Jimmy said, somewhat embarrassed.

"The game was on the line, Jimmy," Nick said. "Lukins would have never called the play, and I would have never thrown you the ball if we didn't believe in you. You kept us in the game."

The room stayed quiet. Everyone knew how hard it would be for Jimmy with Nick gone.

Finally, Jimmy said, "You said you get to come home on leave after basic training."

"That's right," Nick said. "I'll be at basic for six weeks and then I get two weeks off before I leave for advanced training."

"Six weeks?" Jimmy repeated.

"Six weeks," Nick said. "And if you think I'm a stud now, wait until you see me after that. I'll be lean and mean and able to kick all of your asses at the same time, including big Frankie's."

Frankie smiled.

"We'll be here," Jimmy said bravely. "Take care of yourself."

"You too, Nick said. "All of you."

The remaining guys settled into their new routine, but they didn't like it. They worked all day, and by the evening Frankie and Jimmy were too tired from work to go out much. Johnny and Angelo went to Jake's a few times, but it didn't feel right. The place seemed dead and some younger kids were starting to hang out there, giving old Jake their quarters just as fast as they could. On Friday nights the four of them went to dances at the firehouse, run by a DJ from Philly. The dances were crowded and they met plenty of girls, but everyone started looking younger. Each week they felt more and more out of place there too.

Then Frankie's mother died suddenly from complications with her diabetes. Frankie took it surprisingly well, at least outwardly. She had been sick a long time, and it was not totally unexpected. During the mourning period, Johnny spent every minute with his friend, remembering all too clearly when Frankie had sat with him for hours at the log when his father died. Frankie confided that his mom had prepared him for her passing for a long time. They had already done their crying together, and, in a way, Frankie had already done his grieving. Still, it was hard. Frankie's aunt in Delaware offered to take him in, as did his uncle Vince in town, but he declined. He was eighteen, he explained, and could manage just fine. Anna had made him the same offer, telling Frankie that he and Johnny were like brothers anyway, so he might as well move in, but he declined her offer as well. Anna had to settle for a promise that he would eat with them several times a week and visit every day.

Nick came home as promised in late October, looking just as fit as he said he would. He seemed older and more serious than he was six weeks earlier. He had made platoon leader in basic training and his commanding officer encouraged him to take the test for the Green Berets. It sounded like serious stuff. When Johnny joked that they do covert operations like wedding crashes, Nick barely smiled. The army had changed him a lot.

"Any chance of you ending up in Vietnam?" Frankie asked.

"There's an absolute chance," Nick said. "I volunteered."

"Volunteered!" Angelo said. "Are you nuts?"

Nick let the outburst slide. "We have a job to do," he said evenly. "We've made a commitment to help those people defend themselves against communism."

"Jesus!" Angelo said. "What's happened to you?"

"Okay guys," Jimmy said. "Let's change the subject. How about if we get some beers?"

Nick ignored him. "I learned a lot since I've been gone," he said. "I've made friends who've been to Nam and others who are going. Only one out of two hundred and fifty applicants become Green Berets. I have a chance to be one, and that's what I want to do."

Nick's two-week leave passed by quickly, and then he was gone.

In late 1966 the war was still raging. The United States was approaching the level of a half million troops, and thousands had already died. Draft calls were up, and Nick wasn't gone long before Jimmy received his notice. He was scared stiff before he left. He wanted to talk with Nick, but couldn't reach him. Even Nick's parents couldn't contact him. So Jimmy had to leave for the army without the assurances from Nick that he had grown to depend upon.

On the morning Jimmy left, Angelo, Johnny, and Frankie waited outside Jimmy's house as he said good-bye to his parents. His mother looked broken up. Frankie took Jimmy's bag when he got to the front gate, and they walked with him the two blocks to the bus depot. Johnny tried to make small talk, but Jimmy remained quiet. At the depot, they all hugged and Jimmy did his best not to cry as he boarded the bus and took his seat by the window. They returned his wave as the bus slowly pulled away from the curb.

"This is absolute bullshit," Angelo said softly.

20- Charlie Gario

January 1967

Charlie Gario sat with his legs dangling from the roof of his parents' garage, holding a half-finished bottle of his father's Jim Beam, staring at the driveway eighteen feet below. He could hear *Ruby Tuesday* blaring on the radio through the open garage door. Each swig of bourbon seared his chest and made his head spin even more. It was cold, but not as bad as it could be in late January, and the bourbon was making him sweat as it bolstered his courage.

For months he'd been plagued by the same anxiety about Vietnam that other guys felt, but with no real friends to lean on, he faced his fears alone. He saw what was happening to some of his Bristol High classmates. Nick Hardings had been crazy to sign up, and Jimmy Wright wasn't smart enough to get out of it. Charlie knew that sooner or later his own time would come. Then the letter arrived, confirming what he and his parents had dreaded all along. He was scared, and the look in his mother's eyes only made things worse. He was doing this for her too. He removed the letter from his jacket and looked at it again. The words hit him like a fresh punch to the face, and he knew what he needed to do. His watch read 4:35; his parents would be returning from work in ten minutes. He didn't want to embarrass them. Dad was vice president of one of the banks in town, and mom was a loan officer in the same branch. They were always worried about proper appearances, but Charlie was convinced he could pull this off without embarrassing anyone.

It was time. He replaced the cap on the Jim Beam and carefully tossed the bottle to the grass, hoping it wouldn't break. It didn't. He decided things would go better with one shoe on and one off, so he pulled off the left one and dropped it to the driveway. Watching it fall scared him a little. Slowly he pulled his feet up under him and stood. His head was really spinning now and he had trouble balancing on the peaked roof. He tried closing his eyes, but decided against it. Instead, he looked straight ahead, and, for the first time in months, he felt in control of his future. Finally, with surprising ease, he jumped.

He heard the bone crack as he hit the driveway. There was a moment of numbness, then a searing pain that exceeded anything he'd anticipated. Reaching for his leg, he found
blood and exposed bone and thought he was going to vomit. From the garage, the disc jockey boomed, "This is WIBG in Philadelphia. Your WIBBAGE time is 4:43. It's thirty-seven degrees and cloudy. Here's Van Morrison's *Brown Eyed Girl.*"

As Charlie lay coiled in pain, he prayed that his parents would be home in time to help. Then, just before he passed out, he smiled, knowing he would fail his draft physical on Tuesday.

21- The Home Front

By February of 1967, Angelo, Johnny, and Frankie were the only members of the old gang still in town. They made it a point to see each other once or twice a week, but it was nothing like before. On most days Frankie was even too tired to make it to Johnny's. He'd just drag himself home from work and collapse on the couch. The apprenticeship was going well, but it was hard work. Johnny finished his delivery job each day, had some dinner and then went to his night classes at the community college. The courses were tougher than he had anticipated and Johnny decided pretty early that college wasn't for him. He hoped the electrician's union thing opened up soon. Angelo worked from seven to seven at the store six days a week. By nightfall, he usually wasn't in any mood to socialize.

There wasn't a lot of communication from Jimmy or Nick. Jimmy wasn't much of a writer, but it was clear from his notes that his adjustment wasn't a smooth one. He wasn't mixing well with the other guys, and he disliked his commanding officer. Jimmy's company had already been told they would be shipping out to Vietnam as soon as they completed training, and that really had him spooked. The only thing helping him keep his sanity was the physical training. He was one of the smallest men in the platoon, but he wrote that he could run, climb, jump and crawl better than anyone, which came as no surprise to those who had gone through football camp with him. He simply never tired and always welcomed physical activities over mental ones. If the news from Jimmy wasn't good, at least it was something. The guys heard even less about Nick, who virtually disappeared. He sent no letters to any of them, and his parents didn't volunteer much information. The Special Forces stuff seemed to be pretty secret.

The American public no longer overlooked the war. The *County-Times* started printing statistics on war casualties in the upper right- hand corner of their front page. The two-inch box had bold black borders and carried the number of American deaths. By the end of 1966, over 7800 had died, and the 1967 number was growing at an accelerated rate.

On April 15, 1967, there were large anti-war demonstrations across the country. An estimated 300,000 people demonstrated against the war in New York, and over two hundred protesters burned their draft cards in Central Park. Angelo, Johnny, and Frankie were in Johnny's basement and saw the protest on TV.

"That's what we should do," Angelo said. "Burn our damn draft cards."

"It's against the law," Johnny said. "They can be arrested."

"Who cares?" Angelo replied. "I'd rather be in jail than die in Vietnam. The protesters are right."

"How can you say that with Jimmy and Nick there?" Frankie said.

"That's exactly the point," Angelo snapped. "They shouldn't be there. No one should be there. If I had the guts I'd take off for Canada like other people are doing."

Frankie shook his head. "What's stopping you?"

"I can't run out on Pop. He wouldn't be able to run the store by himself," he said. "But if I ever get drafted, I might leave."

"I can't believe you're saying that." Johnny said. "This is our country, we owe it something. If you get called, you go. That's what our fathers did in the other wars."

Angelo waived him off. "Have you really been following this thing? I mean, really following it? Eight thousand guys have died already. Let that sink in. Their stories are in the paper every day. Every day we hear the news of ten more or twenty more. After a while people aren't shocked. They just shrug it off. I see it in the store every day. Customers come in to buy a newspaper. They read the headline, shake their head sadly, grab a quart of milk, bitch about the weather, maybe tell my father a joke, and then leave. Where's the outrage?"

"What are they supposed to do?" Johnny asked.

"How about getting pissed off?" Angelo shouted. "That would be a good start."

Johnny hadn't heard Angelo this excited before and tried to calm him down. "Take it easy Angelo."

Angelo ignored him and plowed on. "I saw a show on TV the other night that said three-quarters of the guys in Vietnam are from working class families. It's people like us who are getting killed, not the rich guys. Don't forget where Billy and Ralph are right now. I mean, I love those guys, but they're off in college in the back seat of some car groping their favorite coeds while Jimmy's sorry ass is headed for Vietnam. How come they got free passes and he didn't?"

"That's just bad luck," Johnny said.

"Bad luck my ass," Angelo said. "They got college deferments from the draft because the law's designed to help the rich kids. I can't afford full-time college and neither can the two of you."

Johnny shrugged it off. "But don't forget why we're there. We're fighting communism. I listened to what Nick had to say when he was home, and it made sense. Either we fight 'em there or we'll fight 'em here."

"Do you really believe that crap?" Angelo said. "For God's sake, those people work in rice paddies. What threat are they?"

"You're missing the big picture." Frankie said. We're there…"

Angelo didn't let him finish. "Look, I'm not going to argue with you guys. Save it for someone who buys that crap. I read the paper every day in the store. Eight thousand guys are dead," he said as he stood and moved toward the door. "The other night on the news some senator... I can't remember his name, but he was somebody important. Anyway, some senator said we couldn't win. He was a goddamned senator; he should know what he's talking about."

"Yeah, well I heard that a lot of senators still support the war," Frankie replied.

Angelo held back. He was sorry he started the conversation.

After a few seconds, Frankie broke the silence. "Look, maybe I don't know all of the facts, and maybe I should learn them. But I just think that if your country goes to war, you support it, whether you like it or not."

Angelo looked at the floor and shook his head. When he looked up, he forced a smile and said quietly, "I'll see you guys later."

He opened the door and left.

Anna Francelli overheard the boys' argument that night, and it seemed to her that the same heated rhetoric extended beyond her basement recreation room and engulfed America. It dominated the news each time she watched it. The country was growing increasingly polarized. Prominent figures from politics, sports and entertainment proudly referred to themselves as "doves." Martin Luther King, Jr. reacted to the death toll among blacks in the war by calling the United States "the greatest purveyor of violence in the world." Others, like Bertrand Russell, condemned the United States for its use of chemical weapons like Napalm in violation of international law. In October of 1967, 50,000 protesters surrounded the Pentagon and almost 700 were arrested. Benjamin Spock, America's best-known pediatrician, became one of the most recognized opponents of President Johnson's war policies.

Democratic Senator Eugene McCarthy was becoming an outspoken critic of the war and Johnson's policies.

The pro-war response was strong and swift. Equally prominent members of society proclaimed themselves "hawks" and spoke forcefully of America's duty to defend freedom throughout the world. Law and order advocates wanted a crack down on anti-war activities and labeled agitators communist sympathizers. Protesting was viewed as being disloyal to our troops. People wanted limits on speech. Some wanted demonstrators prosecuted for aiding the enemy. Proud, elderly veterans of World War II and Korea condemned protesters as cowards and draft dodgers. Several leaders in Washington called for a more aggressive policy to win the war.

To Anna's dismay, in spite of the rising rhetoric on both sides, most Americans still managed to treat the war and the debate it prompted as annoying background noise. They were far more occupied with the daily demands of family, jobs, and whatever else occupied their lives. In the congressional elections the year before, only fifty-five percent of registered voters bothered to vote, hardly the turnout one would expect from a public that should have been engaged. If asked, most people would say they were concerned about the war, but consciously or subconsciously, they still managed to filter it out.

Johnny was still working part time at the flower shop making deliveries. He hated the job, but he enjoyed the happy faces of the customers when they opened their doors and noticed their gifts. The tips were modest, but they helped.

In early October he arrived at the shop and noticed a note from Frankie on the windshield of his delivery truck. All it said was, *Meet me at the log tonight at 6 o'clock. It's important.*

Johnny hadn't seen Frankie for several days and was glad to hear from him. But why was he being so mysterious, and why the log?

It was a cold night for mid October, and it was almost dark when Johnny arrived. He found Frankie sitting on the log with his head in his hands.

"Hey, big guy. What's up? Johnny said. "This better be important."

Frankie looked up but didn't smile. "Thanks for coming Johnny." His voice was barely audible. He looked terrible. Johnny sat next to him and waited a few seconds.

Without speaking, Frankie reached inside his jacket, removed an envelope and handed it to Johnny. The envelope looked official. In the remaining light Johnny could make out some sort of government seal. He removed the letter and strained to read it, but he didn't have to.

"It's my draft notice," Frankie said.

The words took Johnny's breath away.

"Drafted?" Johnny said, barely able to get the word out. Johnny examined the letter, hoping Frankie was wrong.

"I have to report for my physical in two weeks. I leave on October 20th."

"Damn," Johnny said. "What are you going to do?"

"I'm going to go," Frankie said softly. "What else can I do?"

"I don't know what to say, Frankie," Johnny said quietly. "This... I don't know..."

"I'm scared Johnny," Frankie said, barely audibly. "I'm really scared."

Frankie decided to keep on working as long as he could to put some money away. Four days later, he and his uncle were gutting a house with a crew on Pear Street when they heard a horn honking outside. Frankie's uncle went to the window and said,

"It's your friend Johnny in the flower truck," he said. "We need a break anyway. See what he wants."

When Frankie got outside, Johnny was laughing and still honking the horn.

"Big Frankie!" Johnny shouted, as he kept on honking.

Frankie had to laugh. "Stop it man. My uncle will take his hammer to your truck."

Johnny stopped.

"What are you doing here?"

"We're going together!" Johnny said, smiling broadly.

"Going where together? Who?" Frankie said, enjoying his friend's good humor. "What are you talking about?"

Johnny spoke slowly, exaggerating each word, "You and I are going into the army together."

Frankie didn't understand. "What do you mean together? You're not drafted are you? What's going on?"

"Jump in," Johnny said. "It's cold."

Frankie got in and said, "Start again."

"I've enlisted," Johnny said, lifting his own envelope from the dashboard.

"I asked around and found out that the army has a program called the Buddy System. It allows guys to sign up together and go through basic training and other assignments as a team. I checked it out with the recruiter on Mill Street, and he guaranteed me that if I signed up I would be placed in your induction group. We'll go through the whole deal together."

Now Frankie was speechless. When he gathered himself he said, "Johnny, you're crazy. Why did you do this?"

"Look, it's pretty obvious that it's just a matter of time before I get drafted. I'd rather control my own schedule than sit around waiting for them to take me. I hate taking classes at the community college. Besides, what would I do around here with you gone? You've got me Frankie, whether you like it or not."

"I like it." Frankie said. I like it, but I think you're crazy." Then he added, "Are you sure you can trust this recruiter?"

"Look," Johnny said, showing him his papers. "I'm already scheduled for my physical on the same day as you. It's a done deal."

"How did you get your mother to sign the papers?" Frankie asked.

"I'm nineteen! I don't need anyone but myself to sign up."

"What does she think of it?"

Johnny's enthusiasm faded, and he got quiet for a moment. Then, in a low voice he said, "I haven't told her yet. You're going to help me."

22- Dinner at Anna's

Anna Francelli greeted Frankie with her usual warm hug.

"Frankie!" She said. "Where have you been? I hardly see you anymore."

"Come on, Mrs. F, it's only been three days."

"Well it seems longer. I missed you."

Her words stung a little, because they reminded him that he'd be leaving soon and missing a lot of people, including her. She looked as good as ever. Frankie remembered that in seventh grade the guys at the log had voted her the best looking mom, with no disrespect intended. They would never do that to Johnny. It was just one of those dumb games that pre-teens play. One of them would holler something like, "best pizza joint" or "best pro quarterback" or "cutest girl at St. Therese's." The other players would call out answers, hoping to name one a majority would accept. But when someone called out, "prettiest mom," there was only one answer- Anna Francelli. She was aging a little now, showing some strands of gray in her dark black hair. But she was still slender, very pretty, and wore an almost constant smile. Even more important, she was a kind, generous, and intelligent woman. For years she had fed, tutored, and counseled every friend Johnny invited into her home. Every boy who experienced her warmth and hospitality loved her and would do anything for her, especially Frankie.

"I've been pretty busy with work," he said. "I'm putting in a lot of hours."

"Well, you should never be too busy to at least stop in for a quick dinner," she said smiling. And who cleans your house? I've told you that Sissy and I would be happy to stop in now and then and give it a good cleaning.

"I'm fine Mrs. Francelli. Really. The place is clean."

Anna smiled. "I was so happy when Johnny told me you were coming tonight. I just wish I had more notice. I could have made the stuffed olives you love."

"It was spur of the moment," he said. "I hope you didn't go through too much trouble."

"No trouble at all," Johnny called out as he came down the steps to join them. "She's been cooking for the past two hours." He put his arm around his mother's waist and kissed her on the cheek.

"The only reason I invited you was to get a decent meal," he said. "Tonight, we're having cavatelli with meat sauce, spicy like you like it; roasted chicken with plenty of juice; garlic bread; salad with extra croutons, so you don't have to steal mine, and homemade cheese cake."

"You left out the eggplant," Mrs. Francelli said proudly.

"Oh yes," Johnny said. "And fried eggplant, one of Frankie's many favorites."

"Thank you, Mrs. Francelli" Frankie said. "You really didn't have to do all of that."

Her smile faded slightly and her voice grew softer. "Frankie, I'm still so upset about your draft notice. I wish there was something I could do. I want you to know that I'll be praying for you every day you're gone, and I'll write to you at least once a week, even if you're too busy to write back, and I'll make sure Johnny writes too."

Frankie shot an awkward glance at Johnny. "Thank you Mrs. Francelli," he said, and gave her another hug.

"Hey, let's eat!" Johnny said, trying to break the mood.

"Sissy's not here tonight," Mrs. Francelli said, as they made their way to the dining room. "She has a date. She asked me to tell you that she would have broken it if she knew sooner that you were coming."

"That's a lie," Johnny kidded. "She's flipped over this guy and wouldn't break the date if the Pope were coming."

Frankie had eaten enough of Mrs. Francelli's food over the years to know that dinner would be both abundant and delicious. It was. Italians like to cook big. Mrs. Francelli once explained that they called it a *budanza*. A dinner party for four should have enough food for at least eight. People should feel that they could eat all they want, and she would never consider not having enough food for an unexpected guest.

The conversation was light and filled with laughter. The boys shared stories about their experiences in grade school, the times they got in trouble, and trips they took together. They confessed to deeds they had long denied, like forged excuse notes for school, ringing doorbells in the neighborhood and running away, and getting Angelo to prank call the house to scare the girls at Sissy's sleep-over party. When Mrs. Francelli told them she already knew all this, they laughed even harder.

Seeing her so happy made Johnny's task harder. Although he had given his enlistment careful thought, the reality of actually breaking the news to his mother, face to face like this, was killing him. And he knew that it would soon be killing her too. But he remained committed. It was time to move on, to see things, to experience life outside of Bristol. Almost all of his friends were gone, and his best friend was leaving. Johnny wasn't involved in any serious relationship with a girl either. He still used all of his will power to resist thinking about Allison, because it still hurt too much when he did.

The boys ate until they were stuffed and Mrs. Francelli marveled at how much they could consume, especially Frankie. When they were finished she cleared their plates and brought out the homemade cheesecake. As she started to slice it Johnny said, "Sit down, Mom. There's something I have to tell you."

He said all of the things he had rehearsed in preparation for the moment. He told her he had enlisted. He reminded her that it was probably just a matter of time before he would be drafted anyway. He told her that Frankie didn't know anything about his plans until after he had made them. He told her that the electrician's job hadn't materialized yet and probably wouldn't. He told her he was unhappy at the community college and wanted to use the GI Bill to go to college some day later. He told her he loved her and that leaving her was the most difficult thing he would ever have to do. As Johnny said all of that, Frankie wished he were in Vietnam or in the Outback wrestling alligators or any other place than at that dinner table.

Anna sat in total silence, looking like everything good in her life had just drained out of her. She pushed the cake dish away and put her hands on the table. They were shaking. Her lips were quivering slightly, as if she was about to cry, but still she said nothing. Finally, Johnny leaned forward and placed his hand on hers.

"Mom, ever since dad died you've taught me to be independent, to take responsibility for myself. At the same time that you gave me the best, most loving home a kid could have, you always told me that I had to prepare myself for the day when I would be on my own. You said there wouldn't be many people I could depend on to help me and I'd have to prepare to face tough things alone. You said the time would come when I'd be a man and life's decisions would be mine." He stroked her arm gently and said, "I love you more than anything, Mom, but it's time."

23- 401 North Broad Street

Johnny and Frankie's pre-induction physicals were scheduled for 8 AM. They boarded the bus in Bristol at six-thirty for their trip to the Armed

Forces Examination Station in Philadelphia. The facility was located at
401 North Broad Street, an address that had become infamous among
draft age men throughout the region.

On the bus they joked about the stories they'd heard of guys who tried
to skip the service by flunking their physicals. Some of the country-
club crowd used their connections with doctors and psychiatrists to get
notes documenting any number of physical or psychological ailments,
while others claimed conscientious objector status. The less connected
resorted to more drastic measures, including self-inflicted wounds and
even incarceration. Occasionally guys concocted colorful schemes to
take advantage of the military's ban on homosexuals. None of these
options applied to either of the boys.

"I guess we just don't know the right people," Frankie said.

"There aren't too many doctors hanging around Jake's," Johnny
agreed.

"And we both like girls," Frankie said.

"And I'm too chicken to shoot myself in the foot or jump off a roof,"
Johnny added.

"Do you really think Charlie Gario jumped?" Frankie asked.

"Who knows?" Johnny replied. "But that's what people are saying.
What was he doing on the garage roof?"

"He claims he was working," Frankie said.

Johnny shook his head. "I think the only thing he was working on was
getting out of the draft. Maybe he should have claimed to be one of
those non-violent guys, a conscientious objector, instead of messing up
his leg like that."

"As far as being non-violent, we were monsters on the football field. We
really kicked ass, so we can't claim that," Frankie boasted.

"Then I guess the army needs us," Johnny said.

The boys arrived twenty minutes early. The building was drab, with a
simple black and white sign above the door that read:

United States Department of the Army
Armed Forces Examination and Entrance Station
401 North Broad Street

Below it was a green banner with yellow lettering that proclaimed the facility to be "Freedom's Front Door." Both boys appreciated the irony in that.

Johnny was more nervous than he thought he would be and knew that Frankie was too.

To lighten things up he said, "Hey Frankie, wouldn't it be fun if we found some uniforms and crashed this place, pretending to be on the job?"

"Yeah, great fun," Frankie said. "But we don't need to crash this party. We're invited."

Once inside they found the facility to be every bit as depressing as they had expected. The walls were olive green and white. The reception area was filled with rows of long wooden benches. On the wall directly in front of the doorway were labeled photographs of President Johnson, Secretary of Defense McNamara, and Selective Service Director, General Lewis B. Hershey. Flags of the United States and the Department of the Army flanked the photos.

Neither boy had any idea who Hershey was, but they knew of the other two well enough. If Johnny remembered correctly, McNamara had announced his resignation as secretary the previous November and would be leaving the cabinet soon, but not soon enough in the eyes of many. He was viewed as the architect of the war and, along with the president, had received the brunt of its criticism. As for Johnson, the war had been dubbed "Mr. Johnson's War" by the protesters. Johnny doubted that there were men more disliked by people of draft age than those pictured on the wall before them.

There wasn't a happy face to be found or even a pleasant one. No one on the staff said "hello" or "good morning" or anything close to being civil. Most of the soldiers on duty were either expressionless or wore a permanent scowl.

The recruits who had arrived early passed the time by looking around or introducing themselves to other guys. Johnny tried to pick out the ones who came with a plan of getting out. There was one guy who had a cast on his arm and wore it in a sling. He looked hopeful. Another had a bandaged patch over one eye. He looked to be in genuine pain. One recruit, in particular, was catching some attention. He had close-cropped bleached-white hair, a nickel-sized loop earring in each ear, and wore blue pastel sweat pants with a matching loose-fitting sweatshirt. The look was accented with just a hint of mascara and eyeliner.

Johnny elbowed Frankie and whispered, "Keep an eye on little boy blue over there. This could be interesting."

"Maybe he's for real," Frankie said. "Maybe he'll get out of it."

"Maybe," Johnny replied.

As more recruits filtered in, it looked as though there would be about a hundred men examined that day. Almost all of them looked profoundly sad but resigned to their fate. Even the volunteers looked uncertain. Johnny would never admit it, but he began to wonder if he had made a terrible mistake.

One of the guards ordered everyone to sit quietly and not to speak unless spoken to. There was a civilian employee doing paperwork at her desk near the front of the room. She looked pretty old, with silver-blue hair loaded with hair spray. She wore a very proper dress and a string of imitation pearls with matching earrings. After waiting for several minutes, the recruit sitting next to Frankie decided he should explain to someone why he shouldn't be there. He had introduced himself to the boys earlier as Robert from Rosemont. Rosemont was a fairly affluent town on the Main Line of Philadelphia. "I'm getting out of here," he whispered to his new friends as he stood. He must have decided there was a better chance that the woman would listen to his problem than one of the guards. He pulled an envelope from his pocket and approached her desk quietly. Frankie elbowed Johnny.

"Pardon me miss," the recruit said in a low, timid voice, "I would like to…"

The woman interrupted him in mid- sentence. "I thought you were ordered to sit down and be quiet," she shouted for everyone's benefit. "Stick that envelope in your pocket and take a seat like everyone else. It's time you learn to follow directions." This silver-haired beauty was obviously nobody's sweet grandmother.

Robert looked shaken, and when he started to respond she barked, "Sit down!" He retreated to his seat without protest.

"Nice job," Johnny thought.

Eight o'clock came and went and nothing happened. Nor did anything happen at eight-fifteen or eight-thirty. The recruits continued to sit without direction or explanation. The benches were uncomfortable, and Frankie whispered that he felt like walking around.

"Why not take a little walk to grandmom's desk," Johnny whispered back. "I'm sure she'd like to meet you."

"I'd take my chances with chisel face over there first," he said, nodding in the direction of a guard who looked like he was cut from a quarry.

At eight thirty-five, Sergeant Samuel Keller entered the room. "Everybody up!" He shouted. It didn't take long for Johnny to decide that Sergeant Keller was both the most frightening and most comical figure he had encountered in a long time.

The sergeant was an imposing presence, with lean muscular features, and he was flat out nasty. He shouted everything he had to say, and his directions were given with such exaggerated importance that Johnny had to struggle not to laugh.

"My name is Sergeant Samuel L. Keller," he screamed. Johnny noted that the reception hall had a nice echo to it. It would have been a good place for the Tone Kings to practice.

"You will refer to me as 'Sir,' or 'Sergeant Keller.' Is that clear?"

It seemed like a rhetorical question, and no one replied.

"I said, is that clear?" He asked again, his voice growing even louder.

Now a few recruits hollered out, "Yes."

"Yes what?" Keller demanded.

The responses seemed equally split between, "Yes sir" and "yes Sergeant Keller." Many still didn't respond at all because they didn't know which answer to choose. A few others, like Rosemont Robert, didn't respond because they still refused to cross the barrier of submission.

"You will respond to my questions with 'Yes sir!' Is that clear?"

Now the group was more in unison. "Yes sir," they replied.

"I can't hear you!" Keller barked.

"Yes sir!" The group said, much louder now.

Johnny screamed it at the top of his lungs, and Frankie nudged him. He didn't want Johnny to get in trouble for being a wise guy. But he knew what Johnny was like. Going back to the brutal days of summer football camp with Coach Lukins, Johnny always reacted to authoritarians by proving that he could do everything they wanted and more. It was a good trait actually, unless the tough guy thought you were showing off.

Two privates appeared carrying piles of dark green duffle bags. Behind them on a table were stacks of army green t-shirts and trunks.

Sergeant Keller shouted, "These are your government-issue duffle bags. You will wear government-issue shirts and trunks during your physicals. After you change into your trunks you will put your civilian clothes into the duffel bags until it is time for you to go home. Is that clear?"

"Yes sir!" The response resonated throughout the hall.

Johnny had to fight the urge to ask him to repeat the directions.

"When you receive your bag you will hold it in your left hand. You will hold your induction paperwork in your right hand. Is that clear?"

"Yes sir!" They boomed. They were getting pretty good at it and Johnny expected Keller to compliment them at any minute.

Keller was giving more directions when he noticed Little Boy Blue. The sergeant stopped speaking and moved to him slowly, examining him from head to toe. Keller's face was a mixture of curiosity and anger, as if he hadn't seen a creature like this before and was outraged that such a pest would invade his orderly world. He stopped just inches from Blue and stared at him long and hard. Blue looked scared, but he didn't budge. Then in a low, menacing voice, Keller said, "the only thing worse than a faggot is someone who pretends to be a faggot."

"This sergeant is crazy," Frankie whispered. "Why doesn't he leave the guy alone?"

"Careful," Johnny whispered back. "He'll turn on you next."

Keller looked as if he could commit murder. "Get in the bathroom and take that crap off your face right now. And flush those earrings down the toilet or I swear to God I'll rip them right off your earlobes." Blue was shaking a little, but he still held his ground.

"You can't do…" he started to say, when Keller put a vice-like grip on his shoulder and yanked him forward. The two privates dropped their bags and rushed to separate the sergeant from the recruit. "We've got him sir," chisel face said, and the sergeant quickly let go. Keller's fists were clenched, and the veins in his neck looked like ropes under his skin. His face was flushed, and he had a wild look in his eyes. Johnny thought a stroke wasn't out of the question.

Keller struggled hard to compose himself. When he spoke he was surprisingly calm. "Clean him up," he said. "Get rid of the make-up and the earrings and give him a t-shirt and a pair of trunks. Put him in room seven, and we'll process him later."

He made room seven sound like a place from which people never returned. Johnny was sure the room reference was part of a routine, but he had to admit it was effective.

Then Sergeant Keller turned his attention to the group. He stood with his legs spread slightly and his fists on his hips. He scanned the men for a long time before speaking. "This country is at war," he bellowed. "I have friends in Vietnam. I've lost friends in Nam. Maybe you have too." He paused to let his words sink in. "This isn't fun and games here. We don't have time to cater to cowards or mamma's boys. It's time for all of you to man-up and do your duty to your country."

He paused again, and for the first time Johnny thought there might be some substance to the sergeant. Johnny glanced at Frankie and noted that Keller had his full attention.

Keller lowered his voice and continued. "In a couple of months some of you will be in Vietnam. Your lives will depend upon the men next to you. I want you to ask yourselves what type of guy you want by your side covering your ass."

The answer was obviously not Little Boy Blue.

For the rest of the day they moved from station to station, where they were checked, prodded, and poked by the army physicians. Attendants took vials of their blood. They were ordered to produce urine samples. They read eye charts and demonstrated their coordination and reflexes. When it was Frankie's turn at the weighing station, the scale registered 227. The sergeant at the station called out 210 to the attendant recording the information. When Frankie respectfully mentioned that he didn't weigh 210, the sergeant replied gruffly, "you will when we're finished with you."

Following the physicals, the men were tested for literacy and aptitude, although there was no evidence that it was possible to actually fail these tests.

They were finished by twelve-thirty and told to report to the same address on the 7th of November for induction, unless notified differently. They were given more paperwork with details about their preparation for the seventh and allowed to leave.

The boys were starving and they stopped at a street vendor and bought hot dogs, soda, and roasted peanuts.

"Are you okay?" Johnny asked.

"Yeah, I guess so," Frankie replied.

"How about you?"

"I'm fine," Johnny said. "But I'll tell you what. We're not going to let Sergeant Keller or anyone like him get the best of us. Let's spend the next two weeks getting in shape for boot camp, just like we used to for Lukins and summer football practice. If we're going to be soldiers, we're going to be good ones. Then we'll kick ass when we show up at Fort Dix."

"Sounds good," Frankie said. "It's been a while since I've worked out."

"Finish your hotdog Frankie. Tomorrow's a new day."

24- Frankie's News

It took days for Anna to recover from Johnny's announcement. She had been jittery ever since Nick and Jimmy left, knowing it was likely that Johnny could be drafted. But she held out hope that the fighting would end before it was his turn. She never dreamed that he would enlist, especially without telling her first. She was proud of his sense of duty, and even more so of his loyalty to Frankie, but she was nevertheless shocked and terribly hurt by his decision. She thought back to her husband's days in Korea and how she waited over a year for his safe return. She wasn't mentally prepared to go through that again, but she would have to.

Her son had always been the shining light in her life, and she needed something positive to hold on to after Johnny was gone. Determined to make their remaining days happy ones, she pushed any feelings that might jeopardize that to the background and gradually started to talk again. They shared meals, laughed and joked a little, and prepared for their separation.

The boys started their conditioning the day after their physicals. For old time's sake they ran on the path in the woods where they once trained for football camp. Johnny also got permission from Coach Lukins to use the high school weight room.

Johnny tried to keep things loose as they jogged
"Our drill sergeant is going to love us, Frankie. He'll be screaming at the other guys."
"I wonder what the other guys will be like," Frankie said.
"Mostly southern crackers and black guys from the cities. At least that's what I'm told," Johnny replied. "I'm not crazy about the crackers. Can't see myself hanging out with a bunch of guys who want to marry their fourteen year old cousins," he added lightly. "Where do you get these ideas?" Frankie said. "That stuff's not true."
"Are you kidding? What about Jerry Lee Lewis? What about Elvis? Didn't Elvis start dating Priscilla when she was twelve or something?"
"I think you're exaggerating," Frankie said.
"Okay, Frankie, if you say so. But if some cracker invites you home to meet his sister, find out if she's out of eighth grade before you go. I can see it now, you polishing off two pounds of greasy fried chicken and then settin' on the porch swing holding hands with some twelve year old Ellie Mae, while her Mama and Grandma peek out the living room window, wondering when you're going to ask her to marry you. My God Frankie, promise me you won't ruin your life over fried chicken and some freckled- faced adolescent who can't read."
Frankie played along. "How do you know she won't be able to read?"
"She's from the south!" Johnny said. "Didn't you learn anything in social studies class?"
"I learned about stereotypes. Apparently you didn't."
Johnny ignored the comment. He was having too much fun.
"Next thing you know, they're going to make you turn Baptist. They don't like Catholics down there."

Johnny mimicked his imaginary Ellie Mae. "'Frankie, Mama and I was thinkin' that it might be nice if you was to let Reverend Turner bring you into the Lord this Sunday. Weren't we, Mama?' Then Mama would call Reverend Turner on one of those phones you have to crank up."

"They don't have those phones anymore," Frankie interrupted.

"Of course they do." Johnny said. "And by the way, where do you think they go to the bathroom? I hope you know it's not in the house."

"It's 1967, Johnny. They have bathrooms and normal phones," Frankie said.

"You'll see." Johnny said before returning to his imaginary phone call. "'Reverend Turner, Ellie Mae's got her one of those soldier boys from up North. We was wonderin' if we could bring him by for services on Sunday.'"

"I'm staying a Catholic," Frankie said.

Johnny was on a roll now. "You won't have a choice. Do you know how they baptize you? They dunk you in the river. They don't even let you hold your nose. Damn, Frankie, you don't even like to swim. The *County-Times* will run a story, Former Football Star Drowns in Alabama."

Frankie laughed. "I'm not going to drown in Alabama."

"Okay, fine. Let's say you don't. Sooner or later you're going to have to bring the girl home. But you won't even be able to bring her to Jake's to meet the guys." Johnny said. "Do you know why?"

"No," Frankie said, laughing. "But I can't wait to find out."

"Because Jake wants everyone to wear shoes. He's pretty strict about that."

"You're sick Johnny, do you know that?" Frankie said.

"I'm just trying to look out for my best friend like I always do. That's all."

A week before their induction date, Johnny came home from work and found Frankie sitting on his front step. Frankie looked terrible.

"Hey Frankie," Johnny said. "What are you doing out here? Why didn't you go inside?"

"I don't think I can face your mother," Frankie said quietly.

"What are you talking about? The two of you have talked plenty of times since I gave her the news. She's coming around, and she certainly doesn't blame anything on you."

"I know," Frankie said. Then his eyes filled up, and he shook his head slowly.

"I don't know what to say," he sobbed. "I can't believe this is happening."

"Can't believe what's happening?" Johnny demanded.

Once again, Frankie pulled a letter from his coat pocket and handed it to Johnny.

"I didn't know this, Johnny. I had no idea. Maybe I should have known because of my mom, but I didn't."

It was another form letter from the Department of the Army. Frankie's tests showed that he had elevated blood-sugar levels. The army reserved the right to test him again within the next year, but for now, his induction was canceled. Frankie Mayson was rejected for military service because he was a diabetic.

25- Frankie Takes Off

Telling Anna turned out to be the most difficult thing Frankie ever did.

"It's my fault," he sobbed. "All of this is my fault. I'm so sorry."

"There's nothing you can do," she said flatly. "You shouldn't blame yourself." But as hard as she tried to console him, her words seemed empty, and she looked as if she was in shock.

Frankie turned to Johnny. "You don't know how much I wish this was the other way around. I was afraid before, but right now I wish I could go in your place."

Johnny forced a smile. He was devastated, but he hated seeing his friend suffer this way. "I know," he said bravely. "Don't sweat it. Things will work out."

Frankie didn't respond, but he wasn't buying it. Things wouldn't work out. Things were screwed up. He was ruining the lives of people he loved and he felt ashamed. He needed to leave and tried to say good-bye, but when he came apart again, he just turned and ran out.

Anna and Johnny sat in the living room, too stunned to speak. Johnny was too confused to know for sure what he was thinking, but his main concern was for his mother. He didn't know what to say. They sat quietly until he could compose himself.

"Look Mom," he said, "I know this is really messed up. And I admit I'm disappointed. But this doesn't really change anything. I'd be going either way." She was barely listening, so he tried something else. "Maybe I won't even go to Vietnam. Maybe I'll be sent to Germany or someplace." It didn't work. She shook her head sadly and said, "I just wish you would have told me first, Johnny."

She hated herself as soon as she said it, but Frankie's news had rekindled all of the fear and anger she'd been fighting so hard to suppress. At times she'd been so angry about his enlistment that she wanted to grab and shake him, slap him even, to release her pent up feelings. But she didn't. Sometimes, when alone in the house, she'd have bouts of uncontrollable crying. She'd asked herself over and over how he could have done such a reckless thing. But she kept all of this inside, because her fears of separation were even worse than her anger, and her instinct was to pull him to her, to cradle him in her arms as she had when he was a child. She fantasized about running away with him, taking him to Canada or some other place where he would be safe. She struggled to think of people she might know who could undo his terrible mistake, but she could think of no one.

So, on the night of Frankie's news, she accepted reality, just as she had tried to before. She wasn't the first mother whose son was going off to war. Johnny had made his decision to serve his country, and she took pride from that. She wasn't going to send her son away burdened by the image of a distraught mother. As difficult as it would be, she would force herself to support him. "I'm going to make dinner," she said, and left the room.

Johnny knew she was hurting; he was too. But he was relieved to see her putting up such a good front during dinner. He did the same, refusing to think about what Frankie's news meant for him. So they performed for each other, making small talk and forcing smiles. Later, as he helped with the dishes, she told him that she wouldn't be surprised if Sissy and her boyfriend Tom got engaged soon. They'd been dating for a year and seemed serious.

"Do you really think they might be getting engaged?"

"Sissy has dropped some hints. She says that Tom is the kind of guy who might want to settle down. God knows Sissy has dated her share of boys. I think she's finally stopped looking."

Johnny stood next to her and put his around her shoulder. "It sounds like there're going to be some big changes in your life coming all at once. I'm worried about you Mom."

She smiled and kissed his forehead. "You just take care of yourself Johnny. I'll be fine." He wished that she sounded more convincing.

"Besides," she said a little more upbeat. "I've got some things to help keep me busy. Father Creeden called yesterday and asked me if I wanted to work part time at the Rectory. Mrs. McCaskill retired as the bookkeeper, and Father wants me to keep records and pay some bills."

Father Creeden was a long-time friend of the family. When Johnny's Father died he was an incredible source of support for all of them. Even now, he was a dinner guest a couple of times a month. Sissy absolutely adored him, and Johnny and his friends felt as though he was one of the guys. He was funny and outgoing, and he loved sports. They didn't mind having him around. Sometimes, on Sunday afternoons, he came over after Mass to watch pro football with the guys and eat Anna's meatball sandwiches.

But Father Creeden's best attribute was the sermons. They were the best and the shortest of all of the priests at St. Therese's. When he spoke, he made everyone feel like he was talking directly to him. And the message was positive. People left church feeling good and ready to face a new week.

Johnny thought back to a conversation he had one night with Frankie at the log. Frankie had said, "I want to ask you something, but I don't want you to take it the wrong way."

"Hey, we're at the log, remember? Ask whatever you want."

"Okay. But I want you to know that I'm really not trying to be disrespectful."

"Frankie," Johnny said. "Will you please ask the damn question?"

Frankie cleared his throat. "Do you think that maybe Father Creeden is interested in your mother?"

"Interested?" Johnny asked, taken aback. "Do you mean like a guy interested in a woman?"

"Yeah," Frankie said cautiously. "Like a guy would be interested in a woman."

"Jesus Frankie, he's a priest."

"I know," Frankie said. "Look, forget I asked it. It was a dumb question."

"Right," Johnny said. "Out of the blue you ask me if Father Creeden is interested in my mother, and I'm supposed to forget it. You brought it up, now finish it. What made you ask?"

"Don't get mad, Johnny. I said I didn't mean any disrespect."

"I'm not mad at all," Johnny said lightly. But if you don't tell me why you asked the question, I'm going to smash this rock on your head."

As always, Frankie took Johnny's threats good-naturedly, even though he could break Johnny in half if he wanted to. He sighed before responding.

"I'm not sure why I asked it. It's just that there are times at your house when I see him looking at her in a funny way. That's all."

"What do you mean a funny way?" Johnny asked.

"Stop busting on me Johnny. You know what I mean. I see him looking at her the way a man looks at a woman. That's what I mean. I know it's crazy."

Johnny thought for a while and then said, "I've seen it too."

"No kidding!" Frankie said, jumping to his feet. "You have?"

"Calm down," Johnny said. "It's no big deal. I saw something that caught my attention maybe once or twice. I'm sure I misread it."

Frankie sat down again, considering the possibilities.

Johnny said, "Have you ever seen her looking that way at him?"

"No," Frankie said flatly.

"Really?" Johnny asked.

"Really," Frankie said. "I'd tell you if I did."

Frankie picked up a twig and snapped it. "What about you? Have you noticed her looking at him?"

"I'm not sure," Johnny said. "Maybe. I'm not sure."

Frankie tossed the broken twigs into the darkness.

"You don't think they're …" He paused to find the right words. "You don't think they're involved, do you?"

"No way." Johnny said. "That would be messed up. I'm sure they're just friends."

"Me too," Frankie said, trying to sound convincing. He popped open a can of beer he had sneaked out of the house and took a swig. Then he said, "Do you know that my mom didn't go on a single date in all the years after my father ran out on us?"

"My mom hasn't been on one either since my father died," Johnny said.

"When I was little I used to hear her cry sometimes in her room at night," Frankie added.

"Me too," Johnny said. "Sometimes I think I can still hear her."

"It's a bitch to be lonely," Frankie said.

Johnny didn't reply.

From that day on the boys paid closer attention to Father Creeden and Mrs. Francelli when they were together. They concluded that the looks, although very discrete, were indeed real, but they also agreed that there was no evidence of anything going on beyond looks.

Now Anna Francelli was being offered a job at the parish rectory.

"A job at the rectory?" Johnny said. "What about your real job?"

When Johnny's father died the family received a modest insurance settlement from the accident. Mrs. Francelli supplemented their income by going to work as a bookkeeper at a small garment factory down the street. She'd worked there full-time ever since.

"I'm keeping it. The job at the rectory is only two nights a week, from 6 until 9. It will give me an excuse to get out of the house, and the money will help too. Our bills aren't getting any smaller."

"That's great, Mom," he said, giving her another hug. "It sounds just like what you need."

He wondered what he meant by that.

Johnny was worried about Frankie and wanted to look for him. He also needed to get away for a while to clear his head about what had happened over the past few hours.

But then Anna said, "Why don't we spend a quiet night together? We can eat snacks and watch TV. Sissy might be home soon and we can spend time together."

"That sounds great, Mom," Johnny replied, putting his arm around her waist. "Let's do it."

26- Johnny Leaves

As Johnny prepared to report for duty, anti-war activists were gearing up for the presidential election the following year. The American death toll in Vietnam was approaching twenty thousand, with no end in sight. Hundreds of college students were heading to New Hampshire to help Minnesota Senator Eugene McCarthy take on President Johnson in the democratic primary. McCarthy became the darling of the peace crowd by boldly challenging a president from his own party on the war issue. Now, instead of staging sit-ins and burning draft cards, activists would hand out McCarthy's literature and work his phone banks. They were getting "clean for Gene," as the slogan went, by shaving their beards and cutting their long hair, hoping to win at the ballot box what they'd be unable to win in the streets.

Meanwhile Johnny made his good-byes. He began with long, private talks with his sister. He knew that Sissy dealt with problems by repressing them, so he wasn't surprised when Vietnam didn't come up. Instead, they reminisced, especially about their infamous trip to Washington. They laughed and hugged and promised to write often. With most of the guys away at school or in the army, making the rounds through the gang didn't take long. He spent some time with Angelo, and although they both avoided any talk of politics, it was clear that something had changed in their relationship. Next he said good-bye to some girls he knew. He even stopped by to see Jake and Stella at the joint. But he saved his longest good-bye for the friend he cared about most – Big Frankie. He wanted to make sure that things were right between them before he left. It wasn't easy.

Frankie had disappeared after announcing he flunked his physical. He didn't go home, report to the union hall, check in with his uncle, or stop by Jake's. Finally, after three days, he showed up at Johnny's door unshaven and wearing the same cloths as when Johnny last saw him. "Jesus Frankie, where've you been?" Johnny said as he led him in. Frankie reeked of body odor, stale beer, and cigarette smoke. "God, you stink!" Johnny said smiling. But Frankie wasn't smiling back.
"I've been at the Claremont," Frankie said almost inaudibly.
"The Claremont!" Johnny said, taking another step back.

The Claremont Motel was a dive just outside of town, used mostly by truckers looking for some sleep before getting back on the road.

"What were you doing at that flea trap?" Johnny asked.

"Thinking," Frankie replied with his eyes were fixed on the floor.

"Let's grab a beer and go down to the basement," Johnny said. "Mom's upstairs, and she'll be upset if she sees you like this."

Johnny got two beers from the kitchen, and they went downstairs. "Mom's been asking me about you ever since you left that night," Johnny said. "I've been telling her you're fine."

Frankie was studying the photos on the wall he'd seen a hundred times.

"How is she?" he asked, still with his back to Johnny.

"She's been pretty good. She's a tough lady. We've spent a lot of time together, and she seems to be doing okay."

Frankie took a swig of his beer.

Johnny continued. "Last night she took me, Sissy, and Tom out for pizza. We went to Cesare's and had a pretty good time, lots of laughs. She wanted you to come too, but I told her you had to work late with your uncle. Remember that if she asks about it. I don't like lying to her, but I didn't want to upset her."

"She wanted me to come?" he sounded surprised.

"Sure she did!" Johnny said, his voice rising. "Why the hell wouldn't she? She's taken you everywhere since we were kids."

Frankie moved to a section of the wall near the dartboard where his favorite photo was hanging. It was a candid shot of the football team in the locker room after the big game with Morrisville. Guys were bunched together, struggling to get their smiling faces in the picture. Some had their fists thrust triumphantly in the air, others made victory V's with their fingers or hoisted their helmets. Frankie stood with his arms around the necks of Johnny and Nick, pulling them toward him. It looked more like a stranglehold than an embrace. Jimmy held a football high, blocking another player's face. Billy Moyer toasted his father, the photographer, with a half-full bottle of coke. It was a great shot.

Frankie studied the scene for a few seconds, and he began to cry, quietly at first, and then openly. "I'm so sorry Johnny," he said, struggling for control. "I'm really, really sorry."

"Damn it Frankie!" Johnny shouted. He glanced at the steps, afraid that his mother might hear, and lowered his voice. "I'm getting tired of this crap." He motioned to the couch. "Sit down! We've got things to talk about."

Frankie did, still fighting to regain his composure.

"Listen Frankie. I was going to be drafted anyway. That was guaranteed. I'm a big boy and I made a decision. You didn't twist my arm or even hint that I should join."

Frankie didn't respond, but Johnny could tell he wasn't buying it. He pressed on. "You're making me mad Frankie, real mad. You and I are best friends. And on the week I'm going away, when I need you the most, you take off for days and when you come back, you're a whimpering pussy. A smelly, whimpering pussy."

Frankie still didn't respond, but he started to calm down.

Johnny lowered his voice. "I need some things, Frankie. Can you help me?"

"Anything," Frankie said, wiping his runny nose on his sleeve. "I'll do anything."

"Okay. First of all," Johnny stopped to gather himself, "I need you to take care of my mother."

Frankie looked uncomfortable. "I can't," he said.

"Listen to me Frankie. You know she's self-sufficient, and she enjoys her trips down the street to Bono's to buy her groceries. Sissy can help her with things like that. I mean take care of her by stopping around now and then for a visit. That's all. Be there for her."

"I can't," Frankie repeated. "I can't face her."

Johnny shook his head. "Frankie, please don't make me kick your fat ass right here in my basement." Frankie wiped his nose again and smiled.

"You have to face her," Johnny said. "She'll need you. You're a second son to her. Seeing you will make a big difference." He sat back and took a sip of his beer.

"Promise me you'll do it, Frankie. I need your word."

Frankie nodded. "I'll do it," he said solemnly. "I swear I'll do it."

"Great," Johnny said, giving him a playful punch on the arm. "That's really great."

Frankie smiled again. "Know what Johnny? When you get back I'm gonna give you the real ass kickin' you've had coming for a long time." Then he turned serious.

"What about Allison? Does she know you're going?"

"Allison's in Boston. Might as well be a world away," Johnny said quietly.

"Call her," Frankie said.

"No way. Allison's gone, and that's the way it is," he said abruptly. Frankie shook his head. "Okay, I'll visit your mom, maybe even eat her food if she twists my arm. Anything else?"

"Yeah, Frankie, there's one more thing," Johnny said. "I need you to get drunk with me tonight."

———

The night before Johnny reported for duty, Mrs. Francelli hosted a dinner party for Johnny, Frankie, Sissy, and Tom, with enough food for at least a dozen people, including stuffed olives, Frankie's favorite.

Although Anna's heart was aching, she was determined to be upbeat. Johnny was relieved to see her interacting with Frankie so well and enjoyed seeing Sissy and Tom so obviously happy together.

Johnny had an early bus to catch in the morning, so the party broke up right after dinner. Tom and Sissy left the table to do the dishes, leaving Anna and the two boys alone. Frankie and Johnny had agreed earlier that they wouldn't go through a long sloppy good-bye. They had already said everything they needed to say and wanted to put on a good front for Mrs. Francelli. So, true to his word, Frankie got up at seven-thirty, looked at his watch and said, "Well, we both have an early day tomorrow. I'd better be going." He gave his hostess an extra long hug. "Thanks for another wonderful dinner, Mrs. Francelli," he said as they embraced.

"You're welcome Frankie," she said, with tears welling in her eyes.

"Keep me in mind the next time you make the stuffed olives," he said as cheerfully as he could.

"You're the reason I make them," she said. "I promise to have them often."

"Thanks," he said, with just a hint of difficulty.

Then he turned to Johnny. "Well buddy, this is it. You take good care of yourself. Show those guys what a Bristol kid is made of."

Johnny took a deep breath and said, "You take care of yourself too, and send me a letter after you learn how to write. Maybe mom can teach you."

Frankie smiled, gave him a playful tap on the arm, and forced out a "see you soon." Then he turned abruptly, walked to the door, and left without looking back.

The house never seemed so quiet. Johnny wished he could board the bus for the induction center right then. In many ways he'd been saying good-bye to his mother for weeks, and he just didn't have anything left. He was determined not to break down in front of her and was afraid he might. Oddly, Anna felt the same way. They had shared some beautiful times together over the last two weeks, saying things mothers and sons should say, but often never did. Now she was settled on the idea that the sooner he left, the sooner she'd have him home again.

Johnny broke the silence. "Mom, I need to run out for a half-hour. There's someone I have to see."

She smiled. "A girl?"

"I told you Mom. I'm not seeing anyone who really matters to me. I just need to go out for a few minutes."

She wished he had a girlfriend to write to him. But she knew there hadn't been anyone special since Allison. There'd been plenty of girls, but no one special.

"You go along, " she said, "I'll be fine. Sissy and Tom will still be here for a while."

"Are you sure Mom?"

"I'm positive. Go. But I'm going to be right here waiting up for you tonight."

He kissed her on the forehead. "I won't be long. We'll watch some TV when I get back."

Johnny climbed the porch steps of the Victorian home and paused before ringing the doorbell. Then he shrugged and pushed the button hard. There was no response. He was about to ring it again when the intercom box crackled and the familiar voice asked, "Who is it?"

Johnny leaned in and said hesitantly, "It's Johnny Francelli."

"Hold on, I'll be right down."

When Father Creeden opened the door he was wearing his black shirt and pants, but his priest collar had been removed and he was drying his hands with a kitchen towel.

"Johnny," he said smiling. "It's good to see you."

"I'm sorry to bother you so late Father," Johnny said.

"Nonsense," the priest replied. "Come in."

Father had invited him to stop by for a talk before he left, and Johnny had said that he would, even though he had no intention to. But he changed his mind during dinner, and Father Creeden was obviously glad.

The rectory was a source of pride for the parish. It had dark mahogany woodwork, accentuated by ivory painted walls. The floors were polished hardwood and the wall hangings, all depicting religious figures, were tastefully done.

"Is anything wrong?" Father asked. "Your mother told me that you leave tomorrow. I had given up hope of seeing you before you left."

"No," Johnny said. "Everything's fine. I just wanted to stop in to say good bye."

Father beamed. "Well, I'm glad you're here. Come on back."

He led Johnny down the hallway to the kitchen.

"Our cook is gone for the evening, and I was just making some hot tea. Would you like a cup or a bottle of soda?"

"No thanks," Johnny said. "I'm fine."

Father motioned to a kitchen chair. "Please, sit down." He poured his tea and sat across from him. "I'm so glad you stopped by," he said again and took a sip. There was an awkward silence before Father Creeden filled it again. "So what time do you leave tomorrow?"

"I have to be at the bus station at six o'clock. I guess I'll get up about five or so."

"Only priests and soldiers get up that early," Father joked.

The room was silent again.

Finally, Father leaned forward and asked, "Johnny, is there something wrong?"

"No," Johnny said, squirming slightly on his chair.

"I think there's something you want to talk about." Father said.

Johnny took a deep breath and exhaled slowly. He looked at Father Creeden and then dropped his gaze to the tabletop. "I'm scared Father," he said softly. "I'm afraid to go away."

Father Creeden put down his cup and folded his hands on the table. "That's perfectly natural Johnny and nothing to be ashamed of."

"I know," Johnny said. "But I just needed to tell someone how I feel, and I didn't want to upset my mother or my friends."

"I'm glad you came to me," Father said. "You know, Johnny, you'll have plenty of people praying for you while you're gone."

Johnny considered that for a while before responding. "Don't take this the wrong way Father, but lots of people don't have their prayers answered."

The priest nodded knowingly. "That's because they're praying for the wrong thing," he said. "Most people treat prayer like a child's visit to Santa and give God a list of requests. As long as people do that, they'll often be disappointed."

"Isn't that what we're supposed to do?" Johnny asked. "What else is there to pray for?"

Father gathered his thoughts. He wanted to get this right. "When we pray, we should ask God to give us the strength to deal with all of the things that will come our way, some of which can be very bad."

Johnny looked like he needed more.

"Johnny, lots of people who go through terrible things lose their faith. That's because they never really understand what faith and prayer are all about. Mothers ask God to spare their children from disease and then lose their faith when their prayers aren't answered. Men in combat lose their best friends and blame God for not protecting them. If all of these types of prayers were answered, nothing bad would happen. But in this imperfect world, very bad things happen all the time. So when I pray for you, I'll be praying that God will give you the emotional and spiritual strength to deal with everything that comes your way."

"Sounds like God's not offering much," Johnny said.

"I disagree. He's offering everything. He's offering inner peace on earth and the promise of eternal life later. If we go through life thinking we can control things, we'll frequently be disappointed. It's only when we surrender ourselves to Him that we can have real courage," Father said.

Johnny didn't respond, but he was listening.

"When I was in the seminary we had a motto, 'Let go and let God.' Put yourself in his hands and face what comes your way with inner strength, knowing God is with you."

"I like to be in control of things," Johnny said. "I'm not going to sit back and hope I don't get killed."

"And you shouldn't," Father said. "God doesn't expect you to. Whatever we do in life should be done to the fullest of our abilities, including your training as a soldier. All of that may very well keep you safe. But beyond that, you'll still have to place yourself in God's hands. You'll only find your inner strength if you accept that God's plan is eternal, not just of this world." Father Creeden paused and studied Johnny's reaction. "I know this isn't what you want to hear Johnny. But it's the only truthful answer I can give you and the only one that will stand the test of time."

Johnny bit his lip and nodded his head slowly as Father continued. "Johnny, I could tell you that everything will be fine, that God will protect you, that you may not be sent to Vietnam. But we both know that they would be empty words that would evaporate quickly, and in times of trouble, my credibility and God's would be gone."

"I hope you'll be fine. I hope you won't be sent to Vietnam. I hope the war ends quickly. But I don't know any of that. What I do know is that God will be with you if you let him."

Johnny always liked Father Creeden, and this conversation reminded him why. He thought back to when his father died. People treated him like he was fragile. For a time the kids at school, other than Frankie, shied away from him. His mother said it was because they didn't know what to say. But he felt isolated. The sisters at school babied him, and let him get away with things other kids were punished for. Neighbors had what he called a "poor Johnny" look on their faces whenever they saw him. No one really asked him how he felt. He hated it. He just wanted to be like everyone else, and their reactions just made things worse.

Father Creeden was the exception. He called him into his office and told him how truly sorry he felt and how unfair he thought it was. He said he wouldn't blame Johnny for being angry or confused. When Father asked him how he was feeling, Johnny could tell he was sincere. They talked for a long time, and Johnny was grateful for the chance to get things out. Father encouraged him to speak to his mother freely and often, to not keep anything inside. It was a good conversation. Towards the end, Father didn't sugarcoat anything. He told Johnny that things would be much harder for him with his father gone and that he'd just have to be a little braver and a little tougher than the other kids. He told him in a kind way not to use the loss of his father as an excuse for failure. Then he told him he had confidence that he could handle things, but he stressed again that he should always go to his mother or him if he needed to.

Father had given him straight talk then, and he was doing it again now. Johnny leaned back in his chair and said, "I'll take that coke now."
Father got him one. As Johnny took a sip Father continued.
"Do you know the first commandment of the New Testament?"
Johnny thought for a minute. "I am the Lord thy God…"
Father interrupted him. "That's the first of the ten commandments that God gave Moses in the Old Testament. What I want to know is, what is the first directive of the New Testament that a messenger of God delivered on earth?"
Johnny thought briefly and then said, "I have no idea."
"That's okay. Most people don't." He left the room briefly and returned with a Holy Bible. He thumbed through the pages and then placed the book in front of Johnny, opened to the first chapter of Luke. "I'm sure you remember the Annunciation, when the Angel Gabriel appeared to Mary to announce that she would be the mother of the messiah. Seeing this strange image and hearing the news, Mary was scared out of her wits. And the first command that God's messenger conveyed to earth was 'Be not afraid.' God knew what would happen to Jesus when he reached maturity. He knew the trials Mary would suffer, and yet he said, 'Be not afraid.'"
Father just kept going. "Let's talk about when the apostles were frightened and huddled in secrecy. If you remember, Jesus has been crucified and the apostles were terrified that they would be next. So they hid in the upper room and planned to stay hidden until things cooled down. So what happened next?"
This time Johnny knew the answer. "Jesus appears to them."

"Exactly!" Father exclaimed. "And guess what his first words to them were?" Father Creeden smiled. "He said, 'Be not afraid.' Later, they are told to go out and preach to all nations- not an easy task." Father sat back again and assessed Johnny. As far as he could tell, the young man was still listening. "Do you know what happened to the apostles Johnny?" He didn't wait for an answer. "They were eventually killed, martyred for their faith." He let that sink in. "So what was Jesus up to, Johnny? He says 'Be not afraid' to a group of guys he knows will eventually meet a tragic end. He was telling all of us that no matter what we may face in life, we are not alone and something better waits for us. If we allow ourselves to think about it, it's really the only way we can cope."

Father paused again. "Tomorrow you'll be leaving everyone you know. But you won't be alone. I'll be praying for you and planning a big celebration for your return."

Johnny felt as if a weight had been lifted from his shoulders. He had been concealing his fears for days, but they'd been growing. Now, by accepting the dangers he was facing, he actually felt less burdened by them. He could feel the anxiety draining from him. He had visited Father Creeden to be told that everything would be all right. What he got instead was far more reassuring.

Johnny smiled. "Thank you Father," he said softly. "I mean it. Thank you very much."

"You're welcome Johnny," Father said, returning the smile.

Johnny got up to leave and Father walked with him to the door.

Father said lightly, "Please don't forget to write to your mother. Every day if possible!"

Johnny looked at Father for a few seconds as though he wanted to say something but thought better of it.

Father noticed, "Was there something else?"

Johnny brushed him off. "No, it was nothing," he said as he reached for the doorknob.

"Come on Johnny!" Father said lightly. "There was something else you wanted to say. My curiosity will kill me if you don't say it."

"Okay," Johnny said. "It's just that I was wondering…" He didn't finish.

Father persisted. "Johnny, do you need something? You know you can ask me?"

"No. It was just a question. But forget it. It would be way out of line. I'd better go."

"Are you kidding?" Father Creeden asked as he placed his hand on the door. "If I have to lock you in the closet, you're not leaving until you ask the question."

Father was right. There was no turning back now. Johnny cleared his throat and summoned his courage.

"This is crazy, so please don't be offended," he said.

"I'm a tough guy," Father replied. "Ask the question before my curiosity kills me."

Johnny chose his words carefully. "I was wondering if you viewed my mother as someone who is more than just another parishioner."

Father looked uncomfortable, but managed a nervous smile.

"That's not quite the type of question I expected."

"I know," Johnny said. "I'm sorry. Forget I asked it."

"No. That's okay," Father replied. What he said next was surprising.

"Is it that obvious?"

"A little," Johnny said. "If you look closely enough."

Father Creeden rubbed his eyes and exhaled slowly before responding. "Johnny," he said, "I wouldn't normally have this conversation with a parishioner, but given the circumstances, I will."

He glanced down the hallway to make sure none of the other priests were around.

"I was a man long before I was a priest. And I have the same instincts that other men have. Your mother is a beautiful woman. Even more important, she is very intelligent and very spiritual. She's also been lonely without your father around all these years." That was something Johnny knew.

"A priest's life isn't exactly filled with close relationships either. I enjoy your mother's company very much, and I think she enjoys mine. But I want to assure you that I have never violated my vows with her or anyone else, and I have no intention to. Our relationship is one of friendship, a friendship I value very highly. It will remain that way."

Johnny smiled. "Thanks for your honesty, Father; I appreciate it."

"You're welcome Johnny," Father said warmly.

Johnny reached for the doorknob again, but stopped.

"Father, I do need to ask one last favor."

"Of course. Name it."

"Please take good care of my mother while I'm gone."

"I will Johnny," Father said solemnly. "I promise."

27- The Tunnel Rat

Pvt. Jimmy Wright sat against the tree cleaning his Smith and Wesson .38, the weapon of choice of most Vietnam Tunnel Rats. His eyes were fixed on Lieutenant Timmer, his commanding officer. Every day for the past two months Jimmy had fantasized about killing the lieutenant. He was pretty sure he would never do it, but he thought about it constantly.

Jimmy was a tunnel rat, the most terrifying job in Vietnam, and he had Timmer to thank for it. The Viet Cong used an elaborate system of man-made tunnels throughout the south for hiding troops, storing weapons and ammo, and launching surprise attacks. The VC concealed the entrances so well that they were rarely uncovered. The tunnels allowed the VC to launch an ambush and then vanish as quickly as they had appeared. The brass knew the tunnels existed and wanted the weapons and intelligence information they held. The challenge was to find and neutralize them.

The tunnel network dated back to Vietnam's long wars of liberation against the French and had taken decades to dig. The largest were part of the massive Cu Chi underground system northwest of Saigon. But there were countless other, smaller networks, especially in the Iron Triangle region, where Jimmy's company was on patrol. Carved in the red Vietnam clay, the tunnel walls became as hard as rock after the first dry season and could last forever. The entrances were small, barely large enough for an undersized man to pass through. The shafts remained narrow for the first twenty to thirty yards, before broadening to rooms or caverns large enough to hold several men and supplies. The shafts near the entrances were carved with sixty-degree turns before straightening out toward the larger underground rooms.

There were several early theories about how to deal with the tunnels. At first, when the army found a tunnel entrance, they'd hit the hole with grenades, automatic weapons or even flame throwers when they had them, to soften up the enemy that might be inside. But grenades and bullets don't turn corners, and were ineffective against the angled shafts. Some thought of simply sealing off any men or supplies that might be inside by caving in the entrance. But many of the tunnels had a second entrance that could be anywhere within a fifty yard radius. In the dense jungle, it was unlikely anyone would find it, if it existed at all. So in the end, it was decided that the best way to determine who or what was in the tunnels and whether or not there was a second exit was to send in a tunnel rat to investigate.

The rats had to be small enough to fit in the entrance, similar in size to the average Viet Cong fighter. They would crawl on their guts, almost completely flat. It was impractical to carry the standard M-16 into the tunnel; it was too heavy. But even if they could manage the weight, it would be impossible to use the weapon effectively in such close quarters. So the rats were armed only with a pistol and a flashlight. Although the standard issue was a Colt .45 automatic, many rats, like Jimmy, preferred the lighter Smith and Wesson .38. The flashlight was just as important as the pistol, because the tunnels were pitch black.

The rats kept their flashlights off for most of the ordeal to avoid tipping off any VC who might be in the tunnel. They had to crawl in the dark as quietly as possible, and would use the flashlight only after they came upon the larger opening or room they were looking for. If the opening was dark, it either meant that the tunnel was free of VC and the rat would live, or it meant that the VC heard the rat coming, extinguished their lanterns ahead of time, and were lying in wait in the darkness. In that case, the rat would more than likely die. It was like playing Russian roulette.

The first time the company uncovered a tunnel entrance, Lieutenant Timmer selected Jimmy to go in because he was the smallest guy in the platoon. Jimmy was terrified, but he was trained to do what he was told. He'd seen other guys do dangerous things under orders, like take the point in patrol or search for booby traps, so he was willing, although reluctantly, to do his part, even though he didn't really know what to expect. As the Lieutenant explained his assignment, Jimmy's fear rose.

By the time he entered the hole he was shaking badly. He was crossing the threshold into a black chasm, and it was unlike any fear he had ever experienced. As he crawled in the darkness, his mind was racing with possibilities. Soon, he felt things crawling on his arms, and he imagined they were spiders. As a child, they were his worst fear. He brushed his arms as well as he could, while still holding the pistol in one hand and the flashlight in the other. He thought about bats. He knew some species lived in caves. He wondered if he would encounter any like the ones he'd seen flying at night in the jungle. Some were as big as squirrels. He fought off the image and moved on. Each time he made a turn in the darkness he expected to confront the enemy. He thought about going back, just crawling out and telling Timmer that he didn't find anything, but the shaft was much too small for him to turn around. He'd have to back all the way out, and that wouldn't fool the lieutenant. His instructions were to turn around when he found the room, one way or another. So he continued to crawl, slowly and as silently as he could in the darkness, guided only by the confining, nearly suffocating tunnel walls. His arms ached and his knees throbbed, but he kept crawling. There was nothing else to do. He cried silently as he crawled. He prayed, asking God to not let him die, not like this, not in a tunnel. He offered God deals. He reminded God that he'd never really done anything bad that he could think of, at least not really bad. Some small stuff, but never anything to hurt someone, never anything he should be ashamed of. He apologized if he did. He kept crawling as he prayed. He thought of his parents. Be a good soldier, his father had said. Listen to your officers; their job is to keep their men safe. Do what you're told and you'll be fine, his father said. He remembered his mother's face as she waved good-bye. She would be so sad if he didn't make it back. He wondered what they would tell her. He saw the faces of his best friends, the guys who walked him to the bus the day he left. Finally, the walls became wider and he sensed that he was nearing the cavern he was looking for.

He stopped. He laid there in the darkness in total fear, trying not to breathe heavily, listening for the sound of others breathing, others who would kill him. But he heard nothing except his own pulse in his ears. He imagined a handful of Viet Cong in the room with their weapons aimed at the shaft, waiting for him to make himself visible. He rested his cheek on the ground and waited. After what seemed like an hour of silence, but was probably less than ten minutes, he gathered his courage and turned on the flashlight. No one shot him. No one threw a grenade. No one was there. Jimmy took a deep breath and exhaled slowly. He had a sense of elation. For a moment he wanted to sing. He thanked God. He felt like someone had fired a revolver at his temple and the chamber was empty. He was safe.

He surveyed the room. It was about four feet high, just enough to stand semi-erect, and was roughly fifteen feet square. Against the far wall he noticed two crumpled skeletons, still dressed in the black pajama clothing of the Viet Cong. Word was that the VC dragged their wounded to nearby caves or tunnels after fire fights to treat them until the area was safe to leave. These guys didn't make it. Better them than me, Jimmy thought. He counted seven boxes of unused ammo and some medical supplies; other than that, the place was empty. Clearly, this was not a major weapons depot. He panned the room carefully with his flashlight looking for other exits. There weren't any.

He sat with his back against the wall, trying to regain his strength for the trip back. His rest didn't last long. As the reality of his ordeal sank in, his feeling of well-being evaporated. He was in an underground cave thirty yards or so from the outside world. He was exhausted. His arms felt like lead. He tried to light a cigarette, but his hands shook uncontrollably. He never smoked before entering the army, never even experimented with the guys at the log when they were younger. The army changed that. It changed a lot of things.

Suddenly, he was overcome with a fear that the battery on his flashlight would go dead. He didn't want to be in the dark anymore, not even for a minute. The fear quickly turned to panic. He couldn't face that tunnel again without a light. He wouldn't make it. He turned and began crawling as fast as he could back to the entrance, back to daylight. The trip out should have seemed faster, but he had reached his emotional limit. He needed to get out. He thought about the walls collapsing. He felt them for reassurance; they were hard and firm, but still, he thought, it was possible. There could be a weak spot. He moved faster. His breathing became labored and uncontrolled. He ignored the crawling insects. He could feel moisture on his knees and elbows; he was bleeding now. His stomach was raw from crawling, but it didn't matter; he needed to get out.

He thought about discarding his pistol to move faster, but a soldier never gets rid of his weapon. He decided that if he saw a bat he would shoot it. Maybe not, he thought. Maybe the shot would cause a cave in. Maybe his buddies would think he was VC trying to get out. He crawled. He aimed the flashlight wildly and crawled. Ironically, the knowledge that he had just made the same trip in the dark spooked him even more. How had he done it then, when he could barely finish now with a light in his hand? He cursed Lieutenant Timmer. He cursed the Viet Cong. The gooks actually dug these tunnels so they could use them. Hide in them! What sane person would do that? The ordeal seemed just as long as before, even longer. Finally, in the distance, he saw a narrow shaft of light from the entrance. He hollered to his buddies outside. No one answered. He hollered again, but there was still no response. They can't hear me, he thought. Still too far away. It didn't matter. He had made it, he thought. He could see the entrance. He wasn't going to die. Now he was laughing and crying and crawling all at once. The opening was farther away than it seemed at first, so he crawled faster. He kept moving, hoping his strength would hold out. The last two minutes belong to us, Coach Lukins used to preach. We're the toughest and fastest when everyone else is tired, he'd say. Move faster, Jimmy thought. Faster.

Finally he reached the end. The platoon was gathered at the entrance and cheered when they saw him. They took his pistol and flashlight and pulled him out. One of the guys, Jack Higgins, offered him a canteen, and he drank like a camel. His hands shook so much that most of the water ran down his shirt. Every inch of his body was covered with red clay dust. The blood on his elbows formed clumps of dark mud. His pants were torn at both knees, and he could feel blood running down his legs. The sunlight hurt his eyes. He rubbed them with his crusted hands and made them worse. He poured some of the water on his head. He wanted to wash away any trace of where he had just been. It was his baptism, his rebirth from the living death he had just experienced.

Guys were patting him on the back, saying "good job" and "way to go man," everyone except Lieutenant Timmer, who was all business. He wanted to know what Jimmy had found, how big the cave was, whether or not there was another exit. After he got the information he wanted, he said, "Okay, get cleaned up, we're moving out soon." And then he walked away. That was it.

It took a few days and several nightmares for Jimmy to begin to recover emotionally. He tried to block out the experience as much as possible, but he enjoyed the newfound acceptance he received from the rest of the platoon. Higgins and another black kid named Tyrone Willis were regular guys. He had proven himself to them. He was a man, nineteen years old, but a man. He wasn't sure his new status was worth the price he had paid to earn it, but he embraced it. Things settled down for a few days as they continued their patrols. Then they found a second tunnel entrance.

Roosevelt Woods, a towering black guy from Camden, New Jersey, saw it first. Woods and Jimmy had become good friends once they learned that they were practically neighbors back home. Woods was a big time Phillies fan just like Jimmy. Camden was just over the Walt Whitman Bridge from Philadelphia and Roosevelt went to Phillies games a lot. Richie Allen was Roosevelt's favorite player. Jimmy's was Johnny Callison. The two of them found plenty to talk about. Jimmy had latched on to Woods like the leeches they'd all come to know in the jungle. But Woods didn't mind; he liked him.

Woods was walking point that day and motioned for everyone to stop when he saw a small spot in the vegetation, maybe a foot in diameter, that contained a cluster of dead leaves. Some vines had grown over them, but he could still see the dead leaves below the new growth. At first he thought it might be a land mine or some other booby trap. That's what a point man is trained to look for, booby traps and mines, and that's how they avoid having their legs blown off. He motioned to

Timmer, and the Lieutenant took a closer look. Carefully, they poked at the leaves until they were sure there wasn't a concealed mine. What they found instead was a small bamboo door covered by two inches of dirt and new growth. When they pulled it open, it revealed another tunnel shaft.

Timmer stepped away and used the radio to report his find, then he returned to the platoon. "Okay guys," he said. "Headquarters wants us to check it out. Wright, get rid of your gear and get ready to go in." He said it so casually that Jimmy couldn't believe what he was hearing. He just stood there, expressionless.

Timmer moved to within inches of Jimmy's face. "Is there a problem private?" It sounded more like a threat than a question, but Jimmy still didn't respond.

"I'm talking to you, private," Timmer said, menacingly.

"With all due respect Lieutenant, I went in the last time," Jimmy said.

"I know that, private. And you're going in again. This is a war boy. This is what we do," Timmer shouted.

Jimmy couldn't imagine going into the hole again.

"Lieutenant, I thought maybe the men would rotate." He knew that idea wouldn't be popular with the rest of the platoon, but he didn't care. He'd done his part. After the first episode, Roosevelt had told him that the army had teams of small guys who actually volunteered to be tunnel rats. They were even trained for it. Jimmy thought that if his platoon was going to keep finding tunnels, then they should rotate, or the army should send volunteers to do the searching.

"Private, do you see the size of that opening?" Timmer said. "Do you see anyone here besides you who could fit into that hole?" Jimmy knew that no one else would, but he just stared at the Lieutenant without answering. Now Timmer stood even closer. "Private, you've got five seconds to shed your gear and prepare to enter that hole, or I'll have you in military court for insubordination. And if you ever resist an order of mine again, I might just take a rifle butt to the side of your head. Is that clear?"

That was the first time Jimmy thought about shooting the lieutenant. But he stripped off his gear and steeled himself before he climbed into hell again. This episode was no less terrifying than the first. It wasn't something a person got used to. Fortunately, the shaft was a little shorter, and when he reached the small cavern, he found that it held more weapons than the last cave, but no men, dead or alive. In the end, there was the same sense of panic and the same mad rush to get out. But the reception was different on the outside. The men looked at him differently. Some looked on with pity, others with resentment for suggesting that they go into the hole instead of him. If Timmer wanted Jimmy to go into the hole each time they found one, that was fine with most of the platoon. Even Higgins and Willis were quiet about it. Only Roosevelt gave him support. "It ain't right man," he said, as he helped him clean the blood from the reopened scabs. "It just ain't right." But Roosevelt couldn't be much help, even if he wanted to. He was well over two hundred pounds.

They found another hole about three weeks later, and Lieutenant Timmer ordered Jimmy in again. Again he did what he was told. Fortunately, there were no VC, but the cave contained a substantial amount of weapons and ammo. Timmer was thrilled and radioed headquarters with the exact coordinates. Later he said that HQ was sending an air strike to pulverize the area. He said finding the weapons would save American lives. But never once did he give Jimmy any credit or encouragement. Never did he indicate that Jimmy would be replaced with another guy. As far as Jimmy could tell, Timmer would keep him going down into the tunnels until Jimmy was killed or shattered emotionally. And Jimmy didn't think his luck would hold out much longer.

Jimmy missed Nick. Nick would know what to do. He always did. But Nick was off somewhere in the Special Forces. He hardly ever wrote, and when he did he wasn't allowed to say much about what he was doing.

So now, as he polished his pistol and stared at the Lieutenant, he thought about killing him. He thought about waiting until the next firefight with the VC, and then just sending a bullet his way. He knew he would never do that, but that's what he thought about every day.

28- Boston College

Debbie Myers was only nineteen, but wanted to die. Sitting through Dr. Taylor's music class was torture. He had been droning on about Rossini for almost an hour, and she doubted she could take much more. She didn't need music appreciation, at least not taught this way. She expected better from Boston College.

The course description had sounded decent enough. *Linking Classical Music to Popular Culture*, it said, but she soon learned that Dr. Taylor could be deadly, especially in a lecture hall with a hundred students. Today's lesson was a shining example. Taylor would drift into what Debbie called the Taylor Zone, where he would stare off in the distance and lecture. There was no inflection, no passion, just his trademark monotone. Taylor taught with complete disregard for the pain he was inflicting and shared his facts without concern for the class's attention or interest. No one ever interrupted him or asked a question, nor did Dr. Taylor ask questions of the class. An unwritten rule had emerged between teacher and students, a kind of, I don't bother you and you don't bother me mind-set. What bugged her most was that the class seemed content with this arrangement. They happily drifted off to their private thoughts, allowing Taylor to abuse their intellect without complaint. Only their body language spoke to him, but Taylor either couldn't read it or didn't care.

Debbie had an urge to shake up the class. She wanted to stand up and order him to stop speaking. She wanted to demand a tuition refund, right there in front of everyone. She wanted to ask him what he thought about Ray Charles, whom she considered a genius, or Janice Joplin, whom she thought was suicidal. That's what they should have been talking about in music class. Life was too short to accept this stuff, she thought.

She was fascinated by Taylor's appearance and mannerisms. He was short and slender, with thinning blond hair. He wore the same dark gray suit each day and a white shirt with no tie. He seemed too young to be a professor. She guessed he was thirty-five. At random times, he had a habit of rising on his toes for a few seconds, as if he wanted to make himself taller. He'd be talking and then suddenly, just like that, he'd be up on his toes. But that wasn't all. Sometimes, while on one of his toe lifts, he would thrust his head back, clasp his hands behind him, and lecture directly to the ceiling. Debbie had tried it once in her dorm room and twisted her ankle.

He was doing it now. His heels were off the ground and he was looking straight up. His hands were behind him. Debbie decided he was either picking his butt or talking to God. She just wasn't sure. She tried to tune in again to the lecture. "After retirement, Rossini divided his time between Paris and his native Italy," Taylor said while scanning the ceiling. "He enjoyed considerable prestige in both places."
Fascinating stuff, Debbie thought. She glanced at her watch; there were three minutes left. She was going to make it after all.

Taylor was oblivious to the time, and was in mid sentence when the bell sounded, but no one waited for him to finish. Debbie watched as the students quickly gathered their things and scrambled for the door. Exits were usually quick, but today was more of a stampede. Taylor ignored the mass exodus and finished his point. "It is impossible to calculate the full value of Rossini's contribution, " he said without raising his voice. Then he told the near empty room to have a nice weekend, closed his book, and left.

In a way, Debbie saw Taylor's course as a blessing. Each class was like a near death experience. If you survived it, you saw the world differently.

You appreciated things more. Once outside, she felt reborn. She inhaled deeply, savoring the late autumn air. She scanned the sky, the colorful leaves, the tranquil campus setting, and the easy movement of people on a Friday afternoon. She was alive again!

She planned her schedule as she walked. She'd check her mail at the student center, take a quick nap, eat a light snack, begin her beauty ritual, and then leave at eight for the fraternity party.

The mail check was important, because she was expecting money from her parents. She was happy to see a letter in her box, but she soon realized it wasn't from home. The return address read Private John Francelli, Company C, Fort Jackson, Columbia, South Carolina. It had to be a mistake. She didn't know a John Francelli. She was sure of it. But the letter was addressed to her. She checked the postmark. It looked real enough and was dated two days earlier in Columbia. Everything seemed authentic. She sat down, opened it and began to read.

Dear Debbie,

You don't know me. My name is Johnny Francelli. I'm in the army, stationed at Fort Jackson in South Carolina. I'm in the final days of boot camp. I hope you don't think I'm a crackpot for writing to you. It took a lot of time to get your name, but time is something I have plenty of at "beautiful" Fort Jackson, in this "gorgeous" town of Columbia. Actually, this is one of the ugliest and most depressing places I have ever seen.

Anyway, let me explain a few things. First of all, I guess you're wondering how I got your address and why I'm writing to you. I'm writing because of your roommate, which I'll explain in a minute. To get your address I used one of my buddies in Company C, who has a sister at Boston College. We used her to find your name and address in the campus directory. We knew your roommate's name, and by finding her dorm room number and seeing who had the same number, she was able to figure out that Allison O'Brien's roommate was you, Debbie Myers. I wanted to explain it so you wouldn't be worrying or thinking I'm a nut.

So why am I writing? It's actually pretty simple. You and I have something very important in common. You are Allison's roommate right now, but in about three years I intend to be her roommate. I've thought about it for a long time, and that's what I've decided. I fell in love with Allison before we were teenagers, and I've loved her ever since. When her college and my military service are over, we're going to start our life together.

You're probably wondering why I'm telling you all of this. It's because there's a slight snag. Allison and I have had some problems. She hurt me pretty bad. In fact, it hurt so much that I thought the only way I could avoid being hurt like that again was to keep a distance. So, I went out with other girls, girls who didn't mean anything to me, and I watched her go out with other guys. It was hard, but I felt safer that way.

We almost got together again, but it fell apart. That was probably my fault. But anyway, lying here in my bunk night after night without her knowing my feelings didn't seem right. Life is too short and the future to uncertain for that. So when I met a guy in my company who had a sister at Boston College, I saw it as a sign that I should do something. So here I am, letting you know that I've decided to spend the rest of my life with Allison.

Knowing Allison, I'm sure she's seriously involved with some big time important guy in Boston. Maybe he's an athlete, or president of the damn glee club, but none of that matters. When the time comes, I'm going to show up, take her by the hand, and we'll walk off together to begin our new life. That's the way it's going to be. I know she loves me. I'm certain of it. We used to ride our bikes together in the rain in the summertime. Really. If we were doing something together and it started to rain, we'd jump on our bikes and ride to the park. You don't do that with just anybody.

So I need your help. I need you to tell her my plans. Break it to her easy, but tell her. I think it's important that she knows what she's going to be doing with her life before she messes things up by trying something different.

I know that sooner or later I'll have to speak to her myself. But I was afraid I'd screw it up the first time. So I'd appreciate it if you'd help me just this once. I feel like I know you already, and I think it would be neat if Allison asks you to be in the wedding when the time comes.

Until then, please give her the good news, and, every once in a while, try to figure out a way to mention my name to her. I'm counting on you.

Thanks,

Johnny Francelli

Debbie exhaled deeply. Now this was exciting, she thought. The letter was like a jar of nitro; if used the wrong way it could explode. Johnny was right about a lot of things. Allison was seriously involved with Steve Conner. He was the president of his fraternity and, just as Johnny predicted, he was an athlete, a varsity swimmer. He was great to Allison. As far as Debbie knew, the two of them never even had a fight. Overall, he was just about perfect. Half the girls on campus would love to change places with Allison. But she couldn't really say that Allison was crazy about Steve. Content might be a better word, but not crazy. Maybe this guy Johnny deserved a chance.

But on the other hand, Steve had been the best thing to happen to both Allison and Debbie. He was their ticket to BC's social life. Because of him Allison and Debbie had been invited to every party the fraternity had, and Debbie met a new guy each week. She'd probably meet another one at the party tonight. She and Allison saw doors opened that had been closed before. They rode on the fraternity Homecoming float.

They had great seats at campus concerts. People on campus knew who they were. Life was good for both of them with Steve around.

Don't rock the boat, Debbie thought. Why create trouble and get in the middle of a mess? If this guy Johnny has something to say to Allison, he should say it himself. She decided to can the letter and not get involved. If necessary, she could always say that she never received it. She folded the letter and put it back in the envelope. Then she looked at the postmark again. She thought of the guy living in a barracks in South Carolina. She thought of Professor Taylor, droning on and her classmates allowing it to happen without complaint. And she scolded herself again.

This was life. This was exciting. Maybe it was time to shake things up a little, just for the heck of it. Help create a juicy triangle and see what happened. This guy Johnny might be a nut, but she liked his letter. Maybe Allison would too. He planned to just show up one day out of nowhere and walk away with Allison. Debbie visualized the confrontation with Steve, and Allison's dilemma. This could be great stuff. Johnny Fran-something had put his feelings on a billboard. Maybe they deserved to be seen. She put the letter in her book bag and hurried off to the dorm. She couldn't wait to show it to Allison.

29- Angelo's Trip

"Hey, stranger!" Jake shouted when Frankie walked in. He came out from behind the counter and gave him a bear hug. "Where have you been keeping yourself?" he asked. It was Frankie's first visit in more than two months.
"Good to see you, Jake," Frankie said, returning the hug. "It's been a while."
"Damn right it has. None of the old gang comes around anymore. Look at this" Jake said, gesturing to the group of kids in the joint. Most

looked like they were still in junior high. "Sometimes I feel like I'm running a kindergarten. They're so damn young, eighth, ninth grade tops," he said. "You know, it's like having your own kids. They grow up and leave. But for Stella and me it's different. Every four or five years, we get a new group."

Frankie recognized a lot of the young kids from the neighborhood.

"You guys were like this when you first started showing up," Jake said. Frankie agreed. Being old enough to hang out at Jake's was a rite of passage in town. He remembered what a big deal it was when he first started.

"How are they treating you Jake? Are they spending any money?"

"More than you guys did," Jake kidded. "All you guys wanted was a warm place to shoot the bull. The pinball machines got rusty waiting for you to put some money in."

Frankie laughed. "We were poor Jake; we did our best."

"I know you did," Jake said, putting his hands on Frankie's shoulders and sizing him up. "I miss you guys. It was great having you around."

Jake dropped his hands and stepped back. He looked older, Frankie thought. It had only been a couple of months, but there was a definite difference.

"How's Stella?" Frankie asked.

Jake smiled. "Stay single Frankie. She's killing me, always bustin' my chops about going to the track too much, not paying the bills, same old crap."

"You love her, Jake. Everybody does."

Jake smiled. "I love her almost as much as the ponies, and that's a lot. And she's doing fine. She'll be sorry she missed you."

"Say hello for me," Frankie said.

Jake changed the subject. "So what's everybody doing? Who do you hear from?"

"I don't hear much," Frankie said. "Ralph and Billy are away at college. Might as well be on Mars. And with Jimmy, Nick and Johnny in the service, the only guys around are me and Angelo. I don't even see guys like Charlie Gario."

Charlie had been an occasional visitor at Jakes.

"Charlie Gario. Did anything ever happen to him for jumping off the roof?"

"No," Frankie said. "Everyone knows he did it to avoid the draft, but he still says he fell, and the government can't prove otherwise. So he got away with it, I guess. No Vietnam. But his leg's messed up pretty good. I heard it might always be that way."

"The crazy bastard crippled himself," Jake said.

Frankie didn't respond.

"What about Angelo? What's he up to?"

"We don't see each other much. I've been working a lot. Still learning the trade. The work's been steady. I'm making good money and I'll be in the union soon."

"That's great," Jake said.

Frankie looked over Jake's shoulder. Jake had wallet sized army photos of Nick and Jimmy taped to the cash register, the kind in dress uniform that the army takes after boot camp. Jake followed his eyes.

"They look good, don't they? The boys mailed them to me, just like they promised."

"Yeah, they look good, real good. But what about Johnny? Where's his?"

"Didn't get it yet," Jake said. "But it will be up there as soon as I do."

"I'll get one for you from Mrs. Francelli," Frankie said. "Johnny belongs up there."

"That's great Frankie. You get me one." Then he added. "What do you hear about them? I got those photos after boot camp, but nothing since."

"Not much. Jimmy isn't much of a writer. But the last I heard, he was having a hard time, hates the army and wasn't mixing well with the other guys. Nick took good care of Jimmy around here and Jimmy misses that. Jimmy's a little different. People have to get to know him."

"It's a shame," Jake said sadly.

"What about Nick?"

"I talk to Nick's parents every once in a while. Sounds like he's eating up the army. He's in some sort of Special Forces. He's not allowed to tell them much about what he's doing. But it sounds like he loves it and is doing pretty good. His dad was a military guy, so he's all gung-ho about the whole thing. Nick's okay."

Jake knew that Frankie's biggest concern was Johnny, because of the way things unfolded for the two of them. "So tell me what you hear from Johnny. How is he?"

"He says he's good." Frankie sounded like he wasn't sure he should believe it. Then he smiled. "You know Johnny. He says he really kicked ass in boot camp. Says he was the fastest guy on the obstacle course. His sergeant loves him and made him squad leader."

"That's no surprise," Jake said. "Kid's a natural leader."

Frankie was enthused now. "Here's the kicker. He qualified as a sharpshooter or expert, something like that, for firing a weapon. He never held a gun in his life, and now he's hitting the bull's eye."

"That should help," Jake said. "What's he think of the guys he's with?"

"He said it's a pretty mixed group. There're lots of Blacks and Puerto Ricans, and he's okay with that. Growing up here, playing sports with guys like that, it's no big deal. But he said it's a problem for some other people. There're a lot of farm boys from Iowa, places like that, lots of southerners too. He doesn't mix as well with them, but he says they're okay. One thing though, they're definitely not interested in any do-wop music."

"You watch," Jake said, "Johnny will have those crackers singing his stuff soon."

"What's a cracker?" Frankie asked.

"Damn if I know. That's what we called the Southerners when I was in the army. Some of those guys would rather go barefooted than wear boots. Good soldiers though. By the time I got out I was real good friends with some of them." He paused for a moment. "If you want to survive in the army, you learn to get along with everybody. Rock the boat and you get your ass kicked, no matter how tough you are. They'll give you a blanket party."

"What's that?" Frankie asked.

"Guys will wait until you're sleeping in your bunk. They'll throw a blanket over your head and beat the crap out of you. It sends a message; either stop pissing people off or the next visit will be worse. I know; I saw it happen."

"Sounds great," Frankie said sarcastically.

"It won't be a problem for Johnny. He gets along with everybody."

Jake could see that Frankie was still tormented by the whole draft thing.

"Listen, Frankie, things are going to be okay for Johnny. You'll see."

"I know," Frankie said without conviction.

"How's Johnny's mother?" Jake asked. "See her much?"

"At least once a week," he said. "Sometimes she has me over for dinner. Sometimes I pick her and Sissy up for church. We share letters from Johnny. She's good."

"That's great, Frankie. Real good."

Better move on, Jake thought. "So what brings you here today?" he asked, in a lighter tone. Then he whispered, "Is there a horse you're interested in? You're old enough now. Maybe you had a dream about a number you want to play."

"Nah, Jake, no horses or numbers. I work too hard for my money. "

"Get lucky the right way once," Jake winked, "and you don't work anymore."

Jake had been waiting a very long time to get lucky in the right way, Frankie thought. There was no evidence of any luck yet. Jake certainly wasn't living in luxury.

"Actually," Frankie said, "Angelo told me to meet him here to shoot a game of pool, just like old times." He checked the clock on the wall. "He's late."

"Great," Jake said. "I'll get to see him too. I better heat up the grill. He always gets a cheese steak with fried onions."

"Sounds good," Frankie said. "I'll probably have one too when he comes."

"Fries?"

"Not for me," Frankie said. "Doctor said to lose weight."

When Angelo arrived he got caught up with Jake for a few minutes, then he and Frankie had a few laughs watching some kids play pool. The kids looked thirteen, but were trying their best to be hard guys. They had cigarettes in their top pockets and cursed after each missed shot. They didn't make many.

"Think that's how we looked when we started here?" Frankie wondered.

"Nah," Angelo said. "We didn't miss as many shots."

They told Jake to start cooking and took a booth along the wall.

Jake's cheese steaks were a foot long and fantastic. He could have made a living just making sandwiches if he wanted to, but he wanted to be a bookie. So he sold just enough food to make his storefront legitimate with the IRS. That, plus five pinball machines and a pool table, provided all the stress Jake wanted outside of booking bets. So if the food business got too brisk, he'd just announce that the grill was broken, and things would calm down. It was probably the thing that he and Stella fought about the most. She obviously preferred the prospect of a steady income to the up and down world of gambling. But that's the way Jake was, and she knew she'd never change him.

Jake brought out a mountain of fries and two cokes along with the steaks. "If you want more, just let me know," he said, smiling at Frankie. "And go easy on the ketchup, it adds calories." He left the boys alone.

They hadn't had cheese steaks from Jakes in a long time, and they savored each mouthful. They made small talk between bites about Frankie's job, Angelo's girlfriend, Donna, basic stuff. Then Angelo changed the tone.

"Where the hell have you been, Frankie?"

"What's that supposed to mean?" Frankie asked.

"It means that no one has seen you for a long time. Ever since Johnny left you've disappeared."

"Like I told you, I've been working a lot. I come home, eat, watch some TV and fall asleep on the couch."

"Listen, Frankie, you've got to stop beating yourself up over this Johnny thing. It's not your fault that you flunked your physical, and its not your fault that Johnny enlisted. He makes his own choices. He always has. He told me himself that he would have signed up anyway. He believes in this war, and was going to enlist whether you got drafted or not. That's no bullshit. That's what he said."

Frankie took a sip of his coke. "Like I said. I work hard and I'm tired at night, so I stay home."

"Sure, Frankie, whatever you say. Torture yourself until Johnny gets home. It makes a lot of sense."

They ate quietly for a while until Frankie said, "Are we really here to shoot pool?"

"No," Angelo said. "But we can if you want to."

"No thanks, you're terrible. It's no fun beating you."

Angelo ignored the poke and ate another French fry.

"Okay, we're not here to play pool. Is your lecture over?"

"I didn't come here to lecture you."

"Okay. No pool, no lecture, so why are we here?"

Angelo pushed his empty plate away and leaned back in the booth.

"Donna and I are leaving," he said.

"What do you mean leaving? Where are you going?"

"Canada," Angelo said calmly. "Donna and I are going to Canada."

Frankie looked uneasy. "Why? You going on vacation or something?"

Angelo put his head back and sighed. Then he said quietly, "I've been drafted."

Frankie stared blankly, and when he didn't respond, Angelo continued.

"I got my physical notice, a couple of days after Johnny left. I'm supposed to report to Philadelphia tomorrow."

Frankie bolted forward. "You waited until now to tell me!"

"No offense, Frankie, but I didn't think you were in the right frame of mind to hear about my problems so soon after Johnny was gone."

"There's nothing wrong with my frame of mind," Frankie shot back. "So why are you telling me now?"

"Because Donna and I are leaving for Canada tomorrow. I'm here to say good-bye."

"Tomorrow! You're moving to Canada just like that?"

Angelo smiled and tried some humor. "We want to be settled up north before Christmas."

Frankie didn't laugh. "Donna is going with you?"

Angelo nodded.

Frankie thought Angelo had lost his mind.

"Angelo, you can't do this. You just can't."

"Watch me, Frankie. I will not fight in this stinking war. No LBJ body bag for me. This is a civil war between the Vietnamese, and we shouldn't be involved. Everyone knows it but us. The truth is, I think we know it too, but we don't know how to get out. I'm not going to hang around while they try to figure it out. I'm not dying for that kind of crap."

Frankie shook his head. "Angelo, you'll be a criminal. You won't be able to come home. If they find you, they'll prosecute. Guys have gone to jail."

"They won't find me. I'll make sure of it."

"This is crazy, Angelo. You've got to think this through. Where will you live? What are you going to do for money?"

"I have thought it through. Remember when Ralph told us that if he ever got drafted his family would send him to college at McGill University in Montreal? That's where I'm going."

"You're going to college?"

"No way. I don't have any money. I'll have to work when I get there. We're going to live in Montreal near the university, because a lot of

Americans have moved there since the war started. We'll hook up with them. We'll make friends. It'll be like home. "

"Where do you think you'll find work? You don't know anybody."

"I've been looking into it for a long time, long before my notice came, because I knew it was just a matter of time. I've been talking to people too, people I meet at anti-war rallies. Remember when I went to that rally in New York? I met some people who told me things. There's a place called Saint Catherine's Street. It's got plenty of action, nightclubs, bars, restaurants. It's near McGill. I'll get a job tending bar, waiting tables, maybe I'll even be a short order cook. I cook at the store all the time; I can do it. Donna can wait tables too. We'll be fine."

Frankie still wasn't buying it. "You're making a mistake, Angelo, a big mistake. Where are you planning on living?"

"Look, Frankie, I know you don't get this, but there are a lot of people out there against this war. There's a network to help guys like me. When I get to Montreal, I'll ask around. People in the anti-war movement tell me we'll get all the help we need."

Frankie couldn't believe it. Angelo was determined to make a mistake that would ruin his life. He tried again.

"What about your parents? You may never see them again. Have you thought about that?"

Angelo looked at him hard. "It's all I've thought about. Believe it or not this is their idea, my mother's actually."

Frankie thought he was dreaming. "Your parents know about this?"

"Remember I told you that my parents had a baby girl before they had me. She was four years older than me and was hit by a car and killed when she was six?"

"Sure I remember. What about it?"

"I was too young to remember anything, but my father says mom was devastated. They both were but especially her. She almost didn't recover. When this war started she told my father flat out, that her son will not go to war under any circumstances. She refused to allow another child of hers to die."

"I never imagined," Frankie said.

"I didn't know their feelings about Vietnam, but when I started speaking out against the war at home, they agreed. I was surprised. I thought they'd give me a hard time, because otherwise, they're pretty average citizens, not very political, but patriotic. Anyway, I didn't think much of it, but when the draft notice came, my mother freaked out. I mean she was hysterical. It was amazing because I had already looked into the Canada thing, never really thinking that I'd actually do it. I couldn't leave them, because they need me to run the store. But when they brought it up, it blew my mind. They said I can't help with the store if I'm in the army, so what's the difference if I'm in Vietnam or Canada? One thing led to another, and now, I'm going."

"And they can handle that you'll be leaving forever, that you'll never see them again?"

"They plan to visit, so I'll see them. Plus, I plan to come back. It won't be until the war is over in a year or so, but I'll be back. There's some talk in the anti-war movement that some day the government will let us back in. There are too many kids of powerful parents who've already left. They'll figure out a way to get them back. I'm sure of it. When they get to come home, I'll come home with them."

"And what if you're wrong?" Frankie asked.

"If I'm wrong, I'll watch Canadian football the rest of my life. I hear it's crazy. They use twelve men on a side instead of eleven, wider field too. But I'll get used to it. Who knows, maybe I'll even learn to like ice hockey!"

"Come on Angelo. This is no time to joke around."

"Nobody's joking. This war has gnawed at me for a long time. You and I and Johnny talked about this months ago. I told you then that the protesters were right and that if I could, I'd go to Canada. Now I'm going."

Frankie sat there, not knowing what to say. Angelo was frustrated that Frankie wasn't seeing things his way and tried a different approach.

"Do you know who Senator Fulbright is?" he asked.

"No," Frankie said weakly.

"Well you should, damn it! I'm in that damn store all day long and I watch the news while I work. I read the papers when things are slow, and know what? I learn things. Fulbright is the chairman of the Senate Foreign Relations Committee. He's a distinguished senator who specializes in foreign policy. He's not one of those wacked-out peace nuts. He's a democrat, a member of Johnson's party, and he says we can't win. We shouldn't be there. He talks about the arrogance of American power, thinking we can get people to do what we want by bombing the hell out of them until they see things our way. Should I die, should anyone die, fighting for a cause that a guy in the know like Fulbright says we can't win?" Frankie had never seen Angelo so passionate, even when they discussed the war before.

"Where do you get all of this stuff?" Frankie asked meekly.

"Damn, Frankie, I read it! Guys are dying every day over there. People have an obligation to get answers."

Frankie slumped a little. Maybe he didn't know all of the facts. Maybe Angelo was right, or maybe he wasn't. But to Frankie, it all boiled down to something very personal. "What about our friends over there? Do we just write off Johnny, and Nick, and Jimmy? As long as they're there, my heart is there with them."

Angelo sat back again and took a breath. When he spoke his voice was much softer.

"Look, Frankie, I love those guys as much as you do, and I respect them. Their country called and they answered. It's noble. It really is. I'm not trying to be a wise-ass. But in this case, they answered the wrong call, because their country is fighting the wrong war.

And do you know what else? After the big shots realized we made a mistake, they decided to fix it by sending in more men and dropping more bombs. Only it's still not working. They're talking about a peace conference to end the war, and in the meantime, guys are dying. Can you imagine dying in a war that the big guys have already decided should end? Not me. It's not Johnny's fault or Nick's or even poor Jimmy who got drafted. They all did what they thought was right. But I don't think it's right and I won't do it."

Frankie remained silent, torn between what Angelo was saying and wanting to support his country and friends.

Angelo plowed on. "Millions of wonderful, well-intended Americans back the war because they believe it's right to support their government. They trust the government's judgment. The war is not fair to them either because they are going to look back on it someday and know they were wrong. They're looking at the protesters in the streets and saying that they are un-American. Damn it, Frankie, I'm not un-American. I love this country. And I love my friends who are fighting. But I believe in all my heart that the best way to help them is to not fight. If we all did that there wouldn't be a war. Would there?"

He leaned forward and looked into Frankie's eyes. "The war has torn this country apart. I don't want it to tear us apart too. I'm not asking you to agree with me; I'm just asking you to try to understand. I don't want to lose your friendship, but I have to do what I think is right. That's it."

Frankie looked around the joint, awakening countless memories. He saw Jake's makeshift gallery of their high school pictures taped to the wall, surrounding a small hand printed sign that read, "The Boys." They were images of happy times: football pictures, some prom poses, a group shot of everyone gathered behind the pool table. There were candid shots of guys playing the pinball machines. Someone had even taken a picture of the Tone Kings singing out front. They all reflected rock solid friendships that they had sworn would last forever, but now, things were screwed up badly.

Frankie didn't want to talk politics anymore. He wasn't going to change Angelo's mind, and he wasn't even sure he should.

"What about Donna?" Frankie asked. "Do you think she'll be happy?"

Angelo smiled. "The girl's crazy about me. If I'm there, she'll be happy."

Frankie tried to smile. "I'm serious. This is a giant move for her."

"I know," Angelo said, "and I was only kidding. The fact is Donna and I truly love each other. We always have. Neither of us has even dated anyone else. We seriously want to get married. I don't know what the laws are, here or in Canada, but as soon as we can, we're getting married. As for her parents, the sad truth is that she thinks they'll be glad when she's gone. There's nothing there between them. They value their booze more than their daughter. She swears she's okay with it."

Donna's family life and bad relationship with her parents was well known, and Frankie thought Angelo was probably right on that point.

"As far as leaving town goes, she'll miss her friends like I will, but this will be over in a year or two and we'll be home. She sees it as an adventure."

Frankie nodded. The fight had gone out of him. He was emotionally spent.

Angelo saw it. "I need you to be happy for us Frankie. I really do."

Frankie took out his wallet and counted out all the cash he had, a hundred and forty dollars. He peeled off a twenty and stuck it back in his pocket and handed the rest to Angelo.

"Lucky for you, I got paid today," he said.

Angelo looked at the wad and shook his head. "Put that away Frankie; I'll be fine."

"It's not for you," he said, trying a smile. "It's for Donna. I don't want her starving in Montreal."

Angelo still didn't reach for the money.

"You can't afford this, Frankie. You keep it."

"I told you, I've been working. I get paid. Now either stick this in your pocket, or I'll stick it down your throat."

Angelo reached for the money. "Thanks, man. I won't forget it."

"If you get in a jam, call me. I'll send you something if I can. But don't make a habit of it."

"I won't," Angelo said.

"There's one thing I need you to do for me," Frankie said.

"Name it."

"Your parents aren't getting any younger. I want you to tell them that if there is anything they need, any way I can help, I want them to call me."

"Thanks, Frankie," Angelo grinned. "I already told them."

30- Soldier Boy

Allison sat on her dorm room floor wearing her favorite flannel pajamas and cradling the dozen roses Johnny sent her that day. His long-awaited letter was resting on her lap. Next to her was a half-finished bottle of cheap wine. Debbie sat by her side, holding her own near-empty bottle.

It was Debbie's idea to celebrate Allison's surprise with a private wine party.
"Great!" Allison had said. "But I don't drink. And come to think of it you don't either."
"Are you kidding?" Debbie countered. "After a letter like the one you got today we have to drink this one time."
"I guess you're right," Allison said giggling.

Johnny's earlier letter to Debbie had been just the bomb-shell Debbie hoped for. Allison told her all about Johnny- their once great relationship, her screw-up with Drake, Johnny's refusal to get back together, his friends, his singing, his football days, everything. She talked about how she watched his games as a cheerleader, wanting so much to be with him after each game, and how much it hurt when he dated other girls. She explained everything up to when she stormed out of their last meeting at Frankie's house. That was when she had finally given up on their relationship, keeping him in her heart but not in her plans. But all of that changed when Debbie read her the letter.

Allison immediately distanced herself from Steve, making up one excuse after another. Debbie warned her that he was becoming suspicious, but Allison didn't care, and Debbie loved it. This was life; this was exciting.

She waited three weeks, with growing anxiety, for Johnny's promised letter. Finally,

Allison's anxiety ended happily when Johnny's flowers and letter arrived that afternoon. That was four hours earlier, now they were sloshed.

"My stomach feels a little funny," Allison said after another sip of wine.

"Did you coat your stomach with milk like I told you to?" Debbie asked.

"A whole glass," Allison slurred. "But I don't think it works.

"You'll be fine," Debbie said cheerfully. "You can't be sick for a celebration like this."

Allison looked as though her eyelids were getting heavy, so Debbie tried to perk her up.

"I know," Debbie said, "let's have a cigarette. It will make you feel better."

"I don't smoke," Allison replied. Then she added, "Hey! You don't smoke either."

"Tonight I do! Look, I bought these for both of us." She held up a pack of Salem. "Don't wanna smoke," Allison said heavily. "Bad breath. Smoking gives people bad breath. I need to be fresh for Johnny."

"You won't be kissing Johnny tonight. You can have a mint before you see him."

"Fresh as spring for Johnny," Allison mumbled.

Debbie was losing her and tried something else. "Hey, what happened to our music?"

They had put an album on the turntable earlier and hadn't noticed when it finished.

"Stay awake, Allison; I've got something special for you to hear."

After a quick search, Debbie proudly produced "Soldier Boy" by the Shirelles. She played the record full blast and Allison perked up. Pretty soon the girls were singing along.

They were sitting side by side now, swaying back and forth.

… first love…

"First love," Allison shouted above the music. "That's me. Really," she added, looking serious. "Johnny was my first love."

Debbie laughed. "I know. I know. Your first love. Now let's sing the rest."

"Wait!" Debbie exclaimed. "Wait. Start it again. From the beginning."

Debbie picked up the needle and carefully placed it at the beginning.

…I'll be true…

"This time I will," Allison said. "I always will."

By the time the song was over, both girls were crying.

"That's beautiful," Allison said, wiping her tears with her flannel sleeve.

"Beautiful," Debbie agreed.

"Let's read the note again," Allison said with great difficulty.

"Okay," Debbie slurred, "But I better do it, you're in no condition."

"Why, because I'm in love?" Allison asked before letting out a short burp.

"No, because you're drunk and can't read," Debbie said.

Just then Allison screamed, "Oh my God, we lost the note."

"Calm down," Debbie said. "It's right there silly."

"Where?"

"In your lap."

Allison looked down and laughed hysterically. Debbie joined her. When they finally calmed down, Debbie reached over and started the record again. They sang a few lines.

Allison stopped mid way through and said, "Let's read the note."

"Didn't we just read it?" Debbie asked.

"I don't think so. But I have it right here."

She held it up, and Debbie snatched it out of her hand.

"This note," Debbie said, waving it in front of Allison's face. "This note is the best note ever written." Then she added, "by anybody, ever!" Allison leaned over and smelled the roses. "These are Johnny's beautiful flowers. Smell them," she said, trying to lift them closer to Debbie. Debbie ignored her. "I'm going to read the note again."

"Great idea. Read Johnny's note." Allison looked as though she would be asleep at any second.

Debbie made a big deal of sitting up straight and clearing her throat before starting.

"Dear Allison," she began. Then she held up her hand and said, "Wait. Wait just one second." She took another chug of her wine.

"Okay, here we go."

Dear Allison,

I hope you're okay and I hope you like the flowers. I'm doing fine. I've finished my training and our company is being sent to Vietnam real soon. But I'm okay with it. It's a great group of guys and we're well prepared. Don't get me wrong; I'd rather be in high school singing with Frankie and the guys than doing this, but I'm fine.

There was a time when I thought I'd write you a real long, complicated letter, telling you everything I've done and felt since I saw you at Frankie's, and asking you a thousand questions about what you've been doing and thinking. But I've decided that there is really only one thing I want to say to you and only one question I want to ask. So here goes. I want you to know that I love you. I've always loved you and I always will. That's it, simple and honest. The only question I need answered is do you love me?

I'm sorry for dumping this on you before I leave for Vietnam. I told myself I wasn't going to do it until I got back, but I had to. I was afraid you'd marry somebody while I was gone. So anyway, I love you, and I think you know that I always have. Now I just need to know if you feel the same way.

They tell me that the army is pretty good about delivering mail in the field. So please write to me at the address below, and I'll get it.

Love,
Johnny

By the time Debbie finished both girls were crying again.
They sat quietly for a while, wiping their tears.
"I want a letter like that," Debbie sobbed.
"Me too," Allison said.
"You've got one!" Debbie shouted.
"I know," Allison said, and they both laughed and then fell silent again.

"I want to write back," Allison said.
"Now?"
"Yes, right now. Will you write it for me? I'll dictate."
"Sure," Debbie said. She reached up to her desk and grabbed a tablet and pen.
"This is so romantic," Debbie said, arranging the tablet on her lap. "Okay, shoot."
"Okay, here we go. Write this. Dear Johnny."
"Dear Johnny," Debbie repeated as she wrote.
"Okay," Allison said. "First word." She paused for a second. "Okay. Here goes. Write this. Yes!" She exclaimed. "That's it. Write, Dear Johnny, yes!"
Debbie shrieked. "Great!"
"Okay. Second word."
Just then Allison didn't look good at all. Without saying anything else, she stood and raced to the wastebasket. She made it just in time. Debbie felt like she might have to join her.

31- Rat 2

Jimmy crawled in the darkness. Except for the bleeding that had stopped once his elbows calloused, the assignments hadn't gotten any easier. They were every bit as terrifying, worse actually, because Jimmy was convinced that his time was running out. Lieutenant Timmer had ordered him into the tunnels eight times, and Jimmy still hadn't encountered the enemy. The odds were that sometime soon there would be VC waiting for him with AK-47s pointed at his face, and he had a growing feeling that this would be the time.

Physical danger wasn't his only problem; he also felt his mental condition deteriorating. Every day he was consumed by his mounting hatred of Timmer and the fear that the platoon would stumble upon another hole. He was getting to the point where he thought he might crack.

There was a brief time when he felt he might get used to the tunnels, that the fear would diminish, but he fought the idea. He didn't want to be a tunnel rat. Give the job to one of the crazies, he thought. There were some wacked-out guys in the army, guys who loved danger and loved to kill. They were different from average guys who showed real courage in the face of the enemy, guys who did heroic, fearless things for the good of others. Jimmy respected and even envied them, but Jimmy knew there were also sick guys who thrived on combat. They sought out danger and yearned for blood. They put themselves at unreasonable risk, as though they had a death wish. These were guys who laughed after battles and scoffed as they glared at the grotesque corpses of their victims. While most guys were haunted by the knowledge they had killed someone, however necessary it was, the crazies celebrated, even taking souvenirs from the dead. Jimmy didn't know if they had come to Vietnam that way or if Vietnam had made them what they had become, but it didn't matter. He was afraid of death and afraid of killing. He was determined not to be like the crazies, so he resisted getting used to his insane assignment, no matter how many times he was ordered to do it.

He was sickened by his obsessive desire to kill Lieutenant Timmer. The feeling was real, and it was growing, almost exploding inside of him. He considered the ways he could do it without getting caught. The more he thought about it, the more disgusted he became with himself. Jimmy had never been in a fight in his life, not even a schoolyard scuffle. He didn't like trouble. He wasn't perfect, but he usually tried to do the right thing. Now, the thought that he was even considering killing a fellow American turned his stomach. Still, he wanted to survive and was convinced Timmer would get him killed if he didn't stop him first.

He knew that no matter how carefully he planned, he'd be caught and be sent to the brig for life or be executed. He laughed at the irony of his choices: be killed by a gook, be executed, rot in prison or go crazy. He felt trapped, as trapped as he was now while crawling through the tunnel.

By now the men in the platoon were sympathetic to Jimmy's plight, especially the guys closest to Roosevelt. After seeing Timmer's routine over and over, they thought that no one deserved to be treated like that. Roosevelt and Higgins even went to the lieutenant to speak about it, but Timmer wasn't an easy guy to talk to. He was aloof, detached. He rarely fraternized with the men. Still, they approached him. They told him they thought Jimmy had done enough. Since they were finding more tunnels than they had expected, they suggested that he request to have some trained tunnel rat volunteers choppered in to join the unit.

Roosevelt told Jimmy later that the lieutenant had been studying a map and never looked up the whole time he and Higgins spoke. When they were finished he told them that things were fine as they were, and the conversation was over. Roosevelt even thought he saw a hint of a smile on the lieutenant's face. There was something wrong with the guy, Roosevelt said. Jimmy already knew that.

"I thought he was one of those ninety-day wonders from OCS," Roosevelt said. "But I found out he's a West Point guy. Some of 'em are great and some ain't. Timmer ain't."

That was three days earlier. Today they found another hole, and Jimmy was back in the tunnel. He moved quickly, eager to finish and get back outside. He moved silently, knowing that if he did encounter any VC, his only hope was to hear them before they heard him. He traveled almost as lightly as he had on the first mission, with a flashlight in one hand and the Smith and Wesson in the other. As always, the flashlight was off to avoid detection. The only other things he carried were in his back pocket. After his bout with panic on the first trip, he always carried two extra flashlight batteries. He wanted light on the way out. He also carried the two stones that Roosevelt had given him. They were smaller than ping- pong balls, but larger than marbles. Each was very smooth and almost perfectly round. Roosevelt said that the Chinese used similar balls to relieve stress. They would hold the spheres in their hand and slowly rotate them over and over. Jimmy had tried it and found it to be soothing. He carried them ever since.

After crawling for several yards, Jimmy's head struck a small chime suspended from the tunnel ceiling. It was impossible to miss it in the pitch-black eighteen-inch shaft. The VC put bamboo chimes in some tunnels to alert them of someone approaching. The chime didn't make much noise, but Jimmy cursed it just the same. He backed up slightly, put down his weapon and flashlight and waited. He didn't hear anything. Then he carefully groped in front of him for the chimes. They were small, about the size of a screwdriver handle. Moving very slowly, he carefully wrapped his hand around them to muffle the sound. With his other hand he followed the wire up a few inches to the top of the shaft. The wire was attached to a nail imbedded in the clay ceiling. Carefully, he pried it loose. He couldn't take the chance of any more noise, so using the butt of his flashlight, he dug a small hole in the clay beside him. The clay was hard, and the digging was difficult. When the hole felt like it was three inches deep, he buried the chimes. He waited a little longer and listened. When he didn't hear anything, he continued his crawl.

Jimmy had learned that the lack of vision in the darkness could be replaced with a keener sense of smell. The VC ran their air vents down into the larger caverns at the ends of the tunnel shafts. After investigating a few tunnels, he had learned that the air quality improved as he moved from the stale air of the tunnel to the wider opening of the ventilated cavern. This gave him a clue of when he was approaching a cavern. If anyone were hiding, it would be there.

As he crawled, he sensed the air was improving, so he slowed down. After a few more feet he felt the tunnel begin to widen. Now he was sure he was at a cavern entrance. The darkness was a good sign that the tunnel was unoccupied, unless they had heard the chimes earlier and extinguished their light. He had no way of knowing. In the previous tunnels the rooms had been small, maybe ten feet by ten feet, and used mostly for storage. He had no idea how large or small this one would be.

He rested his head on the ground and waited, listening for the slightest sound. After several minutes he decided it was time to make a move, time for another game of Russian roulette. He would turn on his flashlight and either be relieved to find another unoccupied room or he would be in a gun battle that he was sure to lose. He took a long quiet breath. Just as he prepared to turn on the light, he heard something. He was sure of it. It was very slight, but he definitely heard something.

He waited. His heart was pounding now, and he struggled to control his breathing. His mind was racing faster than his heart. Maybe he was imagining things, he thought. Maybe he heard a rodent. He wasn't willing to take the chance, so he waited longer. Then he swore he heard something again. It was very faint, like a person shifting his weight, just a slight movement. He wanted to turn on the light and get things over with, just take on his unseen adversary and let the chips fly. But he knew if VC were there, their weapons were aimed at the opening, and he'd be dead the instant he could be seen.

He waited some more, thinking. Then he had an idea. He reached back into his pocket for Roosevelt's stones. It was difficult because the tunnel was so narrow, but he found them and brought them to his face. He was going to throw the stones into the cavern. Hopefully the noise would provoke a response. Maybe he could flush them out and then fire in the direction of their movement, or muzzle flashes if they shot. Finally, he said a Hail Mary. He was pretty sure he was going to die.

He threw both stones with one hand and heard them hit wood, probably a supply crate. Someone in the room fired wildly in the direction of the noise. In that split second he saw two sets of muzzle flashes next to each other. He fired in the direction of the flashes. Someone groaned. There was another muzzle flash, a single one this time, and Jimmy felt the bullet sail by him. He returned fire in the direction of the flash and heard another, more muffled groan. Then it was quiet. He waited, hugging the side of the small shaft as tightly as possible. He was aware of the blood rushing through every part of his body. There was pulsating pain behind his eyes. His hands shook. He waited a long time, trying to figure out what to do next. Then he had another idea. He reached into his back pocket again and pulled out the extra batteries. He would repeat the process. With one hand he steadied his pistol in the direction of the last muzzle flashes. With the other, he threw the batteries in the same spot he had thrown the stones. They struck wood again, but this time there was no response. Jimmy wanted to be relieved, but he wasn't. His only remaining option was to turn on the flashlight and deal with whatever happened. There was no use agonizing about it. He aimed the gun again and pressed the flashlight switch. He saw two bodies next to each other in a sitting position. Instinctively, he fired a shot into each of them. Neither one moved.

There was no one else in the room. Along the far wall there was a stack of crates where the stones had hit. He forced himself to look at the two VC again. He noticed both had previous wounds. One had a bandage around his ribs, and the other had one around his shoulder and upper chest. Jimmy tried not to notice where his bullets had struck, but it was obvious that one VC was missing half of his face. The guy looked even younger than Jimmy.

Jimmy turned and threw up. Then, he just sat there next to his vomit and stared at the mess he had made. Slowly, just like before, he began to shake. Lately, he was always shaking. Oddly, there was no urgency this time to get out of the cave. Instead, he felt very tired and wanted to sleep. He hadn't slept well in so long. His sleep was always disturbed by dreams of the tunnels. Maybe this would be a peaceful place to sleep, he thought. He tried to lie down, but he was shaking too much to rest. He tried not to think about what just happened, but he couldn't help it. He had just killed a man, two men. He wondered what they were doing in the cave. They were obviously wounded and probably too weak to travel. Maybe they had been left there to recuperate while others went for help or supplies. He was sure they had been as terrified as he was moments earlier. He imagined that they had been listening for his breathing while he was listening for theirs. Maybe they had heard him hit the chimes and sat in the darkness waiting for the battle. He thought about the exchange. They fired and he fired. He got lucky in the dark, and they died. It was as simple as that. He was still alive, and they were dead. He wondered who was waiting for them back home. What were their families and friends like? He wondered where Viet Cong guys hung out when they weren't fighting wars.

He, Jimmy Wright, had become a killer. He imagined introducing himself to other people after the war. "Hi, I'm Jimmy Wright," he'd say.

"I used to play high school football and hang out at Jake's. I once killed wounded guys who were just as scared-shitless as I was."

As he sat there trying to pull himself together, he made himself a promise. He would never go into a tunnel again. Even if that meant that he would have to shoot Timmer between the eyes in full view of the platoon, he would never go into a tunnel again.

32- Timmer

The platoon was exhausted by the time Lieutenant Timmer finally called off the patrol.
"Why stop so soon?" Tyrone whispered to Higgins. "We've only been walking for six hours."
"If the VC don't kill us, Timmer will," Higgins replied. By now most of the men had had enough of Timmer's leadership. At times it seemed like he ordered the men to do things just to establish his authority. He was arrogant, overconfident foolish, and that made for a dangerous combination.
"Hey, I'd rather walk than shoot," Honk Hudson said. "Any day without a fire fight is a good day for me. Ain't that right, Jimmy?"
Jimmy nodded and dropped his gear next to Roosevelt and Sonny Malanaldo, a Puerto Rican kid from Chicago. Jimmy and Roosevelt liked Sonny. He was a rabid Cubs fan, and the three of them spent hours arguing about the Cubs and the Phillies.

Roosevelt and some of the other guys had been by Jimmy's side ever since he came out from the hole three days earlier, when Jimmy had been quiet, almost trance-like, after his search. As usual, Timmer pumped him for information, but Jimmy just brushed by him and sat by a tree. When Timmer followed and ordered him to stand, Jimmy ignored him and stared out at the jungle. He looked pretty spooky, and even Timmer had the sense to back off. He motioned for Roosevelt.

"Find out what happened down there and what's in the hole." Then he walked away. Gradually, Jimmy told Roosevelt everything, including the promise that he would kill Lieutenant Timmer if he ever ordered him into a hole again. He said it loud enough for everyone to hear, except for Timmer, who by then was off by himself. Few could blame him, and no one told Timmer.

Jimmy had barely spoken since, so Roosevelt was relieved when Jimmy started kidding Sonny about baseball. "The only reason you like the Cubs is because you think Ron Santo is a Puerto Rican," Jimmy said. "That's not true," Sonny replied. "I know he's not, but he's still the best third baseman in the game. Everybody knows that." "Not me," Roosevelt chimed in, "Richie Allen is a way better hitter." Roosevelt knew that statement would ignite things.

"Richie Allen!" Sonny exploded. "Are you serious? Do you wanna compare their stats?" Jimmy was smiling and that was a good sign. "I agree with Roosevelt," Jimmy said, "I think Allen is better."

It was then that the shot rang out. Higgins hollered "sniper," and everyone dove for cover. Before Sonny could get far, the sniper fired a second shot that hit him in the throat and knocked him back. Jimmy saw blood sprouting from Sonny's carotid artery. Roosevelt saw it too and dragged Sonny to cover. Jimmy grabbed his M16 and crawled to a log. He scanned the trees in the direction the bullet had come from. There was a clearing of about fifty yards that ended with a tree line, and he looked there first. It was dusk, and the platoon couldn't see much. But for Jimmy, it seemed like mid-day compared to the blackness of the tunnels.

Viet Cong snipers followed a routine. Fire one shot, two at the most, and then hide. They liked to attack at dusk, wait and then slip off in the darkness that would soon follow.

Some gook bastard shot Sonny, Jimmy thought as he scanned the trees. He moved his eyes slowly, trying to pick out something unusual. He was looking straight ahead when he saw a slight movement in a tree at the edge of the clearing. Jimmy focused more closely and saw a figure in the classic black Viet Cong garb. The sniper was about thirty feet off the ground and made a sharp silhouette against the remaining light. Stupid gook, Jimmy thought.

"I've got him," he whispered to the guys around him. "He's at twelve o'clock, about two-thirds up a tree."

Roosevelt was putting pressure on Sonny's neck and didn't answer. Tyrone said, "Where is he man? I don't see him." "Me neither," Higgins said.

"I've got him," Jimmy repeated calmly. There was no hesitation. The sniper had just shot Sonny. He needed to die.

Jimmy took a breath and fired. The rest happened in slow motion. The VC's rifle fell and a second or two later his body tumbled silently to the ground.

"Great shot!" Tyrone said. To the guys who were pinned down, it was a beautiful sight.

They kept their cover as they congratulated Jimmy for the kill. There was still a chance of another sniper. They scanned the trees more but saw nothing. Finally Honk said, "Let's light it up,"

"Damn right," Higgins said. There was an eruption of gunfire as they laid down a steady barrage along the tree line. Jimmy was closest to the perimeter and could feel the bullets from the guys behind him sailing over his head. The noise was deafening. Branches split, and leaves flew as the men sprayed the area. Finally the shooting stopped.

Everyone gathered around Roosevelt, who was still working on Sonny, but his efforts looked futile. Both men were covered with blood and Sonny's neck gushed like a fountain with each heartbeat, but it was dissipating now. Soon it stopped and Sonny was gone. "Son of a bitch," Tyrone said. "The guy was engaged."

They stood there in silence as Roosevelt knelt next to Sonny and cried. Jimmy put his hand on Roosevelt's shoulder and stood there wordlessly. Higgins made the sign of the cross and whispered a prayer. Slowly, guys began to move away, some to gather their things, others to decompress from the attack. Then someone shouted, "Timmer's down!"

A Second Lieutenant in Vietnam had one of the shortest life expectancies of any rank in the military. The Viet Cong were trained to recognize and take out an officer every chance they had, so VC snipers always made an officer the first target. Most officers knew this and took steps to blend in with the men, like removing the officer's bars from their helmets. But Timmer was different. In addition to being arrogant and cold, Lieutenant Timmer was foolish. He always kept a distance from his men when the platoon was at rest, preferring to sit off by himself. And he was constantly studying his maps in the open. To a VC sniper, holding a map was like holding a sign that said, "Shoot me; I'm an officer."

As the men rushed to the lieutenant, it was clear that he was dead. He was still clutching a map in one hand as he lay on the ground. His lifeless eyes were wide open, and there was a look of surprise on his face. It was obvious now that the sniper's first shot had hit Timmer. Judging from the bloodstain, the bullet passed through Timmer's heart. "That VC son of a bitch had a pretty good aim," Higgins said. "Two kill shots with two bullets."
Jimmy had stayed with Roosevelt and Sonny when the men first rushed to Timmer. He left them now and joined the group gathered around the lieutenant. "He's dead," Honk said when Jimmy stepped up. Jimmy edged closer to get a better look and stared at Timmer's body for a long time. He felt no sympathy or compassion; he just wanted to make sure that the bastard was really gone. Finally, Higgins reached down and closed the lieutenant's eyes. A couple of guys took off their helmets, but the gesture was more mechanical than out of respect. No one shed

any tears. The men stood there briefly and then moved on to be with Roosevelt and Sonny.

Tyrone patted Jimmy on the back. "It's over man," he said.

Jimmy nodded. In the span of five minutes he had killed a sniper, lost Sonny, and was liberated from a sadistic, possibly homicidal tyrant. He looked at the dead lieutenant again and thanked the faceless VC he had just killed.

33- Lunar New Year

On February 1, Anna Francelli settled in to watch the news. It was a big mistake. The Viet Cong had launched a massive attack during Tet, the Vietnamese New Year holiday. They hit provincial capitals throughout the country, including KheSanh and Saigon.

Casualties were heavy on both sides, and the marines at Khe Sanh were in danger of being overrun. But the symbolic focus of the story was Saigon, where a team of VC commandos stormed the American embassy and made it inside the compound before being repelled after fierce fighting with marine guards. Although the attack failed, television images of the bullet- ridden embassy seal, and word that one thousand Americans died in the offensive, had a dramatic effect upon American public opinion.

For months the White House and the Pentagon had told Americans that the war was going well, the cities were secure, and the South Vietnamese people were with them. The images on the television screen told a different story. Like millions of Americans who watched the news that night, Anna wondered what was really happening in Vietnam.

34- Landing in Country

Johnny had never been out of the country until his flight to Vietnam. He heard about the trips to Asia aboard C130s where the soldiers sat for hours on nylon web seats. So he was grateful that the army had chartered commercial aircraft to handle the latest troop build-up. During their evening takeoff from Fort Lewis, he enjoyed the beauty of the lights that dotted Spokane and the Pacific coastline. Someone once described the view of the ground during night flights as looking down at the stars, and now he knew what they meant. He slept for a while but awakened as the sun came up behind them. It was spectacular. He remembered the sunrises on the beach at the Jersey shore: the golden glow on the horizon reflecting off the ocean's surface, the crashing waves against the shoreline, and seagulls diving for food. He fought off another wave of homesickness.

They landed briefly in Hawaii to fuel. Johnny expected to see hula dancers on the tarmac. Instead, he saw concrete runways lined by metal hangers. His anxiety was high, but he knew that the other two hundred guys on board felt the same way. When they took off again, the pilot announced that they were officially leaving the United States. As far as Johnny was concerned, he had left long ago. For him, Bristol and the shore were the only parts of the country he ever really knew. Leaving home had been difficult enough, but all of the lonely feelings resurfaced when they left the west coast the night before. He was going as far away from home as he could be, to face things he could only imagine. He needed to stop his imagination from running wild and wished the trip would end. If he had to go to Nam, then he wanted to get it over with.

He thought about what his Drill Sergeant said in training. Fear is okay. Fear is what keeps you alert and staying alert keeps you alive. Johnny did well in training. He was a natural, his sergeant said. They made him a squad leader, kind of a first among equals. The men liked him.

He made friends and learned his job well. He swore he'd do the same in Vietnam once he got there.

Nate Conroy, a native of Conneaut, Ohio, sat next to Johnny, and Sam Johnson, a black kid from Oakland, sat at the aisle. The three of them had met for the first time at Fort Lewis two days earlier and quickly became friends.

Nate eased his anxiety by studying the geography, climate, and culture of Vietnam. He had a book about the country and several maps. He said he read and studied them throughout boot camp and declared himself an expert. Johnny couldn't disagree.

Sam seemed more nervous about flying than he was about where they were going, and he talked to Nate and Johnny non-stop. When they tired of listening, he spoke to the guy across the aisle or walked to the restroom and talked to guys along the way.

The pilot announced they would be landing in twenty minutes. Nate had a map of Southeast Asia spread across his lap, and he was lecturing Johnny and Sam.

"Francelli, you've got to be Italian, right?" Nate asked.

"That's right," Johnny said. "Both sides."

"Most Italians are Catholic. Are you?"

"Full breed," Johnny said. "Why?"

"You'll fit in well in Saigon. There're lots of Catholics in South Vietnam, especially in the cities."

"How'd they get there?" Johnny asked.

"The French," Nate replied. "They occupied Vietnam forever and brought their language and religion with them. Lots of the upper class people in the cities, especially Saigon, speak French and send their kids to French-speaking schools. Ho Chi Minh studied in Paris."

"No kidding," Johnny said. Suddenly he wished he knew more about Vietnam.

Nate continued. "Remember, I'm talking about the cities in the South. Once you're in the countryside your ass will be in trouble. Most of the peasants are Buddhists. Some people say this war is more about religion and culture than communism. The gooks fought to get rid of the French, who they thought were ruining their culture, and now there're fighting to get rid of us. Did you ever see the pictures on TV of Buddhist monks setting themselves on fire?"

Johnny had been horrified by the image. "Those guys had to be nuts," he said.

"They did it to show that the South Vietnamese government was pro western, and pro Catholic, and oppressive toward the Buddhists and the poor. They wanted everyone to know it. Some say the war is about getting westerners out of their country. That's what the Viet Cong are fighting for."

Johnny wasn't up on most of what Nate was saying. "But the VC are still communists," Johnny said. "And that's really why we're fighting."

"They're communists," Nate conceded, "but I'm not sure why we're fighting."

"I think the government knows a little more about this than we do," Johnny said. "We're fighting because our government needs us. It's our job, just like our parents and grandparents fought. It's our turn."

"Sure," Nate said. "If you say so."

Sam jumped in. "Screw that stuff," he said. "I'm Baptist, and I know there ain't no Vietnamese Baptists. Are you going to tell us anything about those maps or not?"

"Sure," Nate replied.

"There are several important geographic regions to Vietnam," he said, running his hand over the map. "The Highlands and the Red River area in the North, the Central Highlands, the Costal Lowlands, and the Mekong River Delta in the South."

"If you're so damn smart, what are you doing in the army?" Sam asked.

"I thought I told you yesterday. I knocked up this girl. It was either marry her or join the army. I picked the army," Nate said. "I would have married her, done the right thing," he continued, "but I barely knew her. It was our first date, the first time we ever had sex. It wasn't fair. What's the chance of her getting pregnant after just one time?"

"Jesus, Nate," Sam said. "You smart white guys can be pretty stupid. You know all about Vietnam and don't know squat about sex. You should've read a book. Didn't you learn nothin' in health class?"

"Sure, we learned about the parts of the ear, things like that. It was really useful stuff, y'know, inner ear, middle ear, outer ear."

"What about making babies?" Sam said. "What'd ya learn about that?"

Nate ignored him. "We did a lot with hygiene. It's important to dry between your toes thoroughly. Use dental floss; brushing's not enough. Drink three glasses of milk every day."

"What about making babies?" Sam pressed. "Did you learn about that?"

"I learned about that when I got old Sue Ellen pregnant. That's when I learned about making babies."

"So you picked Nam over Sue Ellen," Sam said.

"No. Sue Ellen's father picked Nam for me. He was real mad, threatened to kill me. Things happened pretty fast and here I am."

"So you're going to Nam to keep yourself safe?" Sam said, laughing.

"That's about it," Nate said smiling. "The VC don't give a hoot about Sue Ellen."

"Makes sense to me," Sam said.

"What about you, Sam? How'd you get in?"

"I got a personal invitation from Lyndon Baines Johnson. It was real nice. Came with a photo of the president and his family. There was LBJ, Lady Bird, Lucy Baines, Linda Bird, a couple of pet Beagles. They probably had a bird in their names too. They all invited me to come. So I packed a few things and hopped on the first plane. I'm hoping they'll be waiting to meet me at the airport."

Then Sam leaned forward to get a view of Johnny. "What about you, Francelli. How'd you get here?"

Johnny was more interested in looking out the window. He was anxious to see land.

"Not important," Johnny replied. "I'm here; that's all." Then he changed the subject.

"Tell us more about the map."

"Sure," Nate said. "If Sam is done grilling me."

"Finished," Sam said.

"This here's the Mekong River, which flows into the delta region and then into the sea. We're going to be landing at a base called Bien Hoi, North of Saigon. From there it's anybody's guess where we're going."

The pilot came over the intercom again. "They're a little stacked up at Bien Hoi airfield," he said. "You're not the only guys arriving, so we're going to run a circular pattern for a while, farther to the south. I didn't want you guys to think that we're lost."

"Funny guy," Nate said, when the captain clicked off.

"Smart ass," Johnny added. He was getting more edgy by the minute. After a while Johnny could feel the plane's descent. They flew through some heavy clouds and Johnny chuckled. His mood was dark enough without the added gloom of the darkness outside his window. Then the sky cleared, and Johnny could see land in the distance. Slowly, the gray black water turned dark green. Then it became lighter as they approached the coastline. As the landform came into focus, Johnny was struck by its lush, green appearance. It was beautiful. As they got closer to the shoreline, the water was much lighter and Johnny could make out the reddish sand of the beaches. Nate was leaning against Johnny to get a view from the window too.

"Look," Nate said. "There's the Mekong River, and there's the delta." From the distance the river looked like an arm lying flat across the landscape with the delta forming fingers that reached for the ocean.

Slowly, Johnny noticed changes in the green landscape. "Those are rice paddies," Nate said, pointing. They looked just like the photos in his book. "Those things that look like roads are dykes. They control the water source for the paddies."

As they got closer they saw the large grayish area of Saigon. From a few thousand feet up the city offered an unappealing contrast to the countryside. That was funny, Johnny thought, because everyone knew that if you had to be in Nam, Saigon was the best place to be, and the countryside was the worst. Saigon offered relative safety; the jungles and the countryside offered something much different. Finally, they received clearance to begin their landing pattern and the pilot changed course to Bien Hoi.

They began their final descent, and the closer they got to the ground, the uglier Bien Hoi looked. It was an airbase surrounded by a small city. The base resembled the same drab image he had seen in Hawaii, but the houses and other structures were far worse. They landed smoothly.

As they walked down the steps to the tarmac they were overwhelmed by the heat and humidity. A waiting sergeant read their faces. "Don't worry; you'll get used to it," he said. "For now, drink plenty of water."

Sam tapped Johnny on the shoulder and motioned for him to look back. A tow motor was unloading caskets from the cargo area of their plane.
"They're empty," Nate said. "Let's keep them that way."

"I'm sure you guys are hungry," the sergeant said. "Get yourselves some food and a good night's rest. Tomorrow you'll get your equipment and orientation. In a day or two you'll be shipping out to your new base."

The food wasn't great, but there was plenty of it. The guys were so hungry that they hardly spoke as they ate. Back at the barracks Johnny, Sam and Nate took three bunks in a row. They introduced themselves to some other guys, but they were too tired to talk much. They tried to figure out what time it was in Nam compared to the West Coast, but they gave up on it. Sam said he didn't care what time it was. He was tired and the sergeant told them to sleep, so that was what he was going to do.

Johnny laid flat on his bunk thinking. He'd been sleeping in barracks for months now, all through boot camp and advanced training and had gotten used to it. But this was different. This was Vietnam. Throughout training the DI's had made constant reference to Vietnam. When you get to Nam you'll have to do this or that, they said. This will keep you alive in Nam, they said. When they reamed somebody out they said things like, "Boy, I'm trying to help you survive!" Johnny listened to every word they said. He did everything he was told, and more. If he was ordered to dig a two-foot deep trench, he dug it two and a half. If he was told to line it with four rows of sandbags, he used five. When he was told to keep his weapon clean so it would fire properly, he cleaned it every chance he got, sometimes twice a day. He was commended for his marksmanship. The M-16 became an extension of his body. He also learned how to use the M-60, although it was way too heavy. He mastered the M-79 grenade launcher. He learned how to set a Claymore mine. He didn't want to mishandle one, so he paid close attention. He learned the importance of keeping your men spread out during patrol. He learned how to recognize booby traps. He learned that the guys who paid attention could find them; the guys who were distracted or lost their focus did not. The price was high for the latter, so Johnny paid attention. He scored near the top of his company on the obstacle course. He mastered basic first aid. He did it all. And he tried to make sure that the guys around him did it too because he believed that their lives depended upon each other. That's why everyone liked him. That's why he was made a squad leader in camp. Now they were starting all over again. He was determined to prove himself to these guys too.

He pulled a handful of photos from his bag. He had one of his mom and Sissy, sitting together on the glider in their backyard. They looked great. There was a photo of the gang. Johnny's mother had taken it on prom night of their junior year. Everyone was wearing a tux. They were arranged on the steps leading to Johnny's porch. Guys had their arms on each other's shoulders, and everyone was smiling except Jimmy, who decided it would be cool to pose like a tough guy. He had his arms folded across his chest and a scowl on is face. The funny thing was that he was wearing brown Hush Puppies with his tux. Everyone else had polished black shoes and Jimmy was wearing brown Hush Puppies. For months after, guys would bark every time Jimmy walked into Jake's. Johnny laughed out loud thinking about it. The next item was a holy card of St. Therese that his mother had given him. It had a prayer on the back.

"Family, friends, and faith," his mother had said the night before he left. "Those are the things that get us through difficulty in life, Johnny. And they are the things that will get you through this."

He flipped the card over and read the prayer.

When he finished, he shuffled the prayer card to the back of the stack and turned his attention to the graduation photo of Allison that Frankie had given him. He didn't have his own because he and Allison weren't speaking when the class exchanged photos. He cursed himself for being so stupid for so long. He should have let her know how he felt sooner instead of wasting all of that time apart. He viewed time differently now; it was much more important. He looked at her hair, her smile; she looked terrific. He had another photo of her as a cheerleader. He had cut it out from one of his old football programs. It was one of those shots where she was jumping in the air with her arms outstretched, holding pom-poms. He marveled at how she could still smile naturally while jumping two feet of the ground. It reminded him of her tom-boy days, and he smiled again.

Sam leaned over to take a look. "Damn Francelli, she's all right! Is she your girl?"

"I don't know," Johnny said. "I hope so."

35- Orientation

The next day the men received their immunization shots, weapons and other equipment and lined up for their company assignments. Johnny, Sam, Nate and three other guys were peeled off to fill out a squad that would be dispatched to Alpha company.

A sergeant took them aside and started their orientation.
"I'm sergeant Tim Boyd. This squad will be working with me. In a day or two we'll be leaving Bien Hoi and be choppered out to a base camp fifty miles east of the Cambodian border. It's nasty out there. There are reports of heavy North Vietnamese infiltration and there's plenty of VC."
At least this guy isn't sugarcoating things, Johnny thought.
"Let me make something clear," the sergeant said. "I intend to stay alive, and I intend to keep you alive too. But that really depends on you." He scanned the group, sizing up what he had to work with.
"Here's a little fact for you. A lot of guys buy it in their first few weeks in the bush. A majority of the time they buy it because they do something stupid. Or, even worse, because somebody in their squad does something stupid."
He let that sink in a little. He had their full attention.
"This is gonna be the smartest damn squad in Nam. You and I will not tolerate stupidity. We will not tolerate slackers. We will not tolerate carelessness. Is that clear?"
The men nodded. Sergeant Boyd continued.
"You will learn damn quick to support each other, to protect each other. If you don't, there's a good chance you will die. I can't make it any plainer than that."
That's pretty plain, Johnny thought. He appreciated the sergeant's honesty. It was the same theme every DI had lectured about all through training. Johnny wanted to live, and he bought into the logic that a cautious, prepared soldier was a safer soldier. He hoped the other guys in the squad were listening.

Then Boyd softened and added, "I am here for you. If there is something you need, tell me. If there is something bothering you, tell me. And if there is something you don't understand, you damn well better tell me." Boyd paused to let that sink in and then he asked, "Do you guys know each other?"

"A little bit," Sam said. "I don't know everybody."

Boyd made them introduce themselves. Sam went first, followed by Nate and Johnny. Then the three guys they didn't know introduced themselves. Norman Wallace was a black guy from Savanna. At well over six feet tall and muscular, he was the biggest guy in the squad. Tommy Phillips, another black guy, was from New York City. The last guy, Kevin Paige, was from Trenton, New Jersey. Johnny flipped when he heard that. Bristol was only about ten miles from Trenton.

"That's great," Sam said. "Maybe you guys can travel home together on weekends." Then he added with a grin, "Hey, sarge, do we get to go home on weekends?"

Boyd smiled. He wanted these guys to develop a chemistry. They would need someone to keep them loose between patrols. Boyd would make sure they were tight during patrols.

"I know you guys had plenty of training about booby traps and land mines, but you're gonna have some more." Then he added, "Remember, you only get to be wrong once."

They spent the rest of the day looking at dummy mines and simulated booby traps, setting up claymores and trip wires, and firing their weapons. Each had practice using the M-16, M-60 and M-79 grenade launcher. Boyd decided that the hulking Norm Wallace would carry the M-60, but he wanted everyone to be able to use it.

Then Boyd had them dig trenches and line them with sand bags.

"We'll be establishing our own base out in the field. The better the trench, the safer you'll be. Dig the hole and use the dirt to fill the empty sandbags. Make yourselves safe." Johnny soaked in every word Boyd said. Boyd noticed.

When they finished Boyd said, "We're moving out in two days. Get to know each other. Relax a little. There won't be much time to relax in the field. If you need to buy smokes, buy them now. Now's a good time to write a letter too. Mail call is at five at the mess hall. You can send or pick up then. Any mail addressed to you since you left the states should have been forwarded here. Enjoy a good hot meal. They won't be that good where we're going next."

36- On Patrol

Johnny was killing time with Wallace, Phillips, and Paige, when Sergeant Boyd approached with Nate Conroy and Sam Johnson. The sergeant was all business.

"Intelligence says VC entered a friendly village ten miles from here and roughed them up a little. The captain wants us to look for clues of a larger operation. There's a buildup going on and the captain wants to know where. We'll gather information and leave. Should be a piece of cake. We're moving out as soon as the chopper gets here."
The group exchanged uneasy looks.
"This will be your first chopper landing in hostile area, but you've heard this before. Choppers make noise. So if there are VC in the area, they can hear us coming long before we land. Problem is that choppers need an open landing zone, and the VC know where the zones are. They're surrounded by heavy vegetation, a perfect set-up for an ambush. So get this." He scanned their faces for emphasis. "Each time we exit a chopper, we assume that the LZ is ringed by hostiles ready to open fire."

Conroy and Paige looked at each other. No one looked real comfortable.

"When we get to the drop zone, the chopper won't land. It takes too long and makes an easy target. We'll get to within five feet of the ground if we're lucky, and we'll jump, just like in training. The drop should take less than thirty seconds before the chopper is gone, so get out fast. There's nothing to think about. When the ground gets close, you jump. And keep your knees flexed. Got it?"

Everyone nodded, but Phillips' eyes looked like they would pop out of his head.

"If we do get enemy fire, the chopper will provide air cover. The Huey carries a couple of M-60s and phosphorous rockets. They help."

Paige looked terrified as Boyd continued. "What do we do when we hit the ground?"

No one answered.

"Damn!" Boyd boomed. "Have you guys been through training or not?"

Johnny spoke up. "We spread out fast sir!"

"You're damn right you do, Francelli. Good job. Spread out. Give the enemy a tougher target."

He turned to Norm Wallace. "Wallace, you'll carry the M-60. If we're hit, get on the ground and lay down fire as fast as you can."

Wallace nodded. "I'll spray their ass good, sergeant."

"Conroy, you'll carry the ammo belts. Make sure Wallace gets a steady feed. The M-60's no damn good without bullets."

"Got it!" Conroy snapped.

"The rest of us will stay low and return fire."

He paused to let things sink in.

"Now listen to me." His voice had more of a bite to it. "Our first job is to survive. But if you back off from an ambush, you will die. The best way to survive is to go right at 'em."

This was a hard sell, and Boyd wanted to make sure he made the point.

"The VC don't want a long firefight. They want to hit us hard in the first few seconds we land and then get out of there. Hit and run. That's how they do it. But if we forget our jobs, if we panic or back off, they'll just keep firing. If we do what we're supposed to do, and hit back hard, go at them, they'll take off."

The men nodded. They heard it before in training, but now it was very real. Scary, but Sergeant Boyd was convincing.

"So, Phillips, how do we survive an attack in a clearing?"

"We go right at 'em," Phillips snapped.

"That's right, Phillips, return fire, stay low and move forward. Got that, Johnson?"

"Got it, sergeant," Sam winked.

Boyd turned to Kevin Paige and shouted, "Are you scared, Paige?"

"Scared shitless, sergeant!" Paige shouted back.

"Good, you better be. You all better be. Keeps you sharp."

Boyd looked at Johnny. "Francelli, who are you counting on?"

"I'm counting on everyone, sir!" Johnny bellowed.

"You bet you are," Boyd said. "We're all counting on each other. This is no place for cowboys and it's damn sure no place for cowards. We need each other. We need to be scared, focused and doing our jobs."

They could hear the Huey approaching in the distance.

"There's our ride. Here's one more thing. I've looked into the future and I've seen myself as an old man, sitting in my rocker on the porch, watching my grandkids play. I like the image." He let them visualize it. "I'm the best damn sergeant you'll ever have. Do what I tell you and maybe you'll grow old with me. Let's go."

Johnny ran to the chopper and climbed in with the others. Sam was the last one in and was barely on board when the Huey lifted off.

"I told you," Boyd shouted as he gestured to the crew, "these guys don't like to be stationary for long. You've got to move." He could barely be heard above the rotor noise.

They traveled low over the trees and no one spoke. Johnny checked his equipment a dozen times. He remembered the first time he was in full gear at boot camp. The M-16, the ammo, grenades, rations, backpack, helmet, and other gear weighed a ton, but he got used to it. Now, in the intense heat and humidity of Vietnam, the weight seemed to double.

After another fifteen minutes the pilot got Boyd's attention and pointed in the distance. Boyd nodded and shouted, "Five minutes! Check your gear and get ready."
Johnny's heart was pounding. Conroy blessed himself. Tommy Phillips began a nervous hum. Kevin Paige gave everyone the thumbs up, and Sam Johnson winked. They were good guys, Johnny thought. He hoped they were good soldiers.

"There's the LZ," Boyd shouted. Johnny could see a clearing two hundred yards in the distance. He prayed the VC weren't nearby.

The chopper dropped quickly. When they were six feet off the ground Boyd shouted, "move, move." Paige hesitated and then jumped. By the time he did they were hovering at four feet. Johnny went next. He hit the ground hard and rolled with the impact. The whole squad was out in seconds, and the chopper was already climbing. The dust from the blades added to the confusion.
"Go, go," Boyd shouted, and the men spread out. So far there was no shooting. The nearest tree line was thirty yards away. Boyd pointed and said, "Go!"
They moved quickly. Conroy was having trouble with the ammo boxes and Johnny helped him. In less than a minute they were out of the clearing. There was no ambush. They regrouped at the tree line and caught their breaths. Phillips and Johnson shared a high five. Johnny was giddy with relief.

Boyd counted heads. "Good job. No VC this time. We were lucky, maybe next time, or the time after that. Who knows?"
Boyd checked his compass and map. "The village is three klicks from here. Spread out. Francelli, take the point, and everybody remember,

booby traps, mines, trip wires, no mistakes! We all go back with two legs. Stay focused, Francelli. Move out."

Johnny took the point, a terrifying place to be on his first patrol, but, except for Sergeant Boyd, they were all on their first patrol, cherries, as Boyd called them. As he walked, he talked to himself, "Stay focused, trip wires, mines, booby traps, snipers. Keep your eyes moving." He walked slowly. Boyd would tell him if he needed to pick up the pace. He was surrounded by distractions. Fear, humidity, and forty pounds of gear made for an ugly combination. He was dripping with perspiration. Gnats stuck to his face and his knee ached from the jump.
He caught himself thinking about Allison and forced her out of his mind. Thinking of her now could get him killed. He was thirsty, but was afraid to take a drink. He had a flash of Jake and Stella back at the joint. He shook it off. Why in the world was he thinking about Jake's joint now? He struggled to stay focused.

Soon the vegetation thinned and Boyd whispered for him to stop. When the squad caught up, Boyd said, "My guess is we're getting close. As soon as you see the village, stop. We don't move in until I say so."

Five minutes later they were there. The village was small. Johnny counted thirteen huts and thirty to thirty-five people, mostly elderly or children. The adults looked busy, clearing debris and repairing huts, while the children squatted and played in the dirt.

Boyd spoke briefly on the radio, then turned to the squad. "Fan out. We'll approach the village from three sides. Remember, if our intelligence is right, these people have had VC visitors recently. They're probably traumatized. They're going to be scared stiff when they see us and won't want to cooperate. Stay alert. We don't know what's inside those huts, but stay cool. No sudden movements. Don't do anything to spook them. Let's go."

The first woman who saw them screamed, and the other women joined in. Children ran to their mothers crying. An older man approached them cautiously, shaking his head and gesturing for them to go away. Boyd slung his weapon and raised both hands in a sign of friendliness. He kept walking toward them, and the other men moved in closer.

"Lower your weapons, but stay alert," Boyd said, without taking his eyes off of the villagers.

The noise was subsiding, but some of the women and children were still wailing. When Boyd got close enough, two of the elderly men approached him. Johnny couldn't tell what they were saying, but they were clearly pleading for the Americans to leave.

Boyd still tried to calm them, and Johnny was surprised to hear Boyd speak an occasional word in Vietnamese. Boyd asked a one-word question, and the two old men shook their heads emphatically. Another word and the women started sobbing again. They were pointing toward the wooded area at the opposite end of the village. They held up fingers in response to another question from Boyd.

"As far as I can tell," Boyd said, "The VC took the young men from the village with them to fight. Looks like there were more than twenty bad guys. They ransacked some huts to teach the village not to help the Americans. Right now, these people want no part of the VC or us. This one keeps calling himself a farmer. He says the VC headed north, in the direction he was pointing. But why would they tell us the truth if their young men are with them?" Finally Boyd said, "Search the huts, and then let's leave these people alone."

Sergeant Boyd and Johnny entered one of the huts together. An old woman was squatting next to a body that had been prepared for burial. She shrieked when she saw them and wouldn't stop. The only word Boyd could make out was "son."

"These are the kinds of animals we're dealing with Francelli. Don't ever let anyone tell you that the VC are freedom fighters. They're ruthless thugs who kill and abduct their own people."

When the search was over, Boyd took some hard candy from his pack and tossed it in the direction of the children. None of them moved. He said something to the old man who had done most of the talking. Then he said, "Ok, let's move out." As the soldiers withdrew, the children scurried for the candy.

As they made their way back to the LZ, Boyd reminded them about booby traps. "By the way," he added, "The VC like to ambush us boarding choppers just as much as they like to when were getting off. Only now they've had all day to know we're here. Expect it."

Johnny's heart sank and, judging from the looks on the squad's faces, so did everyone else's. Boyd radioed ahead for the Huey and they moved on.

They heard the chopper minutes after they made it to the edge of the clearing. The rush to board was even more chaotic than the earlier exit. It's a lot harder to climb into a chopper than it is to jump out of one. As the chopper lifted off, Boyd took off his helmet and sat on it. Then he smiled at Johnny. "The VC like to shoot through the bottom of the chopper. Lots of guys get it in the ass." Johnny took off his helmet and did the same and Boyd laughed.
"Your first patrol. You guys did ok," Boyd shouted. Everyone nodded, too drained to speak.
"Relax," Boyd said. "We haven't fired a shot yet. How many days have you been In Country?"
"Today is number five sir," Johnny said.

Boyd laughed hard. "Not bad, only three-hundred and sixty days to go."

37- Allison's Letter

Johnny was still shaking when they returned to camp. A full day of fear left the squad emotionally drained, and no one spoke from the time they left the chopper until they collapsed on their bunks.

"Damn," Phillips said. "Will we be doing that every day?"

"Don't see how we can," Johnson said. "Won't make it."

"Wait 'til Charlie starts shooting at us, that'll change things a little," Paige said.

"Damn well better shoot back good," Wallace said in his deep voice. It was a command, not a request. Wallace was an imposing figure, and Johnny was glad to have him near-by. He reminded him a little of Frankie.

"Does anyone have any idea why we're here?" Conroy asked.

"In the bunk?" Johnson asked.

"No, genius. In Vietnam."

"Not this again!" Paige said.

"Screw you Paige!" Conroy said. "I want to know if you saw anything in the bush today that makes it worthwhile to be here."

"I did," Paige said. "I saw a village terrorized by the VC. I saw a mother guarding her murdered son. Didn't you see that stuff, Conroy?"

"I'll tell you what I saw," Conroy said. "I saw a bunch of primitive farmers who don't know the difference between a communist and John D. Rockefeller. I saw people who don't give a damn about anything except their pigs, chickens, and rice paddies."

Paige tried to interrupt, but Conroy kept talking. "I'll tell you what else I saw. I saw a jungle where gooks can hide and pick us off just about any time they want to."

"Nice thought," Phillips said. "Thanks."

"None of that crap matters," Johnson said. "We're here for three hundred and sixty-five days, then we're going home. I'm gonna shoot anyone, communist or not, who gets in the way of that. That's what I think."

"He's right," Wallace said. "Survive and go home. Don't matter nothing else. Survive."

"We'd survive a lot easier if we stayed near camp instead of going out in the bush looking for trouble," Conroy said. "Why not just protect Saigon and a few other cities and let the gooks have the bush and the rice paddies?"

"Look at that," Paige replied. "One patrol and Conroy's an expert. Share your plan with the president. Tell Sergeant Boyd you've got to talk to the man right way."

Conroy flipped Paige the finger and then turned to Johnny.

"What about you, Francelli? You were on point today. What do you think?"

Johnny checked his watch, then he swung his feet off the bunk to get up. "I think it's time for mail call, and I'm gonna see if I got a letter."

"Me too," Johnson said. "I'm expecting a letter from my honey."

"Hell, Johnson, you still pretending you got a woman back home?" Wallace said smiling.

"Got me a beautiful honey back home. Name's Yolanda. You'll meet her some day. I'll bring her to see you."

"Hey, Conroy," Paige added. "Why don't you go with them to check the mail? Maybe the father of that girl you knocked up changed his mind. Maybe he wants you to come home and marry his daughter after all."

"Back off, Paige," Conroy said, taking a step toward him.

"Easy, man," Johnson said. "He's just bustin'. It's too dangerous to go home. You stay here in Nam where it's safe."

Johnny was relieved to hear his name at mail call. He took the letter and quickly checked the return address. It was from Frankie.

"Is that from that foxy cheerleader I saw in the picture?" Johnson asked.

"No," Johnny said, trying to hide his disappointment. "It's from a buddy of mine, my best friend."

"That's too bad, man. The girl I mean." He winked. "Mail here's screwed up. Don't worry; she'll write."

"I know," Johnny said, turning to leave.

Johnson grabbed his arm. "Wait until they call my name, man. We'll walk back together. It'll only take a minute."

"Ok," Johnny said. "I'll be outside."

Johnny sat on an empty ammo crate and opened Frankie's letter. He appreciated the regular news from home. Between his mom, Sissy and Frankie, he was averaging almost four letters a week since boot camp. He expected that from his family, but Frankie's friendship was special and he loved him for it.

The letter was short, but filled with plenty of news items. Everything was fine. Frankie was visiting Johnny's mother for dinner at least once a week. He wrote that she still gets a little teary eyed now and then, but she's keeping busy and doing okay. Father Creeden placed a picture on the side altar of parishioners serving in Vietnam. There were pictures of Johnny, Jimmy, Nick, and two older guys Frankie didn't know. Every Sunday, Father Creeden asked the congregation to join him in saying a Hail Mary for the soldiers.

Sissy seemed fine and was still going strong with Tom. Jimmy wrote now and then, but didn't sound like he was doing well. No one ever heard from Nick, but no news was considered good news.

That was about it. Just as Johnny finished reading, Johnson came out, holding two letters. "Hey, Francelli, know anybody in Boston?" he asked smiling.

Johnny jumped up.

"They called your name again after you left." He tapped the letters in is hand. "Looks like we both got lucky," he said handing Johnny a letter. "One from your honey and one from mine."

Johnny beamed and snatched the envelope.

"Let's go, man," Johnson said, wrapping his arm around Johnny's shoulder. "These letters need to be read in a private place."

Johnny laughed nervously. They almost ran back to the hooch.

They found the guys playing pinochle. Conway and Paige were partners and the earlier tension was gone. Johnson headed for his bunk, and Johnny said, "I need some space. I'm going outside."

Johnson winked. "Sure, man. Catch you later."

The heat was still oppressive and Johnny sat studying the envelope under one of the few trees in the camp. Seeing Allison's name and return address made his heart pound. He smelled the letter. There was no sign of perfume, but something about it smelled good, fresh like he remembered her. This is it, he thought. I took my best shot; now it's time to find out. He opened the letter and started to read.

Dear Johnny,

I received your beautiful letter. You have no idea how happy you can make a person. My answer is a big, fat, emphatic yes! Yes, I love you. I've always loved you and I always will. Sound familiar? I got goose bumps when you wrote that.

Like you, I've thought of the things I'd say if we ever got the chance to talk. And like you, I find it much too painful to think of the time that we wasted apart. So I've blocked out the bad stuff. What I want to write about instead is our FUTURE.

I can't wait to see you. My roommate Debbie, (you'll love Debbie, and she already loves you) said that sometimes soldiers in Vietnam get to go to Japan for a vacation- R & R. I'll fly to see you when you get yours. I'm serious. Debbie said she would come with me, but you'll have to fix her up with a cute guy.

Johnny, I've always dreamed that we'd spend our entire lives together. We'll have kids and teach them to play touch football- I can still catch a football! It will be wonderful.

I'm not sure what you're going through in Vietnam, but I want to know everything, and I want you to promise me that you'll be careful.

Your letter, from "Dear Allison," to "Love, Johnny" was 271 words. If I stop now, I'll be able to say I love you one more time and still come in at 270. I'm still competitive!

So here goes- I Love You!

Count 'em lover boy- I gotcha!

Love,
Allison

Paige was laying down a run in spades when he heard Johnny scream, "Yes!" at the top of his lungs. Johnson smiled.

38- Listening Post

It was clear something big was happening as Sergeant Boyd began his briefing.

"This time we'll be going out as a full platoon," Boyd said. "We'll be choppered to a drop area thirty miles from Cambodia, where intelligence says the VC are planning an offensive. Captain Walters wants Alpha Company to establish listening posts, so the five platoons will set up camps in the area and see what happens. We'll be poking at the enemy, trying to flush him out."

"Like stirring a bee hive," Conroy muttered under his breath.

"Shut up and listen," Paige whispered.

"After our initial deployment, we'll move a little each day. If Charlie's out there, one of the platoons will make contact."

"Then what, Sarge?" Conroy asked.

"We disrupt their ability to organize. If there's enough of 'em and we can pin down their location, we order up air strikes," Boyd said.

"That's it baby! Search and destroy." Johnson said. "Hit those guys with some phosphorous and napalm. Cook their asses!"

"That's right," Boyd said. "Find 'em, help the fly boys cook 'em, and then we come back." Then he turned to Johnny. "Francelli, remind the squad of what they learned in training about calling in air strikes."

"We communicate," Johnny replied. "We make sure we call in the right coordinates, and then get out of there."

"You got it, Francelli. Call in the numbers and split." Boyd said.

"Hey, Sarge," Johnson said smiling, "You just let me know when the canned heat's comin' and I guarantee you my ass will be gone."

"Just pay attention," Boyd said. "You'll know. Okay, like I said, we'll have a pretty good chance of making contact with the bad guys sooner or later. Lieutenant Keaton's the platoon leader and he'll be calling the shots, but when things heat up, I want this squad to keep your eyes on me and do what you're told."

That's a given, Johnny thought.

"Our platoon will go in four choppers, thirty-six men. We'll hit the LZ at the same time, which should be pretty exciting, but you've done it, so you'll know what to do. There's less chance of being hit when we land because we'll have much more fire power. Check your gear and get ready to move out."

As they roared over the tree-tops an hour later, Johnny thought that if the VC could hear one chopper approaching, then they certainly could hear four. He hoped the Sergeant was right about the VC laying off.

The drop went smoothly. The sight of the men spilling out from the four birds, and dispersing quickly impressed Johnny. It felt good to be with a larger team. Boyd was right about an attack too. There was none.

As they waited for the other squads to regroup, Boyd got on the radio with Lieutenant Keaton. Then he said, "We're moving west a few miles. Since we're the raw squad here, we're taking up the rear. If you guys get a chance to prove yourselves, you better do it. Right now, keep your eyes open. Let's go."

The raw squad, Johnny thought. They had less than two weeks experience each. Most of the other squads had been in country for months.

They had humped for a couple of hours when Boyd said, "Okay boys, this is where we sleep. Now we do the things that'll help us live through the night." Boyd had an interesting way of keeping the squad's attention. "Our squad will guard the south side of the platoon's perimeter. We've got plenty to do before dark. I want holes dug there, there, and there. Deep. Remember, get lazy with your defenses and you give Charlie an easier shot. Simple. I want three guys to a hole. Wallace, set up the M-60 in the middle. After the holes are dug and the dirt bags are set, Francelli and I will lay out the trip wires and the Claymores. You guys will watch. Learn fast. We're be doing it all over again at tomorrow night's location, and the night after, and maybe every night until you get back to the world."

Each man carried several small burlap sacks with his gear. They filled the sacks with the dirt they dug and built small walls around the holes. When they finished, it was time to set up their wider defensive perimeter. Surprise was the VC's friend. To prevent being overrun at night, the squad needed to extend the kill zone by keeping the enemy a good distance from their dug in position- not easy in dense vegetation. They started by running trip wires with flares that would illuminate the area if anyone hit one. The wires were placed thirty to forty yards outside the perimeter. Next came the lethal Claymores. They were the size of a paperback book and sat on small, four-inch scissor legs. They were attached to an electronic blasting cap that could be activated from thirty yards away. The platoon set them up with care. When detonated, they unleashed over seven hundred steel pellets in a sixty-degree horizontal arc that could kill anything within forty yards. They were great defensive weapons, but if mishandled or misplaced, they could wipe out the entire platoon.

Sergeant Boyd and Johnny laid them out carefully, as the other squads did the same on the other sides of the perimeter. When they were finished, they went back to the foxholes and Boyd placed his men.

"Francelli, Johnson and Philips, you'll take the hole on the left. Wallace, Paige and Conroy, you'll take the center with the M60. The rest of us will be in the hole on the right. Now let's talk about our line of vision during our watch. If we don't overlap, one of those black pajama bastards can crawl close enough to lob a grenade in your lap, and you won't know it until you're dead." Boyd laid out a plan that had each group scanning the area in front of them and overlapping each other's field of vision.

"Remember, we scan our area and we overlap. Now the most important point, we shoot any damn thing that moves. Anything! Got it?"

"Got it, sarge," Paige said.

Phillips said, "Sarge, what about the Claymores?"

"You've got to use restraint. If you panic and trigger those babies too soon you may be wasting them and giving up your best line of defense. You use the Claymores if we are under full attack, and you use them before they get too close for it to matter."

It was amazing how unprepared these guys were, Boyd thought, but with the growing list of causalities, replacements were needed quickly, which created a vicious cycle. The more casualties they suffered, the quicker they needed replacements. And the faster they pressed inexperienced boys into combat, the more casualties they suffered. That's why they were given Boyd as their sergeant; he was a good teacher.

"Okay," Boyd said. "Time to rest. Eat something and then get some sleep. When you're out here in the zoo, you sleep whenever you get the chance because Charlie usually determines when you have to wake up. One guy in each hole will take the first watch. We'll start with Johnson, Wallace and me. We're on for one hour and then we'll switch. Keep your eyes open!"

He surveyed their work one more time and then said, "Johnson, who are we depending on?"

Johnson smiled. "We're depending on each other, sir."

"Damn right we are," Boyd said.

They ate some c-rations and settled in. It was their first night in the field since arriving In Country. As darkness fell and clouds blocked whatever moon light there may have been, they were isolated from everything except the sounds of the blackened jungle.

Johnny took the second watch. About mid way through his hour Johnson whispered, "Hey Francelli, are you awake?"

"It's my job," Johnny said.

"Just checking."

A minute later Johnson said, "Hey Francelli, can you see anything?"

"Not a damn thing without my scope. Can you?

"I can't see the hand in front of my face. Course, my hand's black. Can you see yours?"

"No."

"So how we supposed to see Charlie coming?"

"Why do you think we have night scopes? And what do you think the trip wires and flares are for?" Johnny said.

"What if Charlie don't trip nothin? What if Charlie steps right over that baby? What if Charlie's two feet away right now, listenin' to us talk?"

"Go to sleep, Sam," Johnny said. "You're making me nervous."

"Phillips here has been sleeping like a baby."

"Good for him. Now you sleep too," Johnny said.

It got quiet for a while and then Johnson said, "Hey Francelli, tell me about the girl you got the letter from."

"Like what?"

"Like, are you gonna marry her?"

"Definitely."

"Ah, that's nice. When you gonna do it?"

"As soon as I get home. Maybe the same day."

"Same day? Damn. You already make the plans?"

"Yeah. My plan is to marry her. That's it."

"What about all that bride stuff they like? Arrangements. You plan that? You gotta make arrangements."

"I guess we'll have to do that."

"I guess you will. Girl ain't gonna marry you without all that complicated bride stuff goin' on. You gotta make arrangements 'til there're comin' out of your ears. Then you get married."

Johnny hoped Johnson was finished, but he wasn't. "Hey Francelli, I was just thinkin'; ain't you gonna get engaged?"

"It would be nice," Johnny said. "But there's no time. We'll skip that and go right to the wedding."

"No way, man," Johnson protested. "Girl's gotta have a rock on her finger. No rock, no wedding. Where the hell you been man?"

Johnny knew Allison didn't care about that, but Johnson still had a point. Allison should have a ring. He imagined himself buying one at the jewelry store in town. Every time his mom needed to buy jewelry, she went to see Mr. Mignoni on Mill Street. She bought Sissy's Confirmation necklace and his own Confirmation watch there. She bought other things too. Johnny decided he'd go there as soon as he got home.

There was more quiet for a while, but Johnson's mind was still racing. "Francelli, how long you been datin' this girl."

There was a long pause on Johnny's end. "We've been broken up for a while, almost two years. We dated a lot before that."

"Two years! You haven't dated for two years and you're getting' married?"

"Definitely."

"Damn, Francelli. That's interesting."

Johnny wanted to change the subject. "Tell me about Yolanda."

"Yolanda! Now you're talkin'. She's my baby. You've gotta meet her when we get back to the world. She's waitin' for me. See, our relationship's different from yours. We actually date! I'm sure we'll be getting' married real…"

The first mortar landed behind them, in the center of the perimeter. Then the world erupted in flashes and explosions. Phillips woke up with a scream. Boyd was yelling, "Mortars, mortars, stay low in the hole." Johnny, Phillips, and Johnson sunk as low as they could. The explosions were lifting dirt in the air and dropping it on them. Then, the sky behind them was aglow; the VC must have tripped the wires on the other side of the perimeter. Johnny heard shouting as the squad on the north side opened fire.

"What do we do, sergeant?" Phillips shouted. "Do we help them?"

"Hold your ground!" Boyd shouted. "They may come from two directions. Keep your eyes where I told you to keep them."

Johnny strained to scan his area. The light from the dying flares behind them helped, but he couldn't see much. Then Johnson shouted, "I think I see something. I see something!"

"Where?" Johnny said.

"Over there," Johnson pointed. Right there at ten o'clock. He was jumpy as hell; they all were.

"I don't see anything," Phillips said, looking through his scope.

"It was right there," Johnson said, pointing again.

Just then the wire in front of them was tripped and the sky lit up.

"Holy shit!" Johnny yelled. "Look at this." There were at least thirty silhouettes coming at them, about thirty yards away. Most had made it past the trip wire without disturbing it.

"Light it up!" Boyd screamed from the next hole. The noise was deafening as the men opened fire. Wallace was spraying the area with the M-60 and bodies were dropping, but the VC kept coming. Johnny saw one clearly in his scope and fired. The image fell. He saw another and fired again.

"Get ready with the Claymores," Boyd shouted.

As soon as Johnson heard claymore, he panicked and detonated his. The C-4 exploded, and five or six bodies fell. More fell as the other Claymores went off. It looked like the remaining VC were pulling back. "Hold your fire!" Boyd screamed. The other end of the perimeter was quiet too.

It all lasted less than two minutes, but the effects were devastating. Philips was shaking uncontrollably. Paige was screaming that Conroy had been hit. Wallace slumped back in his hole exhausted after spraying several hundred rounds. Johnson let out a victory cry that seemed forced.

"Everybody shut up!" Boyd screamed. "This may not be over, and some of those bodies out there may not be dead. Stay focused. You may still get a grenade lobbed at you, and there may be another assault."

Now Phillips was really shaking. If there was another attack, he wouldn't be much use to them, Johnny thought.

"Get a medic to tend to Conrad, quick. The rest of you, scan the area and shoot anything that moves, including bodies on the ground. If you're not sure if it's moving shoot it."

"Sarge! They're dead," Wallace protested. Shooting the dead didn't seem right.

"Dead or faking?" Boyd said. "Just do what I said, damn it."

The men began shooting, and a VC with a grenade, not more than fifteen yards away, jumped up and ran toward them. Wallace stopped him cold with a burst from the M-60, and the grenade went off in the VC's hand, pulverizing what was left of his bullet- riddled body.

Johnny doubted anyone would question Boyd again.

"Stay focused," Boyd said. Keep looking. This still may not be over."

The flares were out by now, and they scanned the darkness quietly with their scopes. Suddenly, the silence was broken by Paige's scream.

"No, goddamn it. No!"

Boyd left his hole and crawled to Paige's, where the medic had been working on Conroy. "What the hell's going on Paige?

The medic replied for him. "This man is gone sir. Conroy is dead."

39- Waiting for Daybreak

Johnny sat in the darkness struggling to keep his focus. His assignment was to scan his area for a repeat attack, but with two hours before daybreak, his mind was flooded with other thoughts. Conroy was dead, just like that. There had been three guys in the center foxhole when the fighting started. Paige and Wallace ended up fine and Conroy ended up dead. How does that work? Johnny wondered. Does it all come down to luck?

He scanned with his night scope, but he kept seeing images of the VC he had shot. It had happened so quickly. He saw the charging figure; he fired and the gook fell. Then he did it again. Had he killed a man? Had he killed two? He must have. The whole Vietnam thing finally hit him. The army wasn't a game about being strong or in shape or following orders. Ultimately, it was about killing people. They attack and you kill them. If you don't, then they kill you.

Now he was a killer. So were all of the guys in the squad. Twenty or thirty VC had attacked. Maybe some of them escaped, but most had been killed. If Johnny killed a couple, and he was sure he had, then the other guys must have killed their share. Wallace certainly did with the M-60. And what about the Claymores? Whoever detonated them must have killed some. Now they were all killers. Not murders or criminals, but they had taken the lives of others, and they would never be the same.

He knew he'd feel guilty, but strangely, he also felt a sense of relief. In a span of two horrific minutes, he had faced the supreme test, and he had passed. He had done what he had to do to survive when his life was on the line. As long as he was in Nam, people would try to kill him. Now he knew he could kill to defend himself. He didn't want to end up like Conrad, and he was terrified that he would, unless he fought as fiercely as necessary.

For the first time, he hated the war that put him there. His mother hadn't raised him to do this. All he wanted was to see her again, and Allison, and Sissy, and Frankie, and the rest of the guys at Jake's. He wanted to go home, marry Allison, get into the electrician's union or maybe get a job at the steel mill, earn some decent money. He wanted to do simple stuff, like have Sunday dinner at his mother's and watch the Eagles, play some cards with the guys on Friday nights. Most of all he wanted to take long drives with Allison along River Road, through Yardley and the state park at Washington's Crossing. Bucks County had such beautiful places, and Allison belonged in beautiful places. He'd take her picture in front of one of the quaint, old covered bridges that spanned the Delaware Canal, just like the ones he saw on calendars. They'd go to Bowman's Hill together and read about General Washington's encampment there. Then they'd drive further north. Central Bucks County was a different world. They'd visit a winery and taste the selections. Maybe they'd spread a blanket and share a bottle and some cheese under a shady tree in a grove. He'd seen that in a movie once and it looked cool. Maybe they'd stop for ice cream in New Hope and stroll along the shops and boutiques. Girls like that stuff. And he would do it. He'd do whatever it took to make Allison happy, but first he had to fight this war, and he still had more than ninety percent of his time left.

He thought about the men he had shared the night with. For a few chaotic minutes, they'd been totally dependent upon each other. These guys that he barely knew shared the most terrifying experience of his life with him, and they had done the job and saved each other's lives. As the first hint of light appeared on the horizon, he looked at Johnson and Phillips, two black guys he barely knew, from places far away. The three of them had dug a hole together and defended it. Johnny had always valued the bonding that people experience when they go through a tough time together. He had seen it a hundred times before: in the locker room before games, in boot camp, in the squad's first patrol together. But this time he and his new friends had shared an exceptional experience, and he felt something toward them that was far more powerful than he had ever experienced before. It was strange, because he hardly knew them, but it was real.

He thought about Conroy and felt profoundly sad. He thought about how the guy had left Ohio to escape the wrath of the pregnant girl's father. He remembered laughing about the irony of it on the plane. He wondered when the baby was due and what the mother would tell it about its father. He thought about Conroy's hometown of Conneaut, and wondered if they would erect a small plaque in his honor, maybe something at the post office. He wondered if the young mother would take the child there when it was old enough to read its father's name. Conroy had been the only guy in the squad to openly question the war. Somehow it didn't seem right that he was the one to die.

Johnny felt confused. After just one night in the bush, he was struggling with his reasons for fighting. He still felt a sense of duty, but other things were beginning to overshadow it, like fighting for personal survival. The VC attack had made that pretty clear. And beyond survival, he wanted to win, whatever winning meant, not just because his country asked him to, but to provide some purpose to Conroy's death. The war had become personal. Maybe survival and revenge were reasons enough to fight, he thought. Maybe he'd just leave the political stuff to the big guys in Washington. Then he thought about Sergeant Boyd who was obviously shaken by Conroy's death. No one had earned his respect as quickly and completely as Boyd had. He was good at what he did, and he obviously cared about his men. Johnny's respect for Boyd gave him more to think about because he knew that Boyd truly believed in the political issues they were supposedly fighting for. If a solid guy like Boyd believed in the war, Johnny thought, maybe he should too. Maybe survival and revenge weren't enough of a reason to fight.

And so, in the predawn hours, in a jungle clearing near the Cambodian border, as far away from home as he could be, Johnny Francelli, a nineteen year old kid from Bristol, Pennsylvania, a boy at heart in a man's uniform, a fun-loving, willing volunteer who had just killed a man, or maybe two, sat in his foxhole, confused about the war, but certain of what he had to do to make it home.

Two Cobra choppers buzzed the area several times at dawn, searching for remaining VC. The gun-ships were an imposing sight, and with the air support in place, Boyd led them out of the perimeter to do a body count. They found eight bodies, but the VC obviously left in a hurry, and there were enough discarded weapons to indicate at least another dozen casualties. Boyd said the VC did a good job of pulling their dead and wounded away in the darkness. The captain would want a report showing a total of twenty-two enemy killed or wounded. Maybe there were, maybe not.

Johnny refused to look at the faces of the dead. Killing was bad enough without personalizing it, but he couldn't avoid what was going on with his comrades. Conroy was the only American KIA, but a guy on the northern perimeter had been seriously wounded, and the platoon waited for a bird to take the wounded soldier and Conroy away. When it was time, Wallace and Paige slid Conroy's body bag into the chopper, and the squad stood in silence as it lifted off.

Boyd's face was hardened, and his blood vessels looked like they might explode, but when he spoke, he said something different than what Johnny expected.
"We lost a man last night. It happens. Conroy didn't do anything wrong. He wasn't reckless and he followed orders. It's just bad luck. It could happen to any of us. That's why you have to get it out of your mind. That's how you survive. You pay your respects and you move on. If you become a coward in the face of death, then we can't depend on you, and both of us might die. If you become a cowboy looking for revenge, then you'll make reckless mistakes and maybe get all of us killed. We can mourn him when the war is over. For now, keep your focus if you want to live."

As the men stood there dripping in the oppressive morning heat, thoughts of Conroy gave way to the dread of another sweltering day in the zoo that was the Vietnam jungle, the mines and booby traps and lurking VC.

"Break down this site and get your gear ready," Boyd said. "We're moving out."

40- The Rectory

Sunday nights were a mixture of work and pleasure for Anna. She and her friend, Betty Sweeney, would meet Father Creeden at the rectory where they would count the Sunday collection. The ladies would record the contributions on the parish donor cards, separate cash from checks, count the money, and prepare deposit slips for Father's Monday banking. Father appreciated their efficiency and discretion. A family's contribution was a private matter, and Father Creeden knew he could count on Anna and Mrs. Sweeney to maintain confidentiality.

After their bookkeeping they'd quickly review the week's calendar of weddings, baptisms, funerals, and other parish events. Then they'd move to the parlor for coffee, dessert, and some light conversation until it was time for the Ed Sullivan show.

Mrs. Sweeney was telling a funny story when Anna stopped her in mid sentence. "I received a letter from Johnny yesterday."
Mrs. Sweeney and Father exchanged glances.
"Really?" Father said, surprised by the remark.
When Johnny first went overseas people inquired about him at church, the grocery store, the dry cleaners, everywhere she went. After a few weeks, Anna had politely let it be known that she'd prefer that people stop asking. She appreciated their intentions, but found it too difficult to respond. She had learned to cope with Johnny's absence by keeping

herself occupied, and the less she dwelled on what he was doing, the better she felt.

Her closest friends knew that if she wanted to talk about Johnny she would initiate the conversation and they, of course, would give her all the attention she needed. Otherwise, she saved her thoughts of Johnny for quiet moments alone, with Sissy or during Frankie's visits.

"Yes," she said, forcing a smile. "It came in the mail."

Father Creeden and Mrs. Sweeney caught each other's eyes again. Something about Anna didn't seem right.

"What did the letter say?" Father asked gently.

"It said he's doing well. He loves his sergeant and likes the boys on his team or platoon or whatever it's called."

"That's wonderful," Betty said.

"Yes it is," Father agreed.

"There's even better news," she said. By now she looked as though she would cry.

"He said that he and Allison O'Brien had been exchanging letters and were getting back together. He said that she's the only girl he ever loved."

"That's great!" Father said. "She's a wonderful girl, from a good family."

Anna had just recorded the very generous O'Brien donation to the collection. The car business was obviously doing well.

"Yes," Anna said. "It's great." She looked as if she was about to fall apart.

"She's a beautiful girl," Betty offered carefully. "They'll make a splendid couple."

"Yes they will," Anna said. "They'll make a wonderful couple." With that she broke down and slumped in her chair sobbing.

Father Creeden leaned forward and asked softly, "Anna, what's wrong? Don't you approve of Allison?"

"No, it's not that at all. I'm thrilled," she said, crying harder now.

"Then what is it? He said he likes his sergeant and the men he's with. He said things are fine. So what's wrong?"

Anna struggled for control.

"My son is a wonderful boy. He's kind, compassionate, considerate, adventurous, everything a mother could hope for."

"Then what's wrong?" Father asked.

"My son is a terrible liar. He always was. He says things are fine, but I can tell from his letter that they're not. Something's wrong."

"Oh, Anna," Betty said. "Maybe you're reading too much into things. Maybe things really are fine."

"I'm his mother!" Anna snapped. "I can tell!"

Betty sat back without speaking.

"I'm sorry," Anna said, crying again. "I'm just so scared."

"That's okay, honey," Betty said. "I understand."

Father Creeden left his chair and squatted next to hers. Taking her hand in his he said, "You have nothing to be sorry about Anna. You've been so brave, and it's about time you let things out."

"He's my baby," she sobbed. "This war has ripped him out of my arms, snatched him like a thief. I want him back. I want him home again."

She buried her face on her priest's shoulder and continued to cry.

Father patted her back gently. "It's okay Anna; it's okay."

"I should have done more to keep him here," she said sobbing. "I'm his mother. I'm supposed to protect him. I should have stopped him somehow."

"There was nothing you could have done, Anna," Betty said.

"There had to be something," Anna protested. "I'm afraid I won't even recognize him when he comes home." She glared at both of them and then really lost control. "He's in a war for God's sake," she shrieked. "He's fighting in a war!"

Anna straightened up, and Betty crossed the room and handed her a tissue.

"Anna, you've been doing this alone. You've got to let people help you," she said. "You've got to talk with people."

"It won't help," Anna said. "I just want him home."

Father Creeden stood and went to the cabinet across the room. He returned with a small glass of Brandy.

"This will help," he said, handing her the glass.

She took a generous sip and slid back in her chair.

Betty said, "I read about a group called the Blue Star Mothers. They're mothers of boys serving in Vietnam. The organization started back in World War I and has continued through each war since. They meet once every two weeks to give each other support. The article said only a mother with a son in Vietnam can appreciate what another mother is going through. Maybe you should join. Maybe it would be good for you."

"No!" Anna said firmly. I won't do that. I can't do that." She put down the brandy.

"Why not?" Father asked, taking his chair again. It sounds like a good idea."

"I went to a meeting already. There were seven of us there, all very nice people, all were trying to be strong, upbeat, but I could see the fear in their eyes. They were frightened for their sons, terrified. Each time I saw their suffering, it made me feel worse."

"But it's a support group," Betty protested. "You're supposed to get comfort knowing that you're not alone, that other people who can appreciate your feelings are going through the same thing."

Anna shook her head. "I get no comfort from someone else's suffering. It only hurts more. I don't want to talk about my son with anyone except my daughter, Frankie, who I consider a second son, and the two of you."

Father didn't want to push things any more. "Then that's fine, Anna. We'll keep it at that."

Anna blew her nose on her tissue. She was getting under control again. She stood. "It's late and I'd better go."

"Stay as long as you like," Father said.

"No, I really should go," she said.

"Then I'll drive you," Betty said. Anna only lived four blocks away and usually enjoyed the walk, but she was still looking unsteady. "Thank you," she said. "That would be nice." Then she forced another smile and said, "Thanks to both of you. I didn't mean to burden you with this."

"I'm not even going to respond to that," Father said.

Betty patted her arm and said, "I'll get our coats." As she went to the closet, Father took another tissue and dabbed gently at a tear in the corner of Anna's eye.

"Anna, I hope you know we all love you," he said tenderly.

"I know," she said, dropping her gaze to the floor.

"Promise me you'll turn to us when you need to," he said.

"I promise," she said.

41- New Hampshire

Angelo sat in their third floor efficiency drinking a beer and killing time until Donna's shift ended at midnight. It was February 12, 1968, almost two months since they had moved in, and he was getting used to the cramped surroundings. They shared a small living room, an even smaller bedroom and a galley kitchen too small to eat in. But the place had a decent bathroom and shower, and the rent was cheap.

The flat was on Stanley Street, two blocks from McGill University, where Angelo had hooked up with the small but growing group of exiled Americans living in Montreal. They set him up with the apartment and found jobs for him and Donna. Angelo worked as a short order cook at a breakfast and lunch joint near campus. Donna worked as a cocktail waitress at a club around the corner on St. Catherine Street. They both hated their hours. He cooked from six in the morning until two in the afternoon. Donna served drinks from seven until midnight, which didn't leave them much time to be together. But they needed the money, and there wasn't much else out there.

The phone rang and Angelo cursed. It was ten after eleven, and a call at that hour meant that Donna was working until closing again.

Angelo always met Donna after work to walk her home. It was hard enough staying awake until midnight when he had to get up at five-thirty; staying up until closing time at two made the morning almost impossible. But there were some seedy characters at her club and there was no way he'd have her walk home alone with them around, especially with the outfit she had to wear. There wasn't much to it, and her body made her the main attraction in the place. So he met her every night and walked her home. Each time he asked her to quit, she reminded him that she earned the best tips in the place and that she could handle herself with the creeps.

"Hello," he said, with an exaggerated edge to his voice.

"Angelo, it's Scott," the voice said.

Angelo was surprised. Scott Mitten was a fellow expatriate from Madison, Wisconsin. He moved to Montreal the day he got his draft notice two years earlier and helped get Angelo and Donna established. He sounded excited.

"Are you watching the news?"

"No," Angelo said. "Should I be?"

"McCarthy is kicking LBJ's ass in the New Hampshire primary."

Angelo sat up straight. "Are you serious?"

"Damn serious," Scott said. "McCarthy's not actually winning, but they're projecting that he'll receive forty-two percent to Johnson's forty-nine. Canadian television is calling it a big moral victory for McCarthy and a huge embarrassment for the president."

"Damn!" Angelo said.

"McCarthy's a nobody," Scott continued. "To take on Johnson as an anti-war candidate and do this well is saying something. I guess the 'Clean for Gene' crap really helped."

"I guess it did," Angelo said.

Hundreds of anti-war activists from across the country had braved the New England cold and snow for six weeks to volunteer for McCarthy. They shaved their beards, cut their long hair, and replaced their jeans and sweatshirts with sport jackets and slacks. They knocked on doors, worked phone banks, and manned the polling places on election day. The result had dramatic implications.

"The Wisconsin primary is next!" Scott said. "McCarthy can beat him there. I know the campus at Madison will be going nuts. It has one of the strongest anti-war movements in the country. I wish I had the guts to go back."

"Bad idea," Angelo said. "It's way too dangerous. You get arrested for something stupid, they run a check on your record, and you're in prison for draft evasion."

"I know," Scott said. "I'm just saying I wish I could. But if this McCarthy thing continues, we all may be going home sooner than we thought."

"We'll see," Angelo said. "Too bad Bobby Kennedy didn't have the stones to take on Johnson."

"Screw Kennedy," Scott said. "McCarthy stepped up when we needed it; Kennedy could have done it instead. Now, McCarthy's a folk hero."

"I guess he is," Angelo said. By now Angelo had switched on the TV. McCarthy was speaking at a post election rally to hundreds of young, ecstatic volunteers.

Angelo said, "But in the long run, McCarthy can't win and Bobby Kennedy can. If we want to end the war, we need someone who can beat Johnson now and the Republicans in the fall. McCarthy can't do that. Kennedy can."

"Stop dreaming," Scott said. "Kennedy's not a candidate, and McCarthy is, and he just sent the government a message about Vietnam. Let's enjoy it."

"Thanks," Angelo said. "I'm enjoying it. I'll catch up with you tomorrow."

Angelo remained glued to the news until Donna walked in at ten after twelve.

"Hey, Sir Lancelot, where the hell were ya?" she said jokingly. "I had ten guys who wanted to take me home. Some even spoke French. I needed your protection."

"Jesus, Donna," he said, checking his watch. "I'm sorry. You should have called me. I lost all track of time."

She looked at the TV, "Ice hockey?"

"No. Something a lot better. Sit down; you're not gonna believe this."

They watched for a few minutes. Then Donna took a sip of Angelo's beer and said, "Let's celebrate."

42- King

April 1968

Johnny's days in Vietnam blended into weeks, and in time he became fatalistic. He was doing his job, listening to Boyd, and staying focused, but he knew that he'd still need a dose of good luck to survive, and he hoped for the best. Fortunately, the search and destroy missions became less frequent. They had encountered the enemy in a brief firefight only once since Conroy's death, with no American casualties. The platoon spent about half its time in the bush, with the rest spent in the relative safety of the base.

There was plenty of news from home. Allison wrote every day, easing his fears that she would eventually lose interest once the thrill of their reunion wore off. Her letters were filled with her dreams about the future: their marriage, their children, even the type of house they'd have. She was the Allison he always knew, happy and exploding with vitality, and each letter was more uplifting than the last.

Debbie also wrote occasionally, assuring Johnny that Allison had shut herself off from the social scene at Boston College, choosing to spend her time "studying her brains out," as she put it, and talking about Johnny. Johnny wondered what the people on campus were thinking about the war, but he wasn't going to ask. He wanted the letters from Allison and Debbie to be about them, not the war. Debbie obviously enjoyed the role she had played in getting Johnny and Allison back together, and Johnny was glad that she was around for Allison while he was away.

His mother wrote twice a week, carefully avoiding too many emotional references, which Johnny knew was her way of coping. Instead, she wrote about events in Sissy's life, her weekly dinners with Frankie, and gossip from around town.

Anna carefully avoided politics or the war, which was strange. The news was his mother's passion, yet she made no mention of Johnson's miserable showing in New Hampshire or Bobby Kennedy's subsequent decision to enter the race. Kennedy advocated a gradual pull back to guarded sanctuaries, in effect ceding the countryside to the VC while protecting the cities and coastal areas. Most guys who served in the bush knew that the VC owned the countryside anyway. Short of an even greater escalation, few could argue with Kennedy's plan. It was on the mind of everyone In Country, but Johnny's mom never mentioned it or Johnson's shocking announcement in late March that he was dropping out of the race. Johnny remembered LBJ's words printed in the *Stars and Stripes*, "I shall not seek, and I will not accept, the nomination of my party for another term as your president." Reading that, most guys thought the war would be over soon. Some were angry, thinking that Johnson had abandoned them and feeling that a negotiated settlement would cheapen the sacrifices of guys like Conroy, but most just wanted to go home. For the first time, Johnny heard someone say that he didn't want to be the last American to die in Vietnam. Predictably, Boyd told the squad to ignore the news from home and keep focused. There'd be plenty of fighting left to do and lots of chances to get hurt if they weren't careful.

Frankie wrote too, although he didn't have much to say. Most of the guys were gone, and he didn't have a girlfriend, so he devoted his time to developing his carpentry skills, working long hours, and making decent money.

Johnny went to the mess tent to eat and wait for the mail call. After filling his tray, he found Johnson and Phillips alone at a table and joined them.

Johnson smiled, "Hey, Francelli, it's about time you ate something; gotta keep your strength up."

"I'm still strong enough to kick your ass," Johnny ribbed.

"Ouch," Johnson said, grinning. "You hear that, Phillips? The man's a fool. Hell, Francelli, maybe if Phillips helped you, then maybe, and I mean maybe, the two of you would come close, but I doubt it."

"What do you think, Phillips?" Johnson asked. "Maybe the two of you together?"

"Just eat, Sam," Phillips replied.

"The man don't say much does he?"

"He's smart," Johnny replied.

Johnny started to eat and Johnson said, "Hey, Francelli, that dinner invitation still on at your mom's house?"

"Still on," Johnny said. "As soon as we get back: you, me, Phillips, Wallace, Paige, the whole squad and my girl. I want her to meet you guys. Maybe Boyd will come too."

"Nah, Boyd won't come," Johnson said. "He only eats nails, not that fine Italian food you brag about. It is good right? I'll be coming all the way from Oakland."

"It's the best food you'll ever eat. Guaranteed," Johnny said.

"Sure she won't mind having a couple of brothers like me and Phillips at the table?" Johnson teased.

"You don't know my mother. She won't mind."

After a few bites, Johnny decided to work on Johnson a little.

"Hey, Johnson, I didn't know your nickname was Mo."

"It's not Mo," Johnson said. "The name's Sam."

"So why the tattoo on your arm that says Mo inside a heart?"

"It's a long story," Johnson said.

"I've got plenty of time," Johnny said. "Three hundred and eighteen days, and so do you."

"Three hundred and seventeen," Johnson corrected.

"Isn't today April 5?"

"Yup," Johnson said.

"Then we have three hundred and eighteen days left," Johnny persisted.

"We would, Francelli, but I wrote to the Pentagon and asked them to let our whole squad out a day early. Told 'em we have an important engagement."

"Really," Johnny played along. "Did they write back yet?"

"Not yet," Johnson said, "but I expect to hear something any day now. I'll yet you know."

"Good, now tell me the story."

"In my senior year I told my mama that I wanted to get a tattoo, but she said no. So I pestered her until she couldn't stand it. Finally, we cut a deal. I could get a tattoo under two conditions. I make the honor roll all year, and the tattoo hadda say Mom. She said I could get a little bit done after each good report card."

Phillips chuckled as he ate his Jello.

"Phillips here knows the story and thinks it's funny, but it ain't funny at all," Johnson said.

"Tell him." Phillips said grinning.

Johnson when on. "The first marking period I made the honor role and got the heart put on."

Johnny nodded.

"Second marking period, honor roll again, so I got the M."

Phillips was trying hard to hold in his laughter and Johnny was smiling.

"By the third marking period, I'm damn near Valadictim or whatever it's called. So I got the O."

"Here it comes," Phillips said, laughing out loud.

"Shut up and wipe that Jello off your chin," Johnson said. "This is serious."

"Okay," Johnny said. "So you got the heart, the M and the O. Then what happened?"

"I met Yolanda in the beginning of the fourth marking period and my grades dropped."

"Your grades dropped?" Johnny said.

"I was so much in love that I damn near flunked my senior year."

By now Phillips and Johnny were howling. Even Johnson was having a good laugh.

"Tell him," Phillips prompted.

"My mom was so mad that she wouldn't let me get the last letter, said I didn't deserve it. She said I messed up my chances to get a scholarship and go to college."

"So that's the end?" Johnny asked.

"No," Johnson said. "I figured I'd wait a couple of months until things cooled down, then ask her again."

"And?" Johnny said.

"And I got my ass drafted. So here I am, with a goddamn Mo on my arm."

While they laughed Phillips said, "There's more."

"Shut up," Johnson said. "That's the end."

Then Phillips spoke more words than Johnny ever heard him say at one time.

"With the heart and all, Wallace thinks Johnson loves some guy named Mo." He laughed so hard he almost slid off the bench.

"It's true," Johnson said snickering. "I told Wallace the story, but he doesn't believe me. Thinks I love some guy named Mo. I think he told Paige too. Now they both look at me funny."

"There's more," Phillips said, still trying to contain himself.

"I swear to God, Phillips, I'm going to stab you with this fork if you don't knock it off."

Johnny could tell Johnson liked telling the story as much as they liked hearing it.

"Yolanda," Phillips said to Johnny while sliding further away from Johnson. "Ask him."

"Okay, I'll bite," Johnny said. "Tell me about Yolanda."

"Well," Johnson said. "Yolanda has a little problem with it too. She wants to believe me, but since I had the tattoo before I met her, she said she's a little," he paused and looked at Phillips. "What's that word I told you she used?"

"Skeptical," Phillips said.

"That's it," Johnson said. "She said that she was a little skeptical about the whole thing. She wants to know who Mo is."

"That's understandable," Johnny said.

"Tell him about Saigon," Phillips said.

He smacked Phillips on the arm. "I'm coming to that."

Then he turned back to Johnny and said. "Am I boring you?"

Johnny grinned. He was having more fun than he'd had in a long time. "Tell me about Saigon."

Johnson looked pleased. "Well, I got this idea. I'm thinking that if we ever get to go to Saigon for some R and B like the other guys do…"

"You mean R and R," Phillips interrupted. "R and B is rhythm and blues, you mean rest and relaxation."

"Yeah, that's it. If I ever get to Saigon for some R and R, I can find me a gook tattoo guy to change my Mo to Yo."

"Yo?' Johnny said.

"You know," Johnson replied, "Yolanda!"

Johnny rubbed his chin and smiled. "Sounds like a great idea to me."

"I thought so," Johnson said. I wrote Yolanda a letter about it and she likes the idea too."

"It'll make her less skeptical," Phillips added.

Johnson smacked his arm again.

"Do you think they can do it?" Johnson asked. "Change my Mo to Yo?"

"Are you kidding?" Johnny said. "They say we're gonna try to land a man on the moon within a year. They can sure as hell change your damn tattoo. Science man."

"I hope so," Johnson said. "I'm tired of telling the story. If they fix it and somebody asks about my tattoo, I'll be able to say, 'Yo's my girl.' It's simple. I'll just say, 'Yo's my girl', that's all."

"Life will be easier," Johnny added.

"Damn right it will," Johnson said.

"Just don't break up with her," Phillips said.

"Never," Johnson said. "Yo's my girl."

They were about to leave when Wallace stormed in looking as if he wanted to kill someone. "They did it!" He shouted. "The dirty bastards finally did it!"

His deep voice penetrated every inch of the huge mess tent. The place fell silent, and all eyes were on his hulking figure in the entranceway. He just stood there with his fists clenched, breathing heavily and shaking his head. Finally, Johnson said, "Did what?"

"They shot Martin Luther King!" Wallace thundered, "Killed him!"

The words hit like a shock wave.

"Killed him?" Johnson said, incredulous.

"You heard me; they killed him! I just heard it on Armed Forces Radio."

"Who did it?" someone asked from another table.

"How should I know! Some Klan son of a bitch or the FBI! I don't know."

"Where did it happen?" Johnson asked, as if it mattered.

"Memphis. That's all I know. They said he was shot in Memphis. They said he was dead, and they didn't know who did it yet. That's all I know."

Wallace sat at their table and rested his head in his hands. Then he slammed his fist so hard that the trays rattled. "The one guy we had, the one decent leader who tried to do some good and they blew him away. I hope the young studs in the cities become Black Panthers tomorrow. Screw this system."

Johnson tried to redirect the dialogue. "I'm buyin' the KKK doin' this, but the FBI might be far fetched, don't you think?"

"Don't matter what I think; he's gone. Hoover and the FBI have had it in for King for years. Lately, he's been bitchin' about the war, sayin' it's a poor man's war, saying too many brothers were doin' the grunt work and the dyin'. Look around; was he right?"

Almost half the platoon was black, so were most of the men in the mess tent.

"Do we make up half the population back home? I think they wanted him and they got him," he said, without defining "they."

"Still, man, my money's on the Klan," Johnson said. "Some cracker did this."

Johnny thought about the nice couple he met at JFK's viewing and how proud they were to have heard King's "I Have a Dream Speech." This was messed up, really messed up. Johnny was just as numb as anyone else in the tent, but as he searched for the right words to say, he came up empty. As the only white guy at the table he thought it best to keep quiet.

"This stinks," Phillips said.

"Really stinks," Johnson added.

Johnny just nodded.

"Know what?" Wallace said, "We're supposed to be here to defend freedom. I've gotta ask myself, what the hell am I here for?"

43- Where's Nick?

Mrs. Francelli always invited someone to join her for her weekly dinners with Frankie. Usually, it was Sissy and Tom, but if they weren't available she'd include a friend like Mrs. Sweeney. When Frankie arrived he found Anna and Mrs. Sweeny watching news coverage of the national reaction to Dr. King's death. They gave Frankie a warm hug, but each looked shaken. Black America was angry, and for the past two days prominent African-American leaders, entertainers, and sports figures made appeals to the black community to respect King's philosophy of non-violence. But riots broke out anyway in cities all over America. The news had been filled with images of burning buildings and National Guardsmen on patrol to prevent looting in the cities. In a humanitarian gesture, Senator Robert Kennedy offered Mrs. King his personal jet to transport her husband's body home from Memphis. While some saw the move as politically self-serving, to those who knew Kennedy's strong civil rights record, it was seen as a sincere act of kindness.

Nineteen sixty-eight was an incredible year for news. In the time since Johnny left for the service, the Viet Cong's Tet offensive had surprised the military brass, McCarthy had shocked President Johnson with his strong showing in New Hampshire, Johnson had stunned the nation with his decision to drop out of the race, and King's assassin set back race relations at least a decade. As if that wasn't enough, Bobby Kennedy had stirred the political pot by entering the presidential race. And all of this was happening against a backdrop of an anti-war movement that was gaining steam, fueled by an increase in draftees and a rising death toll in the field.

Mrs. Francelli put out her usual feast and, although he had something on his mind and didn't feel much like eating that night, Frankie put on a good front for the ladies.

"You should sell these stuffed olives," Frankie said as he downed the last of several. "That would take the fun out of it," she said.

"Besides," Mrs. Sweeney added, "You wouldn't be able to afford them- beef, veal, pork, hours of preparation. I can't imagine what the price would be."

"Well, it doesn't matter because they're not for sale," Mrs. Francelli said. Then she changed the subject. "Frankie, we've been so occupied with the terrible news of Dr. King that I haven't really had the chance to ask how you've been this week."

It was time for their weekly game, and Frankie was determined to play it well.

"Great," Frankie lied. "I got another letter from Johnny."

"Really?" Mrs. Francelli said excitedly.

"Tuesday," Frankie said. "I think it's official, he and Allison are truly flipped over each other."

Mrs. Francelli was beaming. "I'm so happy they've gotten back together, she's such a nice girl. I think she'll be good for him when he comes home," she added.

"It's about time they're together again," Frankie said. "She's the only girl he ever really cared about."

"That's so sweet," Mrs. Sweeny said.

"How about you?" Frankie asked. "Hear anything?"

"Yes," Anna said. "I received a letter too. Johnny said it was terribly hot there, but he's fine with it. She added smiling, "He's made some nice friends from different parts of the country. He said some day he wants me to meet all of them. So overall, I'd say he's doing just fine."

"Sounds that way," Frankie said. "That's great."

It was the game they played each week. Johnny had made Frankie swear that he would never tell Mrs. Francelli any of the real news he wrote from Vietnam, like Conroy's death or the patrols into the bush, and Frankie kept his promise. For her part, Mrs. Francelli gladly shared the light news she received from Johnny's letters, as if repeating it would make it reality. She must have known that Frankie knew more than he shared, but she accepted Frankie's censored reports. So the news for this week was comforting. Johnny had a girl, the food was good and, unfortunately, the weather in Vietnam was hot.

After dinner, they watched some of the taped coverage of Dr. King's funeral held earlier that day. The procession was huge and included President Johnson, Vice President Humphrey, Bobby and Ted Kennedy, Gene McCarthy, Governor Rockefeller from New York, presidential candidate Richard Nixon, and scores of other political luminaries, as well as countless icons from the entertainment industry, both black and white. Dr. King sent one last message in support of the poor and oppressed by requesting that he be buried in a simple pine box and transported on a cart pulled by mules.

When the news was over, Frankie got a big hug from the ladies and said good night. He got into the car and glanced again at the newspaper beside him. He'd studied it several times before going in to dinner. The lead story read, "Local Man Missing in Action." Below it was a photo of Nick in his Special Forces uniform. The brief story said that Nick and three other Green Berets had disappeared while on a reconnaissance mission. No bodies had been found, and they were classified as missing in action. No additional details could be released.

Frankie gripped the steering wheel hard to steady his shaking hands. Then he started the car and drove out of town. He drove along Radcliffe Street to North Radcliffe, through Edgely, past the beautiful homes that lined the Delaware River. He continued on to Tullytown, the peaceful little place that seemed frozen in time, past his uncle's home on Main Street, near Cheston Avenue, where he spent a week each summer as a little boy. He promised himself he'd stop for a beer someday at the local watering hole, The Tank, just as his uncle had done every day. He continued on past Warner Lake, where his uncle used to take him swimming. Sometimes he'd take the whole gang: Johnny, Nick, Jimmy, all of them. They'd eat hot dogs from the concession stand, play ball on the shore and swim in the water that always seemed frigid.

He thought about Nick. Was he alive? Was he a prisoner? Was he hiding somewhere, maybe seriously injured? In spite of her silence, he was certain Mrs. Francelli knew Nick was missing. She was a news hound who soaked up the print media as readily as the TV news. Besides, it was a small town, and everyone was buzzing about it. And then there was Mrs. Sweeney to consider. Nick was a parishioner of St. Therese's, so she would have known. But the rules of the game were clearly understood, there would be no discussion of bad news of any kind from Vietnam, and that was it, even something as important as

Nick's disappearance. Frankie wondered if that was healthy. He knew that people cope in different ways, and if that was how Mrs. Francelli chose to cope with Johnny's absence, then Frankie had to respect it. So, once a week, he would meet with Mrs. Francelli and take part in her conspiracy of denial.

He drove toward the steel mill, on the same stretch of road where Johnny's father had died when they were in fifth grade. A couple of weeks after the accident Johnny's family doctor recommended that the family drive by the spot where the accident had occurred. He said it would help frame the event for Anna and the children and give them closure. So, reluctantly, they went. Ed Stoudt, Mr. Francelli's friend at the steel mill, drove Mrs. Francelli, Sissy, and Johnny. Of course, Johnny had been adamant about Frankie coming along, so he went too.
Mr. Stoudt knew the spot. He had left the mill parking lot just a minute or two after Mr. Francelli on the day of the accident and was the first to arrive on the scene. Frankie remembered wondering what it must have been like for him to find his best friend like that.

When they arrived at the spot, there was little to see. Aside from some skid marks, there was no evidence of an accident. The twisted wreckage of Mr. Francelli's car was gone, as was the tractor-trailer that hit it. Mr. Stoudt had slowed to a crawl as they got close, and there were no sounds in the car as everyone looked. Finally, Mrs. Francelli said it wasn't necessary for them to stop, and slowly, Mr. Stoudt pulled away. Johnny and Frankie were in the back seat and they turned and stared at the spot as it shrank in the distance. They drove home in silence, and, from that day on, no one from the Francelli family ever drove down that road again.

As Frankie passed the spot now, it was still sad. Anymore, it seemed that everything was sad. Frankie never swore, but as he drove, he thought about his friends and he swore. He punched the horn on the steering wheel over and over as he drove and he swore.

Later that night Anna Francelli knelt beside her bed and prayed for Nick. Then she got into bed and cried herself to sleep.

44- Boston Common

May 1968

Allison was handling the war the same way Anna was, by trying not to think about it. She was terribly worried about Johnny's safety, and used her studying to keep her mind occupied. As finals approached she studied even more, so much so that Debbie couldn't take it any longer. Finally, after much pleading from her roommate, Allison agreed to take a break from cramming by leaving campus and going to Boston Common for a morning walk and a leisurely lunch at the Union Oyster House. The weather was sunny and mild as they strolled Beacon Street, and the Common was alive with people walking their dogs, playing touch football or relaxing with something to read.

"Did I ever tell you that I was a good touch football player?" Allison asked.

"Several times," Debbie said. "I'm glad you've become civilized."

"Sometimes I still get the urge to mix it up a little, bloody a few noses like I used to with Johnny's friends."

"Did you really bloody noses?"

"Not really. But I held my own, and I could run a pattern and catch."

"I'm sure you could," Debbie said. "But no football today, we're here to relax."

They passed some tourists waiting to buy tickets from a man in colonial garb, hawking double-decker bus tours of Old Boston. Another man, who looked to be eighty, was sitting under a tree playing the harmonica. The tune wasn't recognizable, but Debbie dropped a dollar in his tip can anyway. He winked at her and said, "thanks baby," before continuing with his music.

"See Debbie," Allison said. "Guys are still interested in you."

"Sure," Debbie said, "if I pay them."

"I'm serious. You're beautiful, and you had more guys than you could handle before we stopped going to fraternity parties. You just have to get back on the circuit."

"Well, that won't happen this year. One more week of finals and we'll be gone for the summer."

"Speaking of summer," Allison said, "Remember, you have to spend at least a week with me in Bristol, and you're coming with my family to the Jersey Shore over the Fourth of July weekend."

"Are you sure that's okay?" Debbie asked.

"Positive, I've talked to my parents and they insist that you come. We've rented a beautiful house on the beach at Stone Harbor. We'll have a room to ourselves. Remember, I'm an only child. If I have to be at the shore alone, I'll die."

"Can't wait," Debbie said.

"We'll have fun in Bristol too. Johnny asked me to visit his mother over the summer. You can come with me the first time for support."

"Oh that should be a blast," Debbie said. "You really owe me, big time."

"It'll be fine, and you're right, I do owe you."

"Maybe you can introduce me to some of Johnny's friends while I'm in town," Debbie said. "Do any of them plan to become doctors? I'll need to marry one to support my life style."

"Well, that's a problem. First of all, except for Frankie, Johnny's friends don't speak to me. It all goes back to the stupid break up we had in high school. They're a very tight group and very protective of each other. But Johnny loves them, and I'm sure he'll patch things up when he comes home."

"I guess they're a lot like us. Mess with one of us you mess with both of us."

"Exactly," Allison laughed. "You'll meet them at the wedding."

"The wedding!" Debbie shouted, and they both laughed. A young couple was passing by on a horse-drawn carriage. The girl was resting her head on her partner's shoulder, and they looked completely at peace.

The rhythm of the horse's hooves on the cobblestone added to the tranquility of the moment.

"Hey!" Debbie shouted, "My friend is getting married."

The couple smiled and the carriage driver tipped his colonial hat. Allison was embarrassed, but joined in.

"It's true; I am," she shouted with her arms thrust into the air.

"Good luck!" the girl called to her as the carriage moved on.

Everyone laughed and Allison said, "We're crazy."

"In elementary school my teachers said I was hyperkinetic," Debbie said. "I thought I had a disease."

"You do," Allison said, "A mental one, and I'm afraid I'm catching it." Allison got back to the previous topic. "Are you really that hung up on marrying a doctor?"

"Totally, that's why I'm changing my major to art appreciation."

"I don't get it." Allison said.

"Doctors make lot's of money, but it's stuffy, narrowly focused work. They don't want a spouse at home who wants to talk about corpuscles or x-rays all the time. They need someone to provide cultural balance to the relationship. That's me."

"So you and your doctor husband will talk about art?"

"It's more than that," Debbie said. "Hubby will make the money and I'll run the benefit art auctions for the hospital. I'll probably be president of the ladies auxiliary and sponsor balls and cocktail parties. I'll give interviews for the society page of the paper."

"I don't think Johnny's friends are what you're looking for," Allison said.

"I'm talking long term here, but for now I just want a good time with a cute guy, so let's keep an open mind."

"Let's do that," Allison said.

Debbie saw a crowd gathering at the far end of the commons. "Must be something going on today."

"Must be," Allison said, sounding distracted. Her attention was drawn to a billboard-sized bronze relief between the sidewalk and the common.

It depicted a group of Civil War soldiers marching, with one soldier on horseback.

"Okay, little miss art major," she said, motioning to the sculpture, "what do you think of that?"

Debbie looked at it and smiled. "What do you think of it?" She said.

"I think it's neat, but you're the art major, and I asked you first."

"Well, I really don't want to show off," Debbie said.

"Oh please do," Allison said, feigning a high society tone. "Perhaps I will buy it at the hospital auction."

"Very well, Madam," Debbie said, putting on airs of her own. "If you insist. The piece is a brilliant bronze relief, crafted by the noted sculptor Augustus Saint-Gaudens, an Irish-born immigrant who came to the United States before his first birthday. It depicts Colonel Robert Gould Shaw and the 54th Massachusetts Regiment that served under him during the civil war. Aside from Shaw and its other commissioned officers, the entire regiment was African-American."

Allison looked at Debbie, shocked by her knowledge. Debbie plunged on.

"The work was commissioned by the Massachusetts legislature for several reasons. As you know, Boston had a proud anti-slavery tradition prior to the Civil War and was a haven for runaway slaves. You'll remember that the legislature even passed Personal Liberty Laws in resistance to the Fugitive Slave Act."

Both girls were struggling not to laugh as Debbie's show continued.

"However, perhaps the driving force behind the commissioning of the work was that Colonel Shaw was the son of a prominent abolitionist Boston family that resided right here in the Beacon Hill section of the city. In keeping with military regulations of the time, African-Americans could not be commissioned officers, so all such African-American regiments were commanded by whites. The Shaw family was deeply honored that their son was chosen to lead the first African-American regiment."

Allison couldn't contain herself any longer and screamed, "You are unbelievable!" But Debbie held up her hand for Allison to be quiet. She wasn't finished yet.

"Saint-Gaudens used exceptional detail to capture the features of the marching soldiers. Note how he conveys nuances of their African-American heritage by using texture instead of color. Note the determination and quiet strength of the men who already had their freedom and yet risked everything to liberate those still in bondage. Note the dignity of Colonel Shaw, sitting tall in his saddle, proud to lead the regiment. Above him is the floating image of the Angel of Death. She is holding poppies, a common symbol of death, and an olive branch, the symbol of peace."

Allison was totally floored by Debbie's performance and wanted to interrupt, but Debbie held up her hand again.

"This is a brilliant piece of art that commemorates a war that had a clarity of purpose, a truly a noble cause." A group of senior citizens had stopped to admire the work and were listening to Debbie's speech.

Still addressing Allison, Debbie said, "As for your interest in purchasing the piece, I must inform you that it is priceless to the people of Boston, and it's impossible to conceive of a circumstance under which the city would entertain proposals for its sale." Then she winked and said, "Perhaps I can interest you in a marvelous Andy Warhol production of a Campbell Soup Can instead."

"Oh, my God!" Allison shrieked. "That was incredible. How did you do that?"

"I cheated," Debbie said. "Saint-Gaudens is on my final on Monday and my professor loves this piece."

"That was great," Allison said, hugging her friend. "You can definitely do the art auction."

"I know," Debbie said. The two of them laughed again and the senior citizens began to clap. More people, thinking the girls were street performers, stopped to see what they were missing. Finally, the girls parted, gave everyone an embarrassed smile and wave, and moved on.

"That was so good," Allison said. "You should have put a tin cup out; you were better than the harmonica player."

"I'm going to ace that final," Debbie said. "I have to. Some day my marriage may depend on it."

As they walked Debbie was gushing with excitement. "Nothing like a Saturday visit to the Boston Common," she said. But the Saint-Gaudens piece reminded Allison of Johnny and the war. "I'm worried about Johnny," she said.

"That's what happens when your nose isn't buried in a book. You start thinking too much. You've got to learn to enjoy some free time."

"I know," Allison said, but didn't sound convincing.

When they got to the Park Street corner of the common, across from the Massachusetts State House building, they noticed a crowd of young people had gathered and someone was setting up a portable sound system.

"What's going on?" Debbie asked a policeman overlooking the crowd. The officer eyed the girls. "You with them?" He wore sergeant strips and his nametag said Reilly.

"No," Allison said. "Who are they?"

"Anti-war crowd," Sergeant Reilly said with a level of disgust. "Trouble makers, draft dodgers, you name it. They come here every Saturday to rip the hell out of America, and I have to listen to it. Free country and free speech." He sneered when he said free speech. He pointed with his nightstick to other cops who had taken positions around the commons. "As soon as it gets vulgar, we shut 'em down."

It was a pretty grungy group, even by college age standards. Most of the guys wore faded jeans, and there was plenty of long hair and beards. A lot of the girls wore long loose dresses and sandals. There were peace symbols everywhere. Some held signs with slogans like, "Stop the War Now," and "LBJ has blood on his hands." Debbie noticed one that read, "Free the Draft Dodgers- Imprison the Baby Killers," and decided it might be a good idea to steer Allison in a different direction.

"Let's go," she said. "The Union Oyster House is waiting with a marvelous lunch." But Allison was transfixed. "In a minute," Allison said. "I want to see this."
With a hundred or so people gathered, the speaker began.

"Okay people, you know the score. We protest, we vote, we demonstrate, but nothing changes because the power brokers of this country have no intention of letting it change. They're making too much money." The crowd cheered. Someone hollered, "Damn right!" The speaker held up his hand for quiet, and continued. "The aircraft industry, the chemical companies, the munitions makers, they're rakin' it in while people die." There were more cheers.

"As long as the money men run this country, it won't matter who's President. We'll still be in Nam." People on the far side of the crowd started yelling, "Stop the war now." As they repeated the chant, it spread through the crowd, and the speaker let it take on a life of its own.
The scene fascinated the girls. When the chanting died down, the speaker continued.
"Remember the old slogan, 'What if they gave a war and nobody came?'"
The protesters nodded knowingly. Some shouted agreement.
"Well, it's time we start calling a spade a spade. This war won't end until the guys in uniform lay down their arms and refuse to fight." There was a roar of approval.
"They need to say 'screw you' to their officers and the criminals in Washington and on Wall Street, and refuse to be a part of the slaughter going on."
Fists were thrust into the air amid more angry cheers. People waved their placards.
"If they don't do that, then we'll have to start treating them like the fascist baby killers that they are."

There was another roar, and another familiar chant started. "Hey, Hey, LBJ, How many kids did you kill today." It spread quickly and was repeated several times.

Allison couldn't believe what she just heard.

"What did he say?" She screamed so Debbie could hear her above the chant.

"It's okay, Debbie said," moving to position herself between Allison and the demonstration.

"It's not okay," Allison said, struggling to see around her. "That jerk just called Johnny a baby killer!"

The speaker nodded smugly as he waited for the chant to fade.

Just as he was about to speak, Allison shouted from the corner, "Hey, creep! Who are you to call my boyfriend a baby killer?"

The crowd turned in the direction of her voice.

Officer Reilly smiled and whispered, "You tell him kid."

Surprised that anyone would dare interrupt his tirade, the speaker was searching for something to say when someone shouted, "Kiss my ass honey."

Debbie was still trying to subdue Allison when she shouted back, "If Johnny Francelli were here he'd kick yours!"

Finally the speaker shouted, "Go home Barbie!" and smiled proudly at his retort.

"Barbie!" Allison fumed, "Barbie!"

Debbie jumped in. "You can shove that microphone you know where," she yelled.

With that, the speaker let loose a string of profanities and the crowd booed the girls. Someone threw a rock in their direction.

Sergeant Reilly stepped in front of the girls and spoke into his radio. "Okay boys, this will be a short one. Shut it down; this rally is over." Then he said to the girls, "Good job. Now get out of here. Head down Bowdion Street, and you'll be fine."

The girls didn't want to look like they were running away, but Reilly repeated, "Get going. I've got work to do."

As they moved reluctantly to cross Beacon Street, Sergeant Reilly called to Allison, "Hey, sweetie. Tell your boyfriend we support him."

45- June 6, 1968

Anna awakened at six still feeling great from the letter she received from Allison the day before. It was a wonderful letter filled with all the spirit and energy that were her trademarks as a younger girl. She wrote of her newfound happiness with Johnny and noted that she was estimating when Johnny would be home, as if Anna hadn't already calculated the time to the second. Allison went on to say that she'd be in Bristol for the summer and planned to visit her often.

Anna hoped things weren't moving too quickly for them, especially given their previous break-up, but it was a light, cheerful letter, and she appreciated Allison's effort to connect. It was quite nice actually, and the thought crossed her mind that Allison could one day be her daughter-in-law, and they would have some bonding of their own to do. She allowed herself the luxury of thinking about Johnny's life after Vietnam. She tried to visualize him as a married man, as a father. She knew he'd be as wonderful a companion and provider as her Jack had been. It was a pleasant thought.

Things were looking good on the political front too, at least from her perspective. Bobby Kennedy had surged to the lead for the democratic presidential nomination, and Anna felt that his disengagement plan for Vietnam offered the best prospect for her son's safety.
The night before she watched the results of the California primary until nearly eleven-thirty, when the networks finally declared Kennedy the winner over Vice President Humphrey and Senator McCarthy. The victory virtually assured Kennedy the nomination at the Chicago convention that summer. She went to bed happy and awakened feeling just as good.

After putting on a pot of coffee, she turned on the television, and was horrified by what she saw. Bobby Kennedy had been shot just minutes after delivering the victory speech she had seen the night before. The bullet struck the back of his head, leaving him in grave condition. Anna sat paralyzed as the film was replayed of Kennedy lying on the floor, his unblinking eyes wide open, and his head resting in a pool of blood. Her mind was swirling. This couldn't be happening again, she thought. As supporters held out hope for his survival, it was clear that the prospects were dim.

Coming just sixty days after Martin Luther King was gunned down, Anna feared this would be too much for a fragmented nation to endure. Kennedy's youthful charm and charisma, his boundless optimism, and his healing rhetoric had become a shining beacon for Anna and millions of other Americans. Now that light had been extinguished. She prayed that he would live, but knew that his presidential prospects, and his plan to extricate the United States from Vietnam, had already died.

Later that day, Frank Mankowitz, Kennedy's press secretary and long-time friend, delivered the news that everyone anticipated. Robert Francis Kennedy was dead. As she watched him, Anna thought that his grief-stricken face reflected the face of the nation.

46- The Bristol Train Station

The *County Times* ran a story on the Kennedy funeral arrangements. After a Requiem Mass at St. Patrick's Cathedral in New York, the senator's body would be transported by train to Washington, where he would be laid to rest at Arlington National Cemetery, just a few yards from President Kennedy's grave. The train would travel along the northeast corridor, and would slow considerably at each station to allow mourners along the tracks the chance to pay their last respects. The train would be passing through town between 1:30 and 2:00 PM and slow down as it passed the Bristol station. Anna thought about the trip her kids had taken to Washington five years earlier. Impulsively, she picked up the phone.

It was an uncomfortably hot day, with the temperature in the upper eighties and high humidity. Frankie arrived at 1o'clock, and Sissy and Anna were outside waiting for him.

"Tom had to work," Sissy said, as she climbed into the back seat. "Mind if I come?"

"Of course not," Frankie said. "I'm glad you're here."

"Hello, Frankie," Anna said as she slid into the front seat. "Thank you for doing this, I feel silly for not walking. It's so close."

"It's better this way in this heat," Frankie said. "There are steps to climb and you might be waiting in the sun a long time. Save your energy for that."

The tracks ran near the edge of town and were bordered at the station by Garden and Prospect Streets. The tracks rested on "the highlines," a twenty-foot high birm, covered with dark crushed shale. There were steep steps on each side that led to the northbound and southbound platforms. The old platforms and passenger rooms reflected the quaint architecture of the golden age of railroads, but they had fallen into disrepair.

The commuter parking lot on Prospect Street faced the Grundy Park and Delaware Canal. Beyond the canal was the old Grundy Mill, where hundreds of residents had worked over the years. Joseph R. Grundy had been a highly successful turn-of- the- century industrialist who later became a United States Senator and philanthropist. His generosity provided significant benefits to the town for decades, and, through his endowment of a charitable foundation, the senator saw to it that the benefits would endure.

The most notable feature of the mill was the fourteen-story tower with illuminated clock faces that overlooked the town in four directions. Fifteen feet in diameter, they were like huge, benevolent eyes, keeping watch over the residents. Folklore had it that townspeople grew uneasy if they ventured from sight of the Grundy clock for an extended period. Anna wondered how long it would be before Johnny and the other boys would see it again.

They parked in the commuter lot and used the pedestrian tunnel that connected the north and southbound steps. It was the same tunnel where the Tone Kings once practiced their singing. They always sounded better with the tunnel's acoustical enhancement, and Frankie smiled at the memory.

"We used to sing here," he said.

"I know," Anna said, looking at years of graffiti that covered the walls.

"She knows just about everything Johnny did," Sissy said. "It's a small town, and she has contacts."

Anna looked for something Johnny might have scrawled but saw nothing. For a minute, she wished she had a marker in her purse so that she could write, "Johnny loves Allison" or, better yet, "Johnny loves Mom." She chided herself for entertaining such a childish thought.

The platform was already crowded, but they worked their way to a good spot. The northbound platform was crowded too, and people were beginning to fan out along the tracks, even as the police did their best to keep them back a safe distance. The crowd was subdued and Anna saw signs that read, "We Love you Bobby," and "We'll Never Forget." One said, "Our Hearts Are Broken." Several children held small American Flags. She noticed Bristol Mayor John Rodgers and Borough Councilman Tom Corrigan, who used to work with her husband Jack at the steel mill. She knew other people throughout the crowd and passed the time in muted conversation.

Anna noticed Billy Moyer waving from the opposite platform. Frankie saw him too, and said, "There's Billy. He must be home for summer break." Frankie hadn't seen him since his brief visit during Christmas week and was excited that he was home. Billy motioned that he would meet them later in the parking lot.

The arrival time came and went without any sign of the train. At two-fifteen someone announced that it was running well behind schedule because of the crowds along the tracks. As they continued to wait, the heat was taking its toll. Some of the elderly began to leave while others from the street level quickly replaced them. Frankie asked Anna if she wanted to go home, but she refused. Two-thirty came and went, as did three o'clock. More people left, and others took their places. Newspaper accounts the next day estimated that between five and six hundred people were in attendance, with thousands more at the larger Levittown station a few miles north and still more along the tracks that ran between the two towns. Finally, at three-thirty, word spread that the train had passed Trenton and was entering Pennsylvania at Morrisville. At normal train speed, Morrisville was only ten minutes away, but it would take thirty minutes at the slower pace today. Still, there was a sense of relief in knowing the train was close.

Finally, after more waiting, someone said, "Here it comes."
The police asked everyone to step back, as the people strained to get a better look.
The train was moving slower than most commuter trains and considerably slower than the express trains that could rattle windows as they flew by.
A hush fell, as it got closer. At fifty yards it slowed to a crawl. Aside from some black bunting, it had no identifiable markings. It was longer than Frankie had imagined; the newspaper the next day would report twenty cars. As it approached men removed their hats. The police honor guard saluted, as did some older men, presumably veterans, sprinkled throughout the crowd.
Then the train was passing directly in front of them, and people strained to look inside the cars. Some whispered the names of Kennedy family

members they thought they saw. Suddenly, to everyone's surprise, Senator Ted Kennedy appeared on the back balcony of the last car, waving ever so slightly and mouthing the words, "Thank you." As he did so Anna Francelli felt like his eyes were locked on hers, as though he was speaking to her directly.

As the train pulled away, the senator stepped inside, and it picked up speed. As it faded in the distance, Anna felt that any hope for a quick end to the war faded with it.

Most people waited until the train was out of sight, well on its way to Croydon, before they started leaving the platform. Still, almost no one spoke until they were at street level.

In the parking lot, the mood was broken by the reunion with Billy Moyer. He greeted Frankie with a long hug, followed by a kiss for Anna and a warm hello for Sissy. He seemed elated to see them.

"How long have you been home?" Frankie asked.

"I just got in last night. Pretty bad timing."

"How's school?" Sissy asked.

"It's hard work," Billy said. "But its great. It's hard to believe I'm almost halfway finished. I made the Dean's List last semester and I think I did well on my finals this time too."

"Impressive," Sissy said.

"So when do we get together?" Frankie asked.

"Don't know," Billy said, sounding disappointed. "I'm only in town two more days."

"Two days!" Frankie said. "Why so short?"

"I got a summer internship with the Department of Commerce through Georgetown. I have to be back in DC Monday."

"That's too bad," Frankie said.

Billy smiled, "You know I'd rather spend a few weeks at the shore with the guys like before, but this is a great opportunity. I want to get involved in business and government."

"It certainly sounds like a wonderful learning experience," Anna said.

"I hope so. My dad said it's a great way to get my foot in the door."

"I should say so," she replied.

The sun was still beating down, and Frankie wanted to get Anna into the car. Billy looked like he needed to leave too.

"Listen," Billy said, "I've got loads of things to do before I leave, but how about if I call you later? Maybe we can get together for a couple of hours and catch up on news from the guys."

"Sounds great," Frankie said.

Then Billy looked embarrassed. "Mrs. Francelli, I'm so sorry. I can't believe how ignorant I am for not asking about Johnny sooner. I guess this whole funeral thing distracted me. How's Johnny?"

"Oh, that's okay. This has been quite a difficult afternoon, but Johnny's doing just fine."

"Great," Billy said. "It really bothers me that he's there. We were writing for a while, but we kind of dropped off over the last two months. I guess we were both pretty busy. I'll write to him when I get down to DC again."

"I know he'd like that," she said.

He gave the three of them a hug, and when they broke, he looked upset. "I miss you guys. Sometimes when I'm swamped with work at school, I wish I were home with the guys at your house, just foolin' around. They were good times."

"Yes, they were," Anna said. "We'll all do it again sometime."

"Count me in," he said.

They said good-bye again and parted.

As they walked to the car, Anna took a tissue from her purse. When she was sure Frankie wasn't looking, she wiped the tears from her eyes.

47- The Ant Hill

The squad matured just the way Boyd had expected. They did things by the book, and it was clear that the sergeant was pleased. But Johnny sensed that Boyd was edgy about their current mission. Boyd was always sharp, always focused, but Johnny had never seen him like this before. He couldn't bring himself to use the words "Boyd" and "nervous" in the same sentence, but he felt it.

Fortunately, this was to be a one-day exercise. They were going on recon about twenty miles north of the base, to check out what air reconnaissance suspected to be an enemy supply line. Their job was to confirm or refute the route's existence on the ground, without engaging the enemy, and return to base before nightfall.

The drop went well enough. The landing zone was clear, and they made it to cover without incident. When they regrouped, Boyd gave them their directions, and they moved out. Johnson was on point. Johnny was closest to him, ten to fifteen yards behind. As usual, Wallace cradled the M-60 in his massive arms. Boyd, Paige, and Phillips were fanned out behind them. There was no replacement for Conroy yet.

They came upon a clearing of tall grass, at least three feet high. It was about seventy-five yards long. They'd be more vulnerable in the open, and Boyd was reluctant to pass through it, but with a steep ridge to their left and deep slope to their right, he had no choice. He urged extra caution, and they fanned out even more and moved ahead. With the shade of the wooded area gone, they were hit with the full glare of the sun. The heat was oppressive. Johnny had gotten used to a lot of things in Vietnam, but not the heat, or the insects. Each day he struggled with the same decision, should he clog his pores by using the standard issue repellant and make sweating difficult or skip the repellant and get eaten alive. Sweating would keep his body temperature lower, so he had decided to skip the repellent and take his chances with the bugs. Now, as they gnawed at him, he was regretting his decision.

He was watching Johnson, who was approaching one of Vietnam's notoriously large anthills. Over time, Johnny had become fascinated with the country's climate and vegetation, its living creatures and their habitats. The most captivating images of all were the enormous anthills and the giant ants that built them. It was not uncommon to see a three or four foot anthill. They were so large that men actually used them for cover in a firefight. Johnny remembered the small, glass enclosed ant colony that Sister Mary Katherine kept in her fourth grade classroom at St. Therese's. He'd been fascinated by the network of tunnels the colony had created. He tried to imagine what kind of network existed beneath the small mountain of dirt he was looking at now.

When Johnson got close to the hill, he called back to Johnny.

"Hey Francelli, if these ants come out and pull you inside, you're on your own, because I ain't going in after you."

"Thanks Sam," Johnny said. "Just pay attention to what you're doing, and I'll take care of the ants."

"Okay man, as long as you know where we stand."

The next line of trees was thirty yards away, and Johnny was grateful for the shade they'd provide.

He turned his attention back to Johnson and thought about the friendship they'd developed. He looked forward to the day when he could introduce him to the guys back home. He was grateful that he had grown up in a racially mixed town. Although no black guys hung out at Jake's, he'd gone to school with and played sports with them all of his life, and that experience made it a lot easier to mix with the guys in the army. Not everyone at boot camp had as easy a time.

Johnny was still looking at him when Johnson stepped on the booby trap. The small explosion lifted Johnson two feet off the ground.

"Get down," Boyd yelled, and they all took cover in the grass.

As they lay there, they could hear Johnson screaming out in pain. "My leg. Oh sweet Jesus, my leg."

Instinctively, Johnny felt for his own legs and was relieved that both were still there. Johnny was anxious to get to Johnson, but Boyd, still another twenty yards behind him, was shouting for everyone to stay put. Finally, after three minutes of agonizing screams from Johnson and

Boyd's repeated orders to stay down, the sergeant said, "Okay, let's get him, but be careful. This place may be filled with traps." But as soon as they stood, they were hit with heavy fire from the wooded area. They hit the ground again, and the shooting continued.

They were defenseless. They couldn't return fire from the ground with the heavy grass blocking their vision, and if they stood, they were easy targets. Meanwhile, the VC continued to spray the area.

"Stay down," Boyd shouted, "I'm calling in an air strike."

Johnny knew this air strike would be different. There was no way to back out of there before the planes arrived to torch the VC. Even if they wanted to crawl out, they couldn't leave Johnson, which meant they would be awfully close to the tree line when the planes started dropping the napalm, especially Johnson, who was ten yards in front of Johnny and almost twenty yards in front of the rest of the squad.

Johnny could hear Johnson's screams above the shooting.

His mind was racing. How much blood was Johnson losing? How long before the air strike? Five minutes? Ten? And what about the air strike, Johnny thought? It would be way too close to Johnson, even if Boyd could get the aircraft to target the trees.

They had learned that blood loss was among the chief causes of battlefield deaths. Somebody had to get to Johnson soon. Johnny had a small medic kit on his belt, and he made a decision. "I'm getting Johnson," he hollered back and began to crawl.

"Stay here!" Boyd ordered. "It'll be over in ten minutes."

But Johnson might not have ten minutes, Johnny thought. He pretended not to hear the sergeant and began his crawl. He stayed low and could hear bullets hitting around him. He wondered whether Johnson was being hit.

"Talk to me, Sam," he called out as he crawled.

"Francelli?" Sam responded weakly.

"That's it Sam. Talk to me."

"It's my leg. I can't get up," he said, struggling to speak.

"Stay still Sam," Johnny said. "I'm coming."

When he got to Johnson, he couldn't believe what he saw. His right boot and foot were gone, and most of his lower calf was a mangled mass of tissue and tendons. Johnny thought he was going to be sick.

Johnson was screaming again, obviously in incredible pain.

"It's okay, Sam, we're gonna get you out of here."

Johnson just kept screaming. Johnny considered knocking him out to relieve the pain, but Johnson's grip on Johnny's arm was becoming weak. Finally, Johnson's screams subsided, and he passed out.

Johnny opened the medical pack and applied a tourniquet. When he stopped the bleeding as much as he could, he took out a syringe and, trying desperately to remember his first aid training, he gave Johnson a shot of morphine. Next, he slung his M-16 on his shoulder, crouched behind Johnson and put one arm under each of Johnson's armpits. Then, staying as low as he could in the tall grass, he walked backward, dragging Johnson with him. The firing continued, and the squad started lobbing grenades toward the trees. It was difficult to do while lying almost flat, but at least it provided Johnny with some cover.

When Wallace saw what Johnny was doing, he stood fully erect with the M-60 and released a deafening barrage of bullets in the direction of the VC.

Sergeant Boyd was on all fours now and moving quickly toward Johnny to help. When he was five yards away from Boyd, Johnny felt a sharp pinch in his thigh where a bullet had entered, but his adrenalin was pumping, and he continued to pull. A second later the impact of a second bullet felt like he had been punched in the stomach, and he fell backward, with Johnson's upper body landing on his legs. Just then he heard the roar of the jets and felt the intense heat as the planes unloaded the napalm on the trees.

Johnny was having the dream again. The same one he had over and over in his bunk.

He and Allison are thirteen. They're riding their bikes during a summer rain, not a downpour, but a strong, steady rain. Her long blond hair is wet and matted. Their cloths are soaked, and they are laughing, especially Allison, who loves riding in the rain. She spots a pool of water ahead and points it out to Johnny as they ride. The gesture is an invitation, not a warning. The puddle is large, at least ten feet long. They smile and race toward it, pedaling faster as they approach. Just before impact they lift their feet from the pedals and stretch their legs out wide, allowing their momentum to carry them. They are side by side when they hit the water, and the splash from the wheels drenches both of them. Allison shrieks with delight.

They pedal on to Lion's Park, a peaceful, grassy area set along the Delaware River. There's a gazebo there. On Sunday evenings in the summertime, the local Lion's Club hosts free concerts. People bring their lawn chairs and enjoy the music as they watch the pleasure boats go by. On most days, old men sit in the shade and talk for hours, enjoying the cool, river breeze. But now, on a rainy summer afternoon, the park is empty.

Johnny and Allison stop their bikes on the river side of the gazebo and take a seat on the park bench, out of view from the street and the glass enclosed restaurant that faces the park. The gazebo overhang gives them some protection from the rain.

They sit there for a while, laughing, catching their breath, and wiping water from their skin. Neither of them speaks. When the laughter subsides, Allison slides closer to Johnny and rests her head on his shoulder. She smells fresh, like Ivory soap. They sit there without speaking, watching a single sail boat struggle against the current in the rain. They smile at each other and share a kiss. It is longer than usual, and Allison's lips taste like peppermint from her chewing gum. She lowers her head in shyness when their lips part. Still no one speaks.

She is so beautiful, Johnny thinks. He wonders what she is thinking. She looks up and gently brushes a drop of water from Johnny's cheek. At that moment he wishes he could sit on that bench with her forever. Then she giggles again, and, without warning, pushes him away. She runs to her bike, laughing. Johnny races after her. Their trips to the gazebo usually end with a race back to Allison's house. This time, she has given herself a head start.

Johnny is pedaling hard behind her, trying to catch up when his dream is disturbed by a strong voice he recognizes. "Stay with me, Francelli, you're going to be fine," he hears. "Open your eyes man," the voice says. "You've got to stay awake." Johnny tries to open his eyes, but he can't. He is tired and wants to sleep. He wants to dream more, to see Allison again. Then another voice says, "Come on, Francelli, open your eyes. We're with you. Help is coming." Johnny is trying to place the second voice. It is strong and deep. He struggles to open his eyes and sees a face he knows. "That's it, Johnny. Stay with us," the face says. Johnny recognizes Sergeant Boyd. "That's it, Johnny," the deeper voice says, "You're doing fine." He recognizes Wallace.

It is a clear, sunny day, and the light hurts Johnny's eyes. Looking up, he can see the treetops at the end of the clearing, and for a moment, he thinks he's in the woods by the canal in Bristol. When he and Frankie were small, they used to lie on their backs in the woods and look at the trees and the birds. Johnny sees the trees now, but there are no birds. Explosions and gunfire have sent them away. Johnny remembers, he's not in the woods by the canal; he's in a field somewhere in Vietnam, ten thousand miles from home.

He can feel people doing things to his stomach and thigh, pressing on them, applying pressure. He starts to shake. His thigh burns, but the rest of his body is cold. He knows the sun is burning hot, but he's very cold. Drifting off, he sees an image of President Johnson on television. It is nighttime, and Johnny can see the illuminated Grundy clock through the window of the Oval Office. Johnny doesn't want to see the president; he wants to see Allison. But LBJ is on the screen giving a speech. "We're not about to send American boys ten thousand miles away from home to do a job that Asian boys ought to be doing for themselves," the President says. Funny, Johnny thought, he hadn't seen many Asian boys yet, at least not friendly ones.

The President's face is gone, and Johnny can sense the people around him doing things to his body. He feels a sharp pinch. Someone is sticking a needle into his arm.

Johnny is dreaming again. He's sitting at the dinner table at home. Frankie is there, and Sissy. Frankie is wearing his Bristol football jersey, number seventy-six, the home jersey. Frankie gives him a wink. Big Frankie, Johnny thinks, and smiles. Sissy is saying something about President Kennedy's hair, but Johnny can't make out the words. Johnny's mother appears in the doorway from the kitchen. She is cheerful, as usual, voted the most beautiful mom by the guys, Johnny remembers proudly. She is beautiful in every way, Johnny thinks. She's wearing an apron over her simple dress and carrying a tray piled high with huge olives, stuffed with her special mixture of ground beef, veal, pork and spices. Frankie's eyes light up.
"Now I don't want any of you taking any long trips," she says pleasantly, as she puts the tray on the table. "Stay close to home forever." She kisses Johnny softly on the top of his head and messes his hair. He smiles. Her image vanishes as Johnny feels someone squeezing his jaw and moving his face from side to side. He hears Sergeant Boyd's voice again. "It's okay, Francelli, help's coming," the sergeant says. "You've got to stay awake." Then the sergeant screams to someone, "Where the hell's that goddamn chopper?"

The chopper? Where's the goddamn chopper? Johnny repeats to himself. Then he thinks about God and whispers a short prayer.

48- St. Therese's

The funeral service was held at St. Therese's, and Ralph McGinnis' uncle handled the arrangements. Some would say later that it was the most gut wrenching experience they could remember. Anna asked Frankie to ride with the family from the funeral home to the church. As they made the short drive, Frankie thought about what had taken place since Johnny's death. Frankie had raced to Anna's house as soon as he heard and found her and Sissy completely shattered. Anna held him so tightly and cried so hard that Sissy had to pull her away and lead her to a chair. Frankie got the sense that Anna was really holding on to Johnny.

During the weeklong wait for Johnny's body to be shipped home, Anna wanted people around her, lots of people. So the house was filled each day. Frankie took the week off from work to be there. Both mother and daughter were clearly in shock, but after breaking down that first day, they shed no more tears, at least not publicly. Anna spent most of her time sitting quietly, staring off in the distance. Sissy preferred to be alone and retreated to her room. Father Creeden was a frequent visitor and spent his time talking privately with Anna, who gave little indication that she heard what he was saying.

Frankie's life as he knew it ended the day Johnny died. He had carried a persistent guilt ever since his best friend left for Vietnam, sustained by the knowledge that he was the reason Johnny had joined the army. Now, logic dictated that he was also the cause of Johnny's death, and the guilt was replaced by a crushing sense of despair. He was convinced that he would never again know or deserve happiness, that there would be no reprieve from the oppressive pain he felt. Johnny had died because of him, and no one could persuade him differently.

All of the worrying about what horrors might befall his friend was replaced now by a clear sense of finality. In a way, it was liberating.

Frankie could begin his life of well deserved self-torture, free from any more assurances from others that things would turn out fine. They didn't turn out fine, just as Frankie always feared, and he would exact a heavy price from himself in retribution. Frankie thought briefly about taking his own life, but decided that would be an unfair escape from the pain he deserved, just like his failed army physical had been. It would also add to Anna's problems, which was the last thing Frankie would want to do.

Sometime during the long vigil at the Francelli house, he made a pledge that, for the rest of his life, he would help Mrs. Francelli and Sissy in any way he could. He would help Angelo's parents too, and anyone else who needed him. He would start by being strong for Johnny's family at the funeral and worry about his own needs later.

He looked at Mrs. Francelli in the seat across from him in the limousine and hoped that she would hold up under the stress she would face that day. She still held the letter in her hand that she had received from the army. Details of Johnny's death had been sketchy. The army said he died saving a fellow soldier. He had displayed uncommon valor, for which he was being recommended for a commendation. But Frankie knew that Mrs. Francelli didn't care about that. She knew her son too well and feared all along the risks he might take for others. The things that had made him the wonderful son that he was, his kindness, his enormous self-confidence, his loyalty, his sense of adventure, all of these things had combined to bring about his death. She was sure of it. She wasn't interested in any medals, although she appreciated the gesture. She was only concerned about the manner in which he died. She took some comfort in hearing that he had died peacefully, that he bled out in a helicopter while being transported to a MASH center. He had been given morphine to ease the pain and had quietly drifted off from the loss of blood. Sergeant Boyd, who had written the letter, told her he was the finest young man he ever had the honor of serving with. He said that Johnny was loved and respected by his fellow squad members, that he was a natural leader. He closed by writing that there were times while they were waiting for the helicopter evacuation when he swore that Johnny was smiling. It was that part that Anna held on to.

Anna immediately thought of Allison and wondered how she would take the news. Anna had only recently allowed herself to visualize Johnny's future with her, a marriage, children, Sunday dinner together. Thoughts of those things being taken from Johnny at such a young age just made the pain worse.

Anna felt Allison should receive the news personally, rather than reading about it in the papers, and the task fell to Frankie. For two days he tried calling and going to Allison's house to find her parents, but no one was home. Finally he went to her father's car dealership, where he learned the O'Briens were on vacation at Stone Harbor. He was told that Mrs. O'Brien wanted her husband to relax, so she had insisted that they rent a house without a phone. No one at the dealership knew the address of the shore rental either, so Frankie was forced to wait until Mr. O'Brien's scheduled call to the dealership two days later, during which the assistant manager promised to get him an address. Two days before the funeral, Frankie dutifully drove to Stone Harbor and delivered the news in person. It was a horrible experience.

Mrs. Francelli had refused to participate in decisions about the funeral arrangements. She considered them irrelevant. What difference did it make about the shape of his tombstone, or the type of flower arrangements on display. Nothing really mattered now that Johnny was gone. When Mr. McGinnis came to the house to get her input, she reached for his hand and said, "Thank you so much for all that you're doing. You are so kind, but please just do whatever you feel is best." So Anna Francelli, who had done so much for "her boys" over the years, cooking, and teaching, and nurturing, sat silently as Frankie, Sissy, Father Creeden and Mrs. Sweeney helped Mr. McGinnis plan her son's funeral.

There was one exception, one thing that was important to her. Anna agonized over what to do about pall bearers. Johnny's life couldn't be captured by a piece of granite or flowers. Johnny's life was the people he knew and loved. He had a circle of friends as close as anyone could have, and she would be denied the one thing she wanted at this moment- their presence at his funeral. Nick and Jimmy were in Vietnam, and God only knew Nick's fate. Angelo was in Canada, and Billy Moyer was in Washington. Young Ralph McGinnis was still away at college, but she was told he would probably be home in time for the services. Charlie Gario was a casual friend, but not nearly as close as the others, and he was still using a cane from his leg injury. Anna's family was small and couldn't produce enough cousins or uncles for the task. So she finally decided to accept the army's offer of an honor guard from nearby Fort Dix, New Jersey.

The family had gathered at the McGinnis funeral home to accompany the casket to the church. It had been closed since its arrival from Vietnam and would remain that way. Anna was grateful that her last image of her son would be his brave smile on the day he left for overseas. There had been no public calling hours at the funeral home either. In another brief interjection of her wishes, she had insisted that those who wanted to pay their respects could do so where it mattered most, in church.

It was a six-block drive from the funeral home to St. Therese's, and the mayor had stationed a police car and officer at every intersection to stop traffic. The officers were in dress uniform and saluted as the funeral cars passed.

When the procession arrived at St. Therese's, Frankie escorted Anna up the steps, and Tom assisted Sissy. Anna had been stoic throughout the morning, but when she stepped into the church, she was overcome by what she saw. Given the small size of her family, she was expecting a modest gathering and wasn't prepared for the throng that was present. Every pew was full, and people were standing along the side aisles.

Of course there were the people she expected, relatives, neighbors, people from her work place, friends and classmates of Sissy. She appreciated their presence. But there were others whose attendance touched her more deeply, people from the chapters of Johnny's short life. The current youth choir from St. Therese's school was there, as were Sister Katherine and several of the other nuns. She noticed the parents of most of Johnny's friends, including Nick's and Jimmy's. Her heart ached for anyone whose children were still in Vietnam, especially Nick, who was still missing in action. Both couples were sitting next to the aisle, and she stopped to hug and whisper encouragement to each of them. They were there to express their condolences to her, but the looks on their faces conveyed much more. There was absolute terror in Jimmy's mother's eyes, and Nick's mother's suffering was so profound that she could barely sit erect. When Mrs. Francelli leaned over, Nick Harding's mother clutched both of her hands and drew her closer. The look in her eyes said, "Why has this happened to our sons?" This was why Anna had refused to go to the Blue Star Mother's support group. This was something a person could only experience once. Anna held her for a long time, as Frankie and everyone else in the church watched and waited.

Finally, she continued up the aisle. She noticed that Billy Moyer had come home from Washington and was sitting with his parents. Ralph McGinnis was there too. She saw an elderly couple she didn't know. Frankie acknowledged them quietly as Jake and Stella as he passed them. Even in a small town like Bristol, she had never met Jake, and she was pleased to be able to put a face to the name she had heard so often. She thought about the countless hours her son had spent at the arcade. She nodded to him and whispered thank you to Stella. Jake was openly crying. Coach Lukins was in the crowd, sitting with several of Johnny's former teammates. The coach was clearly overcome and was being consoled by one of the boys. Some of the players wore their old red and gray football jerseys. There were scores of other classmates whose names she didn't remember or never knew. There were a handful of teachers from Bristol High School, and each invoked a different memory. The school principal was there, as were the superintendent of schools and several members of the local school board. Joe Gallagher, one of the high school custodians, was there. She only knew him by name, but she knew the kids loved him. Seeing him brought her to more tears. She wondered about the conversations her son may have had with Mr. Gallagher in the halls of Bristol High. She wanted to know how their lives had touched each other. She wanted to soak up and hold on to every relationship, every interaction her son ever had and was profoundly saddened by the knowledge that she never would.

She was in no hurry as she walked down the aisle as she had done thousands of times before. Frankie steadied her by placing one powerful arm around her waist and braced her elbow with the other. Each time she composed herself, something else set her off. When she saw Ding Roberts in the crowd, she brought her hands to her face, and the tears flowed again. Ding was a former co-worker and friend of her husband Jack. They had been union shop stewards together. It was Ding who had saved her and the kids a place by the rope when Kennedy visited Levittown. Now, Ding was an officer for the union. Seeing him brought back wonderful memories of her life with Jack and the terrible reminder of Jack's funeral in this same church. It was Ding who had visited her house three days earlier with an envelope containing three thousand dollars cash to cover Johnny's funeral expenses. He knew that the military funeral allowance wouldn't come close to covering her bills, so he took up a collection from the guys in the union hall. When word spread that Jack Francelli's kid had died in Vietnam, the money came in easily. When Mrs. Francelli explained that the McGinnis Funeral Home was handling the service without charge, Ding insisted that she take the money anyway. He told her more would be coming as collections continued at the Mill.

Frankie thought about his mother's funeral just three months earlier. Even though she'd been ill with complications from her diabetes, and her condition had been worsening, Frankie didn't expect her to pass so suddenly. Life was too hard, and he allowed himself a moment of self-pity before he looked at Anna and shook it off. His job was to care for her today, not worry about himself.

When they got to the front of the church, Frankie was relieved to see Allison and her parents sitting in the second pew. He had met Debbie at the shore earlier in the week, and she was with them. Frankie was grateful that Debbie was able to stay with Allison when he returned to Bristol after breaking the news.

As Anna made her way into the first pew, she turned and embraced Allison. The girl was devastated. She was as beautiful as ever; the shore sun had lightened her hair and tanned her skin, but her normally bright, sparkling eyes were swollen and red. She was sobbing uncontrollably as she squeezed Anna's neck and rocked gently from side to side. Anna hadn't seen her for almost two years, but at that moment she felt she was holding on to a huge part of Johnny's life. "We loved each other Mrs. Francelli," Allison said, still holding on. "We truly did."
"I know," Anna said. "My son told me. He never seemed happier."
When they broke their embrace Allison introduced Anna to her parents. They extended their condolences, and she thanked them warmly for coming. Then Allison said, "And this is my roommate Debbie. In a way she knew Johnny too." Debbie looked as distraught as Allison and was crying openly. "So sorry," she mumbled, as they embraced briefly.
"Thank you so much," Anna whispered. "Please take good care of Allison."
"I will," Debbie said firmly. "Forever."
Anna turned to the front of church in time to see Father Creeden and the altar boys take their place at the foot of the altar. He glanced only briefly in her direction and looked as though he was having trouble keeping his composure.

The honor guard began its walk up the center aisle, escorting the flag-draped coffin as the choir sang, *Be Not Afraid*. Father Creeden used the prayers and rituals of the Catholic Requiem Mass as a welcomed crutch. He seemed almost trance-like as he read from the book of prescribed invocations.

At the appropriate time, Sissy and Frankie did short readings from the old and new testaments. Sissy had insisted upon being a part of the service and, of course, pressed Frankie into playing a part as well. Once again, Frankie gave in to the family's wishes. Both struggled, but got through it. Next it was time for Father Creeden to read the gospel and deliver the homily.

He stood at the podium and scanned the congregation. Aside from Easter Sunday, and midnight Mass at Christmas, he had never seen the church so crowded. He was terrified by the emotional task before him. He knew all parishioners were equals and he worked hard not to show favoritism, but the Francelli family had been different. Father Creeden was an only child, so he had no nieces or nephews, and his parents had passed away. He enjoyed the fellowship of the other priests, but privately, he considered the Francelli's to be his secular family, and this funeral Mass was for the son or favorite nephew he would never have. He needed to be strong.

He compensated for his fear by projecting his voice louder than usual as he read the gospel. He refused to show weakness, when so many people were feeling so empty.
When the gospel was over he began his homily.

"From the time I heard the news of Johnny's death a week ago, I've agonized over what I would say that would somehow bring comfort in the face of such loss. Anna and Sissy and I have talked all week, but still this day loomed as the day we would offer our final goodbye to an incredible human being. Johnny was a young man who had a thirst for life and who elevated everyone around him with his spirit, energy and love."

He paused to take a breath. "I searched for the right words, and I came up empty. I prayed for guidance but received none. I read the materials provided by the archdiocese, but they left me wanting more. So I told the Lord that I'd be patient, and I waited. Wednesday came and I had no answer. Thursday was the same. Normally, I sit down with the grieving family the day before the funeral to learn more about their loved one before preparing my remarks. But I know this family as well as any in the parish. I watched Johnny grow. He served Masses for me. I watched him and his friends play Little League baseball, and high school football. I spent countless hours with them at the Francelli house. We watched Eagles games together on Sunday afternoons and talked sports. I marveled at his emotional strength when he lost his father to a tragic accident. The same is true of his mother Anna and sister Sissy. There was little they could tell me that I didn't already know. So yesterday passed, and when I went to bed last night, I still didn't know what I would say today."

He paused again and looked at Anna. "Then, I realized the reason I couldn't find the words was because I was angry. I was angry with God, and my anger was clouding my ability to hear his message."

He let that sink in before continuing.

"I wonder how many of you are surprised that a priest would admit being angry with God. Well, the truth is that I was, and I'll bet some of you are too. We're only human." He paused again.

"At one o'clock this morning I got out of bed, came to this church, knelt in the very pew where Anna is sitting now, and I had it out with God. I looked at the crucifix behind me and asked, 'Why this kid? Why this family? Why so young?' I stared at the crucifix for the longest time, but there was no reply, nothing stirred inside me. Then a message broke through the clouds of my grief to shine light on the obvious. There was no answer because there is no answer. There is no rhyme or reason to God's will, so there is no use in trying to figure it out. I've always known that, but I was too overcome by sorrow and nearsightedness to acknowledge it.

So now I know that there is something I can say to Anna, and Sissy and the rest of you today. I can say it with clarity and conviction. It's a simple message that you've heard so many times." He stopped speaking and let the silence build for a moment. Then he said, "Johnny Francelli is in heaven. Isn't that the most powerful thing our faith teaches us? Isn't that what gives explanation to the unexplainable? Isn't that what renders all other concerns meaningless? He is now enjoying eternal life. I'm as sure of that as I've ever been of anything, because Johnny Francelli was a good person and a person of faith, and ultimately, that's what God asks of us.

The sounds of people's sobs could be heard throughout the church, but Father Creeden was feeling stronger now and he continued. "Martin Luther King, Jr. died just three months ago. Before his death he was once asked what he wanted people to say about him when he was gone. In his now famous Drum Major Speech he said he wanted people to know that he lived a committed life, and he wanted people to know that he tried to help somebody. That was all. One of the most moral and courageous leaders of our time wanted people to remember him for those two simple things. Now I'm not equating Johnny with Martin Luther King. Lord knows Johnny Francelli wasn't an angel. I can tell you that on more than one occasion I saved him from being banished from St. Therese's because Sister Katherine was at her wits end in dealing with him. And surely Anna had the patience of Job to deal with some of his antics. But both of them knew that he was just a kind, fun-filled kid who loved life and loved people and adventure. It was the adventure part that sister had a problem with." He winked at sister and forced a smile, and the audience enjoyed a much-needed reprieve.

Father allowed people to catch their breaths and then continued. "But there is a loose parallel between what King said and how Johnny lived.

In our numerous talks, Johnny told me that he didn't know what he wanted to do with his life, but he wanted to do something significant. It's uncommon for a boy to say that at such a young age. One could tell that he wasn't speaking of a career in the economic sense. When he spoke of his future you got the sense that there was some sort of calling growing beneath the surface. He hadn't put his finger on it yet, but there was something there. He spoke of it more after visiting Washington to see President Kennedy lie in state at the capitol. Sadly, we'll never know what that calling may have been, but I'm certain that, like King, it involved making a contribution and leading a committed life."

He looked at Anna again. "And so, we are left to dream of what might have been, but we can take comfort in knowing that fame or wealth would not have sustained him. He wanted something more, because Johnny Francelli measured success through his relationship with people." He paused again and scanned the room slowly. "Judging by the turnout in church today, he was already quite successful."

Anna smiled slightly and put her arm around Sissy. Father nodded and smiled back.

"The army tells us that Johnny died a hero, that he lost his life in the act of saving another. I'm reminded again of King who wanted to summarize his remarkable life by asking that people simply remember him as trying to help someone. In the final analysis, that's all Johnny was doing, trying to help someone.

"In one of her darkest moments, Anna told me that this war ripped her son out of her arms like a monster in the night and devoured him. They were strong, painful words, spoken with the true anguish of a bereaved mother." He took a deep breath. "But I have a different thought. I believe that God has been smiling upon Johnny for a long time, and that he gently lifted him from his mother's arms to serve as an example for all of us. That we may never breathe another breath or live another day without being touched by the manner in which Johnny Francelli soaked up all the life he could experience and died in the noblest manner, by laying down his life for another."

By now, Father Creeden was emotionally spent. Choking back his own tears he said,
"May God Bless Johnny Francelli and the Francelli family."

49- Charlie Gario

The reception that followed at Anna's house was a typical Bristol event, with everyone pitching in. Mrs. Sweeney put out meatballs, sausage, and ziti. Billy and Ralph did whatever the ladies in the kitchen asked, while Frankie and Tom kept a tub on the back porch filled with soda and beer. Bono's Market, where Anna bought her groceries, donated a tray of lunchmeat, and almost every visitor brought more food. The house was so jammed that the neighbors on both sides made their bathrooms available to the crowd.

People came and went. Some stayed just long enough to pay their respects; others stayed for hours. When Sissy counted a hundred and eighty-seven names in the guest book, with people still arriving, she told her mother they should have rented a hall.
Anna said softly, "This was Johnny's home, Sissy. We belong here today."
The mayor came, as did the police chief, who positioned a policeman in the street to help handle traffic.

Everyone wanted a word with Anna, and she held up well throughout the day. She accepted countless expressions of sorrow and thanked everyone for their kind support. She wept occasionally, but for the most part, she smiled bravely. Frankie admired her strength, but worried about how she would be when the guests finally left. Gradually they did.

By six o'clock only Sissy, Tom, Frankie, Billy, Ralph, Allison, Debbie, Father Creeden, and Mrs. Sweeney remained. While Mrs. Sweeney put things away, Anna took Allison aside and said, "Let's have that visit you talked about in your letter."

They sat alone in the dining room and talked for a long time. They held hands, and consoled each other as they took turns crying. Once, when Allison started to sob badly, Anna held her until she was calm. After a while, Anna walked to a cabinet and returned with a small stack of photos. Soon they were pointing things out and smiling through their tears. Finally, they stood and embraced one more time, each offering strength to the other. They wiped their eyes, smoothed the wrinkles in their dresses and walked hand in hand to the living room. Allison winked at Debbie and forced a smile. Debbie smiled back and nodded her encouragement.

Soon they were all seated in the living room, sharing fond memories of Johnny. Billy was a great storyteller, and he had everyone laughing. Even Frankie welcomed the emotional release. Then it was time for confessions. The boys admitted things they had done over the years, innocent pranks that were mostly Johnny's idea. Anna knew most of the stories already, but enjoyed hearing every word again.

Billy was in the middle of a great tale about stealing tomatoes and squash from a neighbor's garden to give to the nuns, when the doorbell rang. It was Charlie Gario.

He was still walking with a pronounced limp and he carried a cane. He greeted everyone and crossed the room to Sissy and Anna.

"I'm so sorry," he said, as he leaned over to kiss Sissy on the cheek. He smelled like he'd been drinking. Then he approached Anna and gave her a long hug.

"I'm very sorry, Mrs. Francelli. This is terrible," he said.

"Thank you, Charlie," Anna said. "It's nice of you to come. We were just telling stories about Johnny. Would you like something to drink?"

"Beer would be great," he said, and Tom left the room to get it.

Concerned that Charlie's entrance might break the mood, Debbie said, "So Sister Catherine was telling you guys what good boys you were for bringing her the tomatoes and squash. Then what happened."

Billy's eyes lit up. "Then she says, these are so beautiful; where did you get them?"

"Good question," Debbie said.

"Exactly," Billy replied. "Now there's a code out there. You don't lie to nuns. It's okay to steal a little squash, especially if it's for a good cause, like this was, but we draw the line at lying to nuns. I mean, we didn't think God would really keep us out of heaven for eternity over two bucks worth of squash and tomatoes. But lying to a nun, who knows?"

"So what did you do?" Allison asked.

"We stood there like idiots, not saying anything for a long time. Then, with all the enthusiasm he could muster, Johnny said, 'Vegetables are good for you, sister.'"

There was more laughter. "That's it?" Sissy asked, actually giggling. "That's what he said?"

"That was it. 'Vegetables are good for you, sister.' It wasn't much, but it was all we had at the time."

Sissy stayed with it. "So what did sister say?"

"Well," Billy said. "She didn't know what to say. She didn't want to hurt Johnny's feelings, so she said, 'You're certainly right, young man. Vegetables are good for you.' That's when good ol' Frankie here said, 'Wow it's getting late, we'd better get home for dinner.' Johnny jumped in with a quick, 'bye, Sister,' and we all took off."

Everyone was having a good laugh.

Billy said fondly, "Johnny was a natural leader. He just had something other people don't have."

Charlie was shaking his head. When it got quiet again, he muttered, "What a waste."

Sissy didn't quite hear him and said smiling, "I'm sorry, Charlie; I didn't get what you said."

He spoke louder now. "I said, what a waste."

"How do you mean?" Sissy asked, her smile gone now.

"I mean this war is a stinkin' waste."

Frankie leaned forward and said quietly, "Charlie, this isn't the place…"

"Hey, she asked me," he interrupted.

"My brother is a hero," Sissy said proudly. "He fought for his country."

"Yeah," Charlie said. "And what did that get him. What did it get all of you?"

Anna was visibly upset. "I'm going to get more coffee," she said, leaving the room quickly.

Frankie stood and said quietly, "Charlie, I think it would be best if you leave now."

Charlie stood too. "You know I'm right, Frankie. You know this war isn't worth a damn."

"What a jerk!" Debbie yelled, as Allison started to cry again.

"Just leave, Charlie," Frankie said. "Nobody wants to hear this."

Reluctantly, Charlie moved to the door. Frankie could tell he had been drinking more than they realized.

When he got to the door he looked at Allison and said, "I'm just saying what I feel. I didn't mean to upset anybody. I loved Johnny."

"We all did," Frankie said. "So just leave."

Frankie followed him to the porch.

Once outside, Charlie turned to face him with a menacing look.

"You think I jumped from the garage, don't you? You think I hurt my leg on purpose?"

"It doesn't matter what I think," Frankie said. "Just leave."

He placed his hand on Charlie's back to guide him away. Charlie dropped his cane and gave him a hard shove in the chest. "Don't touch me," he said.

Frankie held back. "I'm not asking you anymore, Charlie. Go."

"Big, bad Frankie," Charlie mocked, reaching down for his cane. "What makes you so high and mighty? Everybody knows it's your fault Johnny is dead."

Aside from football, Frankie had never hit anyone in anger in is life. Now he exploded. He launched a punch just as Charlie swung his cane at his head. The cane broke in half on Frankie's forearm as the punch landed squarely on Charlie's jaw. Charlie fell backward and stumbled down the porch steps. Frankie was on him like a bear. He punched his face again, and Charlie screamed out in pain. He was still holding half of the cane and swinging it wildly at Frankie's head. Frankie ripped it out of his hand and tossed it away. Then he punched Charlie again. He punched him for Johnny. He punched him for upsetting Anna and the girls. He punched him because he knew Charlie right about everything being his fault. He punched him because of the stinkin' war that took his friend. Charlie's screams brought everyone outside. Billy and Ralph tried to pull Frankie off, but he flung them away like rag dolls. Father Creeden and Anna were the last ones out the door, and Frankie kept punching Charlie Gario until he heard Anna scream for him to stop.

Part V
Coming Home

50- Dr. Foster

Debbie was a different person when she returned to Boston College in the fall. She had seen Allison shattered by Vietnam and was ashamed for having lived her life blissfully unconcerned about the war that she now felt was ravaging her generation. In Debbie's previous world, the war had been in some far off place, fought by faceless soldiers and dictated by leaders she didn't care about. Had she taken the time to watch the news, she would have known more, but she had been disengaged, floating from one frivolous activity to another, and ignoring the small but growing number of campus activists vying for her attention. She blamed the government somewhat for her earlier disinterest. As a twenty-year old, she was still legally too young to vote. It never mattered to her before, but now she found it astonishing that Johnny, the dead soldier and Nick the MIA, and all of their young friends who were devastated by the war, were denied the ability to shape government policy at the ballot box. They were old enough to suffer, but not to vote. So for starters, the new Debbie committed herself to two things, to learn as much as she cold about the war and to work to lower the voting age to eighteen.

Allison was different too. Months after Johnny's death, her condition was still fragile. Where she once radiated energy and enthusiasm, she was now sullen and withdrawn. Fortunately, Allison had the ability to escape to her schoolwork, and that helped. It was better than drugs or some other destructive behavior, Debbie thought, but she remained concerned about her. They still had long talks at night, and when they went to bed, Debbie could often hear her crying softly in the darkness.

Debbie was also haunted by the image of Frankie beating Charlie Gario. It was the most brutal thing she had ever seen. But she was bothered even more by Gario's statement that prompted it. He said that Johnny's death was a waste. It had been a stupid, insensitive thing to say. No one could disagree that Johnny was a hero. He had died saving another. But Gario's point was that neither Johnny, nor the guy he saved should have been in Vietnam in the first place, that the whole concept of the war was senseless. Was it? She needed to know. She wanted to keep an open mind. She wasn't about to be transformed into one of the disgusting, anti-war protesters she saw at the Boston Common rally the previous spring. The campus was full of them now. She had seen more anti-war rallies since then, filled with the same empty slogans she heard before. In her view most of the students were there, not because of conviction, but because they had a vested interest in ending the war- the draft. Others were there because it was a happening place to be.

She visited a couple of pro-war rallies as well. Though far fewer in number and sparsely attended, she found their rhetoric to be just as simplistic. She wanted answers, not slogans, and she was determined to get them.

In January she enrolled in a course titled 20th Century American Foreign Policy,

taught by Dr. William Foster, and she liked the class immediately. Dr. Foster was young; she estimated he was in his late twenties or early thirties. He was handsome, dynamic, and engaging. Young handsome professors were a rarity, and they were sure to attract their share of infatuated coeds. Some profs reveled in the attention and even cultivated it. What Debbie liked about Dr. Foster what that he clearly loved history and teaching more than he loved the attention of the girls. He brought a passion to his work that was infectious and could bring life to the dullest topics. The course began with a brief review of early American expansionism: the Louisiana Purchase, Florida, the annexation of Texas, the Mexican war that yielded California and the southwest, the deal with England to acquire Oregon, the purchase of Alaska from Russia, and the annexation of Hawaii. For Debbie, watching the United States grow was like adding so many pieces to a jigsaw puzzle, and the insights Dr. Foster provided were fascinating. Still, this wasn't what she was looking for.

Next, they reached the turn of the century and plowed their way through the Spanish- American War and Teddy Roosevelt. Foster was still interesting, but Debbie was growing impatient. She wanted to understand what was happening now, not sixty years earlier. She decided to do something about it.

It was common knowledge that Dr. Foster spent most of his unscheduled time in McElroy Commons, a place students and faculty frequented between classes to relax or grab a quick lunch. Debbie had seen Foster there on several occasions, sitting in a corner, marking papers and sipping coffee. She decided to look for him now and approach him. She found him at his usual table, engrossed in his reading.

"Excuse me, Dr. Foster," she said.

"Yes," he said, looking somewhat surprised.

"I'm sorry to disturb you," she lied. "My name is Debbie Meyers. I'm in your ten o'clock foreign policy course."

"Oh yes," he smiled. "I'm sure I've seen you out there in the sea of faces. It's difficult with so many students in the lecture hall."

"I'm really enjoying your course," she said.

"I'm glad to hear that," he replied, still smiling.

"I wonder if I could ask you a question," she said.

Dr. Foster's smile faded slightly. He loved interacting with his students, but he'd also learned to keep his relationships professional. "Of course. I have posted hours, and if you're having a problem with the course you can call the department office to make an appointment. You can also get some help from my teaching assistant."

"I'm not having a problem," she said. "At least not in the sense you mean."

"I'm not sure I understand," he said, becoming more guarded.

Debbie pulled out the chair next to him and sat down. Foster glanced at his papers briefly. He was really hoping to spend the afternoon putting a dent in them, and he didn't need the interruption.

"Dr. Foster, I'm really anxious to talk about Vietnam," she said.

Foster relaxed a little. "We will," he reassured her. "But the course is chronological. We have a lot to get through before Vietnam, but I'll be spending at least a week on it in May."

Debbie leaned forward. "Dr. Foster, I just can't wait that long."

Foster shook his head and exhaled deeply. Now he understood; he'd seen the type before, Jane Fonda wannabes, radicals who couldn't wait to argue with the professor in class. They went on anti-war rants that set off the Barry Goldwater types, and before long the hawks and doves would be shouting at each other and learning would cease. Foster was tired of it from both sides.

"Listen Miss."

"Debbie," she added respectfully.

"Yes, Debbie." He forced a smile. "There are plenty of outlets on campus for your views on the war. There are rallies almost every week where you can express yourself. I suggest…"

"I'm sorry to interrupt, professor, but that's my problem. I don't have a view on Vietnam. I don't know what to think and I don't want to find out from a bunch of screaming lunatics."

Foster listened.

"I've been in your class for two weeks. I've heard you analyze things from different points of view. I like that. I'd like to learn about Vietnam that way. I've read a lot of things on my own, but I have a ton of questions."

Foster was impressed. He was disappointed that she knew so little about such an important topic, but impressed by her desire to learn.

"Listen, Debbie. I'm flattered by your comments and I appreciate your desire to get to the more timely topics quickly. You need to know that this is a survey course. It's designed to give you the broad perspective you need so that when we do examine Vietnam, you'll be able to evaluate it in the context of our past failures and successes."

Debbie didn't respond, but he could tell she wasn't satisfied.

"Tell you what," he offered. "If you let me grade my papers now, I'll do my best to pick up the pace of the course. Maybe I can get us to Vietnam a week sooner and spend an extra week on it in the spring. How would that be?"

Debbie didn't answer. She lowered her head, and a tear ran down her cheek. She wiped it with her sleeve.

"Okay," Dr. Foster said. "I give up. Tell me what's going on here."

That opened a floodgate of emotions. Debbie told him about Allison and Johnny, Johnny's funeral, Allison's depression, Nick the prisoner of war, Charlie Gario's statement, Mrs. Francelli's pain, everything.

When she was finished, she said, "So that's what's going on. I left Boston College for the summer and I walked into a world I didn't know existed. I can recite the Greek alphabet forward and backward. I know the lyrics of most of the fraternity songs on campus. I can dance my ass off for four hours straight. But I don't know a damn thing about this war, and I hate myself for it. For the first time in my life I feel like a stupid little girl."

She reached for his napkin without asking and wiped the tears from her eyes.

"I'm sorry to bother you with this," she said. "It was rude of me. I'll see you in class."

She started to leave, but Dr. Foster grabbed her forearm.

"Sit down Debbie," he said softly. "I'm so sorry. You've been through a lot."

She nodded, still trying to compose herself.

He placed his stack of papers in his binder and closed it.

"I'm going to get us a cup of coffee. When I get back, we'll figure out where to begin."

51- Jimmy's Home

Jimmy was the first to come home. There was no fanfare or welcoming parade. In fact, no one but his parents knew he was back until he appeared at Frankie's doorstep late one afternoon.

"Hi, Frankie. I'm home," he said when Frankie opened the door. There was no emotion, no smile. He looked thinner and his eyes lacked the glint they once had.

Frankie was floored to see him. "Jimmy!" he howled, stepping forward to give him a bear hug. "Come in, it's freezing outside."

Jimmy smiled weakly and stepped in from the January cold.

"I didn't know you were back in town, or even discharged."

"No big deal," Jimmy said flatly. "I'm here."

"That's it?" Frankie said excitedly. "You're finished?"

"Yeah, I'm finished," Jimmy said, still without enthusiasm.

"Take your coat off and sit down," he said. "How about a beer? Can I get you a beer or a coke?"

"No thanks," Jimmy said. He took a seat and looked at Frankie without speaking. When the silence became awkward, Frankie said, "So how are you?"

"Better than most guys, I guess," and his eyes started to fill up. Seeing that, Frankie's did too. When he recovered, Jimmy said, "It killed me when mom wrote about Johnny. I can't believe I couldn't be here for the funeral. And Nick," he paused to compose himself again. "The whole thing's been eating at me."

Frankie stayed quiet. For the first time he had something to be grateful for. As bad as the whole funeral experience had been, at least he'd been there. He couldn't imagine what it was like for Jimmy being away. And as for Nick, he was Jimmy's best friend, his protector. The news about Nick had to be tougher on Jimmy than anyone outside of Nick's family.

"Nick's alive, Jimmy, that's huge," Frankie offered.

"Yeah, he's alive. Now we have to get him back."

Two weeks earlier, the army notified Nick's family that his status had been changed from Missing in Action to Prisoner of War. It had been in the papers. Now, months of wondering whether or not Nick was alive had been replaced with anxiety over his condition.

"How about you?" Jimmy asked. "How are you handling all of this?"

"It's been six months since we heard about Johnny, and I still feel like jumping off a bridge every day. But I don't, and I won't. I work a lot and sleep a lot. I visit Mrs. Francelli at least once or twice a week, and I help Mr. Marzo restock the shelves at the deli when his orders come. It's too hard for him."

"Too bad Angelo isn't there to help him," Jimmy said dryly.

"I've got no place to judge," Frankie said. "So I don't. Maybe I'd feel different if I were in your shoes."

"I'm not judging," Jimmy said. "I don't give a damn what Angelo does. He can come home tomorrow or stay in Canada forever. I don't care. Lot's of guys didn't come home, except in a box. Angelo's just another one."

This was a much darker Jimmy than the one Frankie had known for so long.

"Jimmy, I can't imagine what you must be thinking. What you've gone through yourself, and what it must have been like being away while everything happened. You got a bad deal, a real bad deal."

Jimmy laughed sarcastically. "A bad deal? That's one way to put it. Sounds like baseball. The Phillies make bad deals. What happened to me was a little different. I got screwed Frankie. I tried to do everything my country told me to do and I got screwed."

"I'm really sorry," Frankie said softly. "I am."

"You've got nothing to be sorry about. What happened to me had nothing to do with you. It's all just luck. You had some good luck with your physical, others didn't. Everyone understands that."

"Well I don't," Frankie protested. "I was the only guy home. You guys were off doing your duty and I was home dealing with the shame of doing nothing."

"Don't call what I did duty," Jimmy said. "Maybe the other guys, but not me."

Frankie asked carefully, "What did you do?"

Jimmy didn't respond right away. He saw a flash of his friend Maldanaldo right before the bullet entered his neck. He saw the sniper he shot fall from the tree. He saw the dead VC in the cave. He saw the blackness of the tunnels, all the images that visited him each night. "Frankie," he said softly, "don't ask me what I did. Not today or any other time. Just don't ask me."

Frankie nodded. "Okay," he said.

They sat in silence again. Then Frankie tried to break the mood. He smiled and smacked Jimmy's knee. "So tell me about your discharge. You must have been flying high when you got to leave."

Jimmy shook his head. "When my tour in Nam was up, they told me I was getting out a month early. They do that with guys. You've had your training, you've served your stint in Nam, why keep you around a base in the states if they don't need you? So they send you home. Fine with me. They gave me a quick exit physical, and declared me physically healthy. Then they asked me if I had any emotional issues I wanted to talk with someone about. 'Now why would I have any emotional issues?'

I said. 'Just because I spent a little time in Nam? Nothing unusual happened,'" he said mockingly. "I don't need no shrink. They said 'Good,' wished me good luck and said good by. They flew me to San Diego and gave me transportation vouchers for the rest of the way to Philly." Jimmy shook his head again. He looked bitter. "One day I'm in a foxhole in the jungle and two days later I'm on a plane heading home. My whole squad got the same treatment. I knew guys who were afraid to sleep at night. Guys who experienced things they'll never forget, and the goddamned army kicked all of us out the door with a stinkin' transportation voucher."

Frankie listened.

"What's today?" Jimmy asked.

"Saturday," Frankie said.

"Saturday," Jimmy repeated bitterly. "On Wednesday I was in the jungle wondering if every bush or tree was hiding someone who was going to kill me. Now on Saturday, I'm sitting in your house. It doesn't feel right yet, know what I mean?"

Frankie didn't, but he tried to imagine.

Jimmy went on. "I traveled ten thousand miles to get home, and all I'm thinking about during the whole rotten trip is Johnny and Nick." There was a flash of anger in Jimmy's eyes. "Sometimes I just want to hurt somebody." Jimmy rubbed his eyes and ran his hand through his hair. Then he said in a low voice, "I've been sleeping with the lights on."

This was definitely a different Jimmy than the one who left town a year and a half ago, Frankie thought.

"But the hell with that," Jimmy added, showing the first hint of his old mischievous smile. "Mom tells me you got yourself in a little bit of trouble a while back. She said it was in the paper."

"It was blown way out of proportion," Frankie said.

Jimmy leaned closer again. "So tell me about it."

"I'd rather not," Frankie said. "It's over."

There was a look of anger again. "Damn, Frankie, I've been in Nam for a year. One of my best friends is dead. Another one is a POW. Another one took his chicken ass to Canada. I came home to find my father really sick. Mom says he's not gonna make it. He was fine when I left. My whole world is different, and I don't know crap about what's going on, and you'd rather not talk about it," he added mockingly.

Frankie took it all in. Jimmy was angry and had a right to be.

"I need you to tell me Frankie. Start with kicking the crap out of Charlie Gario, and then tell me everything you know about Johnny, his mom, Nick, everything. Please Frankie, I need it."

So Frankie did. He told him about the beating he gave Gario, and how Gario dropped the charges after he realized no one in town would ever talk to him again if he pursued it.

"Gario's an ass. I'm glad you did it, and you should be too," Jimmy said. "You're always feeling guilty about something. You did the right thing!"

Frankie didn't argue. He told him about the funeral, who was there, what Father Creeden said, while Jimmy sat back and stared blankly.

"As far as Nick goes," Frankie concluded, "I don't have anything more than what you probably read in the papers. But everyone is saying that Nixon will never end this war until he gets all of the POW's home."

"Right," Jimmy said. "We'll find out after he's sworn in." He thought for a moment and then added, "If I knew where Nick was I'd get some guys together and go get him myself. I swear to God I would. I'd crawl on my belly for miles if I had to so I could rescue his ass. I would. And I could do it too."

Frankie nodded as Jimmy continued.

"I've got some guys who would do it with me too." Then he perked up a little. "I got this guy named Roosevelt. He lives in Camden. A big-ass black guy. He reminded me a lot of you, big ass and all," with that he actually smiled. Frankie did too. "I love the guy. He saved my life. Not fighting, or anything like that. He saved me mentally. Some day, let's take a ride to Camden and find Roosevelt. I told him we'll go to a ball game together."

"Sure, Jimmy," Frankie said, relieved to see him enthused about something. "We'll do it. You just say when."

"Soon," Jimmy said, looking more relaxed now. "Let's go see Roosevelt real soon."

"Hey," Frankie said, building on the moment. "How about that beer now?"

"Why not?" Jimmy said. "A good cold beer with Big Frankie."

When Frankie returned with the beers, Jimmy was looking at the newspaper. "How'd the football team do this year?" he asked.

"Good," Frankie said. "They got better since we left."

"Impossible," Jimmy said. "We kicked ass. Or at least you did. I just caught a pass now and then."

"Our last Thanksgiving Day game is still the most exciting one anyone can remember. I'm still getting free haircuts for it," Frankie said. Then, without thinking, he added, "They had a short ceremony for Johnny at this year's halftime. They mentioned Nick too." He cursed himself as soon as he said it. Jimmy's mood was rising and he didn't want to destroy anything.

"That's nice," Jimmy said quietly and took a swig of his beer. Surprisingly, he changed the subject. "So, are you making any money?"

"I am, as a matter of fact. I'm working as a union carpenter with my uncle, and things are going pretty good. Right now it's all rough work, studding out walls, stuff like that. But he's showing me how to do trim work, which pays better, and I'm getting pretty good at it."

"That's great," Jimmy said. "When I'm ready to have my first house built, you'll be the guy."

"Deal," Frankie said, taking a long swig himself.

"What about you? What are your plans?"

"First I'm gonna go visit Mrs. Francelli and Nick's parents. Then I'm gonna try to sleep for a couple of weeks. I don't sleep too good anymore."

"You will now that you're home," Frankie said.

"We'll see," Jimmy replied. He didn't sound confident.

"What about making some money?" Frankie asked. "What do you plan to do?"

"They're holding my job for me at the steel mill. I'll guess I'll take it."
He didn't sound too interested.

"Sounds good," Frankie said. "It's good money."

"I guess," Jimmy said. "Money isn't everything."

"How about now?" Frankie offered. "I could spot you a few bucks until you get on your feet."

"Nah, I'm okay. I got my discharge money. Big friggin' deal. It comes out to about thirteen cents an hour. But I should be okay for a while."

"You're gonna be okay, Jimmy, you'll see," Frankie said.

Jimmy looked him straight in the eyes. The smile disappeared and so did the relaxed tone. "Listen, Frankie. Cut the crap. I'm not okay and neither are you, and I'm not sure if we ever will be."

52- Nixon

Five days after Jimmy got back to town, Anna and Sissy watched as Richard M. Nixon was sworn in as the thirty-seventh President of the United States. In his inaugural address he said, "The greatest honor history can bestow is the title of peacemaker." While his supporters were optimistic that he would end the fighting in Vietnam, his critics were wary.

Nixon's election had been close. Not as close as his razor thin loss to JFK in 1960, but close. With Bobby Kennedy gone and Gene McCarthy's campaign in disarray, the democratic nomination had fallen to President Johnson's choice, Vice President Hubert Humphrey. Humphrey faced the nearly impossible task of keeping favor with Johnson, and the party apparatus he controlled, while distancing himself from Johnson's failed war policies. As a loyal Vice President, Humphrey had supported those policies. Now, he had to convince the American people that he would manage the war differently. To make matters worse, the democratic convention in Chicago had been marred by one of the most disruptive political protests in American history. In contrast, the Republican,

Nixon, had reinvented himself. The former cold warrior and communist witch-hunter had offered himself as the peace candidate. The peace Nixon spoke of would be a "peace with honor." He had a "secret plan," he told the American people, a plan to bring the troops home, while preserving America's objectives in South Vietnam and her stature in the world. The contest was complicated by the third party candidacy of Governor George Wallace of Alabama. Wallace used inflammatory rhetoric to present a pro-war platform and reactionary positions on race and crime. The nation was virtually pulsating with divisiveness. Nixon enjoyed a comfortable early lead, but as expected, the race grew closer as the election approached. Ultimately, the American people voted for change, and Humphrey, like Johnson, became another casualty of the war.

Ever since Debbie first spoke to Dr. Foster in October, the two of them had been meeting at McElroy Commons every two weeks. Dr. Foster explained early on that he would help her, but only if she did her part to become informed. So Debbie became an avid student of current affairs. She read what he recommended, watched the news, and attended guest lectures. The more she learned, the more questions she had, and they became the focus of their meetings.

Dr. Foster had been careful to remain professional throughout their sessions. They always met in public, and he often made it a point to keep their discussions formal. In that context, they had become friends, and he enjoyed their sessions as much as Debbie did.

Now it was early May, and they were still at it.
"So how's your roommate?" he asked, when she returned with their coffee. It was her turn to buy.
"She's doing a little better," Debbie said. "She still won't even think about seeing any guys or anything like that, but she's spending some time with the girls, and we're seeing flashes of the old Allison now and then. Mostly though, she just studies."

"Takes time," Foster said. "Is she still talking with Johnny's mother?"

"Not as much as she had been," Debbie said. "But fairly regularly. It's awkward, because she doesn't want to get Mrs. Francelli down, but she's not ready to be upbeat."

"What kind of feeling does Johnny's mother project?"

"That's the thing," Debbie said. "She's very positive. Allison thinks it's an act, but she's trying."

"Then Allison should roll with it and try the same thing."

"I told her that," Debbie said. "And she's making an effort."

"What does she say about the war?"

"Nothing," she said. "Allison doesn't want to hear a word about it. I turn the news off when she's in the room."

"If that's how she's coping right now, that's fine." He took a sip of coffee and said,

"What will she do over the summer?"

"Her family rented a place in North Carolina for the season. They think it's best not to have her back in town reliving old memories yet. She's actually showing some enthusiasm about it. She loves the beach and wants a break from studying. I'm going to visit her for a couple of weeks."

"She's very fortunate to have a friend like you."

Debbie smiled. "It works both ways," she said. Besides, she's helping me pass my other courses, since I spend all of my time on this stuff."

"It was your call," he reminded her.

"I have no complaints," she said brightly. "I might even change my major to International Relations."

"Wonderful," he said with a hint of sarcasm. "The want ads are filled with openings in the field."

"I'll get a job," she said confidently. "Maybe I'll become a professor and have an office next to yours."

Foster wasn't comfortable with any hint of a relationship beyond their meetings in the commons, and he changed the subject.

"It's your nickel. What do you want to talk about?"

"Before we talk about the war, I have a question about you," she said.

He looked uneasy.

"Well, actually, it's about you and the war," she added quickly.

When he didn't protest, she continued. "So many of the profs on campus have taken strong stands on the war. Most are against it; a few are for it. Anyway, my point it is, they get pretty vocal. Why not you? I'm not even sure what your position is."

"This may sound a little bland for you Debbie, but I'm a teacher. My job is to help students think, not tell them what to think. Students can be impressionable. Sometimes the loudest voice can win them over or they will embrace the position of a professor just because they like him. That's not learning or thinking. Neither is all the arguing. I really dislike the rancor that dominates the debate over the war because when the shouting starts or simplistic slogans are thrown at complicated issues, the learning stops. My colleagues can try to impress with their fiery speeches. I prefer a different approach." He smiled. "Is that good enough for you?"

She smiled back. "Good enough. That's why I picked you."

"I'm flattered," he said flatly. "So what's our topic today?"

"Well. We've done a pretty good job with the background. To put it mildly, you're a slave driver," she joked.

By now Debbie understood the origins of the conflict. She studied the French colonization of Vietnam and its impact on the Buddhist peasants. She traced Ho Chi Minh's emergence as a nationalist, fighting against foreign domination. She explored Ho's attraction to communism, his defeat of the French and their retreat from Vietnam. She studied the treaty that temporarily partitioned the country into a communist dominated North and pro-western South. She read how the domino theory prompted our support of the South. Eisenhower had said that if we didn't stop the communists in South Vietnam then all of Southeast Asia would fall to communism. Next, she studied Kennedy's early commitment, Johnson's decision to change our involvement from advisory to combat, the troop build up, and the resulting quagmire the United States found itself in. Now it was time to focus on speculation about what Nixon might do.

"You said you wanted to know how it started," he said evenly. "Now I think you do."

Debbie nodded. "The thing that kills me is that everyone examines the same set of facts, but they interpret them differently," she said.

"Exactly," he agreed. "Some see the background as clear justification to be in Vietnam and to stop the spread of communism."

"And others say it was an unjustified mistake all along," she added. "But while they debate, people like Johnny are dying. So now I want to know what you think. You're the professor. No fiery speech needed, just your opinion."

Foster sat back and savored a deep drink of his coffee. He allowed himself a long pause before responding.

"It really doesn't matter," he said.

Debbie shot forward. "No way, professor! I've killed myself studying everything you gave me. You're not going to get away with telling me your opinion doesn't matter. I want to hear it."

Foster loved her spunk and couldn't help but laugh at her tone.

"A bit inappropriate, don't you think? I am the professor."

Debbie laughed with him. "So what are you going to do, give me an "F" in student lounge discussions?"

Foster smiled again. It was hard not to like her.

"Come on," she insisted, playfully, "I'm serious. I want to know your opinion. Should we have gone there?"

Foster looked at her and shook his head. "You're not listening," he said patiently. "I'm not saying my opinion doesn't matter. My opinion *is* that, at this point, it doesn't matter why we're there or whether or not we were right in the first place. It's done. We're there. What really matters now is how we end this thing. How do we get out? How do we minimize additional causalities and protect our national interests?"

They both sat back and let that sink in.

Debbie spoke first. "You're not talking like winning is an option."

"It's not," he said flatly. "And it hasn't been for a long time, at least not at the price in lives and resources we'd be willing to pay. Secretary of Defense McNamara knew that long before he left office, but didn't have the courage to say it publicly. Johnson knew it when he refused General Westmorland's request for additional troops. Nixon knows it now. We can't win in the sense we're used to winning."

Debbie looked crushed. "You're saying they knew we couldn't win before Johnny died."

"Let me back up," he said. "I don't want to overstate this. I'm saying that McNamara, and other people close to the action had reached that conclusion. Surely there were others who thought otherwise."

It got quiet again. Debbie asked her next question as though she didn't want to hear the answer. "So has it all been a waste? Did Johnny die for nothing?"

Dr. Foster sat back again and exhaled slowly. Academic questions were easy, but when phrased in the personalized context of a young man's death, everything changed.

He took his time. "Listen Debbie. We put young men in extremely difficult positions. Given the circumstances, they've performed incredibly well. Johnny is an excellent example. He served his country willingly. From what I've heard, he was like most guys. He may not have been totally up on the issues, but he did what his country asked him to do, and he is a hero. That has to matter."

"Thanks," Debbie said dismissively. "I've told Allison that a thousand times. Now please answer my question. Has this war been a waste? Will we have accomplished anything when we're finished?"

"That depends upon what Nixon does next," he said carefully.

"I'm listening," she said.

From that point, Dr. Foster did most of the talking. He explained that in his view, the best the United States could hope for would be a negotiated settlement, with some kind of power sharing between the communists and non-communists in South Vietnam. People like news commentator Walter Cronkite had said that right after the Tet offensive, months earlier. A negotiated settlement would be less than what the hawks wanted, he explained, but at least it would avoid an all out defeat.

He explained that, early on, Nixon and his foreign policy advisor, Henry Kissinger, had made overtures to the communist government in Hanoi, indicating our willingness to negotiate. But Hanoi didn't bite. Even though they had been suffering set-backs on the battlefield, they believed that growing anti-war sentiment in America, brought about by a continued American death toll, would only strengthen their position in the future. Hanoi believed that the longer the war dragged on, the more likely Americans would want to pull out, giving Hanoi a total victory. So Nixon was faced with three choices: withdraw the troops immediately, increase our war effort, or prepare South Vietnam to be self-sufficient in its defense. Immediate withdrawal really wasn't an option. No one but the most fanatical anti-war factions advocated a policy that would leave the United States humiliated, hand victory to the communists, and teach our allies that we could not be trusted to honor our commitments. Not to mention that a rapid pull out would be dangerous to our troops in the field. So Nixon settled on a combination of the remaining two, increased military pressure, including more bombing raids, and stepped up training and equipping of a larger South Vietnamese army that would defend itself. Foster explained that Nixon was calling the program Vietnamization. Johnson had Americanized the war; now Nixon was determined to give it back to the Vietnamese.

Debbie was frustrated. "Meanwhile, American deaths are as high or higher than they were under Johnson. Some think Nixon is talking about winding down the war while he is expanding it."

Foster nodded. "There are scattered, unconfirmed reports in the press that say Nixon has secretly ordered the bombing of suspected North Vietnamese installations in Cambodia. But there are those who say that those kinds of raids can actually shorten the war by making it harder for the North Vietnamese to succeed."

"And there are those who fear that the war will widen," she retorted.

"I'm glad you did your homework. Aren't you?"

Debbie rested her elbows on the table and rubbed her temples.

"I read the other day that, as of the end of April, almost forty thousand Americans have died," she said bitterly. "Forty thousand! Almost six thousand just since Nixon took office. How many more deaths will there be before we know if Vietnamization will work?"

Dr. Foster looked at her with empty eyes. He didn't have an answer.

53- Parish Picnic

On June 22, 1969, Mrs. Francelli got up early to prepare for the parish picnic. The event was one of the highlights of the year. It was always well attended and everyone pitched in to set up or provide food. Her contribution would be fifteen pounds of her special potato salad. She had diced and cooked the potatoes the night before, so all that remained was to add the eggs, mayo, and other ingredients. She enjoyed the work and looked forward to seeing people.

It was almost a year since Johnny died, and Mrs. Francelli's days had become bearable. She still cried most nights, and rarely enjoyed a restful sleep, but she was beginning to find comfort in her daily activities. Shortly after the funeral, she resolved not be the somber, grieving mother, at least not in public. She felt that if she became a burden, people would grow tired of her, and she would soon find herself alone. She couldn't allow that. So, regardless of her pain, she worked at putting on a strong front. It was clear that keeping busy helped, so Father Creeden and Mrs. Sweeney kept her schedule as full as possible.

Privately, she continued to feel unspeakable pain. There were times when it hit her suddenly and took her breath away. At other times it came on slowly. She could feel it moving over her, like a vine covering every part of her body, until she felt paralyzed. She would fight it, try to free herself, but she couldn't. It was at those times when the demons would take over, sorrow, grief, and bitterness. They would dominate her, and she'd find herself lashing out at God, the government, or the Viet Cong. In her worst moments, she even lashed out at Johnny, for joining the army, for being a hero, for leaving her in such pain. Then, just as slowly as they had taken control, the feelings would fade, the vines would weaken. She'd snap them one by one and move again. She'd emerge from the darkness and prepare herself to face the next hour, and then the next day.

Frankie remained a frequent visitor and a tremendous source of support. She had always treated him as a second son, and she needed him now more than ever. She sensed that he felt the same way about her, especially with his mother gone. They established ground rules for his visits. There would be no sobbing testimonials, no grief, or pity sessions. Each knew how devastated the other was. It wasn't necessary to talk about the loss of Johnny. But they did agree to talk openly and freely about the Johnny who had lived, whenever a happy thought or fond memory surfaced.

She was glad that she'd see Frankie at the picnic. He had volunteered to shuck clams. The clam booth was next to the beer stand, and the men would eat clams, drink, joke, and talk about baseball. Later, tables would be set up, and they'd play pinochle until dark. Mrs. Francelli enjoyed the rare times when she'd seen Frankie laugh during the past year, and she was pretty sure today would be one of them.

She was slicing the eggs for the potato salad when the doorbell rang. No one she knew ever rang her bell or knocked; they just walked in. She wiped her hands and moved to the front of the house. When she opened the door she was surprised to see two young black men in military uniform. One was slender with pleasant features, the other was massive, with an expressionless face.

"Excuse me, Ma'am," the slender one said. "Is this the Francelli house?"

"Yes it is," she said cautiously.

"Are you Mrs. Francelli?" he asked softly.

"Yes I am," she said. "Can I help you?"

They were obviously nervous, but the slender one smiled. He tried to speak, but stopped to clear his throat. When he started again, he was barely audible.

"Ma'am, my name is Sam Johnson, and this is Norm Wallace." He paused to look down at his shoes. When he looked up he said, "We served in Vietnam with your son, Ma'am. We came to pay our respects."

Mrs. Francelli covered her mouth with her hands. Instinctively, she took a step back, unable to speak.

"I'm sorry, Ma'am. Maybe we shouldn't have come. It's just that we're heading home and we wanted to stop."

She reached out wordlessly, took him by the hand, and pulled him toward the house. Her eyes told the bigger man to follow.

"Please sit," she said.

The soldiers sat next to each other on the couch, and she took the chair across from them. She was still too shocked for words. It was then that she noticed the slender man was wearing prosthesis. It rose out of his right shoe and disappeared into his pant leg.

The man smiled. "I lost my leg below the knee. Stepped on a land mine."

Mrs. Francelli shook her head and said, "I'm so sorry." Her voice was thick and deep.

"It's okay," he said. "I consider myself lucky."

The bigger man still hadn't spoken, and the two men exchanged a glance, as if each was encouraging the other to speak.

The slender one continued. "Maybe I should start again. My name is Sam Johnson and this is Norm Wallace. Like I said on the porch, we served with Johnny in Vietnam."

Mrs. Francelli nodded in understanding. She looked dazed.

Then Johnson added gently. "Ma'am, your son saved my life."

The words jarred her. For a moment she looked like she would lose consciousness. Then, for the first time since the funeral, she cried in front of someone else. Johnson and Wallace sat there quietly, not knowing what to say. Finally, Johnson said, "We're sorry to have upset you, Ma'am, but we just had to come. We'll go now."

"No!" she said, much louder than she had intended. It startled them. "Please don't go yet," she added much more softly.

She left her chair and knelt beside him. She placed her hands on the sides of his face and looked into his eyes lovingly, as if Johnny's essence had taken the form of the man he saved. Then she embraced him and held him for a long time. Wallace, the giant who still hadn't spoken, had tears in is eyes.

"He saved you; he saved you," she kept repeating tenderly.

When she broke the embrace she looked embarrassed. She ran a hand through her hair and sat down again.

"Can you stay for a while?" She tried to sound composed, but the question sounded more like a plea.

"Sure. I have a plane to catch, but we have some time." He looked at Wallace, who nodded his approval.

"I'm so very glad you're here," she said, sounding much better now. "What can I get you? Have you eaten lately?"

"No thanks, Ma'am. We'd rather just visit with you. Although Johnny said you were the best cook we'd ever see. He said he'd have the whole squad over for dinner after..." he stopped and said, "Sorry. That was stupid."

"Oh no," she said. "Don't be sorry. Please tell me everything you can, every word he ever said, every promise he made. Everything you can remember. Please."

Johnson smiled. "Well, can't remember everything he ever said, and Wallace here has lost his voice I guess."

Wallace cracked a smile. He was a nervous wreck.

"But I can tell you a lot," Johnson said.

He began by telling her what an excellent soldier Johnny was, how he had learned everything and how the other men respected and depended on him. He told her about some of Johnny's pranks, how he kept the men loose. After a while Wallace relaxed and offered some stories of his own. They told her how much he seemed to be in love with Allison, and about the day Johnny received her letter saying that she loved him too.

She saw their visit as a gift from God and soaked up every word. In effect, Johnny had left her life the day he went to Vietnam. Her images of him were all from his time in Bristol. Now, she was getting glimpses of the precious short time he had in Vietnam. She could visualize him performing his duties at the camp, playing cards with the squad, writing and reading letters, playing touch football, telling stories. She absorbed it like the last drops of water in a desert.

Eventually, they exhausted their stories and the room became quiet. She wore a strange expression, like she wanted to smile and cry at the same time. In a way, the look was peaceful. Then she braced herself and said, "Please tell me what happened."

Johnson knew what she meant, and looked uncomfortable. He shook his head. "Maybe not, Ma'am. I don't know if that's a good idea."

"Please," she said. Her eyes were begging.

Then Wallace's deep voice came to life.

"We were on patrol, walking through elephant grass. Sam was in front and Johnny was next. The rest of us were spread out behind them. Sam stepped on a mine and got hurt pretty bad. Just then the enemy opened fire. It was an ambush and they had us pinned down good. The whole time the shooting's going on, no one can get to Sam, and we're afraid he's getting hit more."

At that point Sam jumped in. "I'm screaming from the pain in my leg, and bullets are landing all around me. Next thing I know, Johnny crawled through the high grass and he's there. It's scary as hell, bullets flying all over the place. He applied a tourniquet, which the doctors later said saved my life, gave me a shot of morphine, and then he started dragging me away from the action, exposing himself to fire so that he could pull me."

Wallace added, "It was the most selfless thing. It took courage, Ma'am."

She was crying softly now, and smiling through the tears.

Sam leaned closer to her. "Mrs. Francelli, the last thing your son did on this earth was save another person's life."

She nodded bravely and whispered, "Thank you."

They fell silent again, and Sam looked at his watch, but it was obvious Anna didn't want them to leave.

"And what about the two of you?" she asked.

Wallace said, "Sam's been at Walter Reed Medical Center for a few months, having some operations. How many did you have?"

"Seven," Sam said. "It's no big deal."

Wallace ignored the last comment. "Sam was at Walter Reed having seven operations, getting fitted for his new leg, and learning how to walk. I'm stationed back here at Fort Dix, New Jersey."

"Wallace here got himself promoted," Sam said. "He's training new guys. But he reenlisted. Can you believe that? The man is crazy."

"Got no place to go but the army," Wallace said. "Anyway, Sam's been discharged. He's flying back to Oakland tonight."

Sam interrupted. "My family lives there, and my girl Yolanda. She said Sam Johnson with one and a half legs is better than most men with two. She still wants to marry me."

"Of course she does," Wallace kidded. "If she was willing to marry you before with that messed up head of yours, why would a bad leg make a difference?"

They all laughed.

"Anyway," Sam said. "Wallace and I made a plan for me to take a train up from DC. Norm met me in Trenton, and we drove over."

"I'm so glad you did," she said. "You have no idea how important this was to me."

Wallace smiled for the first time. "Mrs. Francelli, can I tell you one more thing?"

"Of course," she said.

"All this stuff about the war, the protests and all. I know it really hurts the families of the soldiers, especially families like yours that lost someone, or men like Sam, who are injured for life. It can make you bitter, but let me tell you. Different guys over there looked at the war in their own way. I think Johnny supported it, but it doesn't matter, because some guys in the squad did, and some didn't. Some volunteered and some were drafted. But do you know what? In Nam, after a week or two in the jungle, none of that stuff mattered. Who's right? Who's wrong? Communism? Capitalism? The only thing that mattered was the guys you were with and the family waiting for you back home. That's it. You try to survive, you try to protect each other, and the war takes care of itself. We had a bond, Mrs. Francelli. We were one."

Now it was Sam's turn. "What Norm's saying is that the day you lost your son, we lost a brother. And that's the truth. I didn't want to go back to Oakland without telling you that there were people you hadn't met, people you didn't know, who loved your son."

Mrs. Francelli was overcome. She nodded her head, but couldn't speak. She wished Frankie or Sissy were there to meet the young men who said they loved Johnny. They would have enjoyed meeting them. Finally, she stood. They exchanged addresses, and hugged one more time, knowing that they'd probably never see each other again.

At the door Mrs. Francelli said, "I received a very nice letter about Johnny from a Sergeant Boyd. Will either of you be hearing from him soon?"

By the looks on their faces, she knew the answer before either of them spoke.

"He didn't make it," Wallace said. "He was killed about three weeks after Johnny died."

54- Fred's Bar

Frankie found Jimmy sitting on the steps of the shoemaker shop that faced Fred's bar.

"Where've you been?" Jimmy said. "You're twenty minutes late."

"Sorry, I fell asleep."

Jimmy looked agitated. "Next time set an alarm clock."

Frankie shrugged. "Why did you wait out here? You could have gone inside."

"I told you. You're my ticket," Jimmy said. "Hell, you look at least twenty-five or thirty. Nobody gets carded when they're with you."

"It doesn't matter here. They don't check ages."

Jimmy ignored him. "Can you imagine? After what I've been through, I'm not old enough to drink!" He mimicked an army officer. "Okay, sonny. Here's your M-16. Here's how you shoot it. Now go kill the bastards, but don't drink a beer when you get back home; you're too young." Frankie guessed that Jimmy had already been drinking.

"When will you be twenty-one?" Frankie asked.

"Exactly one month, May 30, 1970, will be my liberation day."

He thought for a minute and added, "Maybe I should have told the draft board I was too young. 'Sorry, guys,'" he said sarcastically, "I should have said, 'Too young to drink, too young to fight.'"

Frankie felt he owed it to Jimmy to be patient, but sometimes, like now, he got tired of his carping.

"Look, either we go home and wait a month, or you stop complaining and we'll have a beer and shoot some darts." Frankie said. "Which is it?"

"I'm not waiting a month," Jimmy said. "I plan to kick your ass in darts tonight! Lead the way."

Fred's was a sleepy blue-collar bar, a shot and beer place. Frankie and Jimmy slid in, looking as if they belonged there. It was a Thursday night, and there weren't many customers. A few men sat at the bar; two more were shooting pool in the corner. Frankie nodded to the bartender and laid down a ten-dollar bill.

"Two Buds," he said casually, as they climbed onto the stools.

The bartender eyed the ten and left to get the beer.

"I swear to God, Frankie, you look like you're forty," Jimmy whispered. "You could have been served when you were seven."

"Shut up," Frankie whispered back.

The bartender returned with the beers. "Glasses?" he said.

"No, we're good," Frankie said.

The bartender took the ten and returned with the change, which Frankie left on the bar.

"Cheers," he said, holding up his bottle to Jimmy.

"Bullshit," Jimmy replied. But he clinked his bottle anyway.

Frankie just shook his head and took a drink.

Jimmy immediately felt guilty. "I'm sorry, Frankie," he said quietly. "I don't want to be a pain in the butt. Sometimes I just can't help it. What's to be cheerful about?"

"I know," Frankie said. "But the routine is getting old." He didn't want to upset Jimmy, so he added, "Don't worry about it. Things will get better. You just have to work through it."

"I'm trying," Jimmy said, but he didn't sound convincing.

There was a small television mounted behind the bar, and the Phillies were playing.

Larry Bowa was the batter, and he laid down a perfect bunt to get on.

"Look at that!" Frankie said. "Now that's baseball. Bowa can play."

"Yeah, nice bunt," Jimmy said without much interest.

Jimmy's response was a bad sign. He was a Phillies nut before he went into the army. Now he acted as if he couldn't care less about baseball or anything else.

Frankie tried again. "Think they'll bring that Luzinski kid up from the minors this year? He can hit the ball a mile."

"Too young," Jimmy said, half-heartedly. "He's only nineteen. They shouldn't mess with people when they're too young. They can screw them up forever if they do."

Frankie knew Jimmy wasn't just talking about baseball. He gave up on conversation and focused on his beer.

They drank in silence and watched the game. After a while, Jimmy noticed Frankie eyeing him up and down, looking at his hair and his clothes.

"What's up?" Jimmy said.

"Nothing," Frankie replied, turning back to the television.

"No, not nothing," Jimmy said, sounding agitated. "You were looking me over. What's on your mind?"

Frankie exhaled slowly. He looked at Jimmy again and, as tactfully as he could, said,

"I was thinking maybe you could use a little sprucing up, that's all."

"Sprucing up?" Jimmy's tone was confrontational.

"Forget it," Frankie said, returning to his beer.

"Like hell," Jimmy persisted. "Tell me about sprucing up."

Frankie put down his bottle. "You've been letting yourself go a little," he said quietly. "Maybe a shower and a shave, a clean shirt. Maybe you'll feel better."

Jimmy kept his voice low, but he was angry. "What are you, my mother? You giving me a dress code?"

Frankie was regretting the whole exchange. "No, Jimmy, I'm just your friend trying to help."

Jimmy spun the bottle cap like a top on the counter, shaking his head in disgust.

"Like I need this from my friends," he said.

Frankie didn't reply.

"I worked all day," Jimmy said tersely. "I had dinner and sat on the corner waiting for you. Sorry if I didn't freshen up."

"Look," Frankie said. "It was just a suggestion. I wasn't just talking about tonight. Forget I brought it up."

Jimmy stayed with it. "In the bush we got to shower maybe once a month. We shaved once a week with cold water and a dull razor."

"Okay. I understand," Frankie said. "It's no big deal. Forget it."

Jimmy continued. "If you tried to wash off in a river or pond, you came out with goddamned leeches all over your body."

Frankie didn't know what to say. He sighed deeply, took a long drink of his beer and stared at the ball game. Since Jimmy came home, it seemed as if his moods were getting worse. His anger surfaced a lot. Occasionally there would be periods of the old, carefree Jimmy who was constantly fooling around, but the nasty Jimmy was getting more playing time lately. Frankie tried to be sympathetic. He couldn't imagine how bad Nam was, even on the best of days, but he had to get Jimmy out of his depressing mind-set soon. At times Frankie thought he would just take whatever garbage Jimmy threw at him, hoping that eventually, the moods would pass. At other times, he wanted to smack Jimmy around a little, knock some sense into him. The war was over for him. He'd been home for months. It was time to straighten out. He even thought of trying to find someone Jimmy could talk to, a counselor, or a doctor. He didn't know what to do, but he was committed to stay with his friend until he saw it through.

But Frankie had his own problems to deal with. He thought about Johnny's death and Mrs. Francelli every day, and he thought about Nick. The guilt and sorrow were still crushing at times, but he was trying to deal with it. Each time Jimmy acted out, it rekindled all of the fires burning inside of Frankie.

They sat quietly for a couple of minutes and then Jimmy said, "Sorry."
"Forget it. It was my fault," Frankie said. "Bad idea." He held up two fingers, and the bartender produced two more bottles.
Now Jimmy proposed a toast. "To our friends, Johnny and Nick," he said somberly, holding up his bottle.
"To Johnny and Nick," Frankie said.
Jimmy eyed a guy who was eating at the end of the bar. "I need some food," he said.

Fred's only had three menu selections: French fries smothered in brown gravy, pickled eggs, or a plate of hard salami and provolone cheese served with crackers.
He called to the bartender, "Can we get a couple of eggs, please?"
"Some salami too," Frankie said.
The bartender nodded. No one in this bar talked much.
He opened a large jar of pickled eggs that sat on the counter, and he used a pair of tongs to grab two, which he placed on paper plates. He gave each of them a plate and napkin, and disappeared into the back room for the salami and cheese.

Jimmy took a huge bite of his egg. He was still thin, maybe even a little lighter now than when he first left for Vietnam. Frankie guessed he weighed around a hundred and thirty pounds, about half of what Frankie weighed now. But he still had a tremendous appetite. At least that was something.

The bartender returned with the salami and took the money from the bar. The ten spot still covered everything. They both dug in.

"So how are things at the steel mill?" Frankie asked, between bites.

"Money's good," Jimmy said. "But I hate the place."

Another bad topic, Frankie thought.

"Why's that?" He asked reluctantly.

"My boss is always on me, constantly bustin' my chops."

"About what?"

"Everything," Jimmy said.

"Like?"

"I can't explain it. He's just telling me what to do all the time. I've had enough of that crap."

Again, Frankie guessed Jimmy wasn't just talking about the steel mill.

"Has your attendance been any better lately?" Frankie knew Jimmy had been reprimanded for missed work before.

"I miss a day every once in a while. It's no big deal."

"Look Jimmy, I'm saying this as a friend. You've got a good job. It's hard work, but if you work someplace else, you won't earn anything near what you can make right now at the mill."

"I know," Jimmy said. "Or I would have walked a month ago."

"Just try to stay with it."

"I'm trying," he said, stabbing a chunk of cheese with a toothpick.

"Do you have any idea what your foreman is looking for? What ticks him off?"

"Nah, he just has it in for me, that's all."

Frankie doubted that, but he left it alone.

"Just try to stay out of his way and do your job."

"I am," Jimmy said. "But sometimes I just feel like popping him, just one quick shot to the jaw." Jimmy mimicked throwing a jab.

"Don't do that," Frankie said. "You'll be finished."

Jimmy didn't respond.

"Maybe he just wants you to pay your dues for a little while," Frankie offered.

Jimmy gave him a cold stare. "I paid my dues before I even started there."

Frankie nodded.

By now the Phillies were down six nothing in the seventh.

"Wanna shoot those darts?" Frankie asked.

"I don't think I feel like it right now. Mind if we just relax?"

"Fine with me," Frankie said.

Another patron came in who seemed to know all the regulars. He looked to be in his early sixties and wore work clothes.

"Hey, Mike," he called to the bartender as soon as he came in.

"Hi, Herb," the bartender replied without smiling.

Herb joined the guys at the other end of the bar.

"Give me a Schlitz," he said, and slammed down some money.

"You guys hear about Nixon?"

Herb obviously thought that everything he said was important enough for everyone else to hear.

"No," Mike said, drying a glass. He didn't seem too interested.

"They're saying on the news that he's gonna invade Cambodia for God's sake."

"Cambodia?" one of the pool players said.

"I'm not kidding," Herb said. He pointed to a clock behind the bar. It was five minutes to nine. "He's supposed to be on TV in a few minutes," he said. "Change the channel."

The bartender looked at Frankie and Jimmy who nodded their approval. The game was a blow-out anyway. The pool shooters stopped shooting and moved closer to the bar.

A White House correspondent was providing the standard speculation. "There have been growing reports of Viet Cong and North Vietnamese activity in neighboring Cambodia," he said. "The Pentagon claims they are using Cambodia as a staging area to launch attacks against us, and then taking sanctuary across the border. Meanwhile the Cambodian government appears either unwilling or unable to stop it."

"Jesus, what now?" The other pool shooter said.

Soon Nixon was on the screen providing the same information in greater detail. He said the United States and South Vietnamese governments had decided that it was time to end the enemy presence in Cambodia, and that the South Vietnamese army would handle most of the operation. Then the President dropped the really big news.

"There is one area, however, immediately above Parrot's Beak, where I have concluded that a combined American and South Vietnamese operation is necessary.

Tonight, American and South Vietnamese units will attack the headquarters for the entire Communist military operation in South Vietnam. This key control center has been occupied by the North Vietnamese and Vietcong for five years in blatant violation of Cambodia's neutrality." There wasn't a sound in the bar as Nixon continued. *"This is not an invasion of Cambodia,"* the President said. "That's a bunch of crap," one of the pool shooters yelled, but Herb quickly told him to be quiet.

Nixon continued. *"The areas in which these attacks will be launched are completely occupied and controlled by North Vietnamese forces. Our purpose is not to occupy the areas. Once enemy forces are driven out of these sanctuaries and once their military supplies are destroyed, we will withdraw."* Nixon explained that the action was necessary to ensure the safe and orderly withdrawal of American forces over time as the South Vietnamese assumed greater responsibility for the war. *"We take these actions,"* Nixon said, *"not for the purpose of expanding the war into Cambodia, but for the purpose of ending the war in Vietnam, and winning the just peace we all desire."* Mike turned the sound down when Nixon was finished, and the bar erupted. "Who the hell does he think he is?" Pool player number one shouted. "He's the President of the United States," Herb shouted back. "He doesn't have the power to just invade another country. He's acting like a goddamned dictator," the pool shooter bellowed. "That's why we're losing this war," Herb said.

"We're fighting with one hand tied behind our back. Too many rules." Player number two chimed in. "He's not winding down the war; he's expanding it." "If you ask me," one of Herb's buddies said, "we should have dropped the big one a long time ago, just like Truman did." "That's brilliant," player number one said. "Nuke 'em all. Fortunately, nobody asked you." Frankie and Jimmy sat quietly as the barbs flew past them, until the bartender finally told them all to shut up or leave.

"What do you think?" Jimmy asked Frankie quietly when the noise died down. "Is Nixon ending the war or expanding it?" "I have no idea what to think," Frankie replied honestly. "How about you?" "I don't know," Jimmy said. "All I care about right now is getting Nick home safely, and I'll support anything that'll do that. I don't know if this will help or hurt."

55- Kent State

On May 5, 1970, six days after Nixon announced the Cambodian invasion, or incursion as the White House preferred to call it, Debbie walked into McElroy Commons and slammed the *Boston Globe* on Dr. Foster's table. The action was a little more dramatic than she had intended. They hadn't spoken since Nixon's announcement, and she was bursting with frustration.

"I'm sorry," she said, as she sat across from him. "But have you seen this? Students are rioting across the country."

"Hello, Debbie," he said calmly. "Of course I've seen it. It's reprehensible."

She barely heard him. "First Nixon orders an illegal invasion of another country without an act of congress. Damn, he's the commander-in-chief, not the emperor. And now this," she motioned to the newspaper again. Those kids at Kent State were exercising their constitutional right to assemble and protest, and they killed them. Those goddamned Nazis gunned them down!"

She stormed ahead. "Four are dead, nine or ten are wounded, one might be paralyzed! Jesus," she was almost screaming now, "they just fired into the crowd." She stopped to catch her breath. "Some of the victims weren't even part of the protest. They were walking across campus. My God!"

Foster let her vent. There was no use trying to stop her.

"This will go down as one of the darkest events in American history," she said. "Do you know that there are people who are actually saying that the dead students deserved it, that they were taunting the National Guardsmen? Is this country crazy? They're shooting our young, and people are saying it's okay. This is America. We don't shoot people for protesting!"

Dr. Foster thought she was finished and began to speak, but she plunged on.

"The networks are reporting that there are protests taking place at hundreds of campuses across the country. Are they going to shoot at those students too? The country is ripping apart."

Finally, she stopped and looked at him. When he didn't speak she said, "Well?"

"Is it my turn?" he asked cautiously.

"Fire away," she said.

"I'm afraid I don't have any answers. There are several issues here. Were Nixon's actions in Cambodia constitutional? Not in my opinion, although Presidential war powers are vague. Was it a sound military move? Plenty of analysts are saying that it was. It may actually bring the troops home early."

Debbie was incredulous. "You're agreeing with him?" She almost shouted it.

Now Dr. Foster was annoyed. He leaned forward and spoke firmly but softly. "I said that many analysts are saying it may have been a good military move. That's not my opinion; it's the opinion of the analysts." He paused briefly. "Now you need to calm down, because I will not be bulldozed academically."

She sat back and took a deep breath. "Okay," she said. "No bulldozing."

Foster continued, "I have my doubts about the military value, but if this diminishes the ability of the North Vietnamese to attack the South, and thereby gives Nixon more time to train South Vietnamese replacements for our troops, then..." he let the conclusion hang in the air.

"But you have your doubts," she said defensively.

"Serious doubts," he said. "How successful was the incursion? What did we find when we got there? How will China react to us possibly expanding the war? Is this really an escalation intended to win the war rather than get us out?"

Debbie wanted to hear more. "So?"

"So all of this is nothing in importance to the political costs at home. We haven't been this divided since the Civil War, and that's not just rhetoric. Our young people have lost confidence in their government. Yesterday's shooting was terrifying, but even more terrifying is the reaction you mentioned. The nation is polarized between those who were horrified by the shooting and those who think it was justified."

"Exactly!" Debbie interjected. "As for me, my learning days are over. This war is not just in Vietnam any more. It's right here at home. It's becoming a war against our own government. It's time for people to step up. I know you like calm, rational dialogue, but it's hard to speak calmly when our own government is shooting at us." She waited for a response, but when Foster remained expressionless, Debbie filled the void.

"There's a protest rally tomorrow at Boston Common. I'll be there," she said defiantly. "And I won't be just a spectator."

Still there was no reaction. Then she asked the question that she assumed would probably end their relationship. "What about you, Dr. Foster? Are you ready to step up?"

Foster looked her squarely in the eyes and said, "I've already agreed to be one of the speakers."

56- "Peace is at hand."

Richard Nixon's Vietnam policies dominated the news that Anna watched. He was standing firm in the face of the growing anti-war demonstrations, and he had reason to. Polls showed that in spite of the opposition's protests, he still enjoyed a steady core of support for his actions, partly because he was delivering on his promised troop reductions. By the end of 1970, America had 334,000 troops in Vietnam, down from Johnson's 550,000. Causalities were down as well. Regrettably, Americans were still fighting and dying, and the most ardent critics were still screaming for an immediate pullout. Nixon knew he'd never win over the extremists, but he was confident that as long as he reduced our role, cut causalities, and preserved American honor, the majority of Americans would support him.

At the Paris peace talks, Le Duc Tho, the North Vietnamese representative, demanded a complete American pullout and the replacement of the South Vietnamese government with one to Hanoi's liking. Of course, this would violate Nixon's "peace with honor" pledge. So, to turn up the pressure, he sent troops into Cambodia, mined North Vietnamese harbors, and resumed the bombing of the North. He did so without a declaration of war, and in spite of growing congressional opposition. By the end of 1971, America's presence in Vietnam was down to 158,000. Tragically, twenty-three hundred Americans died that year, but that was fewer than one-fifth of the deaths that occurred in 1969. Though a final settlement was still elusive, the endless war seemed to be winding down.

By the spring of 1972, Nick had been a prisoner of war for four years. The enemy knew the POWs were excellent bargaining chips and used them effectively. To help keep concern for our POWs alive, Americans wore copper wristbands engraved with the name of a captured serviceman. Hundreds of Bristol residents wore a band bearing Nick's name. Thanks to Frankie and Jimmy, a poster with Nick's photo and the words *Remember our POWs* hung in the windows of storefronts on Mill Street and homes throughout town. Mrs. Francelli helped Nick's mother organize a letter writing campaign, urging congressmen and senators to keep the POW question a high priority.

Meanwhile, in every negotiation, Henry Kissinger stressed that the United States would never fully leave Vietnam without the prior release of prisoners, and the Vietnamese countered that their release would only be discussed *after* a complete American withdrawal and the replacement of the South Vietnamese government.

In October, prompted by the bombing and the virtual assurance of Nixon's re-election a month later, and concessions made by both sides, Hanoi agreed to a cease-fire and the return of all POWs. Kissinger announced, "Peace is at hand," and Nixon went on to win one of the most lopsided elections in American history. Finally, on January 27, 1973, a week after his second inaugural ceremony, a formal peace agreement was signed. The war was over, and Nick would be coming home.

Part VI
Far From Over

57- Travis Air Force Base

The television cameras followed the giant C-141 Starlifter as it taxied off the runway at Travis Air Force Base. It was February 1973, and the first of the POWs were coming home. The camera panned a fence lined four deep with people waiting to greet the returning servicemen. Like Americans watching across the country, Frankie and Jimmy were fixated in front of Anna's TV screen.

"What a wonderful gift this will make for their families," Anna said.

"Do you see Nick's parents anywhere?" Jimmy asked, his eyes still glued to the screen.

"No," she said, "but thanks to the two of you, we know they're nearby."

Nick's parents had been told that Travis would be a stopover for a few days while the men underwent checkups; then Nick would be flown to the East Coast. They wanted to be at Travis when Nick arrived, but couldn't afford to make the trip to the California air base. When the boys heard that the government wouldn't provide them with transportation to be there for such a short time, they quietly spread the word around town. Within two days, local businesses donated enough money to cover their air and lodging expenses. It was a heartwarming story of small town Bristol generosity, and Anna was surprised by the comfort it brought her. She still suffered from occasional bouts of depression, but thankfully, she was able to rejoice in the good fortune of others and felt blessed when she heard of the return of the POWs, especially Nick, who was one of her "boys."

Initially the North Vietnamese said that they would release the prisoners in increments, with those in need of medical attention first, followed by the others in the order of their captivity. Not wanting to halt the process by provoking the Vietnamese, the Pentagon withheld information about how the prisoners had been treated until all were safely returned. Nevertheless, rumors of torture, isolation, and near starvation, were everywhere. But at least they were coming home.

"Think he'll be on this plane?" Jimmy asked.

"We'll know soon enough," Frankie offered.

Anna placed her hand on Jimmy's shoulder. "I know you're anxious, Jimmy," she said reassuringly. "He might be on this plane or the next, but what matters is that we know he's coming."

"I want him home," Jimmy said firmly, without averting his gaze from the screen.

The plane came to a halt, and medical vehicles made their way to the tarmac. As the plane's giant doors opened, the news commentator said, "We'll do our best to give you the names as they disembark the plane."

Finally, the scene that prisoners and their families had dreamt of, some for as long as eight years, began to unfold. The first figures to emerge were medical personnel guiding a gurney toward the waiting ambulances. The gurney spooked Jimmy, and his mind raced about Nick's condition.

"We're gonna help him," he pledged. "No matter how bad he is, we're gonna get him home and take care of him."

"Whatever he needs," Frankie added.

Anna was touched and nodded her agreement.

At first the crowd wasn't sure how to greet the most injured men. Some decided to clap respectfully, and soon the noise grew to a steady applause. Next came men on crutches and in wheel chairs. As the condition of those exiting the plane improved, the mood lightened and the applause turned into cheers and whoops. Some returnees saluted the gathering, others waved their hats, and the crowd went wild. As each appeared, the commentator, working from a revised list, did his best to give the serviceman's name, rank and date of capture. He was obviously moved by the scene, and at times he could scarcely be heard.

The homecoming evoked complicated emotions for those who watched: joy in seeing loved one's reunited; anger at the sight of sick, and obviously mistreated Americans; guilt from the knowledge that these men suffered while those at home did not; sorrow for the losses they experienced, of time, of relationships, of watching their children grow; and pride in the honor, courage and dignity they displayed. Regardless of ones view of the war, watching these men embrace their homeland again filled the hearts of Americans with a sense of unity that the country so badly needed.

Finally, Jimmy pointed and shouted, "There he is! Is that him?" The man was in a wheelchair. His neck was in a brace, and he looked emaciated, but as the camera zoomed in, it captured Nick's unmistakable face. He was forcing a weak smile. The commentator mentioned Nick's name and was saying something about Special Forces and four years in confinement, but it was difficult to hear above Jimmy's cheering. He stood and thrust his fist in the air. Anna and Frankie stood too, and then they were all exchanging hugs. Jimmy was laughing and screaming, "He's home! He's home!" Then Frankie and Anna clapped as Jimmy danced in the middle of the room. Nick was back, and things would be better.

58- Allison's Letter

America's last combat troops left Vietnam in March. It was a difficult day for Anna. She thought back to Johnny's tour of duty when she held hope that the war would end in time to save him, watched the peace rallies and demonstrations, and followed the McCarthy and Bobby Kennedy campaigns. Roughly twenty-five thousand boys had died since Johnny's death, twenty thousand of them since Richard Nixon spoke of his "secret plan" for peace. Fifty-eight thousand had died in all. In addition to the deaths, she had no idea how many others there were like Sam Johnson who'd been seriously wounded. How many were there like Jimmy, trying to adjust emotionally to "Life after Nam." In addition to the human costs, there was the cost in dollars, over one hundred and fifty billion by some estimates. She measured that in lost opportunities, in education, health care, housing, and job training.

She opened the dining room hutch and took out the small box that held special things about Johnny. Sitting at the table, she opened it and examined its contents. She held his Bronze Star, awarded posthumously, and his Purple Heart. She was angry when she first received them, but they had come to mean much more to her now. Certainly her son deserved a star. He deserved one long before he went to Vietnam. She noticed the letter Sergeant Boyd had written to her after Johnny's death and wished she had met the man Johnny had written so fondly of in his letters. She looked at the small card the funeral home had printed for Johnny's service, with his date of birth and death, and the Prayer of St. Francis. *"Make me a channel of your peace…"* She allowed herself a tear.

Next, she picked up the letter she had received from Allison two years earlier and decided to read it again.

Dear Mrs. Francelli,

Thank you for your thoughtful graduation card and note. It was wonderful to hear from you. I wanted to thank you in person, but Debbie and I are leaving for Europe in a couple of days for a six-week tour. It's our graduation present! We'll be sleeping in hostels and traveling by train. We plan to visit eight cities and countless small towns along the way. Debbie, of course, made all of the arrangements, and I'm just along for the ride, but I am excited.

I'm happy to be leaving Boston College. Although I've loved the city, the school, and the education I received, BC holds far too many bittersweet memories for me. The time between when I received Johnny's letter until I learned of his passing was the happiest period of my life. I did more planning and dreaming in those few weeks than I had ever done before. While that memory will always be precious to me, I think a change will be good.

Speaking of change, I've finally decided that I'd like to be a teacher. Since I've never taken education courses, I have some catching up to do. I've been accepted into a Masters of Education program at Columbia, and I begin in the fall. Living in New York should be quite an experience. It will be easier to travel home, and I'll be sure to visit when I do.

Debbie plans to change the world on a larger scale than twenty or thirty students at a time. She's decided to pursue a career in International Relations and has entered a program at George Washington University in DC. I hope Washington is ready for her! I will miss her enormously, and I'm a little scared, but we both know it's time to move on. We've promised to visit each other often, and I know that we will. Besides, we still have a whole summer in Europe to get sick of each other!

As for moving on, I appreciate your words, and I've come to know that there is a new life for me in the future. What it will be, I'm not sure. But I plan to be positive and open and take things as they come. I know you will do the same. I also know that you and I will always save a giant place in our hearts for Johnny.

Love always,
Allison

Mrs. Francelli replaced the contents and covered the box with the lid. Then she sat alone at the table for a long time.

59- Walter Reed

Frankie drove. It was the first time he and Jimmy had been to Washington since President Kennedy's funeral. They crossed into DC from Maryland and traveled a short distance on Georgia Avenue before they saw the signs for the Walter Reed Army Medical Center. An MP at the gate checked their names against a list on his clipboard and waved them through.

They found the tranquil setting impressive. The grounds were tastefully landscaped, with mature trees and manicured lawns. Beyond them was the hospital, a red brick, Georgian style, three-story structure with four large columns supporting a wooden canopied entrance. A distinctive white cupola capped the roof. Directly across from the entrance was a large circular fountain that generated a soothing cascade of water.

Jimmy was struck by the contrast the medical center offered to where Nick must have been for the previous four years. The brochure Nick's parents gave him stated that the building had been constructed during Teddy Roosevelt's administration to care for wounded and disabled veterans and had been wonderfully preserved. He hoped the care the facility offered was as impressive as its outward appearance.

They entered through the main doors, where the receptionist asked them to wait as she used her desk phone to report their arrival. In a minute, a woman in her late fifties approached the desk and greeted them. "You are right on time," she said cheerfully. "My name is Sharon Larkin." She extended her hand to each of them, and explained that she would be escorting them to Nick's room, but needed a word with them first. She led them to a lounge area in the corner of the lobby and invited them to sit.

"I work with the psychiatric staff of the hospital, and we make it a practice to speak to visitors first, if we think that the patient they are about to see has experienced significant emotional trauma."

Jimmy looked concerned.

"It's the procedure we follow," she said pleasantly.

"Is he bad?" Jimmy asked.

Larkin smiled. "He is doing remarkably well, considering what he's been through. But I still..."

Jimmy interrupted. "What's he been through?"

"Mr. Wright," she said.

"It's Jimmy," he corrected. "Please call me Jimmy."

"Of course," she smiled again, but it was clear she wasn't pleased with the interruptions.

"We're still learning the full answer to that question, but we need to take one thing at a time."

"Okay." Jimmy said. "Can we see him now and talk later?"

Her smile disappeared. "We need to talk first," she said firmly.

Frankie decided to mediate. "Jimmy and Nick are very close," he explained. "He's just a little anxious to see him."

"Damn right I am!" Jimmy said. "I haven't seen him in four years!"

"And you will," she said patiently, "If you'll just allow me to finish."

"It's five more minutes, Jimmy," Frankie added. "No big deal."

"Sorry," Jimmy said. "So what were you trying to say?"

"Sergeant Hardings is making good progress. Physically, he had a rough time. He suffered a broken hip that was never corrected. It's presenting serious problems for him and will require surgery. The damage is four years old and it's a mess, but one the doctors feel they can improve."

Jimmy exhaled deeply as nurse Larkin continued.

"He also suffered an injury that damaged some tendons in his neck. He apparently underwent some surgery for that while in captivity, but it was poorly done, and he has significant scar tissue. He will require surgery to regain more mobility in his neck."

Frankie was shaking his head, and Jimmy looked as if he wanted to throw a chair through a window.

"There's evidence of a prior staph infection, for which he may have received treatment, but it presents a problem for the future surgeries he faces."

Now she was talking about things that Jimmy didn't understand, but it didn't take much to know they were not good.

"Bastards," he said, clenching his fists.

Frankie put his hand on Jimmy's shoulder.

"Finally, there's the issue of nutrition," she added. "He was seriously undernourished when he was released. As a result, he has lost muscle mass, and there may have been some damage to his organs. His problems are not life threatening, and he is beginning to gain some weight."

"I'll get him a couple of pizzas," Jimmy offered.

"Pizza would be fine," she said. "But we have to take things slowly. His body has to be reconditioned to eat large amounts of food again, but he's doing fine in that regard."

"We want him to have the best doctors, and all the help he needs," Jimmy said.

"All of our doctors are highly qualified," she said flatly. "As for the help, there's been a war, and we're a stressed facility. We have a patient load and a staff. We match the two as best we can based upon the patient's needs and condition. Your friend will receive the best attention we can provide within the limits of our resources."

"We don't want him missing anything," Jimmy said, disregarding what he just heard.

Nurse Larkin looked annoyed and Frankie decided to change the subject.

"Is that it?" he asked.

"That's it for the physical issues," she replied. What I really want to talk with you about is the psychological trauma he has suffered."

"Oh man, is he messed up?" Jimmy asked, growing more concerned.

"First, let me say that we normally would not share this information with non-family members, but the patient's parents told us that both of you are very significant in his life. Therefore, you may be significant in his recovery," Larkin said.

"We'll definitely be significant," Jimmy said.

Frankie nodded.

"Okay. So here it is," she said. "The patient has been…"

"Nick," Jimmy interjected. "Could you call him Nick?"

"Certainly," she said. By now she realized that she would have to allow Jimmy more leeway in this conversation than she normally would.

"Nick has been in captivity for four years. Although we don't know the full extent of his experiences yet, we know that they were traumatic, mentally and physically. Patients who have experienced terrible treatment over an extended period may exhibit lasting effects.

They may interact differently with people. They may have difficulty expressing themselves. They may be lethargic."

So far, Nurse Larkin could have been describing Jimmy, Frankie thought.

"They could also be experiencing guilt," she continued.

"Guilt?" Jimmy asked. "Why should he feel guilty? He didn't do anything wrong."

"Exactly," Larkin said. "But, from his perspective, he may be thinking that he did. Maybe he's feeling that he could have done more for his fellow prisoners. Or he's feeling that he did something careless to be captured in the first place. He may have a sense of failure, and may be in conflict with himself over that issue."

Frankie and Jimmy were quiet.

"So with all of this and more possibly going on, it's important that you know that regardless of your prior relationship, he may behave differently toward you."

"That's okay," Jimmy said. Frankie nodded.

"The good news," she said brightly, "is that so far he's been fine. His parents were here as recently as yesterday, and he reacted well with them. That's important."

"Good," Jimmy said. "Can we see him now?"

Larkin ignored him. "When prisoners are released, they often experience a sense of elation, as one would expect. But often the elation gives way to a sense of being overwhelmed. The readjustment is too much. Also, at first the patients do exactly what they are told by the hospital staff, almost as though they are still in their prison environment. But they often develop a sense of independence and even rebellion. They become assertive and uncooperative. The point is that with so much possibly going on in Nick's mind, it's imperative that you take things slowly."

"We will," Frankie assured her.

"He's very bright," Larkin said.

"Smartest guy I know," Jimmy said. Then he cracked a brief smile and added, "Sorry about that, Frankie."

Frankie smiled too, grateful for the break in tension.

"The point is, don't try to fool him. Be truthful. Not blunt, but truthful."

"Okay," Jimmy said.

"His sleep has been fitful, and it appears that he's still experiencing nightmares. We don't want you to raise any questions about what has happened to him. It may be too traumatic. In fact, he's mildly sedated, so he may be tired when you see him."

Again the boys nodded.

"There's one more thing, and then I'll take you to his room." She looked uncomfortable.

"His parents left yesterday. They were here for two days, and they'll be back."

"They don't have much money," Jimmy said. "Hotel rooms are expensive. I think the government should pay."

"I understand," Larkin said. "The word is we will be building some lodging facilities on the grounds here in the future."

"That's good," Jimmy said. "But it doesn't help them now."

Larkin returned to her original thought. "Before they left, we asked his parents if there was anything else in his life that may be a source of trauma for him as he readjusts to civilian life." She lowered her voice. "They said that one of his best friends had been killed in Vietnam and that he didn't know it yet."

"That's true," Frankie said, with a choked voice. Jimmy put his head down.

"The doctors discussed this extensively, and although there is a slight difference of opinion, the general belief is that he should be told as soon as possible. The doctors felt they wanted him to deal with his issues at the same time rather than suffer a set back later after making early progress. I agree."

"I guess that's right," Jimmy said.

"For four years, everything he has heard has come from people who had authority over him, prison guards, military personnel, people like that. Right now, he views the hospital staff the same way. It's normal. The doctors feel that the news of his friend's death should come from someone that he shares a personal relationship with."

Jimmy and Frankie looked at each other.

"We suggested that the parents do it, but they were unable to. It was their strong belief that the two of you would be better suited to give him the news. They said you had a special relationship. Given that information, in the final analysis, the staff agreed."

Jimmy broke down. "I can't do that," he said. "I just can't do it. I know how I felt when I heard about Johnny, and I wasn't even sick. How can I tell him while he's in a hospital?"

Nurse Larkin didn't respond.

Finally, Frankie said softly, "I'll do it. If the doctors think this is the best way to go, then I'll do it."

When they left the lobby to enter Nick's wing of the hospital, everything changed. Men on wheel chairs and gurneys surrounded them. Amid the blur of IV tubes and bandaged faces, they noticed amputees. Although they both saw the same scene, they had different reactions. Frankie's guilt swelled, because they had served and he didn't, while Jimmy felt nothing but anger. Why had this happened? Why did these men have to suffer like this?

Finally, they reached Nick's room.

"This is it," Larkin said. "Remember, most of all, he needs your love and friendship."

"He's got that," Jimmy said.

"I know," she smiled. She checked her watch. "Let's keep this first visit to a half hour."

"Fine," Frankie said. "And thank you."

"Thank both of you for your help," she said and then disappeared quickly down the hall.

They stood at the door, each afraid to make the first move. Then Frankie opened the door a crack. Nick appeared to be sleeping. They stepped inside gingerly. When they were both in, Nick said, without opening his eyes, "I'm a Green Beret you know. If I wanted to, I could have killed both of you ten seconds ago. You're not very good at sneaking up on people." Then he opened his eyes and laughed.

They froze, shocked by what they saw. He looked worse in person than he had on television. The once robust football hero was gaunt and pale. His neck was braced and bandaged, and his right leg was elevated slightly above the bed.

"Damn, that was a joke," Nick said, still laughing. "Come in."

They moved quickly to his bed, and Jimmy got there first. "There he is," Nick shouted happily as they embraced. Next came Frankie. "Hey, big guy," Nick said. "Great to see you." They embraced also. All three were choking back their emotions.

"Damn," Nick said brightly, "I've got nothing but gooks screaming at me for four years, and I finally see my friends and they've turned into friggin' mummies. Are you guys gonna speak or what?"

"I'm talking. I'm talking," Jimmy said excitedly.

"Good to see you," Frankie added.

"It's damn good to see you," Nick replied. "Where the hell have you been? I expected you a half hour ago."

"Red tape," Frankie said. "Seeing you is like trying to see the President."

"So how do I look?" Nick asked cheerfully.

Frankie and Jimmy glanced at each other briefly, and then Jimmy said, "You look terrible."

"My man Jimmy," Nick beamed, raising his hand for a high five, which Jimmy met gently. "I was testing you. You passed."

They laughed again.

"Listen," Nick whispered, "I need a favor."

"Anything," Frankie said, as they both drew closer.

"Take it easy," Nick said. "I don't need a bed pan or anything like that." He glanced around to make sure they were alone. "There're some nurses around here that I've had my eye on. One in particular named Margie. You can't miss her, blond, blue eyes, built well and pretty as anything. Plus she's got the name tag on."

Then he motioned to Jimmy and said to Frankie, "Can he read yet?"

"Still bustin'," Jimmy said.

"It's M-A-R-G-I-E," Nick said. Jimmy was relieved to see Nick so up.

"Anyway, if you see her, would you put in a good word for me? Tell her what a hunk I am when I'm not damn near starved to death. Tell her about my football days. Beef it up a little. Make some stuff up. I don't care. I want that girl."

"No problem," Jimmy said. "She got friends?"

"Sure, she's popular. Hell, we can triple date."

"Done," Frankie said.

"Good," Nick said, still smiling.

Things got quiet, and Nick turned serious. "It's been four years," he said sadly, "four stinkin' years."

Frankie and Jimmy didn't know how to respond.

"So how was Nam?" Nick asked Jimmy.

"Piece of cake," Jimmy said quickly.

"See that," Nick said. "You got the first question right, and right away you blew the next one. I got your early letters; remember? It didn't sound like a piece of cake then."

"Things got better," Jimmy said.

"Okay, you're done. You fail. Next student." He turned slightly to Frankie. He clearly didn't have much mobility in his neck "So how you doing, big guy?"

"I'm doing great," Frankie said.

"Yeah? Well you're the saddest looking great I ever saw. Lighten up, man."

"I'm just tired from the drive."

Nick looked at both of them. "Are you sure you weren't a prisoner too?" he said to Jimmy. "It looks like you lost a few pounds. Then he said to Frankie, "and it looks like you gained the weight he lost."

Frankie smiled. "I gained a few."

"Just more to love man," Nick added, smiling again.

It got quiet again, and after a while Nick said. "Okay, it's your turn."

Frankie and Jimmy didn't get it.

"Our turn for what?" Jimmy said.

"It's your turn to ask me how Nam was."

Jimmy didn't know what to say.

"They told you not to talk about it, didn't they?"

"No," Jimmy stammered. "They didn't ..."

"That's it!" Nick interrupted, "I guess I can't believe anything else you say."

Jimmy put his head down.

"Just kidding, man," Nick said. "They told my parents not to ask too. I could tell. Pretty dumb, don't you think? It's like talking to a guy with two noses and pretending nothing's unusual."

"They just want to take things easy at first," Frankie said. "Maybe get into it later."

"Later?" Nick said. "There isn't gonna be any later. I plan to get out of here pretty quick."

"Right," Jimmy said. "We've got to get you home." He wondered whether Nick knew about the operations that awaited him.

"Look, let me break the ice for you guys," Nick said. "Nam was awful. The worst damn thing you can imagine. And being captured, you can use your imagination for that. As for the secret stuff I did as a Greenie, I'd love to tell you, but how does the saying go? If I told you, I'd have to kill you. And I'm through with killing."

They let that hang for a while, and then Jimmy said, "You're home. That's what matters."

"Yeah," Nick said. "We're home. But let me tell you something. We could have won that war. We were winning. The enemy was hurting big time. They had way more causalities than us. All we had to do was stick with it, but Washington screwed us. We could have and should have won."

Neither of them was about to get involved in a debate with Nick, so they just nodded.

Nick changed the subject. "I have a mission for you," he said to Jimmy, "A favor, not as important as lining up Margie, but it's important."

"Sure," Jimmy said.

"Come over to the other side of the bed."

When Jimmy got there Nick said, "See that table?" There was a small utility table within reach of the bed. It had a single drawer. "Inside that drawer are some loose orange pills. They give them to me to dope me up, like I'm some psycho or something. I've been hiding them in the drawer. Take them out without anyone seeing you and flush them down the john. It's right inside that door."

Jimmy started to protest, but Nick wouldn't let him. "I didn't take drugs when I was in Nam, and I don't plan to start now. Just do it. Close the door and pretend you're using the bathroom in case somebody walks in."

Jimmy opened the drawer and slid the pills into his pocket. Then he went to the bathroom. When he closed the door, Nick quickly grabbed Frankie's arm.

"He looks pretty bad," Nick said. "How is he?"

"He's a lot better than he was when he first got home."

"Are you watching out for him?"

"In any way I can," Frankie said. "He'll be fine."

"Thanks," Nick said. "You know he needs it."

Frankie nodded as Jimmy opened the door.

"Okay," Nick beamed. "You're the man," offering him another high five.

"I hope you know what you're doing," Jimmy said, slapping Nick's outstretched hand again.

"Some guys save them for a different reason. Rumor is that some guys who are really bad save the pills and then try to off themselves by taking them all at once." Nick realized he shouldn't have said that, and he added, "Don't worry; that's not me."

"No way," Jimmy said.

Nick added, "If they want to bring me a few beers, I'll be happy to cooperate, but the drugs, they can keep them."

Nick adjusted his leg. "I've got some problems with my hip," he said. "No big deal."

When he was comfortable again, he said. "Okay, fill me in on the last fours years of news. How is everyone? And where the heck is Johnny? I thought he'd be with you guys."

60- Citizenship

Angelo and Donna observed their seventh anniversary in Canada with a quiet dinner. Over the years they established a decent life for themselves. Angelo left the breakfast joint for a job in a respectable restaurant, and Donna quit the nightclub dive to join him as a waitress. They were paying their bills and managing to save. They developed a wide circle of friends among both exiled Americans and resident Canadians. Overall, things were okay.

But there were still problems, and the mood at the dinner table was melancholy. Angelo's parents postponed a scheduled visit because his father wasn't feeling well. Twice a year his parents boarded a bus to make the long trip to Montreal. The visits were bittersweet, filled with laughter and tears, but mostly tears. During their recent visits, they discussed the option of Angelo coming home, serving his punishment, and starting a new life. The idea was tempting, but Angelo and Donna were afraid.

They came closest to leaving in 1974 when President Ford offered a limited clemency plan. Those wishing to return to the U.S. would be evaluated on a case- by-case basis, with possible amnesty offered in return for an admission of guilt and a commitment to alternative service. But the operative word was *possible*, and few took advantage of the plan. Many, like Angelo, refused to admit wrongdoing for following their consciences and were worried about prosecution. Angelo still had the notice of indictment hanging on his wall as a stark reminder of why they were in Canada. A zealous prosecutor in the Philadelphia US Attorney's office had issued it after Angelo's failure to report for duty. He was facing a felony charge, and it was frightening.

Angelo had been torn for years. He told himself that he did the right thing by opposing an immoral war, yet he was riddled with guilt for the pain he was causing others. For seven years he fluctuated between feeling righteous for following his heart, and cheap for abandoning his family, friends and country. But the damage was done, and returning wasn't an option.

Over the years, word from home only added to his depression. Of course Johnny's death was the most crushing news. Angelo had written to Mrs. Francelli soon after to say how sorry he was and that he would understand if she hated him for resisting the draft. In her beautifully written reply she said she had no ill feelings, and was sure that Johnny wouldn't have either. Her grace and kindness moved him to even more shame. News of Nick's ordeal, as well as Jimmy's problems with post-war readjustment, just added to his misery. He asked himself why he had to be the one who ran, when others stayed and did their duty? Thousands of young men went to Vietnam, hundreds of thousands. Brave, noble, frightened young men had answered the call, some willingly, some grudgingly, but they did their duty. They paid their price, with their lives, or their limbs, or by sacrificing precious time, but they brought honor to themselves, while he fled to Canada. Why him? He asked that question almost every day.

He thought more about his parents as he stared at his dinner plate. They had seen him only fourteen times in seven years. He imagined the shame they suffered at home. He knew their business had suffered because of his actions, not dramatically, but enough to make a difference. Plus, his father's health was failing, and Angelo's presence at the store would have been helpful. Yet they never complained. They wanted him home, but they supported every decision he made. They didn't deserve what he had done to them, he thought.

He looked across the table at Donna, and thanked God he had her. Surprisingly, she adapted to their exile better than he had and was their source of strength. It saddened him that her relationship with her parents had been so bad that she barely mentioned them, but her sacrifices in coming were still significant. He remembered their wedding day, just a few months after receiving their official immigrant status. All through high school Donna had talked about what their wedding would be like, the church, the flowers, the large bridal party, the reception in the hall of one of the local clubs. They had even selected "In the Still of the Night" as their wedding song. It was all planned, but how sadly different their actual wedding had been. They had gone to a local magistrate, accompanied by two new friends as witnesses. It was all so impersonal, and was over in a few minutes. Angelo remembered looking at Donna that day, knowing how disappointed she must have been with the arrangements, yet seeing her smile. She had done it for him, and he loved her even more for it.

Donna could usually be counted on to get Angelo out of his funk, but on this night she was in a funk of her own. There was something she needed to tell him and didn't know how to start.

"How's your dinner?" she asked.

"Great," Angelo said, although he hadn't eaten much.

"How about yours?'

"Mine's good too. You know how I love French food. French Canadian food is the next best thing."

"Tastes good," he conceded, "but there's never enough."

"You American guys are all the same," she said lightly. "You're not happy unless you have a sixteen ounce steak."

"And a baked potato," he added, managing a smile.

She was glad to see it. The hardest time for Angelo was always around their "Canadian Anniversaries," as they called them, and he had been down when they left the house. She wasn't even sure why they continued their little dining ritual to mark the occasion. She remembered how exciting it was the first time they did it, two kids away from home, taking a stand against something, starting with almost nothing and proving they could make it on their own. It was an adventure, a scary but cool adventure. But over time, as reality sunk in, the ritual took on an entirely different meaning. It marked another year away from home, another year in exile. She supposed that neither of them wanted to admit that, so they continued.

"Amanda and Scott are planning a weekend trip to Quebec, and they asked if we want to go," she said.

"Sounds good," he said. "Except there'll be even more French food."

"Pack some snacks if you're that worried about eating," she kidded.

"We'll have to check with work," he remembered. "Weekends are bad."

"I'll handle it. People owe us. I'll get someone to switch."

"You always handle everything," he said. Then he raised his wine glass toward her in a toast. "You are the best, babe. The very best."

She clicked his glass with hers and said, "I know."

The lighter mood awakened Angelo's appetite, and he ate.

The waiter arrived to ask if they wanted more wine. It was eight dollars a bottle, and Angelo chased him away.

"These people should be arrested for their prices," he said. "Small food, big check."

"It's once a year," Donna said. "I'll flirt with the businessmen at lunch tomorrow and get bigger tips."

"That stuff ended when you left that other sleaze joint," he said firmly.

"Hey, the guys in the expensive suits like a hot chick just as much as the dirtballs at the other place," she winked. "The difference is they leave more money."

"You just earn your tips by making sure the food's hot. Nothing else."

"Sure, Angelo," she laughed. "Whatever you say. I wouldn't want you coming out of the kitchen with a meat cleaver to go after some guy. I'll be good."

They returned to their meals.

After a while Donna said, "I've been thinking, if an American kid, you know, someone with American parents, is born in Canada, is he an American or Canadian citizen?"

"I have no idea," Angelo said, dipping a piece of bread into some olive oil.

She let that sit for a moment and then tried again.

"What about dual citizenship?" she asked. "Do you know how that works?"

Angelo shrugged. "I've heard of it, but never paid much attention. Ask one of the lawyers tomorrow when you're serving lunch."

"That's an idea," she said. "I think I'll do that."

He was about to take another bite when it hit him. Slowly, he put his knife and fork on his plate and looked at her. "Why are you asking me this, Donna?"

She lowered her eyes and didn't respond.

He waited a while and then said, "Donna, tell me what's going on?"

She gathered herself and said softly, "We're having a baby."

The words hit him a like punch to his throat. For a few seconds he couldn't breathe or swallow.

Finally, he choked out, "A baby?"

"Yes!" she said emphatically. "A baby. Our baby."

His eyes widened. He didn't know what to say. "That's great," he offered, without much enthusiasm. He had always wanted children someday and knew that Donna did too, but this was a sneak attack, and his mind was racing. He was bombarded with fears about how a baby would impact their lives. Where would they put it? How would Donna work? What about medical bills?

"Wow, babe," he said. "We didn't really plan this."

Donna had been hoping for a little more warmth than she was getting.

"That's why I love you so much," she said sarcastically, "because you're such a friggin' genius! Of course we didn't plan it. Is that the best you can do?"

Now it was Angelo's turn to fall silent.

"This is great," she said sarcastically. "I'm telling my husband the most important news of our lives, and he's acting like his dog just died or something."

"I'm sorry," he said gently. "I really am. You just caught me off guard. It's a lot to deal with out of the blue." Then he flashed a genuine smile.

"This is great," he said. "It really is. It's what we always wanted. We're gonna have a kid."

Donna brightened. "I know," she said.

It got quiet again, and Angelo asked cautiously, "How do you know?"

"Well, I was late, and I've been feeling a little funny in the morning, not sick, but different. So I went to the clinic at the university and got the results today."

"Jesus," Angelo said, turning serious again. "So this isn't just a hunch."

"It's no hunch."

He finished off his glass of wine and looked for the waiter to order more.

"I'm really a jerk," he said. "I feel so stupid. This is terrific news. It's what's life's all about. Please forgive me, Donna. You know I've always wanted a family. We might as well get started."

Donna started to cry.

"What's wrong babe?" he said, reaching out to take her hand. "I'm okay with it. I really am. We'll work things out. I'll get another job. I'll go back to making pancakes in the morning and keep my other job at night. We'll be fine."

She closed her eyes and waited for the tears to stop. Then she said, "I want to go home."

"Okay, no problem," he said. "I'll get the check."

"God you can be dumb at times," she said. "I want to go home to the United States!"

Angelo sat back, stunned again.

"I want to go home," she said again. "I want our baby to be born in America. I want him to have a hometown. I want my friends, my real friends, not these sandal wearing, pot smoking, politicized assholes to help us raise our baby. I want all this protest crap to be over. I don't care about 'the movement' anymore. I'm tired of hearing about what's happening at Berkeley or Columbia or any other place. All that crap is over. We're not fighting anymore. The POWs are home. No one cares about us, or what we stood for. I just want to go home."

Angelo watched as the tears streamed down her face. When he didn't speak, she went on.

"But I also want my baby to have a father. Not a father in prison for draft evasion, a father at home. A father who will do the things my crappy father never did. I want that too."

Angelo squeezed his eyes shut and shook his head as Donna continued.

"But I can't have both, and I won't raise this baby without a father, and I'll never leave you. I love you too much. So I guess I'm stuck."

Now Angelo was filling up too.

She leaned forward and rubbed his hand. "I'm sorry," she said. "But I couldn't keep it inside any longer. Maybe it's my hormones or some damn thing. I don't know. But I had to let you know how I feel. I'm sorry."

Angelo raised his head. "That's okay," he said softly. "I'm the one who is sorry, more than you could know. I screwed up. It's all my fault, and I don't know how to fix it."

"Everything is going to be fine," she said, trying to smile. "We'll make it that way, just like we always have. And our Canadian friends aren't so bad," she added. "In fact, some of them are pretty nice, a little full of themselves, but nice."

He nodded.

"Come on," she said. "Let's go home." Then she laughed at her choice of words. "I mean to our apartment."

61- Like Riding a Bicycle

Nick always had his bicycle with him when Frankie arrived to pick him up for Saturday breakfast. It was a burnt-orange three speed he purchased the day he was released from the hospital. "Looks like a nice day," Nick said as they loaded the bike into the rear of the pickup. To him, any day that didn't include heavy rain or snow was nice. From there, they'd go to Jimmy's house to meet him after his midnight shift at the steel mill.

Nick had spent fourteen months at Walter Reed, enduring seven operations, two on his hip and five on his neck. Somewhere in the middle of it all, he had a breakdown, and his early optimism vanished. It was hard to tell what crippled him more, his injuries, Johnny's death, or the news from Vietnam, but he became bitter and withdrawn. His lowest point came while watching Saigon fall in April 1975. As expected, the North Vietnamese violated the treaty after the last American combat troops left. They swept through the remaining South Vietnamese forces easily. By late April they were on the outskirts of Saigon and panic set in. Thousands of anti-communists flocked to the American Embassy seeking protection. Nick watched in disgust as the news showed American helicopters landing on the embassy roof, lifting refugees to safety aboard nearby ships, while hundreds of others jostled for the next ride. The whole episode sickened him. This wasn't just defeat; it was humiliation. Within days it was over and, in the ultimate insult, Saigon was renamed Ho Chi Minh City. The cause Americans had paid such a heavy price for in lives and resources was lost.

For a time, Nick would lapse into fits of anger. "We could have won," he repeated to hospital staff, or anyone who would listen. "We deserved to win. Good men died trying."
At times he had to be restrained. The doctors said that while his feelings were understandable, his rants concerned them. Over time, medication and counseling helped with the anger, but it also created a Nick who was much more isolated and withdrawn. Even as he continued to progress, he rarely initiated a conversation, even with his closest friends. He'd be responsive if they spoke first, but he never initiated the dialogue. Once, when a therapist asked why, he replied that he simply didn't know how to begin anymore. There were so many things to say. He was feeling better about things and wanted to talk with people again, but he didn't know how. He said he felt "stuck." The therapist suggested that he try

doing what other people do all the time, make small talk, or maybe comment on the weather. The advice stuck like glue. He'd been greeting people with weather reports ever since.

Physically, the operations helped. The mobility in his neck improved after each surgery, until doctors finally announced that they had done all they could. He would have a permanent tilt to his head, but it was dramatically better than it had been. As for the hip, the two operations worked wonders. He was able to walk again, and when doctors said he might eventually do so without a cane, he worked vigorously in physical therapy until he reached that milestone.

When it was time to go home, Frankie and Jimmy made the trip to Washington to pick him up. On the day of his release, he asked his doctor if he'd ever be able to ride a bike. "I'm not sure," the doctor replied. "Right now you don't have enough range of motion to mount or pedal. Perhaps if you work at it, you may, but don't be too hopeful."

As he left his room that day, with Frankie and Jimmy with him, the hospital staff lined the corridor to say good-bye. They had cared for him for fourteen months, from his darkest times to his present state of recovery. Gradually, they had learned his story, not just about his ordeal at Walter Reed, but his heroics in Vietnam. They clapped as he passed. Some saluted, others stepped forward to touch his arm and wish him well. At the end of the corridor he turned to face them one more time. Their sendoff had moved him to tears. He wanted to say something, but he felt "stuck." Finally he said in a strong voice, "How's the weather outside?"

"It's a beautiful day, Nick," someone shouted back.

He smiled and gave them two thumbs up. They cheered.

Now, almost a year and a half later, he and Frankie waited in front of Jimmy's house to begin their Saturday ritual. Nick was much better emotionally. The anger was gone, but he wasn't the same person who had captained the football team and joined the Green Berets. His back pay from his years as a POW gave him a small nest egg, and he had been discharged with an eighty percent disability, which meant he collected a decent pension. He supplemented both with a small income from a job at a local newsstand. He was as smart as a whip, as he had always been, and now he became a voracious reader. During the slow hours at the stand, he consumed the contents of every periodical they sold. Foreign affairs, domestic politics, sports, entertainment, Hollywood gossip, he read it all and became a virtual encyclopedia. But in spite of his intellect, he was unable to focus upon anything except the simplest tasks. He avoided any sort of conflict, and relied upon humor and sarcasm to communicate.

Jimmy arrived at eight-thirty, fresh from his twelve-to-eight "graveyard" shift. He liked the hours. In fact, he requested them. The truth was he had trouble sleeping in the dark, but the night shift was also his way of getting away from the foreman he felt was harassing him. During their conflict, the mill's personnel director had told Jimmy that he seemed to have trouble with authority and was in danger of losing his job because of it.

In typical fashion, Jimmy replied, "I don't have a problem with authority, just that no- good son-of-a-bitch boss of mine."

The union intervened and Jimmy was transferred to third shift, away from the troublesome boss, but there would be no more chances. Fortunately for Jimmy, his new boss was a good guy who liked veterans. There was an occasional problem, but nothing that couldn't be fixed.

"Nice day today," Nick said, when Jimmy climbed in.

"Beautiful," Jimmy said. "Let's go, I'm starving."

"You should be," Nick said. "You worked all night."

"Sweated my butt off," Jimmy said. "Damn blast furnace was cookin' man."

It was just a few blocks to the breakfast joint on the upper end of Radcliffe Street.

"I'll get the paper," Nick said as they piled out.

They took their usual table and ordered enough food for six people. For Jimmy, it was like eating dinner after a full day's work. The other two guys just liked to eat.

The check arrived, and their weekly fight broke out. Paying the bill was a badge of honor, and they all wanted to pick up the tab. This time Frankie snatched it out of the waitress' hand before she put it on the table.

"Come on," Jimmy said to Frankie, "You paid last week."

"Too bad," Frankie taunted. "I'm paying again."

"It's not right," Jimmy said. "You drove. I should pay."

"Driving is driving. This is breakfast," Frankie said. "They're two different things."

"Wow," Nick said to the waitress. "Did you hear that brilliant logic? It's hard to argue with that."

She had stayed for the show and was enjoying it. "I think you're all nuts," she said laughing.

"Hey, watch it," Jimmy said smiling. "You might be more right than you think."

Frankie got back to the issue. "I told you before, we should just make a rule about this. But until we do…" he smiled smugly. "I've got the check."

"No rules," Jimmy thundered. "There're too many damn rules now. I don't need somebody telling me how to pay the breakfast check."

"That's true," Nick said. "Jimmy doesn't like too many rules."

"Fine with me," Frankie said as he taunted them by waving the check around the table.

Nick tried to snatch it, but Frankie pulled it away.

Then the waitress asked the same question she asked each week. "Would you guys consider splitting the bill? Lot's of our customers do that."

"Never work," Nick deadpanned. "I had the French toast, Frankie and Jimmy had pancakes. Jimmy had bacon, but Frankie and I had sausage.

Rye toast, white toast, English muffin, we'd be here until lunch time trying to figure it out."

The waitress laughed. "I meant splitting it evenly."

Nick looked at her as if she were crazy. "That wouldn't be fair. We didn't eat evenly."

Frankie and Jimmy quickly agreed.

With that, she smiled, told them to work it out and left happy, knowing what was coming next.

"Okay," Frankie said heading for the register. "I've got this. You guys leave the tip."

"That's me," Nick said.

"No way," Jimmy countered. "You got the newspaper."

"I said it first," Nick insisted. "I'm leaving it."

"I'm not getting shut out," Jimmy said.

"Looks like you are," Nick laughed, tossing a generous tip on the table.

"Screw you," Jimmy said, and laid down the same amount.

As they left with their honor preserved, the waitress smiled and waved good-bye, grateful for the extra money.

The next stop was the train station parking lot. There were few commuters on Saturday mornings, so the lot was almost empty. The Grundy Clock Tower across the street said it was 9:45.

"We're late," Nick said. "I wanted to get started by nine-thirty."

"Eat less next time," Jimmy said, lifting the bike from the truck.

"I'm feeling pretty good about things today," Nick said, waiting for the bike.

Frankie and Jimmy shot a glance at each other. Every Saturday morning had been the same. Nick would do his range of motion exercises at home all week to prepare for the big test on Saturday. His hope was to be able to lift his leg high enough to clear the bar and sit on the seat. The next big step would be to pedal. For the last year and a half, his bad hip had prevented him from doing either. His current doctors were doubtful that he'd ever master a bike. Nick felt otherwise and was obsessed with proving them wrong.

Once Frankie suggested that he try a girl's bike without the cross bar. Then he'd only have to worry about the pedaling issue. But Nick refused. So each Saturday, they went to the parking lot to see if the week's exercises had made a difference. He wanted Frankie and Jimmy there to spot for him when he rode off, which he was convinced he would do. He had failed every previous Saturday, but he was determined.

He put up the kickstand and walked the bike a few feet away from the truck. Then, with Frankie and Jimmy on each side of him, he tried to raise his leg over the seat and crossbar. He got it about a foot off the ground, grimaced, and brought it back down. He cleared his throat, adjusted his hands on the handlebars, and tried again. Again he couldn't raise his leg high enough. Jimmy and Frankie had learned not to rush him, so they watched in silence. He didn't speak either, but he gripped the handlebars so tightly that his knuckles turned white. The veins in his neck bulged and his breathing became labored. He tried twice more and failed.

Finally, he said, "I guess I need another week," just like he said every other Saturday.

"I think you're right," Jimmy said, trying to sound upbeat. "That might do it."

"Yeah, I'll give it another week," Nick said, still looking at the handlebars.

"Okay," Frankie said lightly, "Why don't we load the bike in the truck and get you home?"

Nick just shook his head as he did every other week. "Thanks," he said, "but I feel like being alone for a while. I'll just walk the bike home."

It was useless to argue, so like every other Saturday morning, they watched Nick begin his walk down Jefferson Avenue toward his home, with one hand on the handlebars and one on the seat.

62- Jimmy Carter

During the 1976 presidential campaign, Jimmy Carter made a stop in Seattle to address the annual American Legion convention and received warm applause as he pledged his support for veterans' causes. But at the end of his remarks, he said, "I plan to pardon draft evaders to heal the nation's wounds." At that point, the veterans stood and roundly booed him. Throughout the fall Carter continued to stress the need for reconciliation, while President Ford and his running mate, Bob Dole, a highly respected veteran, insisted they would continue to issue only limited pardons on a case-by-case basis.

Carter went on to win a narrow victory. On January 21, 1977, the day after his inauguration, he issued Executive Order 11967, granting amnesty to those who had evaded the draft. There was a barrage of protest, but Carter felt certain that his action was right and didn't waver. Donna and Angelo started packing as soon as they heard the news. Now, just two weeks later, and nine years after they fled America, they were coming home.

Mr. Marzo parked at the bus depot on Route 413 in Bristol Township. It was an exceptionally cold night and he kept the motor running. He checked his watch. The bus was due any minute. He turned to his wife and rubbed her knee gently.

"Are you warm enough, Mary?" he asked. "Maybe you should have stayed at the house."

She shook her head. "My son is coming home. I'm fine."

"There's a blanket in the back; would you like me to get it?"

"I'm fine," she repeated absently, focused on nothing but her son's arrival. She strained to look down the road. "Where is the bus?"

"Be patient," he said. "It will come."

She nodded, and turned her attention to her husband. "And how are you feeling?"

"Fine, a little tired and a little nervous, but fine."

"You have to take it easy. Try not to get too excited."

"Don't worry. I'll be okay."

In fact, Mr. Marzo was not okay. His heart condition had slowed him considerably.

"Nine years," Mrs. Marzo said sadly. "Our son has been gone for nine years." She brought her hands to her face. "Did we make a mistake, Angelo? Did we tell him to do the wrong thing?"

She'd been asking the same questions ever since her boy left.

Mr. Marzo moved closer and put his arm around her shoulder. "He's alive, Mary. And he's healthy. That's what we wanted. There's no use looking back."

"I know," she said. "But still…"

"You have to count your blessings. Your son is coming home and you have a new grandson. Think of the future."

She smiled briefly. "Our grandson, his pictures are so beautiful."

"He'll be even more beautiful in person; I'm sure of it. Angelo said he's starting to walk."

"I hope they like their room," she said.

"Of course they will. Why wouldn't they? You saw where they were living in Canada. This will be much better for them."

Her mood slumped again. "And what kind of life will they have? Will our son ever be accepted?"

"He'll be fine," her husband reassured her. "He'll run the store, and in time, things will be forgotten."

The Marzo family had paid a heavy price for their son's actions. When Angelo first fled the country, all but their closest friends became distant. Father Creeden remained a strong source of support and visited often, and Frankie, dear Frankie, kept his promise to Angelo to help them well beyond what anyone could have expected. As for everyone else, conversations were shorter; greetings were polite, but cool; and social invitations evaporated. Later, especially after Johnny died, there was a noticeable change for the worse. Mary was convinced people were saying nasty things behind their backs. Business dropped off as some lifelong customers visited the store less frequently or not at all. In time, as the war wound down, the tension eased, but things were never the same as before. Now, Mrs. Marzo wondered how her son would be treated.

Angelo and Donna agonized over the same issue. They knew they'd have an easier time if they established themselves in a different place, not far away, but somewhere where their history wouldn't follow them. But they had a baby and only modest savings. On top of that, Angelo knew that his father was failing. Without Angelo to help out, the family would lose the business. So he and Donna resigned themselves to their new reality. Their exile was over, but they were about to enter a new ordeal, which, in many ways, could be worse.

The bus arrived ten minutes later and Mr. and Mrs. Marzo went to greet it. Five or six people filed out before Angelo finally appeared. Donna was behind him holding the baby, and Angelo turned to help her down the steps. When they saw Angelo's parents, they hurried toward them.
"Mom!" Angelo shouted as he locked his arms around her. Mr. Marzo was next. "Welcome home, son," he said as the two of them embraced. They turned their attention to Donna who had stayed a step back. Mrs. Marzo squeezed her shoulder and kissed her cheek warmly. "You're finally home," she beamed.
"Hello, Mrs. Marzo," Donna said smiling, "and Mr. Marzo."
Mr. Marzo wrapped one arm around her and the other around the baby.
"And this is my grandson," he said proudly. Under doctor's orders, they hadn't made the trip to Canada for a year and a half and were seeing the child for the first time.
"He'll be a year old next week," Donna said cheerfully.
"And what a party we'll have!" Mr. Marzo said.
The baby was bundled against the cold and Donna moved the blanket to expose his face.
Mrs. Marzo crossed herself and said something in Italian. Then she said, "So beautiful."
"It's freezing, Mr. Marzo said. "Let's get the baby in the car."

"Good idea, Pop," Angelo said. "We just have a couple of bags. We shipped the rest. I'll get our things while you wait in the car."

Mr. Marzo drove. Angelo's license had expired, and the last thing anyone wanted was trouble with the law. "We've fixed your old room and made a place for the baby," Mrs. Marzo said excitedly. "Your father bought a crib. You're welcome to stay as long as you like," she said.

"Just until we get on our feet," Donna said from the back seat.

"Whatever is good," Mr. Marzo added. "There's no hurry. Stay forever!"

"Thanks, Pop," Angelo said. "We'll talk about it."

As he drove Mr. Marzo glanced at his wife. She looked more at ease than she'd been in years. He reached over and playfully rubbed her knee. She smacked his hand playfully and said, "Drive, old man." She was smiling broadly.

He looked in the rear view mirror and saw Donna kiss the baby on the forehead while Angelo stroked the child's hair. It was then that Mr. Marzo realized the dull ache in his chest was gone.

The house was located at the rear of the store. They entered from the side door and Angelo froze in the doorway as he took the place in. He bit his lip as he saw the images of his boyhood, things he hadn't seen for almost a decade. His father patted him on the back and said, "This is home."

Angelo nodded.

Mrs. Marzo took them upstairs to show them Angelo's old bedroom. It was a large room with a double bed and two dressers. In the corner, the Marzos had set up the baby's crib. "We only had two weeks to get ready," she said, "but we had the room painted and bought new sheets for the bed. We didn't know if you wanted the crib in this room or the small room next door. You can do whatever you want."

"It looks wonderful," Donna said. "I love the curtains and bedspread."

"Looks great Mom," Angelo added. "Thank you."

"What about the crib?" Mrs. Marzo asked.

"I think we'll keep it in here at least for a while to see how he adjusts," Donna said.

"That's what I thought," Mrs. Marzo said. "Let's go downstairs and have something to eat, you must be hungry."

"Starved," Angelo said.

When they got settled at the table, Mr. Marzo said, "Angelo, I feel like some hot peppers. Do your old man a favor and get me some from the store."

"Sure, Pop," Angelo said.

He walked down the short corridor that connected the house with the storefront. When he flipped the light switch, he saw Frankie, Nick and Jimmy sitting at the deli table.

Jimmy had one of those small New Year's Eve noisemakers, the kind that uncurls when you blow into it. "Surprise," he said, and blew on the mouthpiece. "It's been a while."

"Welcome home, Angelo," Frankie said.

Angelo stood dazed in the doorway.

Nick said, "It's freezing in here, man. Does the store have a separate thermostat?"

"Come on in," Frankie said. "It's your store."

Still speechless, Angelo almost staggered into the room.

"So how was the bus ride?" Nick asked. "Did the bus have a john or did you have to hold it in all the way from Canada?"

"How'd you like the paint job in the bedroom? It took us three days," Frankie said.

Without responding he studied them from head to toe. Frankie looked heavier, Jimmy looked thinner, and Nick, there was something different about Nick. Angelo was still ten feet away from them, but he stopped and leaned back against the counter. When he spoke, his voice was deep and hoarse. "I'm so sorry," he said, choking back tears. "I'm so sorry I ran out on you guys."

Jimmy shrugged. Frankie smiled and said, "Your parents told us you were coming. We thought a surprise would be nice."

"I didn't expect to see you so soon," Angelo stammered. "I needed time to figure out what to say. I don't know where to start."

"I used to have that problem," Nick said.

Jimmy stood. "Let me start for you. None of us knows what to say. The war was one big friggin' mess." He put his hand on Nick's shoulder. "My best friend here, he did all kinds of honorable stuff before he got his ass captured. He came home banged up. But guess what? He believed in the whole deal and would go back tomorrow if we cranked it up again. So he's obviously crazy. Me, I went through two stages. The first stage was to do my duty for my country. That lasted about three days. In the second stage I was fighting for good old Jimmy Wright and a couple of guys in my platoon. That was it. Everything else was too confusing. That stage lasted for the rest of the war. If I had it to do over again, I'd probably be on a bus heading north with you. So Nick and I disagree, but that's okay. Frankie here, he spent the whole war beating himself up over Johnny. Still does. No reason to, but try to tell him that. Then big, sad Frankie damned near killed a guy and didn't even have to leave town to do it. We had to go all the way to Nam to kill ours; he almost killed Charlie Gario right in front of Johnny's house. As for Johnny, it hurts too much to talk about it, but sometimes we do and most times we don't. He was a hero, a real hero. So was Nick, but Nick won't let us say that about him, so forget I said it. But Johnny's dead so we can say it. The guy was an American hero, and we're proud of him. I think he felt the same way Nick does about the war. At least he did the last time I heard from him. When the world lost him, it lost someone special. He had something. And his mother, you could go crazy thinking about how sad it is.

"Then there's you. I'd say you screwed up your life pretty good for the past few years. You know that better than we do. So this war grabbed all of us you-know-where with one hand while it punched us in the face with the other. As for who got punched the hardest, we gave up trying to sort that out. Stuff like that can make you mad. Some days we really get pissed off about the whole thing, tryin' to figure out what's fair, but most others, we just don't give a crap. Today's a don't-give-a-crap day, so enjoy it."

"This is a really good speech," Nick said. "Is there an intermission?"

"Pipe down, wacko. I'm not finished," Jimmy said. "Aside from the guys in this room, the guys I grew up with, you included, and two or three guys from Nam, there are very few people I care about or who care about me. So I'm not about to kiss off any of them because some smart ass in Washington decided it would be a good idea if we fought in Vietnam. I was mad at you once, but I'm not anymore. So kill the sorry crap and get over here and say hello."

"Yeah," Nick said. "And turn up the damn heat; it's freezing."

Angelo fought back his tears as they hugged, laughed and high-fived each other.

Frankie went to the deli case and took out the six- pack he was storing there. When they each had a beer in hand, Frankie said, "To Angelo and Donna's homecoming and their new son."

"By the way," Jimmy said, "What's the kid's name?"

"Johnny," Angelo replied. "My boy's name is John Francis Marzo." They all drank to that.

Part VII
Reunion, 1991

63- The Invitation

April 1991

All the invitations arrived on the same day. Nick was sitting at the deli table reading his for the tenth time when Jimmy walked in.

"It can still get pretty hot at the shore in mid September," Nick said, without introduction. "Does the place have air conditioning?"

"I don't know," Jimmy said. "Maybe not."

"Angelo thinks it does," Nick said.

Angelo slammed his hand on the meat counter. "I told you five times!" Angelo thundered, "It's in the brochure. Read it!"

"I'm still reading the letter," Nick said calmly.

"How many times are you going to read the damn thing?" Jimmy asked. "You were reading it when I left for deliveries an hour ago."

"He's been reading it the whole time you've been gone," Angelo said. Nick was undeterred. "I'm looking for hidden meanings," Nick said. The note was typed, and Nick read it again.

Dear Jake's Alumni,

I hope this letter finds you well and enjoying life. I know I owe you and the other guys an apology for coming out of the blue like this. I guess when people move away to follow their work, they lose touch, and before you know it, half a lifetime has gone by. In my case, I totally threw myself into building my career and raising a family. I've been pretty lucky with both, but the truth is, I've been thinking about the old days a lot lately.

Believe it or not, 1991 marks the twenty-fifth anniversary of our graduation from good old Bristol High. I'm not much of a class reunion guy. I think they're phony and way too formal. Besides, there aren't that many people from the old class that I'm dying to see. But I am dying to see the old gang, and I think it would be great if we could get together for a weekend. I've been wanting to do that for a long time.

Last year my wife Trish and I bought an old Victorian mansion at the Jersey shore in Beach Haven on Long Beach Island. You might remember the island, it's just south of our old stomping grounds at Seaside. Trish always wanted to open a bed and breakfast when we retire, so we got an early start. We completely rehabbed it and last year was our first season in operation. Trish spends the entire summer there with our two teenage girls, while I kill myself during the week with the law practice in North Jersey and join her for long weekends.

Here's my idea. Our rental season drops off after Labor Day, and I'm thinking that we could block out a weekend, and have you and the whole gang as our guests. We have sixteen rooms, so everyone, wives and significant others included, would have a place to stay. We have a huge dining room that could accommodate all of us, and a large back yard with a pool. We'll eat, drink, relax, and catch up on old times. I've been thinking about the old gang for a long time. Now that the kids are in college and the younger guys are doing most of the work in the firm, I've had more time to reflect, and, as I said, I miss you guys a lot. The date is the second weekend in September. Hopefully, 1991 will be the year that starts a new tradition.

Billy Moyer

At the end of the letter, Billy had added a hand-written note.

Nick,

As I'm sure Frankie told you, I came to visit you at Walter Reed. Unfortunately, it was right after one of your operations and you were sedated. I'm sure you had your reasons for not answering my letter, and I understand. I just want to see you and everyone else again.

Billy

"I'm not going," Nick said, as he folded the letter.
"Neither am I," Jimmy said. "How come you're not?"
"Too fancy," Nick said. "These bed and breakfasts are frilly. Chick stuff. They've got antiques, lace curtains, grandfather clocks with that constant soothing rhythm in the background. All the stuff chicks like. It makes me nervous. I'd probably break some priceless dish or vase from the Ming dynasty and ruin the whole weekend. It's not for me."
Jimmy nodded in agreement.
"What about you?" Nick said. "How come you're not gong?"
"Bathrooms," Jimmy said flatly. "I saw a show on TV once about a couple that turned an old place into a bed and breakfast. It had one bathroom on each floor! No way I'm sharing a bathroom with strangers. What if I have to wiz before I go to bed? Am I waiting in the hallway

while some eighty-year- old broad in a bathrobe, with rollers in her hair, brushes her false teeth? I'm not going."

"Jesus!" Angelo thundered from behind the counter. "First of all, we'll be the only guests there. Second, will you please read the damn brochure?" He wiped his hands on his apron and unfolded the brochure Billy had sent each of them. "It says right here on the cover, 'Combining Victorian Age elegance with modern conveniences, each room is air conditioned and has a full private bath and honor bar. Guests may use the heated pool in the rear or enjoy the beautiful sandy beach.'"

"What's an honor bar?" Jimmy asked.

"They stock the room with those little bottles of booze like they serve on airplanes. You're supposed to keep track of what you drink and pay when you leave," Angelo said.

"Are you kidding me?" Jimmy said. "I'd scam them good. I'd drink four or five and say I had three."

"Then you'd be screwing Billy," Angelo said.

"No, I wouldn't because I'm not going."

"Neither am I," Nick said. "And what's with having a pool at the shore? That's like having a hot dog stand in a restaurant. I don't get it."

Angelo shrugged. "I'm just reading the brochure."

"And what about you?" Nick said to Angelo. "Are you going?"

"I don't think so. It feels funny."

"How?" Nick asked.

"I don't know," Angelo said. "It just doesn't feel right."

Jimmy and Nick nodded. They had no idea what he meant, but were pleased that they had another to boycott the weekend.

Frankie arrived a minute later.

Hey, look what the wind just blew in," Nick said smiling.

"Must have been a gale force," Jimmy added. Proud of himself, he leaned over to high five Nick.

Frankie ignored them, nodded to Angelo, and went to the coffee counter. He looked as if he had something on his mind.

"You get your letter?" Nick asked.

"Yeah, I got it," Frankie said.

"We're not going," Jimmy said. Feeling vulnerable he added, "I'm not, Nick's not and Angelo's not."

Frankie didn't respond. He poured his coffee, grabbed a newspaper and sat down at their table. He started to read, but Nick interrupted him. "Are you going?"

Frankie looked annoyed. "Sure I'm going; Billy's my friend." He returned to the paper.

"Wanna know why we're not going?" Nick asked sheepishly.

"What's the use?" Frankie said. "I'm sure you've got your reasons."

"Lots of reasons," Jimmy said.

"Great," Frankie said. "Just keep them to yourself, okay?"

He turned to the sports page.

"So how come you're going?" Jimmy asked.

Frankie lowered the paper and shook his head. He took a deep breath. "Look, I'm going. We're all going. I already called and told him. So get that into your heads. Billy invited us, and he's our friend, so we're going. It's that simple."

Nick's smile faded, and things got quiet. Then Nick said, "You told him we were going without asking us? Why did you do that?"

"Because I knew you guys would have a hundred dumb ass reasons not to go, so I decided to skip the crap. It's easier this way."

Nick nodded, but he looked mad. Angelo just kept working behind the food counter.

Jimmy said, "What makes you think we'll go, just because you said so?"

"I'm hoping you'll go." He stressed the word hoping. "I'm hoping you'll go because I'm asking you as a favor."

It got quiet again. Frankie didn't ask people for favors; Frankie always did favors.

Nick smacked his lips and rubbed his shaved head. He stood and walked a few feet and then walked back.

"You want us to go, Frankie?" Nick asked.

"I want you to go," Frankie confirmed.

"You think it's important?"

"I think it would be good for us to see Billy," Frankie said.

"Are you driving?" he asked.

"I'm driving," Frankie replied.

Nick banged his palm on the table. "I'm going!" he exclaimed. "If I can find my bathing suit, I'm going."

Jimmy looked startled. "What about me?"

"What about you?" Frankie said.

"He's worried about the bathrooms," Nick said. "I don't know why. It says right in the brochure that they have private baths. Angelo explained it to him."

"I'm not going to stay here if you guys are going," Jimmy said.

"Why don't you come with us?" Frankie said lightly.

"Will there be clams and beer?" Jimmy asked.

"Are you kidding?" Frankie said. "It's the shore. Of course we'll have clams and beer."

Jimmy flashed a wide grin. "Count me in."

Angelo was peeling potatoes throughout the exchange.

Frankie got up and walked to the counter.

"How about you Angelo?"

"Can't do it."

"Why not?"

"No one to watch Johnny."

"That's a load of crap. The kid's fourteen and has plenty of friends. He can stay at somebody's house for one night. You set it up with the parents."

Angelo shrugged.

"What's the real reason?" Frankie said.

Angelo looked troubled. "I don't know, Frankie. It just doesn't feel right."

"Why not?" Frankie said.

"I don't know. Billy went to Nam after he graduated from college. I don't know how he feels about what I did."

"He sent you an invitation," Jimmy said. He shot a quick look at Nick hoping to confirm that he had just made a good point. Nick gave him a thumbs up.

"He was probably just being polite," Angelo said.

"He wants you there," Frankie said.

"He probably just invited everybody from our class," Angelo added.

"Charlie Gario's not invited," Frankie said. "I asked Billy before I said yes."

"I wouldn't eat clams with that son of a bitch," Jimmy said.

"Think about Donna. She'll have a nice weekend in a beautiful setting," Frankie said.

"Yeah, a real chick place," Nick added.

"She doesn't care about that stuff," Angelo said.

"Come on, Angelo," Frankie said. "When was the last time you took her on a vacation?"

"Hey, that's not fair," Nick said. "He brought her to Canada once for an extended vacation."

"Screw you," Angelo said.

"Sorry man, I was just kidding."

"She'll be the only woman there," Angelo said.

"Not true," Frankie said. "Billy's wife Trish will be there, and Ralph is taking his wife."

"Ralph's going?" Angelo said.

"Everybody but you," Frankie said.

"And that son of a bitch Gario," Jimmy added.

"Just drop it about Gario, okay?" Frankie said.

He turned back to Angelo. "Are you in?"

Angelo smiled. "What the heck," he said. "A couple of days at the beach can't be too bad."

"I hope it doesn't rain," Nick said.

64- The Island

Frankie, Nick, and Jimmy rode in the cab of Frankie's pickup, wearing matching sunglasses that Nick picked up at Wal-Mart. Frankie slipped the Beach Boys into the tape deck, and the three of them sang along to "Surfin' USA."

"What a day!" Nick said, when he tired of the song. "This is beach weather."

"Just like old times," Jimmy said. "But we should be heading to Seaside. Man, we used to own Seaside."

Nick elbowed Frankie. "Hey, Frankie. Remember the Tone Kings singing at Seaside?"

Frankie smiled. "I remember."

"How about the crowds we drew?"

"I remember," Frankie repeated. "Those were good times."

"What about the stories we made up to impress the girls," Jimmy said. "That was fun."

"We never needed stories to impress them. We were impressive enough," Nick said proudly.

"Damn right," Jimmy said. "But we did it anyway."

Nick turned off the tape and started singing "Under the Boardwalk." Frankie and Jimmy joined in. Frankie took the deep part. Big, sad Frankie was having a good time. They all were.

They crossed the causeway and entered Long Beach Island. "Six Miles Out to Sea," the sign read. Frankie turned right on to Long Beach Boulevard and headed south, with the ocean on their left and the bay on their right. It was a narrow island, just a few blocks wide in most spots and was far less commercial than the places like Seaside or Wildwood that they were used to. They passed through Ship Bottom, Brandt Beach and continued south toward Beach Haven.

Nick noted that there wasn't a boardwalk.

"The people like it quiet," Frankie said. "They still have an amusement park for kids, but no boardwalk."

Jimmy looked perplexed. "Quiet at the shore?" It didn't make sense.

"It's a family place," Frankie explained.

Nick started singing "Under the Boardwalk" again, but no one joined in this time, and he soon trailed off.

"That was Johnny's song," Frankie said with a touch of sadness.

"He was the best," Jimmy said.

"A magnet for girls," Nick added.

They drove in silence for a while until Jimmy said, "I think we passed it."

"It's a few blocks after the Ferris wheel. Do you see a Ferris wheel?" Frankie asked.

Just then they did. The amusement park was not far ahead on the right.

"Okay," Nick said excitedly. "We're getting closer."

"Did Billy say it's before Center Avenue or after," Nick asked.

"Before," Jimmy said.

"After!" Frankie corrected. "Look," he added. "I've got the directions. I'll handle it."

Soon Frankie turned left and they headed toward the ocean. The street was lined with grand Victorian homes, meticulously maintained. He drove slowly as he checked the house numbers. He didn't have to. When Billy's home came into view, Nick said, "Sweet Jesus."

The building was a wonderful three story Victorian, complete with a turret that extended past the roofline, and a magnificent wrap-around porch. There was a widow's walk above the third floor trimmed with gingerbread. The porch railings were made of spindles painted in a multicolored Victorian design. There was also a small porch on the second floor and a smaller, ornamental balcony on the third. The top panes of the windows were stained glass. It was a marvelous building that was obviously kept in superb condition. The sign above the porch read, "The Moyer House."

Ralph and his wife Judy were standing on the porch. Ralph was wearing an Eagles hat and a Hawaiian shirt. Donna and Angelo were there too. Both men were holding beers, and the girls held drink glasses. They all cheered and raised their drinks as Frankie beeped and pulled into the driveway. Billy heard the commotion and came out to greet them. He had aged well, looking as trim and fit as he was in high school. He rushed to the car and gave Frankie a bear hug. Nick and Jimmy came around and did the same. It was a warm, but awkward meeting and Billy got a little choked up.

When the greetings were over, Billy said, "Trish is out back getting lunch ready. Let's get you settled and have something to eat."
"Sounds great," Nick said.
As they climbed the steps to the porch, Billy noticed Nick's limp and the scar on his neck. There was another round of greetings when they got to Donna, Judy and the other guys. Taking it all in, Frankie felt happier and more relaxed than he had in a long time.

Once out back, they met Trish. She looked like one of those healthy, vibrant women who appear on the covers of women's magazines. She was attractive, with a lean, runner type body and an easy smile. Everything about her, her jogging suit, her sneakers, her haircut, looked expensive, but not lavish. Her personality matched her appearance. She was a gracious hostess and embraced her new guests as though she had known them for a lifetime. Within minutes, everyone felt comfortable.

Billy's backyard was impressive. A large brick patio surrounded a tiled, in-ground pool. Beds of flowers and neatly trimmed shrubbery ringed the patio, and behind them was a scalloped cedar privacy fence.

Near the house, two long tables had been pulled together for lunch. Billy produced a large roll of brown wrapping paper that he used to cover the tabletops. Trish invited Judy and Donna to help her. Soon, the men watched in awe as they brought out trays of shucked clams on beds of ice, corn on the cob, cole slaw, sliced Jersey tomatoes, and potato salad. Angelo helped Billy carry two pots of crabs he had steamed on the outdoor grill. Nick noticed a large tub of iced beer in the corner and smiled. Donna dealt everyone disposable plastic plates, cups and utensils. Trish ran in the house once more and came out with a large pitcher of lemonade and nine nutcrackers for the crabs.

Jimmy's eyes looked like they would leave their sockets. Nick was mentally counting the ears of corn, calculating what his share would be. Frankie thought about the couple of pounds he had just lost, and shrugged it off. He'd lose it again later. When they sat, each of them showed remarkable restraint, waiting at least fifteen seconds before plunging into the food like Huns at a Middle Ages feast.

"This is what you call lunch?" Nick said, wiping corn from his chin.

Trish smiled. "We serve our guests something a little lighter, but this is such a special occasion, and Billy thought you might like it."

"Like it!" Jimmy said. "I'm moving in."

"Eat up," Billy said. "We're not having dinner until nine o'clock."

When lunch was over, Nick said, "We'll help you clean up."

"Wonderful," Trish said, "It shouldn't take long."

Billy dragged over a trashcan and peeled off two heavy-duty trash bags. He and Trish rolled the brown paper, the plastic plates, clamshells and crab claws into two neat bundles and dropped them into the bags. They sealed them and put them into the can. Then she winked at Nick, handed him the nine nutcrackers and said, "Would you wash these for me?" The whole cleanup took less than sixty seconds.

Billy said, "Life's too short to waste time. We're here to have fun, not do dishes. Pool or ocean?"

The pool looked inviting. The water was crystal clear, and there was an attached Jacuzzi.

Nick thought for a minute. "Does the ocean still have sand, salt water, and waves?" he asked grinning.

"Still does," Billy said.

"Then I say ocean." The men agreed, and the women opted for drinks around the pool.

"Okay," Billy said. "Let's suit up and meet here in ten minutes."

Jimmy looked down at himself. He was wearing the same cut off shorts he wore on most warm days. "I am suited up," he said sheepishly.

"Jesus," Angelo said. "You're forty-five years old. Don't you own a bathing suit?"

"Forty-three," Jimmy shot back. "And this is my bathing suit."

"We have extras," Trish said. "I'm sure Billy can find you one if you like."

Jimmy looked embarrassed.

"You're welcome to it Jimmy, but I think the shorts work fine." Billy said.

Jimmy relaxed. "I'll stick with these."

"Okay, let's go," Nick said, breaking the tension. "I haven't seen Ralph ride a wave since high school."

"You never saw Ralph ride a wave, because he can't swim," Angelo said.

Ralph grinned and looked at Judy. "They're always bustin'," he said.

Frankie visited the shore a lot, mostly on fishing trips with his uncle, and Ralph and Judy spent a couple of weeks each year in Avalon. But Angelo, Nick and Jimmy hadn't been to the shore since the summer after graduation. The September beach was almost empty, and they hit it like schoolboys. Any concern they had about how Nick would handle the water vanished quickly when he half limped, half trotted, to the surf and dove spastically into the first wave. He came up squealing with delight, his arms flailing wildly. Jimmy was next. He tried to do one of the running flips he was famous for in Seaside, but he damn near killed himself. Before going in, Angelo tried to pull down Ralph's bathing suit, but Ralph held on fiercely, so Angelo picked him up and threw him in the ocean.

Billy and Frankie stood at the shoreline laughing as the four of them were thrashing and howling at one another.

"This was a great idea," Frankie said.

"I'm really glad everyone came," Billy said, obviously touched by the scene.

"Me too."

They stood there for a minute until Billy broke the silence.

"So how are they doing?"

"They've gotten better over the years, but it's painful to see what the war did to them. Nick's been on disability since he's been out. His body is a wreck and getting worse. He's got constant pain in his neck and hip. The doctors say he still suffers from pellagra, brought on by nutritional deficiency from the POW camp. It left him with a stomach and intestinal disorder. You'd never know it from his eating habits, but trust me; he suffers later. He also has peripheral neuropathy, which is a tingling or numbness in his arms and legs."

"You sound like a doctor, Frankie," Billy said.

"I've been tuned in to his problems for twenty-years, ever since he was released. You get to learn things."

"Yeah, I guess you do," Billy replied. "Is there anything else?"

"He's got what they call traumatic arthritis. The beatings he took in Hanoi turned into permanent inflammation in his joints. It's like the professional football players who are almost crippled later in life from the hits they took when they were younger. I'm sure I'm leaving stuff out, but you get the picture."

Jimmy called to them from the water, "What are you guys waiting for? Come on in."

"We're on our way," Billy hollered back.

"How's Nick mentally?" Billy asked.

"He's as bright as ever, but he can't take any kid of pressure. He worked at a newsstand for years, but now he pretty much just hangs out at Angelo's store all day."

Billy closed his eyes and shook his head.

"The real kicker," Frankie said, "is that he's really gotten jerked around by the government. Don't get me wrong; when he's in a VA hospital he receives excellent care. The problem is getting treatment in the first place. Since he's been discharged he's had to fight for every benefit he has."

"Damn Frankie, I'm an attorney, I could have helped. Maybe I still can."

Frankie waved him off. "Nick has made it his life's work to learn the system. He knows the law and he hounds the Veterans Administration, both for himself and others. Did I mention he goes to the VA in Philly once a week? He's actually helped other guys get their benefits. I think the fight is actually good for him in a way. It gives him something to do, especially when he helps other guys."

The guys in the water were riding waves now, or trying to, and Frankie gave them thumbs up before continuing.

"I'll tell you though. The whole ordeal with the VA bureaucracy breaks his heart, cuts him up inside. The guys he helps got all smiles and promises at the recruiting office and then blank stares when they came back looking for help. Don't get me wrong; he's still a patriot. He claims he'd do it all again tomorrow, but I believe he experiences more pain from his disappointing treatment than the broken body he suffered from the Vietnamese.

"What about Jimmy?" Billy asked.

"Jimmy is fine physically, but he's an emotional wreck. He went through some really bad shit in Nam, some stuff I don't even know about. Then, he was given a handshake and sent home. He should have had some counseling, some transition back to regular life. He was offered it, but turned it down. He shouldn't have had a choice. He was only twenty years old when he got out. What did he know about shrinks? He came home angry, and still has bitterness twenty years later. It's not healthy."

"What does he do for money?" Billy asked.

"He got his old job back at the steel mill. He almost lost it because of his attitude, but he straightened out and hung in there. He retired last year after twenty years. He gets a small pension from the mill, but claims he doesn't need much. He inherited his parent's home, and he doesn't spend much on himself. He's another regular at Angelo's store."

"And how's Angelo?"

"Angelo's the tough guy, but he never recovered from going to Canada. Plenty of guilt because of Nick and Jimmy, and of course Johnny. He hides it by bustin' their chops all the time, but he treats 'em like gold when it counts. He's got a good family life. He and Donna have a boy, John Francis, Johnny. He's fourteen now. Nice kid. Aside from your girls, who we haven't met, he's the only kid in the gang. He calls all of us uncle. It's nice."

"Tell me about you," Billy said. "I've got a lot of catching up to do."

Frankie stayed quiet for a while, and when Ralph hollered, "Hey Frankie. These guys are placing bets over whether you'll sink or float. I say you'll sink."

Frankie laughed and sprinted to the surf.

65- Dinner at Billy's

After the beach the gang scattered. Judy and Ralph took off for Bay Village, a cluster of quaint, upscale shops nearby. Donna and Angelo walked to the bay to watch the sun set. Frankie took a nap. Nick read about historic shipwrecks on Long Beach Island, and Jimmy went for a walk.

By seven-thirty they started to drift back. Billy and Trish were setting the dinner table when Judy burst in, giddy from her shopping spree. Ralph was close behind, loaded with packages.

"We found so many cute shops," she said.

"I knew you'd like the Village," Trish said cheerfully.

Ralph looked at Billy and rolled his eyes.

"Drink?" Billy said, as he fixed himself one.

"Sounds good. I'll take these bags upstairs first," Ralph said.

"Thanks, Ralphie," Judy said, kissing him on the cheek. "Mind if I start without you?"

"Not at all," Ralph said unconvincingly.

She turned to Billy, "Vodka and tonic please, with lots of ice."

Angelo and Donna arrived next, looking like starry-eyed honeymooners.

"The island is beautiful," Donna said dreamily. "We're moving here."

"Yeah," Angelo said. "Right after we hit the lottery."

Donna elbowed him. "I'm serious! You haven't been this relaxed in years. We'll open a deli, do some catering."

"I can hook you up with some contacts," Billy said, smiling at Donna. "People do lots of entertaining on the island."

"The Yacht Club has a catered party almost every night," Trish added. "We could get your foot in the door."

"Maybe next year," Angelo said. "Right now, I care more about my stomach than my foot. I need a beer."

"Frosted mug?" Billy asked.

Angelo nodded, "You're spoiling me."

"How about you, Donna?" Trish asked.

"I drink what my man drinks," she said, resting her head on Angelo's shoulder. "Even if he won't move to LBI."

Nick strolled in next, still holding the book he'd been reading. "I can't believe how many shipwrecks there've been on the Jersey coastline."

"Some say hundreds," Billy said. "And LBI has had its share."

"Fascinating," Nick said. "The book says the island has an old lighthouse."

"It's about fifteen miles from here," Trish said, "on the northern tip of the island. "It's almost a hundred and fifty years old and stands one hundred and seventy-two feet above sea level."

"Wow," Nick said, "You know your stuff."

"Trish is a member of the historic society," Billy said. "Don't get her started."

"Hey, I love history," Nick replied.

"Tell you what," Trish said brightly. "On a clear morning you can see the lighthouse from our widow's walk upstairs. If it's nice tomorrow, we'll check it out."

"Great," Nick said. Then he caught Billy looking at his leg and added, "Don't worry, I can make the climb."

"Then it's a date." Trish said.

Frankie came down the stairs carrying a tin canister for Trish. "These are Italian cookies from Mrs. Francelli, our friend Johnny's mom."

Trish smiled. "Billy told me all about Johnny and Mrs. Francelli. I feel like I know them. This is so nice of her."

"I think they're pizzelles."

"I love pizzelles," she said. "We'll have them for dessert. Please thank her for me."

Frankie glanced at the stairway and then motioned for everyone to come closer.

"Listen," he whispered, "Jimmy is upstairs getting dressed. He'll be down soon."

"So what?" Angelo said.

"I mean he's really getting *dressed*. When he went for his walk he bought a new shirt and tie."

"A tie!" Nick said. "He didn't tell me. I would have bought one too, to show a little respect for the beautiful lady of the house."

"That's so sweet," Trish said. "But it's hardly necessary here."

"There's no tie," Angelo said. "Frankie's just jerkin' us around."

"I swear," Frankie said. "Ralph's up there now helping him tie it. The first time Jimmy tried it the knot was as big as a baseball."

"And why in the world is Jimmy doing this?" Nick asked.

"He said he's tired of being a bum," Frankie said. "I think the bathing suit thing embarrassed him this morning."

Angelo grinned, "This is gonna be a treat."

"Don't bust his chops," Frankie pleaded. "He got the bug to do this and he's nervous about it."

"He should be," Angelo said. "It's a dumb ass idea. We're at the shore, not the prom."

"The prom!" Nick said. "Remember the brown Hush Puppies Jimmy wore with his tux?"

Nick chuckled and started to bark. Angelo joined in.

"Quiet," Donna said. "He'll hear you." The barking stopped and Donna said, "I'm surprised at you, Nick. You're his best friend."

"We're just foolin'," he said sheepishly.

Donna wasn't satisfied. "If any of you guys make fun of him I'll rip your eyes out." Then she glared at Angelo and added, "especially you."

Angelo gave her a sarcastic smile and said, "No problem darling."

"I mean it!" she said. "And lose that stupid look on your face."

Angelo put his arm around her and looked at Billy. "See, didn't I tell you she was a sweetheart?"

The room went silent when Jimmy and Ralph walked in. Despite Frankie's warning, they weren't prepared for what they saw. Jimmy was cleanly shaved and scrubbed. His shoes had been done with liquid polish, the kind that comes with a sponge applicator. They looked shiny and clean, but streaked. His hair was plastered with a heavy dose of tonic. He wore khaki pants and a blue button down shirt still wrinkled from the packaging. Thanks to Ralph, his striped tie sported a smart Windsor knot. He had obviously added a healthy dose of cheap cologne. His hands were in his pockets and his eyes were focused on the floor. Nick took it all in and tried to imagine him at the store by himself buying the stuff. Nick always took Jimmy shopping.

"Hi guys," Trish said brightly. "Join the party."

"I'm making drinks," Billy said. "What would you like?"

Both asked for a beer.

Angelo and Nick caught each other's eyes, and Nick started to grin. Donna shot him a nasty look, and he turned away.

Angelo felt himself losing it, said something about needing ice, and bolted for the kitchen. Trish followed him.

Frankie decided to start a conversation.

"Hey, Jimmy, the Eagles play the Cowboys tomorrow. It's a big game."

"Eagles, no problem," Jimmy said.

"Even with Randall Cunningham hurt? They lost last week without him."

"What's wrong with Randall?" Judy asked.

"He hurt his knee in the first game against Green bay. Tore it up pretty good. He's out for the season," Frankie said.

"Oh my," Judy said. "Randall's a great quarterback."

"The Eagles will be fine," Jimmy said. "My man Reggie White and the defense will take charge."

"The Minister of Defense," Frankie added reverently.

Trish returned in time to hear Jimmy say they had to leave early Sunday morning to be home in time to watch the game.

"Why not stay all day and watch it here?" she said.

"That's right," Billy added. "I'll be watching it."

"Thanks," Jimmy said. "But we always watch the game in Angelo's store. It's tradition."

After a while Trish said, "Why don't we start taking our seats at the table? She draped her arm around Jimmy's and said, "Come on, handsome, I want you sitting next to me."

Jimmy smiled awkwardly and allowed himself to be led.

Soon the second feast of the day began. They started with steaming bowls of New England clam chowder.

"This chowder is sensational," Judy said.

"I wish I could say I made it," Trish confessed, "But we actually bought it. There's a chowder festival on the island each October. It's kind of the unofficial end of the season. Restaurants and chowder joints all over the island compete. We buy the winner's chowder all year."

"It's delicious," Ralph said.

"You should come to the festival next month. It's a good day," Billy said.

"There you go, Angelo," Donna said. "We can move here and open a chowder joint. It would be fun."

"Italian chowder?" Angelo said. "I don't think so."

Donna just shook her head.

After the chowder, Trish gave everyone cotton bibs, each with a matching embroidered lobster and script that read, "The Moyer House, LBI."

Angelo looked at Nick again, dying to say something about Jimmy's tie. Donna noticed and kicked him under the table.

Billy brought in an iron tray filled with sizzling steaks, and his guests ooed and ahhed.

Next came a cauldron of steaming five-pound lobsters. Trish and Donna added melted butter, sour cream and baked potatoes.

The guests were stunned by the spread. After staring at the table for a few seconds, Ralph said, "This is embarrassing. You've done too much."

"Just enjoy it," Billy said, smiling proudly.

"No really," Judy said. "You're way too kind. The lodging, the food, we should share the cost."

"Please don't spoil a beautiful day. This is what we want to do," Billy said.

Trish added, "Believe me, Billy has been like a little kid ever since he knew you were coming. We enjoy this."

Frankie held up his beer. "To Trish and Billy," he said.

"To Trish and Billy," the group repeated.

It was a perfect dinner party. They laughed as they struggled with their nutcrackers, while Billy patiently taught them to crack the lobster claws. They ate, drank and shared memories. Trish loved hearing about the wedding crashes and the Tone Kings.

"Billy has some old tapes of you guys singing," she said. "Maybe we can play them later."

"Forget the tapes," Angelo said. "A few more beers and we'll sing live."

"Better stick to the tapes," Frankie said. "There's not enough beer on the island to make us sound good now."

"Speaking of old times," Trish said proudly, "Billy has a surprise for you guys in our sitting room. The girls and I are going to sit out back. You guys have fun."

After the girls left, Billy said, "Okay, follow me."

Jimmy stopped him. "Billy, mind if I ask you something first?"

"Of course not," Billy replied. "What's up?"

"Well, first of all, thanks for this day. It's been unbelievable. You throw a great party, and Trish is terrific. Beautiful house, beautiful wife, kids, a law practice, you're a lucky guy."

"Thanks, Jimmy. I appreciate that," Billy said. "I count my blessings every day."

Jimmy nodded. "Here's the thing. We've been out of touch a long time, and I know you went to Nam after college, but that's all I know. Can you fill us in?"

The room got quiet. Billy scratched his head and thought for a minute.

"It's history, Jimmy. Everything was a long time ago. I try not to think about it too much.

"That's right," Frankie said, "It's in the past. Let's go see our surprise."

"Yeah, what the hell," Angelo said as he started to stand up. Ralph joined him.

Billy looked at Nick. He looked interested in Jimmy's question too.

Billy shrugged. "It's no big deal. I'll keep it short."

Angelo and Ralph sat down and Billy started.

"By the time I graduated from college, Nixon had replaced student deferments with the draft lottery. I pulled a bad number and was sure I'd be called. I wanted to go to law school, but I didn't want the draft hanging over me, so I went in to get it over with. They sent me to Officer Candidate School. I came out a Second Lieutenant and was in Nam by September of 1970, right after Kent State. We still had a quarter-million men there, but Nixon was pulling them out gradually. Morale was rock bottom. We were fighting in Nam while Lt. Calley was on trial here for war crimes. Kissinger was negotiating a peace settlement and there were rumors that the war could end at any time. All of that just made it worse. It's like you're risking your life for a cause that's already over. We know now the rumors were wrong. The war dragged on another two and a half years. But back then, no one wanted to be the last guy to die and yet guys kept dying all around me, somewhere between three and four thousand while I was there. Our unit saw plenty of action, most of it against North Vietnamese regulars near the DMZ. They were better trained and equipped than the VC, and they were tenacious bastards. I lost some good men."

"How did it end for you?" Jimmy asked.

"Our platoon ran into a full company of NV regulars. They had us pinned down pretty good and guys were dropping. Eventually, I called in an air strike. It was dangerous with the enemy so close, but I had no choice. Anyway, it worked, but I took a pretty good chunk of shrapnel in the shoulder. It was serious enough to get me sent home two months early. The arm went dead for a while, nerve damage, but ninety percent of the feeling came back with treatment. The fact is I was damn lucky compared to a lot of guys. Anyway, I came home and blocked it out, put it behind me."

"I wish I could do that," Jimmy said. "I just get so pissed off sometimes. It's bad enough that the war was a waste, but then they screw the guys who fought. Sometimes..." he let himself trail off.

Nick finished for him. "For the past ten years Jimmy and I have been visiting the VA hospital and outreach center in Philly. Every Wednesday I help guys fill out benefit claims. I know the forms inside and out. The government rejections are unbelievable. It makes you want to scream. Guys with legitimate problems having to fight for their benefits."

Angelo, Ralph and Frankie listened quietly. Everything with Nick was usually humor and sarcasm. Tonight was different.

"I could tell you stories of disabled veterans that would make you cry. And I'm not talking about questionable disabilities. I'm talking about guys who lost limbs or vision and still have to fight the bureaucracy. They get treated well at first, but have to fight later for everything they get. But those are the obvious problems. Then there was the whole Agent Orange thing. How could we turn our backs on it for so long when the evidence was overwhelming? It was a joke. All they had to do was check the cancer rates, the birth defects. But they dragged their feet, made it a battle. And what about psychological damages? There was no exit counseling worth anything. No matter what guys had been through, most, like Jimmy, got a handshake and a pat on the ass. That's it. And the widows, forget it. Do you know what the death benefit was for a guy in Vietnam?"

Nick sat back and exhaled deeply, shaking his head. Jimmy put his hand on his shoulder. The room stayed quiet while Nick took a sip of beer.

"I'm sorry, Billy," he continued. "I don't know why I'm getting into all of this. It's just that I can't get this thing off my back and neither can Jimmy. Seeing you this weekend, seeing how life is supposed to be, seeing how you went through stuff like we went through, but you managed to put yourself together, we're happy as hell for you. But it just makes me think of all the guys who couldn't put it together, who weren't strong enough. That's what I can't shake. Not my problems, but theirs."

Billy's eyes filled up. "I don't know what to say, Nick. Everything you're saying is true. I guess guys like me never looked behind us. We should have."

"That's not it, Billy. You did what you should have done for yourself. I'm serious. My complaint is with the people at the top: presidents, congressmen, senators and generals, they could have done a better job for their vets. They still can."

"Now there are new veterans," Jimmy added. "Desert Storm."

"At least Powell and Schwarzkopf knew how to fight a war," Ralph interjected. "We bombed the crap out of Iraq for five weeks and then fought a ground war that lasted four days!"

"That's the way to do it," Jimmy agreed, "instead of using grunts like me as pawns. Hell, President George Herbert Walker Bush, or whatever the hell his name is, launched the troops in February 1991 and two weeks later some of the first guys were coming home. That's the way to fight a war."

"But here's the rub," Nick said. "Some of those guys have been home for six months and we're already hearing stories of strange ailments. Did Saddam use a chemical agent on our guys? Were they exposed to depleted uranium, radioactive waste? I don't know, but I'll tell you this, already the government's response has been the same as it was for Agent Orange. Same crap. Send them to fight, and then don't listen to them when they get back."

He lowered his eyes and his voice dropped. "I just don't know anymore."

No one spoke for a long time. Finally, Nick raised his head and laughed. He looked around the room and laughed again. "I'll tell you what I do know," he said. "I know I love everybody in this room. Everybody. And I'm so damn glad that Billy is back in our lives."

Now Billy wiped a tear.

"And I know something else. I'm screwing up a great party, and I'm really sorry."

Then, with a glint in his eyes he said, "Let's see this surprise."

"Sounds good," Billy said. "It's in the next room."

66- Video Replay

It was the kind of room they were taught to stay out of as kids, with floor to ceiling bookcases, Victorian furniture and an ornate fireplace. Dimly lit Tiffany lamps and the rhythmic ticking of a grandfather clock created an unlikely mood for what was about to take place.

Billy fussed with a large TV that had been rolled in. "Have a seat," he said, while searching for the power cord.

Jimmy looked around, "We can't sit in here. This stuff's too nice."

Billy laughed. "They're reproductions we buy from our hotel supplier. They're made to sit on. Relax."

They sat and Nick said, "Okay, what's this all about?"

"I told you guys that I wanted to have a reunion."

He held up a videocassette. "This," Billy said proudly, "is Thanksgiving Day, 1965, the Bristol Warriors and the Morrisville Bulldogs."

The room erupted.

"No kidding!" Angelo said. "You've got the tape?"

"Right here," Billy said, pleased with their reaction. "Hope you don't mind sitting through this Ralph," Billy said. Ralph was the only non-player in the room.

"Are you serious? It's the most exciting game I ever saw."

"Where'd you get it after all these years?" Frankie asked.

"In my attic. My Uncle Don had an 8mm camera back then, and he filmed the game. He gave it to my dad. Dad kept it in the attic, and when he passed away last year I found it. I took it to a friend at the camera shop and we converted the highlights to video."

"Fantastic," Angelo said. "I hear they can add background music."

Billy smiled broadly. "We've done better than that." He held up an audiocassette. "This is the WBCB radio broadcast of the game with Buzz Baker and Walter Bracey doing play by play."

"Buzz Baker! There's a name from the past," Frankie said.

"Dad was in the Rotary Club with him. Buzz gave him the tape. And," Billy continued, obviously pleased with himself, "Thanks to my friend at the camera store, we were able to dub in the broadcast. It was tedious, but worth it."

"Let's do it man!" Jimmy said, barely able to contain himself.

"There's one more thing," Billy added. "Because the taping was so time consuming, we skipped the first half. But it was a zero-zero tie anyway."

"Screw the first half," Angelo said. "Nothing happened. We just pounded each other."

"That's what we felt," Billy said. "We also edited out parts of the third quarter for he same reason. But we've got the important stuff."

"Roll it!" Jimmy said.

The video began with the Bristol band doing its halftime show.

The room cheered.

"Where are you, Ralph?" Frankie asked.

"First horn, in the center of the first row."

"All right!" Frankie said.

Then they heard the unmistakable voice of Walter Bracey doing the halftime analysis:

"…Bristol's quarterback, Nick Hardings is doing a fantastic job protecting the football. He's been sacked six times. He's been punished when running the option. He's taken monstrous hits. But each time, he's held on to the football…"

"Damn right!" Jimmy said, patting Nick on the back.

Next came the voice of Buzz Baker.

"Not only that, Walter, he's been an inspiration to his teammates. He just keeps picking himself up and encouraging his team…He's really showing some leadership out there."

As the band was filing off the field Bracey said,

"We've seen Hardings play well all year, but this is by far his most courageous effort."

The video jumped to Morrisville kicking off in the second half. The camera followed number twenty-five, who everyone knew was Johnny, as he returned the kick to the thirty-five yard line.

"Nice run, Johnny," Frankie said quietly.

"Francelli returns the ball to the thirty-five," Baker said.

"That was a nice run," Bracey added. *"And on the play, Angelo Marzo, flattened the Morrisville kicker. I mean he destroyed him. The kicker left the field with some difficulty. It looked like an ankle."*

Again the room cheered. "Just doing my job man," Angelo said.

"Nothing happens in the third quarter, so we edited it out," Billy said. No one cared because they knew what was coming.

The next image of the scoreboard clock showed eleven and a half minutes left in the game.

"Fourth quarter. Now the action starts," Billy said.

In the next scene, Morrisville's gifted running back, number twenty-two, took a handoff, cut back against a wall of defenders and raced down the right sideline.

"Tackle the son of a bitch," Angelo yelled.

"Not this time," Jimmy said, as the runner crossed into the end zone. Baker and Bracey were raving about the run, but no one was listening.

"Damn kid was good," Frankie mumbled.

"I forget his name," Jimmy said.

"Dawkins," Billy said. "The guy was powerful. I won't forget him."

As the teams lined up for the extra point, Baker said,

"Here's Morrisville's Matt Kutler to kick the extra point. You have to wonder if his ankle is okay after that Marzo hit earlier."

Just then, Kutler kicked the ball into his center's back.

"I guess he's not okay," Frankie yelled as Angelo accepted high-fives from around the room.

"That was big man. Real big," Jimmy said. The video showed Morrisville up 6-0.

Baker was speaking.
". . .could be important later in a close game."

Bracey jumped in.
". . . Kutler has gone to the bench. He's obviously more injured than we realized. Morrisville will be forced to use a different kicker for the kickoff. It's number eight. I'm checking my program. His name is Joe Scalfano. The kid's only a sophomore and we haven't seen him today. Let's see what happens."

"Oh Yeah!" Jimmy said. "You'll see."

The camera followed the short kick to Billy, who took it on the dead run, put on a burst of speed, and carried it to the Morrisville forty-five yard line.

"Bam!" Jimmy said. "What was that?"
"A cannon shot!" Frankie added.
The guys were barely in their seats. "Here we go," Ralph said, leaning forward and rubbing his hands.

"Hey, what happens next?" Jimmy asked, giddy with excitement.
"Like you don't know," Angelo said, messing Jimmy's hair. "Damn," he said, looking at his greasy hand, "how much stuff are you wearing?"

Frankie quieted them as Baker narrated.

"It's first and ten for Bristol. Nick Hardings takes the snap from center, hands off to Francelli going left. Wait! Francelli flips it back to Hardings on a flea flicker. Hardings lofts it to Jimmy Wright streaking down the right sideline. It's caught! Jimmy Wright caught the ball! Scott Robinson, Morrisville's all-stater, delivered a crushing hit to Jimmy Wright just as he caught the ball, but Wright held on. Wright is a hundred and thirty pound speedster, and Robinson punished him, but Bristol has the ball on Morrisville's four-yard line!"

There was bedlam in the room.

The camera zoomed in on Jimmy, and Angelo said, "Look for the dripping snot."

Jimmy punched him on the arm. "No snot."

"Like hell," Angelo said. "I saw it."

It was then that Frankie noticed Nick hadn't been saying anything. "Quiet down," Frankie said. "I think we want to see the next play." He winked at Nick, but Nick lowered his head.

The video showed Bristol break its huddle. Buzz Baker was still going nuts.

"Bristol trails six to nothing. Hardings leads his team out of the huddle. Bristol has three receivers split wide. The backs are split. Hardings takes the snap. He's back to pass. There's a strong outside rush. Hardings steps up. Quarterback draw! He's running. He scores! Touchdown Nick Hardings from four yards out!
Hardings spread the defense and ran a quarterback draw up the middle to tie the game!"

Frankie and Ralph were on their feet. Everyone was hooting for Nick, until they realized Nick's head was buried in his hands.

"Good job, man," Jimmy said softly, and gave him a tap on the arm.

Nick didn't respond.

Buzz Baker was screaming.

"... That kid has carried this team on his back today. Plenty of guys have played well, but Nick Hardings held this team together. It's fitting that he scored the touchdown."

They watched as the extra point kick sailed through the uprights. Baker couldn't contain himself.

"Bristol leads this Thanksgiving classic 7-6 with three and a half minutes left!"

The camera zoomed in on the ecstatic cheerleaders, dancing and waving their pom-poms at the crowd. Frankie watched closely as it panned their faces, until he saw Allison's. Her hair was pulled back tightly and her smile was radiant. He thought of Johnny and shook his head over what could have been. He looked at Nick again. Nick's head was up, but his face was expressionless.

Knowing what was coming, Ralph said, "Do we have to watch this next part?"

"Absolutely," Billy said, smiling. "It will only hurt for a while."

They watched in silence as Morrisville came back breathing fire. They hadn't trailed in a game all year, and didn't like it. They moved the ball methodically down the field. And Baker and Bracey spoke of them with reverence. During the drive Morrisville's Dawkins was unstoppable. Finally, they faced a fourth and six at the Bristol twenty-four yard line. The camera showed one minute left on the clock.

Jimmy screamed, "Watch the trick play!"
"Cover the quarterback!" Billy yelled playfully.

The room laughed, but it still hurt to relive the play. Again the quarterback pitched the ball to their star running back. Again, Dawkins ran to his right, but this time he stopped and threw the ball across the field. Again, the quarterback had slipped out of the backfield to catch it. And again, he crossed the goal line untouched, just as he had twenty-five years earlier.

The room moaned. As the camera captured the Morrisville celebration in the end zone, and Buzz Baker called this the most exciting fourth quarter in Thanksgiving history, the guys were screaming at the TV.

"Who cares? Jimmy said.
"Party now," Angelo said. "You're gonna cry soon."
"The game's not over baby," Ralph added.
They talked throughout the failed two-point conversion try.
The next scoreboard shot showed Morrisville up 12-7 with forty-six seconds left to play.

With the final kickoff coming, Angelo said, "This is you, Billy. You ought to bring Trish in to see it."
"Some other time," Billy said. "This is us."

Buzz Baker was singing the praises of the undefeated Morrisville champions and of Bristol's noble effort as underdogs. As he did, the camera showed Coach Lukins talking to his players huddled near the sideline.

"Good ol' Lukins," Jimmy said.
Then they lined up and the same sophomore kicker hit the same lame kickoff he had made before, and Billy Moyer came up again and caught it at the twenty on the dead run.
"Go, Billy," Jimmy shouted.
"Burn their asses," Angelo said.

Again Billy put on the burst of speed, broke through the first defenders and, for a minute, looked like he would score, but Morrisville's Robinson had an angle on him and made the tackle. Billy had returned the ball fifty-five yards to the Morrisville twenty-five yard line.

The Bristol band, located just below the radio booth, was blaring the fight song.

Baker was screaming so loud into his microphone that it was hard to make out what he was saying. But it didn't matter. Billy Moyer had just put Bristol in a position to win with thirty seconds left. At that moment he could have been elected mayor.

"Baboom!" Jimmy said.

"Billy, the lightning bolt!" Angelo added.

"Silver bullet!" Frankie said.

"It happened pretty fast," Billy said. "Next to my marriage and the birth of my kids, it was the best moment in my life."

"Come on, man, we're alone," Angelo said. "Where does it really rank?"

Billy's uncle panned the stands with the camera and the crowd was going wild. People were hugging and jumping up and down. With less than thirty seconds left, people left their seats and moved closer to the end zone to watch the final plays.

As Frankie watched the team huddle, he remembered the real huddle twenty-five years earlier. He remembered Johnny's face as Nick called his play. He remembered Nick's leadership and confidence. He looked at Nick now. His eyes were on the screen, but he was still expressionless.

"Bristol has no time outs left. There's time for maybe two plays."

The room fell silent. This was Johnny's play, probably the most memorable play in the most memorable game in Bristol football history.

Frankie absorbed it all, as though it were in slow motion. He saw Nick's fake. He watched himself pull to get in front of Johnny. He saw Johnny take the pitch cleanly. He saw the linebacker fall down. He saw himself turn up field for the famous collision with Robinson. He saw the hit, and Robinson go down. He saw Johnny's burst of speed into the end zone. He saw Johnny leap into his outstretched arms and hold the ball high, like the statue of liberty. He remembered all of this. Then he saw something he didn't know had happened. On the sideline of the end zone, he saw Allison. She had broken from the squad and had followed Johnny down the sideline for twenty-five yards. As the team swarmed Frankie, who was still holding Johnny off the ground, Allison stood alone with her arms by her sides, wishing perhaps that it were she who was holding the hero.

Aside from the announcer's ravings, the room was silent. There were no catcalls, no shouts. There was no clapping or dancing. Billy had frozen the screen, and they stared at the image, emotionally spent, watching one of the happiest moments of their lives- and watching Johnny.

Finally, Nick stood and walked to Billy. He hugged him, long and hard. Then he walked out of the room without saying a word.

67- Ship Wrecked

Trish returned from her Sunday morning jog, surprised to find Nick sitting on a rocker on the front porch, absorbed by the newspaper.
"Good morning!" she said.
Nick looked up. "Good morning," he replied, standing to greet her as she climbed the steps. "It certainly is a beautiful day. Cool, but clear and sunny. Did you have a good run?"
"Perfect," she said, giving him a peck on the cheek. "You're up early. It's barely six-thirty."

"It's my normal time. And what about you? Up and dressed and finished your run already. You're like that army commercial on TV." He mimicked a TV announcer, "In the army, we do more before nine AM than most people do in a day."

They both laughed.

"Health comes first," she said brightly. "A nice jog, followed by a healthy breakfast." She draped her arm around his. "How about a glass of fresh juice or some coffee while we wait for the sleepy heads to get up?"

"That would be nice," Nick said, as she led him inside.

Trish noticed Nick's bags in the foyer.

"Are you sure you won't stay for the day and watch the Eagles game here?"

"Thanks," Nick said. "But I have season tickets to Angelo's Deli. It's tradition."

Trish smiled. "I understand."

Trish poured each of them a tall glass of freshly squeezed juice and started making the coffee.

"Speaking of football, I understand you saw a game last night," she said.

"Yes we did. Billy did a great job putting that together. Must have been a lot of work, and expensive too. The gang really ate it up."

She looked at him briefly without speaking and then said softly, "Billy wasn't sure how you liked it."

"Me?" Nick shrugged. "I'd rather watch the Eagles."

"Really," Trish said gently. "I'm not sure I buy that. From what I hear, it was a pretty big deal back then, and you were a huge part of it."

"That was a long time ago. I guess it was important then."

Trish looked at him. "We're a product of all our experiences. They shape who we are and how we regard ourselves."

Nick smiled. "That's a lovely sitting room you have out there."

"Thank you," Trish said, disappointed by his deflection.

"The bookcases are beautiful, floor to ceiling, solid mahogany," he said.

"Billy and I designed the room together."

"I saw the pictures of your kids. They look great."

"They are," Trish said modestly. "We're blessed."

"I also liked the way you and Billy have your diplomas on display. I saw Billy's law degree and I saw one for Trish Dobbins, Masters in Psychology from George Washington University."

Trish grinned. "That was a long time ago. I'm retired from my practice. I run a bed and breakfast now. Did you feel like I was conducting a counseling session?"

Nick took a sip of orange juice. Then he smiled and said, "We are a product of all of our experiences. They shape who we are and how we regard ourselves." Then he added, "and others."

She laughed. "Okay, wise guy. You win." The coffee was ready and she poured them each a cup. "I made you a promise yesterday. Are you up for it?" she said.

"Widow's walk?"

"Yup."

"I'm ready," Nick said. "Can we take our coffee?"

"I often do. Can you manage?"

"Sure," Nick said politely. "I'm not an invalid."

Trish leaned on the counter and looked him in the eyes. In an even voice she said, "That's exactly right, Nick, you're not."

They climbed the three flights of stairs to a ten by ten room with triple windows on all sides. The room was stark white and was empty except for two plain white chairs. Trish opened windows on all sides and the cool ocean breeze filled the room. They were just a handful of houses from the water, and they could see over the roof tops to the beach and ocean surf. The sun had risen completely out of the horizon and reflected brightly off the ocean's surface. Seagulls floated at eye level. Nick could hear the waves pounding against the jetties.

"What a room!" Nick said. "You should eat and sleep up here; it's fabulous."

"I've thought of that," Trish replied. "I come here as often as I can."

"Why is it called widow's walk?" Nick asked.

"From here you can see miles out to sea. Folklore has it that rooms like this were built by sea captains so their wives could keep vigils for their return. It worked both ways. Wives would hang lanterns at night so their husbands would know they were getting close to home."

"Neat," Nick said.

"Unfortunately, the captains were sometimes lost at sea and their wives would pace the rooms for weeks or months before giving up. Thus, the widow's walk."

Nick thought briefly of Mrs. Francelli.

"So where's the lighthouse?"

Trish turned him to the North windows and pointed. In the distance, Nick could make out a small figure on the horizon, barely visible, but clearly taller than anything around it.

"The beacon would warn seafarers traveling south that they were approaching the sandbars, shoals, and rocks of Long Beach Island."

Nick stared at the ocean and shook his head. "You had some great books in your sitting room about the storms and shipwrecks off the Jersey shore."

Trish agreed. "Some of the stories are fascinating."

They stood quietly for a while, sipping their coffee and enjoying the experience. Then Trish said, "I'm really glad all of you came. I hope it can become a regular thing."

Nick nodded ever so slightly, but kept his eyes on the ocean.

"You know, Nick, even a retired psychologist can become a good friend to someone. I hope in time you'll know that I can be a good listener."

She sensed him stiffen. Without turning, he said, "I guess people are a lot like ships. Some make it through the storm just fine, while others crash against the rocks."

68- A Quiet Drive

Frankie started the day by taking Mrs. Francelli to Mass. He did that at least once a month. This Sunday was special because it was November 26, Anna's seventieth birthday. It was hard to believe that 1995 was drawing to a close.

Each year the guys celebrated her birthday by meeting at her house to do chores. This year Nick, Jimmy, and Angelo were waiting at nine-thirty when Anna and Frankie returned from church. Jimmy and Angelo cleaned the rain gutters, Nick raked leaves, and Frankie carried Anna's winter clothes down from the attic. They were finished in two hours and sat down for one of Anna's classic brunches.

Anna was as gracious as ever, and the guys were pleased to see her looking so spry.
"Father Creeden called from Chester yesterday to wish me a happy birthday," Anna said brightly. "He asked about all of you."
"How is he?" Nick asked.
"He's doing well. He's going to visit after Christmas and hopes to see each of you."
"Is he still an Eagles fan?" Jimmy asked.
"I'm sure he is," Anna said. "Those loyalties don't die."
Ten years earlier Father Creeden had been promoted to a new, larger parish on the other side of Philadelphia. Frankie knew his leaving was hard on Anna. She'd become dependent upon his friendship, and now, he was lucky if he made it back to town three or four times a year.
"What's he been up to?" Frankie asked.
"He's busy. It's a large parish to keep up at his age," she said. "But he sounds happy. We talked about President Clinton's visit to Northern Ireland next week to start the peace talks. He's optimistic."

Frankie asked about Sissy, and Anna beamed. "She and Tom are doing just fine. So are the grandkids. There're coming tonight to take me out to dinner. I told them that was silly; we should eat here. But they insisted. They don't want me to work on my birthday."

"They're right," Angelo said. "You shouldn't have made this brunch either."

"Cooking isn't work," she said cheerfully. "It's what I do. And speaking of work, Angelo, you should be home doing chores for Donna instead of raking my leaves."

"Don't worry, Mrs. F, I do plenty for her. And besides," he kidded, "you treat me better."

"So how about you two?" she said, looking at Nick and Jimmy. "Are you still making trips to the Veterans' Center?"

"Every Wednesday," Jimmy said.

"And how's it going?" she asked.

"I don't want to be a bore on your birthday," Nick said.

"Well," she said lightly. "It's my birthday and I want to know."

Nick shook his head. "Not good. We're still fighting about Agent Orange. After twenty years of cancer rates and birth defects way beyond the norm, the National Academy of Sciences is finally saying the illnesses may be related to the dioxins used in Vietnam. We've been saying that all along."

"So sad," Anna said.

"What kind of country is this?" Jimmy asked.

"It's not the country," Nick snapped. "I don't believe for a minute that Americans would turn their backs on veterans if they knew what was going on. It's the bureaucrats and Congress. Before a war they allocate billions for everything the generals want. But when it's over, they turn their attention to building roads in their districts. Some give the vets lip service and little else. Only a few really battle for the cause. After a while the public loses interest too. They figure when a war's over, a war's over. They don't realize that for vets, a new battle begins when the shooting stops."

"And you're fighting it," Anna said.

"Darn right," Nick replied. "Like I said, we're just starting to make progress with Vietnam."

"Now Nick's helping the guys from Desert Storm too," Jimmy said.

Nick nodded. "It's been four years since they've come home, and they're seeing the same problems. All the rumors about Saddam using biological weapons, about the questionable vaccine we gave some of our troops, about depleted uranium exposure, all that stuff is having an effect. Guys are complaining and they're hitting a brick wall."

"Uranium?" Angelo said.

"Some of our armor piercing shells were made with depleted uranium. Some of the guys who've become sick handled that stuff or were nearby when the shells exploded. We've got people coming in who've had flu-like symptoms for four years! They're getting the runaround."

"So how do you help?" Anna said.

"The first step is to get them into the system with a claim, even if they don't get help yet. So every Wednesday we go to the outreach center and help them fill out claim forms."

"Good for you," Anna said. "It's wrong to turn our backs on these young people." She shook her head sadly and said, "If you ever need help, I'll be happy to tag along. I may be old, but I can still read and write."

"And cook," Nick said, smiling.

"And cook," she agreed.

Then she turned to Angelo. "And how's my favorite young man, John Francis Marzo? I haven't seen him in months."

"Johnny's great," Angelo said proudly. "You know he's a senior, so he just played his last football game on Thanksgiving. He did well. He's never liked school much though. He wants to go to work when he graduates, but we're still trying to talk him into the community college. He asked me to tell you that he'll visit soon."

"That would be wonderful," Anna said smiling.

Anna caught Jimmy glancing at the clock. It was 12:45. "Now, Jimmy," she said playfully, "you don't have to worry about the time. I checked the newspaper, and the Eagles don't play until 4:00 today."

"I know," Jimmy said. "But I have some things to do."

"Tell the truth," Nick said. "Jimmy gets nervous on game days. He has to move around when he starts to feel it."

Jimmy laughed. "I'll admit it. I hate four o'clock starts because my body doesn't adjust. I still start jumpin' at noon." He checked the clock again. "I'm ready now."

Anna laughed. "Well, I certainly won't interfere with that. Thanks again to all of you. Now get on your way."

"Oh, I forgot," Angelo said, "Ralph sends his regards. He would have come, but Judy had things for him to do."

There was more laughter, and Anna joined in.

"You boys shouldn't tease Ralph so much. He's a devoted family man," she said.

"We're just jealous I guess," Frankie said. It sounded like he meant it.

Frankie dropped Nick and Jimmy off at the deli and told them he'd be back. Sometimes Frankie just felt like driving. He'd head north through Tullytown and Yardley and follow River Road to New Hope. Or he'd stay in Bristol and just cruise around, thinking and relaxing. Today he decided to stay in town.

He thought about the hugs Anna gave the guys when they left. She squeezed each of them, just as she had done when they were in high school. He drove up Jefferson Avenue and laughed to himself when he saw the Grundy Clock Tower looming ahead. He'd spent his entire life under its long shadow. He turned left on Prospect Street and drove toward the train station, slowing as he got closer to the old tunnel where the Tone Kings used to sing. It was silent now.

He turned left at the post office and drove toward one of the more racially mixed sections of town. He saw Wayne Thompson, an old friend and classmate. It had been a while since he'd seen him. Wayne was the funniest black man he knew. He stopped and lowered his window. Within seconds, Wayne had him laughing. As he pulled away he thought of the violence in Northern Ireland and couldn't figure it out. Bristol had been racially and ethnically mixed for Frankie's entire life. It was the only living pattern he knew. People got along. They played sports and attended school together. They grew up friends. He wondered how people in Northern Ireland could kill each other over religion.

He drove down Mill Street, Bristol's once thriving shopping district. There were signs of new life. He headed toward the river and the Bristol wharf. In 1992 a local group erected a monument to mark the 500th anniversary of Columbus's voyage. It was a large, beautifully done bust that projected strength and vision. A gifted local artist named Joe Pavone had sculptured the bust, and it was a source of pride in the town. But Frankie was drawn to the granite pedestal and base. For a hundred bucks sponsors could have their family names inscribed on it. Scores of people did. Word was that other groups in town had plans to erect additional monuments along the waterfront.

Frankie parked. It was getting colder and the wind picked up as the sun disappeared behind the clouds. The weather had chased the normal Sunday crowd away. Aside from a young couple huddled on a bench near the waterfront, the park was empty. Frankie turned up his collar against the chill and walked to the monument. He looked at the names inscribed. Family members had placed most of them there in honor of their parents or grandparents. It felt good to recognize so many. He decided that he was a small town hick, and he liked it. He liked knowing everyone. The newer housing developments made him feel uncomfortable. It took a while for him to figure out why, but he finally did. They lacked a past. They were beautiful communities, but sterile, void of history, kinship, or emotional bonds. He liked it where he was.

Some kids approached on skateboards. He counted six of them, with their baggy pants low on their hips and hats cocked sideways. They rumbled in from nowhere and shattered the peace. The noise was grating and the couple by the water turned toward the intrusion. The kids eyed the monument, assessing its potential for their next set of stunts. Then they caught Frankie's glaring eyes and moved on reluctantly. The couple looked at Frankie and smiled. Peace was restored.

The monument was a tribute to all immigrants and their descendents. Eight granite blocks surrounded the statue and its base, each bearing a different inscription. Frankie circled the structure and read.

"...We dedicate this splendid monument not only to Americans of Italian ancestry, but also to every American from all continents of the world, of every race, color & creed. Living & working together, their sacrifices, struggles & triumphs . . ."

Another block referred to the people whose names were on the base. It was labeled "Quiet Heroes."
"*...most led more simple lives. Like many whose names appear inscribed on this monument, these are the "quiet heroes." Their values, example, & commitment to family constitute a vital contribution to our society.*"

He scanned the names again. Some were prominent, successful people, leaders of the community. But the others struck him-the quiet heroes. The town was full of them. Simple, blue-collar people who worked hard, cared for their families, served their country, and passed on peacefully, obscure to anyone except their families and closest friends. America couldn't make it without them. He cursed himself for not thinking of adding Anna's name when the monument was constructed. Who better fit the description?

The temperature was dropping and the couple on the bench huddled closer. Frankie noticed they had a blanket. He felt a flash of loneliness but shook it off. Maybe someday, he thought. Then he surveyed the glass enclosed dining area of the King George II Inn behind him. He thought back to grade school, when his mom used to take him there occasionally. It was called the Delaware House then. It was actually called Ye Olde Delaware House. He remembered, because he liked saying "Ye Olde" as a kid. Now it was the King George II Inn that overlooked the river. He could see couples at each window enjoying a quiet Sunday dinner. He wanted so much to be one of them, sitting with someone special. He turned away from the image and slowly walked back to his truck to continue his tour.

He drove by Jake's old storefront. Jake was dead now. He had died in the joint five years earlier. Word was that the kids shooting pool called 911 and fumbled to save him, but it was no use. He'd suffered a massive stroke and was gone. The obituary said he was a World War II veteran of the European theater and owner of Jake's Steaks and Arcade. What it didn't say was that Jake's joint had been one of Bristol's unofficial boys' clubs for decades, getting kids off the streets and giving them a place to keep warm on cold winter nights. It gave them a sense of belonging. It also gave them pool, pinball and cigarettes, and a place to plot their next adventure. Jake died poor, a victim of his regular contributions at the track and young customers who had little money.

Frankie thought of the small American flag Jake had mounted on the wall and pictures of his war buddies. Sometimes when Stella wasn't around, Jake would tell the guys war stories. He'd always end with tales about the grateful French girls he helped liberate from Hitler.

The guys went to the viewing. It was small, but Stella was so glad to see them. She cried, looked toward the open casket and said, "Look Jake, the boys are here." It was the last time they saw her. She sold the place and moved to Trenton to live with her sister. The joint was boarded up for a while, until somebody bought it and converted it to an apartment. The new owner asked Frankie to do the carpentry work, but he couldn't bring himself to do it.

He drove by St. Therese's and blessed himself. He remained faithful to his church, but things hadn't been the same since Father Creeden left. The new priest, Father O'Brien, was a nice guy, but he didn't connect the way Creeden did. Plus there was the impact upon Anna. Frankie regretted that Father was gone. He and Anna were two great people who were lonely for different reasons and dependent upon each other. As far as Frankie was concerned, Anna had already lost a husband and son, and it wasn't fair that she lost her close friend too.

He drove by his old house. He sold it after his mother died and kicked himself for it now. He was a young bachelor when she died and he didn't want the added responsibility. Now he wished he had it back. He promised himself he'd buy a house soon, and wished he had someone to share it with. For the second time in a half hour he admitted to himself that he was tired of being alone.

He drove down Wilson Avenue toward the high school and allowed himself to turn left on Garfield Street toward the football field, something he rarely did. The field was flanked by row homes with front porches that overlooked the playing area. The street was less than twenty yards from the end zone where Johnny scored his famous touchdown. Frankie stopped. Some kids were playing a pickup game. They looked to be no more than ten or eleven years old. It had rained the day before, and the kids were covered with mud. Frankie wished he could join them.

He looked at the stands. There were no fans or parents. No band, cheerleaders or referees. There were only the players. He lowered the window and listened. The kids tackled and blocked without equipment. They laughed and cursed, shouted and taunted each other. They argued about almost everything. With no one around to mediate, the arguments ended quickly and the ball would be snapped for another play. It was pure combat, waged for nothing more than the love of playing and the bonding that came with it. Frankie thought about his own playing days. He thought about the trophies in the gym lobby he helped win. They were nice, but they meant little. What mattered was what these kids were doing now, building friendships and memories. He pulled away, mad at himself for having visited. Too much of him remained at that stadium. Before she died, his mother told him that his friends were living in the past and that they were causing him to do the same. She encouraged him to branch out, to go places, experience new things. He'd never meet a girl, she said, until he got out of the deli. Frankie loved his mother, but she didn't understand.

He checked his watch. It was 3:45, fifteen minutes to kickoff. He headed toward Angelo's to watch the game.

Part VIII
Full Circle
2001

69- Get Me to the Church.

"Must be a cold day in hell," Nick said when Frankie walked in.

"What's that supposed to mean?" Frankie asked.

"I was just telling Jimmy that since you found your new honey you don't come to the deli much anymore. And Jimmy said…"

"Wait," Jimmy interrupted. "Let me tell him."

Nick looked disappointed. "Fine, you tell him."

"I just said if I had a girl it would be a cold day in hell before I'd leave her to spend time with us. Know what I mean?"

"I'm in here every morning for coffee," Frankie protested. "Tell 'em," he shouted to Angelo who was grinding beef behind the counter.

"Can't help ya," Angelo hollered back. "Because they're right. You stay five minutes, ten at the most. No time for your friends now. You're spending all of your time at that damn diner, eating American food! That broad's got you whipped, man."

Frankie shook his head.

"How long have you been seeing her?" Nick asked.

"First of all, the girl's got a name. It's Jane. Think you can remember that?"

"We remember," Jimmy said. "It's you we're starting to forget. So anyway, how long?"

"Six months today," Frankie said happily.

"Listen to this guy," Angelo shouted. "Sounds like a middle school kid. Six months today," he mimicked a child's voice. "We've been dating six whole months."

Nick chuckled. "Maybe Frankie should give Jane his old football sweater. They could go steady."

"Or one of those friendship rings from Wal-Mart," Jimmy said. "Probably get one for twenty bucks."

"You guys are just jealous," Frankie joked.

"Exactly," Nick said. "Why should you get a girl when both of us are better looking and have much better personalities."

Frankie ignored him and shouted for Angelo to join them.

"I'm making meatballs. I got beef all over my hands," Angelo yelled above the grinder noise.

"Just come here for a minute," Frankie said. "There's something I want to show you."

"Damn," Angelo said as he turned off the grinder and wiped his hands. "I'm tryin' to earn a living."

Frankie pulled out a chair and motioned for Angelo to sit too.

When the four of them were seated, Jimmy said, "Boy this is special. Wanna play cards?"

"Sure, after you learn how," Angelo said. "Can we hurry please? I've got work to do."

"Me too," Nick said, fanning a stack of papers. "These new VA guidelines, I gotta keep up if I want to help anybody."

"Can you guys be quiet?" Frankie said.

Nick shook his head and smiled. "I sense a lot of tension here."

Frankie reached into his pocket and produced a small box, which he opened and placed on the table.

"Wow," Nick said.

"What the hell's that?" Angelo asked nervously.

Frankie took a breath. "It's an engagement ring."

"Sweet Jesus," Angelo said. "An engagement ring."

The four of them sat there for a long time, just staring at the ring. Finally Jimmy said, "You're getting married?"

"Yup," Frankie said.

"To Jane?" Jimmy asked.

Angelo smacked him lightly on the head.

"Hey, take it easy," Jimmy said. "I was just checking."

They sat there speechless until Angelo said, "Okay guys, take off for a while. I need to talk to Frankie alone."

"Wow," Nick said again, still staring at the ring.

Angelo snapped his fingers. "Okay, move it."

"Are you asking us to leave," Jimmy said indignantly.

"Yeah, I'm asking you to leave."

"You can't do that," Jimmy said. "We work here."

"Okay," Angelo said. "I've been meaning to tell you, you're fired. So leave."

Nick stood, but kept his eyes on the ring. He took Jimmy by the arm and eased him up. "Married," he muttered as he led Jimmy to the door.

"Are we really fired?" Jimmy asked Angelo.

"You're both crazy. I can't take it anymore," Angelo said distantly, still focused on the ring.

"Can we reapply tomorrow?" Jimmy asked

"Get out!" Angelo yelled.

Nick and Jimmy watched through the window as Frankie and Angelo had a long, serious talk.

"What'd ya think they're saying?" Jimmy asked with his face pressed against the glass.

"Angelo's trying to talk him out of it," Nick said. "He's telling Frankie that he's twenty years older than Jane."

"How do you know? I can't hear him."

"I can't either, but that's what I'd be telling Frankie if you didn't get us kicked out."

"Me again. It's always my fault." When Nick ignored him, Jimmy said, "What's Frankie saying back?"

"Frankie's saying he's lonely. He's saying they love each other and he doesn't care how old she is."

"Which one's right?" Jimmy said.

"They both are."

"Think Angelo will talk him out of it?"

"I guess not. Look."

Jimmy refocused. The talk was over and Angelo and Frankie were smiling. If the windows were cleaner, Nick and Jimmy would have noticed Angelo's eyes filling up.

Angelo noticed Nick and Jimmy outside and waved them in.

"Frankie's getting married," Angelo said, sounding his approval.

Nick and Jimmy exchanged looks. Then Nick offered Frankie his hand. "That's great," he said. "I'm really happy for you."

"Congratulations," Jimmy said. "I don't think she's too young." Then he added, "You know what I mean."

Frankie was beaming. "I want you guys to be in my wedding. Angelo's my best man and I want you to be ushers."

"Really?" Nick said. "That's an honor. Really, man. Thanks."

Jimmy looked touched. "Are we gonna rent tuxes? If we do, I'll get real shoes. I won't screw this up."

Nick barked once and laughed.

"Knock it off," Jimmy said. "I'm serious."

"No tuxes," Frankie said. "Jane wants a small thing at the District Justice's office. Just you guys, Mrs. Francelli and Sissy, and a couple of Jane's friends and her kids."

"It's a great thing man," Nick said.

Frankie smiled.

Frankie's next hurdle was to introduce Jane to Mrs. Francelli. They dropped in unannounced, knowing she'd cook for two days if she knew they were coming. Before going, Frankie thought back to when he first told Anna he was dating Jane. He told her all about Jane's past, the hard living, the bad relationships, the kids, her estrangement from her parents, everything.

"I'm worried, Frankie," she had said. "People can change for the better, but sometimes they can't."

Frankie had assured her that she had changed and was doing the right thing, struggling to hold a job and raise her kids. She was a new person. They talked about their age difference and the kids too. In the end he could tell she hadn't been convinced, but she had smiled and said, "Just be careful, Frankie. I want you to be happy."

Anna was excited to see them and the introductions went well. Anna was pleasantly surprised. After hearing Frankie's stories, she had visualized someone far less appealing than the nicely dressed, well-groomed girl she was seeing now.

"Why didn't you call me?" Anna said. "I would have made something. I'm so embarrassed."

Frankie got to the point. "We're not here to eat. Jane has something to show you."

Jane held out her hand to expose her ring and Anna almost fainted. When she recovered, she hugged them both.

"I love weddings, especially when they're in the family." She said to Jane, "Frankie is family you know." Then she added, "This is wonderful."

Anna and Jane hit it off well. Even before they met, Anna's concerns had gradually given way to joy over Frankie's happiness. Now, Jane could sense Anna's acceptance, and the two of them warmed to each other.

Jane told Anna how much her kids loved Frankie, and how good he was with them. Anna smiled proudly. "That doesn't surprise me. He'll be as good a father as he is a friend."

After a pause Anna said, "So tell me about your wedding plans."

She listened politely as the couple described a small ceremony in the judge's office with just the bridal party, Jane's children, and a handful of guests. Anna waited patiently until they finished; then she went to work. By the time she was finished, the plans had changed. There would be a Friday night service at St. Therese's. Anna would ask Father Creeden to visit and perform the ceremony. Her good friend, Mrs. Sweeney, would sing, and another friend would gladly play the organ. Jane was thrilled. Then Anna threw in the clincher.

"I hope you'll do me the honor of allowing me to pay for your dress."

Jane was touched. She had two children and no marriages, and like any girl, she had always dreamed of her wedding day. Now a stranger was treating her better than most people she had known.

"Sorry," Frankie interrupted. "You don't have that kind of money. I'll buy Jane's dress."

"Grooms just don't do that," Anna said. "And as for money, I don't do much, so my cookie jar is full. This will be a wonderful day, and I'd like to have some fun with it." Then she turned to Jane.

"May I?"

Jane's eyes began to fill. "I don't know what to say. You're so kind. But under the circumstances, I'm not sure what kind of dress I should wear. You know?" She looked embarrassed.

Anna smiled. "Are you talking about those silly, old fashioned rules?" Jane nodded.

"You can wear any dress you like. If I were you, I'd buy one as white as snow. Something simple, but white!"

Jane smiled and looked at Frankie.

"Whatever you want," he said.

"Will you help me pick it out?" she asked Anna.

"I'd love to!" Anna said.

They laughed and embraced again.

The preparations took off from there. The guys rented tuxedos, and Jimmy bought black shoes. Frankie looked so good that Nick said he looked like a bouncer in a casino. Jane wore a charming white, cotton eyelet dress. She had three girls in her bridal party to complement Frankie's friends. With the age differences, each pair looked like a father and daughter couple, but it was nice. Besides, much of the attention was focused on Joey, the ring bearer, and Erin the flower girl.

Father Creeden did his usual masterful job. He spoke movingly of the joy of finding true love and how Frankie and Jane's happiness proved that good things were worth waiting for. Mrs. Sweeny sang *Ave Maria,* and another friend, Mrs. Falcone, played the organ. The gang from the deli came and Ralph and Angelo brought their wives and Sissy brought Tom. Pete the Mailman, Jane's boss Duke, and three waitresses from the diner came. Billy and Trish surprised everyone by driving in from Jersey. Frankie also invited a full table of guys from the carpenter's union and their wives. The kids had some friends too.

Frankie rented the Hibernian hall for the reception. Angelo prepared the food in advance and Duke brought some of the diner's best desserts. Pete the Mailman's cousin was the DJ.

During the toast Angelo told Jane that Frankie was a rock, a person who would always be there for her, just as he had been there for his friends. He told Frankie that he had finally found happiness in the girl he had always deserved. Anna cried.

The party started off slowly. But Nick and Jimmy changed that when the DJ played *Shout.* The two of them danced, throwing their arms up with the music and eventually rolling on the floor in a bad version of the worm. The crowd loved it. Soon the girls from the diner were dancing and the party took off. Even the groom got up after considerable coaxing and everyone roared as Frankie, biting down on a rose stem between his teeth and holding a giggling Erin in his massive arm, led a conga line through the hall. Mrs. Francelli couldn't remember laughing so hard.

"This is good," Nick said to Angelo.
"I hope so," Angelo said. "This girl's been around."

For the rest of the party, Jimmy and Nick stood by the door, guarding against crashers.

70- September 11

"It's a beautiful, sunny day," Nick said, looking out the deli window. "We should jump in that truck of yours and take a ride."
"Got gas money?" Jimmy replied. "You still owe me from last time."
"You shouldn't have kept the truck if you can't afford to drive it. Besides, I gave you four bucks last time *and* paid for the ice cream," Nick said.
"What does four bucks do? What about wear and tear on the tires, insurance costs, car washes? Businessmen get money for each mile they drive. That's what I should do."
"You're not a business man. You're unemployed."
"I'm retired," Jimmy said. "Besides, I work here."
"Forget it," Nick said, still looking out the window. "Ralph just pulled up. Maybe he'll take a ride."
"Does he have the beamer or the limo?"
"The limo," Nick chuckled. "Maybe I'll sit in the back and make him my chauffer. I'll read the newspaper while he drives around."
"If you go, I'm coming," Jimmy said.

"Okay, but it'll cost you thirty cents a mile."

"Beautiful day," Nick said cheerfully, when Ralph walked in. "How about if…"
Ralph cut him off. "Where's Angelo?"
"Delivering a brunch tray. He'll be back any minute. Meanwhile, I'm in charge. Coffee's a buck. Leave it on the counter."
"I'm in charge!" Jimmy protested.
"Just the lottery machine," Nick said. "Ralph doesn't buy tickets; he's already rich."
"Turn on the TV," Ralph said impatiently.
"Can't 'till after lunch deliveries," Jimmy said. "Angelo's rule."
Ralph walked behind the counter and turned it on.
Jimmy smiled. "You're in trouble man."
Ralph checked his watch. It was ten after nine. "The radio just said that a plane flew into the World Trade Center."
"New York?" Jimmy said.
"Probably one of those drunks in a Cessna," Nick said. "They oughta…"
Nick trailed off as the image came on the screen.

"…A second plane crashed into the south tower of the World Trade Center shortly after nine this morning… Once again, an aircraft of undetermined origin crashed into the north tower of the world trade center at approximately 8:45 this morning. Apparently, it was a large plane. A second aircraft struck the south tower almost twenty minutes later. Both buildings are in flames with clouds of deep black smoke billowing from the towers."

"Jesus," Nick said.
Angelo stormed in, having just heard the news on the radio. The four of them stared in disbelief as more reports trickled in.

"New York's airports, tunnels and bridges have been shut down and all United States flights have been grounded. Airborne flights have been ordered to land. Incredibly, a third plane struck the Pentagon, dashing all hope that this was all a horrible mistake."

"President Bush was in Florida when he received the news. The First Lady was in Washington. The White House and other government buildings are being evacuated, including the State Department. Secretary of State Powell was in Latin America and we're told is now heading home."

With Bush in Florida and Colin Powell south of the border, Nick wondered who was in charge.

Then the action returned to the images from New York. There were wide estimates of how many people were in the towers. Ten or fifteen thousand, it was said. Some estimates included employees only, while others factored in business visitors. Hundreds of emergency workers were on the scene for the evacuation and rescue effort. As the buildings burned, commentators speculated about who might be responsible.

Then the south tower collapsed. Nick, Jimmy, Angelo and Ralph sat in silence, too stunned to speak. Finally, Nick whispered, "crazy bastards."

Angelo flipped through the channels. The reporting was the same. *"...Horrific...shocking... Ghastly scenes... "* The next channel offered more grim news, *"...officials estimate that hundreds of firemen, police and rescue workers were inside or too close when the tower collapsed and may have perished."*

Within a half hour the second tower fell like a deck of cards. No one knew how many made it out in time. Lower Manhattan was blanketed with powdered debris, as though a snowstorm hit on a bright September day. The morning sky grew dark as clouds of dust rose above the city and remained suspended, defying gravity and filtering out the sun. Scenes of the survivors came next. Some fled in panic, while others wandered aimlessly, choking on the thick, polluted air. Executives and street vendors, gray-haired men and young, smartly dressed women stood trance-like, in shock. Ghostly figures walked in groups, covered with pulverized concrete, their black eyes staring blankly from their gray-white faces.

Just before eleven it was reported that a fourth plane had crashed in western Pennsylvania. Angelo had enough. "I've got an order to prepare," he said angrily as he left the table.
"I'll help," Jimmy said.
"I don't need any help!" Angelo snapped. "Those poor sons of bitches in New York need help!"

Washington was responding. Combat jets patrolled the skies as the FAA confirmed that the planes had been hijacked from Boston, Newark and Washington. The capitol was still being evacuated and border security was increased. Emergency teams were dispatched to New York from the CDC in Atlanta, amid fears of chemical or biological fallout. Rumors flew and imaginations ran wild.

Angelo began preparing chicken cutlets. Nick watched him flatten the pieces with his mallet. As more stories unfolded, Angelo cursed and pounded harder. Jars rattled with each blow. The chicken was thin enough, but Angelo kept pounding. A local business called to cancel its order. Angelo slammed the phone. He stared at the chicken for a long time. Then he grabbed some raw pieces and threw them, one at a time, like fastballs, at the trashcan in the corner. Most missed. One stuck to the wall just above the can. He kept winding up and throwing them, each one harder than the previous one, until they were gone. He walked to the can and kicked it over, wiped his hands on his apron, and sat down, breathing hard. No one spoke.

Frankie arrived at twelve-fifteen looking shaken. "They shut down the job and sent us home," he said quietly. Jimmy nodded.

Angelo flipped the sign on the door from open to closed.
"Anybody need food?" he asked.
Only Ralph said yes, but changed his mind when everyone else declined.

Frankie's cell phone rang. It was Jane calling from the diner. She was worried about the kids. A friend told her that news of the attack had reached the school. The students were scared. Parents were calling, wanting to pick up their children, and word was that school might let out early. She wanted them home. Frankie said he would be there when they were dismissed.

Angelo called Donna at work. She started to cry. She wanted to call their son, but Johnny couldn't receive calls at work.
"Call him later," she said. "See if he can come over for dinner tonight. I want us together. He'll listen to you."
"I'll call him," Angelo assured her. "But he may be busy tonight."
"I want us together!" she insisted.
"Okay, I'll make sure he comes."

Nick started to pace, making a fist and punching his open hand. "Crazy bastards," he murmured, over and over.
"For God's sake, Nick, stop pacing," Angelo shouted.
Nick stopped and stared hard at Angelo.
Angelo softened. "Why don't you get us some beer from the stockroom?"
"Good idea," Nick said, anxious for the chance to do something.
"I'll help," Jimmy said. "We're gonna need a lot."

There was fear that more attacks would follow. President Bush had been flown to an undisclosed location, and his wife was in a "safe location" in Washington. Officials declared a state of emergency in the capital. Warships and aircraft carriers left Norfolk to protect the East Coast from attack. It was felt they'd be less vulnerable at sea than in port. The Pentagon didn't want another Pearl Harbor.

Nick and Jimmy returned with the beers just as Mayor Giuliani started a press conference. He looked strong. Scared and pissed, but strong. Nick liked it. "This guy's a tough son of a bitch," he said. "It's what we need."

"Sure he's tough," Angelo said. "He's Italian."

Pete the Mailman arrived. He saw the closed sign, peeked in, and pounded on the door. Angelo nodded and Frankie let him in.

"Can you believe this shit?" Pete shouted, not waiting for an answer. "It's those God damned a-rabs."

"Damn right it is," Jimmy said. "Beer?"

"Can't, I'll get fired." He went to the soda case and opened a coke.

"What are we gonna do about this?" Pete demanded. "That's my question."

"Somebody's ass has to be kicked," Jimmy said. "Hard!"

"I say we nuke 'em," Pete said. "Turn the whole damn Middle East into a sheet of glass."

"That's brilliant," Angelo said sarcastically. "Then what, park our cars for fifty years and ride bicycles? What about the oil?"

"Screw the oil," Pete said. "We could fix that if we wanted to."

"We need hit squads," Jimmy added. "Trained assassins. High tech stuff, like they have on TV. Kill their leaders, and when they get new leaders, kill them too."

"I thought you were a pacifist?" Nick said.

"This is different," Jimmy said. "This isn't that Vietnam bullshit. We've been attacked."

"Careful," Nick said. "We've got a pissed off country right now. We need to keep our heads."

"Like hell," Jimmy said. "It's like that movie we saw about Pearl Harbor."

"Which one?" Nick asked.

"The one about the green giant," Jimmy said.

"You're talking about Tora, Tora, Tora," Angelo said. "And it's not a green giant, you dimwit."

"Yes it is," Jimmy said, turning to Nick for help. "What's that Japanese admiral say after they suckered us at Pearl Harbor. You remember it."

Nick did. "He said, 'I fear we've awakened a *sleeping giant* and filled him with a terrible resolve.'"

"Right," Jimmy said. "Green giant, sleeping giant, what's the difference? This country is huge, and they just pissed us off. Now they're gonna pay."

"Who?" Ralph asked. No one had an answer.

Frankie's cell phone rang, and he stepped away from the conversation to get it. He spoke softly for a minute and then shouted for everyone to quiet down. All eyes were on him as he listened. Slowly, the blood drained from his face. By the time he hung up, he was ashen. He closed his eyes and shook his head, still not speaking.

"What is it?" Angelo asked quietly.

Frankie panned the room and took a breath. "That was Trish calling from Jersey." He struggled to continue. "Billy had a business meeting at the Trade Center this morning. She hasn't heard from him since the planes hit."

71- Waiting for the Call

Trish's call was followed by an eruption. Nick was pacing again, cursing and punching his hand like before. Ralph sat sobbing at the table, while Jimmy wailed, "Please not Billy," over and over. Angelo went on another rampage and threw a bottle of coke against the wall.

"Leave it alone," he snapped when Jimmy moved to clean it.

"It'll stain," Jimmy said.

"It's my store, and I want it there!"

Nick glared at him. "Back off Angelo; he's trying to help."

Angelo glared back, and Frankie stepped between them.

"It's the God damned a-rabs you should be mad at," Pete hollered. "Not each other."

"Screw you, Pete," Angelo said over Frankie's shoulder. "You didn't even know Billy."

"Are you serious?" Pete exploded. "Do I have to know him? The people in those buildings were Americans, and I'm just as pissed as you are, about your friend and everybody else!"

Frankie had enough. His head was spinning, and his stomach hurt. He needed to escape. "Shut up!" he roared, and the room got quiet.

"We're not helping anything by going off on each other. Let's think about what we can do for Trish and her family instead of all this crap."

Nick nodded and stepped away. So did Angelo.

"Besides, we're not sure of anything yet. With all the confusion in New York there could be plenty of reasons why Billy hasn't called. Communications are down. Maybe his cell phone is dead, and he can't get to a real phone. Maybe he's busy helping people. You know him. He would do that. Maybe he's stuck on one of those ferries we saw on TV, evacuating people from Battery Park. Maybe he's hurt and getting treatment. There're plenty of possibilities."

"He's right," Ralph said. "There are."

Frankie lowered his voice. "I'm gonna pick up the kids at school. I'll let you know if Trish calls again. Try to stay calm."

The pain in his stomach eased as he stepped into the fresh air. He hoped the walk to St. Therese's would help clear his head and calm his fears, but deep inside, he knew, just as he suspected Trish knew, that something was terribly wrong. Billy was resourceful. He would have found a way to contact her if he was all right.

At the moment, the overwhelming national tragedy, the obscene act of violence that had unfolded that day, had been funneled into his concern for Billy and Trish. The catastrophe now had a face, the heartbreaking image of the ideal couple, a couple whose charm, generosity, and love had been a light in the often dimly lit world of the guys at the deli. He was grateful that Billy had come back into their lives. The shore reunions that started in '91 had grown into annual affairs and relationships had flourished because of them. One year, even young Johnny drove up for a day so that Billy could meet him. They hit it off well, and Johnny went back several times to go deep-sea fishing with Billy. They also spent a long time talking and laughing last spring at Frankie and Jane's wedding reception. Trish said Billy always wanted a son and loved spending time with Johnny.

Other relationships grew as well. Ralph came around the deli more often, and Nick and Trish had grown close. Since their first talk in the widow's walk, they had found time for a long conversation whenever they were together. Frankie felt Trish had a soothing effect on Nick and wished they could talk more.

Last year the group celebrated their tenth year of gatherings, with the next one scheduled for the coming weekend. Frankie and Billy had been calling back and forth, planning it for weeks. This was to be the first reunion that included Jane and the kids, and after going stag for so long, Frankie had looked forward to showing off his new family.

He arrived at St. Therese's twenty-minutes before dismissal and waited at the gate with the other parents. He used to feel self-conscious around them because they were so much younger, and they eyed him suspiciously at first. But, in time, as they saw how warmly Joey and Erin responded to him, he became a kind of folk hero, especially with the young mothers, and he enjoyed seeing them and sharing lighthearted stories about raising children. But there wasn't much joking going on today. People had other things on their minds.

Jose' Rivera, a young guy he knew from the dart league, was heading for the gate. He was wearing army fatigues and looked like he was in a hurry.

Frankie eyed the uniform. "What's going on Jose'?"

"Hi Frankie. I'm here to pick up my daughter early."

"What's with the uniform?"

"I just got a call from my reserve unit. We're on alert. I want to make sure I see Jessica in case I get called up." Frankie shook his head. This was real.

"Any inside scoop?"

"Sorry Frankie. I only know what you know." He checked his watch. "I'm gonna get my little girl. See ya around."

"Yeah, good luck Jose."

At dismissal he was relieved to see that the kids were okay, a little concerned and confused, but okay. And they were certainly glad to see him. Erin gave him an extra long hug, and Joey's "hi Dad," conveyed a sense of relief.

He was hoping to shield the kids from the day's events, so his heart sank when little Erin said, "Butchie O'Reilly said we were attacked today. He said lots of people died. Are we going to be attacked again?"

Joey added, "Mrs. Blanch put the TV on in her classroom for current events. The principal made her turn it off. Lots of kids were crying."

Frankie hid his anger. He didn't want the kids seeing the coverage at home or in school.

"Was the TV on in your grade?" He asked Erin.

"No," she said, "But the eighth graders told everyone about it at recess. They said there were fires and smoke and people running."

Frankie gave them a careful explanation of what was going on and assured them that the government was working hard to protect them. After asking a few more questions, they seemed satisfied.

Frankie thought it would be best if the kids didn't see any news coverage that night, so after dinner, Jane went to the video store for a movie while Frankie helped the kids with their homework. Later, they made popcorn and watched *Alf,* but Frankie's mind was elsewhere. Trish still hadn't called and Frankie's hope was fading. At seven-thirty he left to visit Anna. He wanted her to be prepared if news of Billy got out.

He let himself in as usual and found her sitting quietly in the living room. The television was off, and, aside from the small lamp beside her, the house was dark.

"Frankie," she said softly. A slight smile crossed her face, but she looked tired. "It's good to see you."

"Hi, Anna." He crossed the room and gave her a kiss before sitting down.

"How are Jane and the kids?" she asked. "I haven't seen them lately."

"They're okay. A little shook up today, like the rest of us, but they're fine."

"You'll have to bring them around more when you visit. They're wonderful children. I just love them."

"Next time I come, I promise."

"How are Sissy and Tom?" He asked.

"They're fine thank you. I spoke to Sissy just after dinner. Now that their kids are grown, she and Tom are pestering me to move in with them in their nice big house in Langhorne."

"Maybe you should," Frankie said. "Things will be easier for you."

"Things are fine here, Frankie, and this is where I belong."

She smiled briefly. "You know. I love Tom dearly, but there were times before they were married when I hoped that you and Sissy might get together. I think you would have made a good couple."

Frankie lowered his head.

"And there were times when I thought you might feel the same way," she added.

"I had a crush on Sissy for a long time," Frankie admitted.

"I thought so!" she said. "So why didn't you do anything about it?"

"She was two years older," he said lamely.

"Two years!" She smiled again. "It means a lot when you're young, but not so much when you're older."

Frankie understood.

"Anyway, you're both happy now, so it worked for the best. And although you're not my son-in-law, you are my adopted son, and that's just as good."

She sat back and gave a deep sigh. "It's been quite a day."

"Terrible," he said.

"I can't imagine the families," she said sadly. "So much sorrow."

Frankie nodded. The pain was back in his stomach.

Anna regretted bringing up the subject and tried to change it.

"Can I fix you something?"

"No thanks. I just ate."

"How about something to drink?"

"Thanks," Frankie said. "But I'm fine."

"Please stay a while and keep an old woman company."

Frankie studied her. Although he made it a point to see her at least once a week, he always marveled at how well she was doing. At seventy-six she was still fit and enjoyed excellent health. She took no pills and rarely saw doctors. Though her hair had turned gray, and her face was lined, it was obvious that she was once beautiful. Her personality matched her health, always warm and caring and thrilled whenever any of the boys visited, especially Frankie. But tonight she looked different.

"You look tired," he said. "Maybe I should come back tomorrow."

"I'm not tired, Frankie," she said softly. "I'm just terribly troubled."

"That's understandable," he said. But he was concerned. Ever since his mother died he had adopted Anna just as she had adopted him, and he wanted to protect her from any more of life's blows. Yet here he was, ready to deliver more bad news.

"This will bring war you know," she said with deep sadness.

Frankie thought of the guys' reaction in the deli and knew she was right.

"We've been attacked," he said softly. "The payback will be strong."

"I know," she said, barely audible. "We'll go to war against someone, I'm not sure who, and more people will die."

He chose not to answer. He wished there were more lights on. The house was always filled with activity and he needed some now. He checked his watch.

"Will you be listening to the President's speech tonight?"

"I don't think so," she said calmly. "I think I know what he's going to say."

Again the room fell silent. Finally, Frankie said, "Anna, there's something I need to tell you."

She looked at him without speaking, but her eyes said, "not again."

She knew by his expression that it would be bad, and she waited calmly, treating herself to thirty more seconds before she would have to bear more sadness.

"Poor Frankie," she said softly. "You carry so much." Then she nodded. "Okay, tell me. What else can be so bad on a day like this?"

72- For Sale

September 30, 2001

Billy's memorial service was held on September 29. Frankie, Nick, Jimmy and Ralph traveled to North Jersey by train. Young Johnny drove Donna and Angelo. Trish gave a magnificent eulogy to the packed church. Frankie was astonished by her grace and courage as she spoke beautifully of Billy's devotion as a husband and father and of his service to the community. It was one of hundreds of services held in the region, and Frankie felt as if an entire nation was mourning Billy's death. As scenes of grieving wives and tearful children dominated the TV news, a deep sadness hung over the country, and a growing sense of anger and frustration festered beneath it.

The next morning, after walking the kids to school, Frankie went to the deli for his morning coffee. Nick's burnt orange bike with the rusted wheels and faded seat was parked out front. Attached to the handlebars was a hand-made sign that read, *Bicycle For Sale $5.00.* Scrawled beneath the price were the words, *Never Been Ridden.*

Frankie went in and found Nick and Jimmy in their usual spots. Nick was writing a letter and Jimmy sat next to him. Angelo was working behind the counter. Jimmy nodded and Nick said, "Hey Frankie, how's it going?"

Frankie thought for a minute. Something was different, but he couldn't pinpoint it. Then it hit him. There was no weather report from Nick. He caught Angelo's eye, but Angelo shrugged.

"Morning," Frankie said. "What's with the for sale sign?"

"I'm selling the bike," Nick said. "Know anybody who needs one?"

"Why are you selling it?" Frankie asked.

"I can't ride it," Nick said, flatly. "And I won't be able to later, so I figured I'd sell it."

Frankie never knew what to expect from Nick, but selling the bike was a huge surprise. He looked at Jimmy.

"He tried to ride it for twenty-five years," Jimmy said. "I think he gave it an honest shot."

"He gave it a great shot," Frankie said. "But why sell it now?"

"Trish told me too," Nick replied.

"Trish told you that? Yesterday?"

"No, she told me to sell it about eight years ago, back in '93. She said it was a crutch. She said I had to accept that I couldn't ride a bike and that we can't do or get everything we want. Trish and I used to talk a lot," he said sadly.

"I know," Frankie said.

"She said that if I wanted to move on I had to put my past behind me. She said the bike was holding me back."

Frankie poured a coffee. "Okay, seems like good advice. But why now? Why not before?"

"It takes time to learn things," Jimmy said helpfully. He and Nick had obviously talked about this.

"I didn't listen to her before, because I was a hard headed, smacked ass, feeling sorry for myself. Trish said I used the bike to remind everyone what had happened to me."

"That may have been a little harsh," Frankie said. "I didn't see it that way."

"I didn't like it when she said it, but now I think she was right. Seeing her give that eulogy yesterday taught me something. I know how great her relationship was with Billy, how happy she was. She lost everything, but she was so strong. She had the courage to talk about moving on with our lives. She said Billy would want that. I know that he would."

"I think he would too," Frankie said.

"And do you know what Frankie? I think Johnny would too, and the other fifty-eight thousand guys who didn't make it back from Nam. I think they'd all tell us that life's too short to jerk around with it. I've lost a lot of time. I'm not sure where it went, but I've lost a lot of time." Nick's eyes welled up.

"You've done good things, Nick. Your work for the veterans. Other things."

"I know," Nick said. "But I've wasted a lot too. So today, I'm turning the page. That's what Trish said, 'turn the page to a new chapter.' And that's what I'm going to do."

"Good for you, Nick," Frankie said. He reached into his pocket and pulled out a five.

"What's that for?" Nick said.

"I'm buying the bike."

"You can't have it," Nick said. "Put your money away."

Frankie kept his hand out. "Come on, Nick. I'm buying it for Joey. I'll fix it up, change the wheels and get a new seat. He'll love it."

"Sorry, Frankie," Nick said. "I love the kid. You know that. And I'll buy him a brand new one myself. Hell, I'm his uncle; it's the least I can do. But he can't have this bike. I want it gone."

Frankie smiled and said, "I understand."

Jimmy stood up. "Tell him about me," he said to Nick.

Nick shook his head.

"What about you?" Frankie asked.

"Tell him," Jimmy pleaded.

"Nope. You've got some good news to tell. Tell him yourself," Nick said.

Jimmy hesitated.

"Tell him Jimmy," Angelo said from behind the counter. "He'll be glad to hear it."

Jimmy straightened and a smile crossed his face. "Remember the truck I won?"

"Of course I do. It's out front every day!"

"I wrote a thank you letter to the dealership today, and I called the owner to say I'd be happy to take a picture with him."

Frankie smiled. "No kidding?"

"It's true," Jimmy said proudly. "I called him."

"What did he say?" Frankie asked.

"Well, he was half asleep."

"At the dealership?" Frankie said.

"No," Angelo interjected. "The dimwit called him at home at 6:30 this morning!"

"I was anxious," Jimmy said. "His number was in the book."

"So did he say anything?" Frankie asked.

"He thought I was nuts," Jimmy beamed. "But I told him I made a mistake about the truck and I wanted to fix it. He said I was a couple years late, but we could still take the picture if I wanted to. He sounded like a nice guy."

"I guess he is," Angelo said. "He gave you a truck."

"He didn't give it to me," Jimmy said. "I won it."

The rest of the guys decided to quit while they were ahead.

73- Young Johnny

December 2001

The sign on the deli window read, *Closed Today for Renovations*. Inside, Nick and Jimmy were painting the walls while Angelo scrubbed the cooking area. Frankie was putting the final touches on a new countertop.

"There's nothing like a good paint job to make a place look fresh," Nick said.

"Especially white paint," Jimmy added. "What's this stuff called again?"

"Stark white," Nick said.

"That's it. Stark white. Brightens the place up. How 'bout it, Angelo?"

"It looks real good. You guys are talented. Where'd you learn to paint?"

"First grade," Nick said. "Sister Mary Margaret used to let us paint all the time. We wore smocks."

"I still think we should paint a red and green stripe all around the place," Jimmy said. "Make it look real Italian."

"You'd be pushin' your luck," Angelo said. "Straight lines are tough. I'll hang some Italian stuff on the walls when you're finished. Right, Frankie?"

Frankie was clamping glued Formica to the counter. "Hang pictures of Sophia Loren and Gina Lollobrigida, that'll give it an Italian look."

"Damn, Frankie, you're old," Nick said. "Those broads are in the Hollywood retirement home."

"Watch it," Frankie said. "In her day Sophia Loren was the most beautiful woman in the world. Better than those teeny boppers everybody drools over today, like Britney what's her face."

"I was thinking of pictures of pasta dishes and maybe hang some provolone and garlic, some dried peppers. Stuff like that," Angelo said. "Donna would have my ass if I hung pictures of chicks."

Pete the Mailman knocked on the window and Angelo motioned him in.

Pete was impressed. "This really looks good. It brightens the place up."

"Stark white," Jimmy said.

"I'd like to help," Pete said. "But I'm behind."

"Don't forget the letter on the table," Nick said.

Pete put it in his bag and laid Angelo's mail in its place.

"Anything for me?" Nick asked.

"Sorry, Nick. Not today," he called over his shoulder as he left.

Donna arrived next. "Wow, what a difference!" she said.

"Stark white," Jimmy said. "Angelo was just saying he's gonna hang your picture when we're finished. Right here where everyone can see it."

"I'll bet he said that," she said.

"Absolutely," Angelo winked and gave her a kiss. She looked like she'd been crying. Angelo asked her if she was all right?

"I'm fine," she said, wiping her nose with a tissue. "Must be a cold."

Angelo checked his watch. "Long lunch hour?"

"I took the afternoon off. Johnny took me to lunch."

"Johnny? Why isn't he at work?"

"He took the day off. He wanted to talk with his mother."

Angelo looked confused. "About what?"

"He'll tell you himself in a minute. He's parking around the corner. It's no parking today on this side of the street."

Johnny walked in to his typical greeting.

"There he is!" Nick said. "World's handsomest man."

Johnny smiled. "Hey Nick, Jimmy, how's it going?"

"Hi, Johnny. Sorry we can't shake," Jimmy said, holding up his paintbrush proudly.

"The place looks great," Johnny replied.

Frankie came around from behind the counter and gave him a bear hug.

"Frankie. Good to see you."

"Since you got that apartment we never see you," Frankie said. "Must have a girlfriend."

"Forget a girlfriend," Jimmy said. "He's twenty-four. He should be married."

"Hi, Pop," Johnny said, sharing a hug with Angelo.

"No work today?" Angelo asked.

"I took the day off."

"You took your mother to lunch? You could have eaten here."

"I took Mom to the King George for a treat. It was nice."

"The King George! Sounds nice," Angelo said. He looked at Donna. "So we're keeping secrets now?"

"No secrets, Dad," Johnny said softly.

"Johnny has something to tell you." Donna gave Angelo a look that said shut up and listen to your son.

"Maybe we should leave you guys alone for a while," Frankie said.

"Yeah maybe," Angelo said, sounding concerned.

"No, stay," Donna said.

Johnny agreed. "You guys are family. I want you to hear this too."

"Okay," Angelo said. "So the whole family's here. What's up?"

Johnny looked at his mother for support. She nodded encouragement. He smiled and turned back to Angelo. "I'm enlisting."

The words flew through the room and bounced off the freshly painted walls.

"In what?" Angelo asked curtly.

"The army."

Nick rubbed his head. Jimmy and Frankie exchanged glances, but didn't speak.

Angelo turned to Donna. "You knew this?"

"I found out at lunch today."

Angelo walked to the front window and stood looking out.

"Why?" he asked, without turning around.

"It's pretty obvious. I started thinking about it on September 11. I'm not alone. Enlistments are way up."

Angelo turned to face him. "You're thinking with your heart, son, not your head."

"I'm thinking of my duty," Johnny said. "It's been three months since Billy's memorial service, and I haven't been able to get it out of my mind. This is what I have to do."

Angelo looked at Donna. "You're okay with this?"

"No, I'm not okay with it," she said. "I'm not okay at all. I'm real scared, and I told him that. We went round and round at the restaurant, but this is what he wants to do."

Angelo shook his head, but Donna continued. "We make choices in life Angelo. Some are good and some are bad. We made ours when we were much younger than he is. Now, I've got to respect his."

"We should go," Frankie said. Nick and Jimmy agreed.

"I said I want you to stay," Donna said firmly.

Angelo looked at Johnny and squeezed his eyes shut. When he opened them he said, "Is this one of those sins of the father things? Are you trying to make up for what I did?"

"No way, Pop. I respect what you did." He gestured to Nick and Jimmy. "I respect what they did too. You guys lived in confusing times. Maybe I would have done what you did or what they did, I don't know."

"I'm not sure any of us knows what we'd do if we had it to do over again," Donna added. "But this isn't Vietnam," Johnny said. "Things are clearer now." "We've been attacked. Billy's dead. Trish is heartbroken. I want to do this. We've got guys in Afghanistan searching for the animals that killed Billy. There are rumors about Iraq and Syria too. I want to help."

Angelo sighed. "Wars are supposed to be fought by other people's kids."

Johnny smiled. "That's not the way it works, Pop."

Angelo looked to his friends for help, but got nothing. "What do you guys think?" he asked. Frankie said, "The longer I live, the less I know." Jimmy shrugged and Nick diverted his eyes.

"He's got his future to plan," Angelo said to Donna.

"I know," she said. She was crying softly now.

"I'm operating a forklift in a warehouse," Johnny replied. "That's not the future I want. After the army I'll use the benefits to get an education."

Angelo surveyed the store. Then he said sadly, "I guess I didn't give you much of a start in life."

"You gave me plenty, Pop. Now I just need you to give me your blessing."

Angelo pulled his son toward him, squeezed him tightly and said, "Please be careful, son."

Jimmy whispered a prayer.

74 Gulf War Syndrome

February 2002

Nick hung a framed excerpt from Lincoln's Second Inaugural Address on the deli wall so he could see it from the table. Lincoln had given the speech on March 4, 1865, just a month before Lee's surrender at Appomattox. By then there was little doubt of the war's eventual outcome, and Lincoln was sharing his vision for the future, unaware that he would be dead in less than six weeks. The excerpt was taken from the last sentence of the speech and read, "*… to care for him who shall have borne the battle, and for his widow, and his orphan…*" To Nick, that line said it all, caring for veterans and their families was a moral responsibility, a responsibility that wasn't being fully met. He'd seen too many cases where legitimate claims fell through the cracks because guys weren't smart enough or persistent enough to deal with an overworked and under funded Veterans Administration.

It usually wasn't long after a war's end before the public would move on, blissfully unaware of the lasting effects on those who fought it. Nick didn't want to believe that Americans or their elected representatives would knowingly turn their backs on those who had sacrificed. More than likely, people just didn't think about it, or assumed that those in charge would take care of things. But too often, those in charge turned their attention elsewhere as memories of the conflict faded. Nick's memory didn't fade.

After years of helping Vietnam veterans, he was on a new mission. Veterans from the '91 Desert Storm war were showing up at the outreach center complaining of chronic chills, sweats, joint and muscle aches, memory loss or intestinal, heart, and respiratory problems. Some blamed the ailments on exposure to Saddam's low-level chemical or biological agents. Others suspected the vaccinations our troops received before deployment to the region, or their exposure to the depleted uranium used in our new anti-tank shells. Whatever the cause, their difficulties were real and the press had labeled the problem Gulf War Syndrome.

Often, the government refused to recognize the syndrome and rejected veterans' claims. Some were told that their ailments were not service related, or that their problems were mental, the delayed effect of combat stress. Nick wasn't a doctor or a scientist and he didn't know what caused the problems vets were experiencing, but he did know gut wrenching stories of rejection. These guys needed services and someone to champion their cause, and if the system wouldn't do it, then he would. So he became an advocate, working with vets one at a time, counseling and helping them fill out forms.

He thought about young Johnny's enlistment. The kid was the closest thing he had to a son, and Nick had been torn between feelings of pride and dread. That was months ago. Now Johnny was in the Persian Gulf, with a force poised to strike Saddam again if he refused to cooperate with U.S. demands. The administration was saying that Saddam had weapons of mass destruction, chemical, biological, maybe even nuclear, and Americans were scared. Nick knew our troops might have to fight, and he worried about what they would face if they did.

75- Telling Anna

April 2002

Frankie found Anna at her usual spot in the kitchen. She gasped when she saw him.

"My God, Frankie, you look terrible. What's wrong?"

They embraced and he let out a deep sob that frightened her. They parted wordlessly and he handed her a letter. Anna opened it gingerly and read.

Dear Frankie,

No one knows better than you that I can make some awfully bad decisions and I know I'm making the worst decision of my life right now. The problem is that I just can't help it.

I've never had a chance to really have fun. From the time I quit high school my back has been against the wall because of the kids. I love them more than anything, but I resent them too. I've missed so much of my life by taking care of them.

I have to live Frankie. I have to see and do things I've missed. I hope you know that, in spite of what I'm doing, I truly love you and always will. You're too good for me. I guess a shrink would say that I'm leaving because I'm afraid to try to live a normal life, surrounded by good people. Maybe he'd be right. All I know is that I have to go.

Somehow you'll have to explain this to the kids. At least I carried them, and that should be something. But you've given them more genuine love in this short time than I have their entire lives. I know you'll be good to them

Frankie, and that somehow you'll think of something to say to them that won't hurt too much.

Love,
Jane

Anna felt faint and sat at the table. Frankie sat next to her.

"When did you get this?"

"I found it when I went home for lunch."

"She's already gone?"

"All of her things are missing. Her closet's empty."

"Oh Frankie," she said, and leaned over to hold him again. His body was shaking. It was agonizing to see him in so much pain.

"Where are the children?" she asked.

"Donna took them to the mall. I haven't told them yet."

"My God, what will you say?"

"I have no idea. But it has to be clear that they'll be safe and cared for. I have to convince them that I won't leave too."

"You know I'll help you any way I can."

"I know," Frankie said.

Part IX
Inner Peace

76- Myers-Foster

October 2004

The sign on the door read DEBORAH MYERS-FOSTER, CHIEF OF STAFF, but after twenty-five years on Capitol Hill, she still had to pinch herself occasionally to confirm it was real. She'd had it all. Four years at Boston College, followed by a Masters in Government Relations from George Washington University, an internship with a rising-star, Midwestern congressman that turned into a permanent job, a marriage to her former Boston College professor, and a set of twin girls, both seniors at Georgetown. All of this had made life awfully good. But serving at the center of power, and being so good at it- that was something else. She'd worked hard to build her career, and was one of the most respected and sought after staffers on the Hill.

She looked at the thick binder on her desk. She'd been filling it with hand written letters from the same person for over five years, but today was a special day. As she added item number one thousand to its contents, she marveled at the author's perseverance. She'd promised herself that she would do something if that number were ever reached. Today it was, and with congressional hearings approaching, the timing was perfect.

The timing was terrible too. The request was unorthodox and everyone, the congressman included, was up to his ears in work. She flipped through the contents. Over the years she had forwarded copies of every letter to the appropriate agency as she received them, along with a brief cover letter. There was no time to do follow-up, but she knew that a congressional letterhead carried weight, and she was hopeful that it did some good. In some truly exceptional cases she'd even picked up the phone. But she had never pushed for the writer's full request. Today was different. With the arrival of entry number one thousand, she had no choice.

She looked at the author's file from the Pentagon. It was quite impressive. In fact, it was dynamite and would make her selling job to the congressman much easier. Gathering her courage, she picked up both documents and headed for the congressman's office. He was the ranking minority member of the House Committee on Veterans Affairs, and she needed a big favor.

77- Christmas at Anna's

December 25, 2004

Anna was greeted with a chorus of Merry Christmases from Frankie and the kids when she opened the door. "Merry Christmas to you," she said happily. "Come inside, it's cold." Frankie and the kids stepped in.

"Hope we're not too early. The kids were eager to get going," Frankie said, giving her a long hug.

"You could never be too early. I'm so glad you came," she said.

"Me too," Frankie replied. "Thanks again."

"Kids, let me take your coats, and then I want you to tell me what you got for Christmas."

Joey took off his coat to reveal a Philadelphia Eagles jersey with the number 5.

"This is my favorite gift," he said.

"My that's beautiful," Anna said.

Joey turned around to reveal the name on the back. "It's a Donovan McNabb shirt," he said proudly.

"I knew that when I saw the number," Anna said. "I'm a big fan."

"I'm going to play football when I get to high school," Joey said.

"You are?" she said, giving Frankie an exaggerated hard stare.

"Don't look at me," Frankie laughed. "The kid's getting big and he wants to play. I had nothing to do with it."

Turning back to Joey she said, "Well, you be careful young man. Football can be dangerous." Then she smiled and added, "But if you're going to play, work hard at it."

"I will Mrs. Francelli," he said brightly.

"And what else did you get?"

"My dad's taking a friend and me to a Sixers game next week. We have court side seats!"

"That should be great!" Anna said. Then she turned to his sister who was waiting patiently for her turn. "Erin, you look so beautiful!" The girl was well groomed. Her hair was pulled back neatly in a ponytail, and she wore a lovely light blue dress.

"Thank you, Mrs. Francelli," she beamed.

"And what about you? What did you get for Christmas?"

"I got a new flute," She gushed.

"A flute?"

"She's been taking flute lessons at school," Frankie said proudly. "Her teacher says she's good."

"That's wonderful," Anna said. "I hope that by the next time you visit you'll be able to play something for us."

"I can play some things already, but I left my flute home," she said.

"Then you'll just have to visit again tomorrow," Anna said.

They all laughed.

"I also got a shopping spree at the mall for clothes," Erin announced.

"Hey, what's with the *spree*?" Frankie teased. "It's a shopping *trip*. There's a difference."

"We'll see," Erin said, winking at Anna.

Frankie looked at Anna and shrugged. "There's no way I can buy her clothes unless she picks them out," he said. "She's fussy."

"Exactly," Erin agreed.

"Where's Sissy?" Frankie said, looking around.

"They're at Tom's mother's house exchanging gifts, but they'll be here in time for dinner."

Anna led them into the kitchen where Mrs. Sweeney was working.

"Hi, Mrs. Sweeney," Frankie said. "Merry Christmas."

"Frankie!" She gave him a squeeze. "Merry Christmas."

"I'm surprised Anna lets you in the kitchen," he said.

"I'm only allowed to make the salad. I'm not cooking anything."

"How do you like the new cabinets?" he asked.

"They're beautiful," she said. "You did a marvelous job."

"Better than beautiful," Anna added. "I'm embarrassed by such a gift."

Frankie had spent two weeks remodeling Anna's kitchen as a Christmas present.

"It's what I do," Frankie said. "But remember, this is my showroom. If a customer wants to see a sample of my work, you have to give a tour."

"I'll do a commercial on cable TV if you like," she smiled. Frankie was pleased to see her looking so happy.

"I still don't think a woman my age should have such a kitchen," she added.

"You'll be using it in good health for years to come," Frankie said.

Mrs. Sweeney made a fuss over the kids. Then Anna announced she had gifts for Joey and Erin and wondered if they'd like them before dinner. They looked at Frankie, who pretended to be thinking about it and then nodded yes.

Anna went to the tree and returned quickly with two packages.

Joey got the newest Playstation and Madden football game, and Erin got a pink ipod. Both were thrilled.

"Anna!" Frankie said in protest. "This is too much."

"Be quiet Scrooge. It's Christmas."

Then Erin gave Anna her gift. It was a photo album filled with shots of the kids. Anna loved it. They looked at the photos together and Erin explained each one. When they were finished, Anna noticed Joey looking at the play station box and said,

"Do you know how to set that up?"

"It's easy," he replied. "My friend has one."

Then why don't the two of you set it up on the TV in the basement and you can play with it until dinner.

"Great," they said, and scurried downstairs.

When they were gone Frankie said, "Anna, you really went overboard."

"Are you kidding Frankie? You gave me a kitchen!"

"But you've been feeding me for forty years!" Frankie protested. "We're not close to being even."

"Still, a woman my age doesn't need such an extravagance."

She smiled briefly, before turning serious. "The children are beautiful, Frankie. You're doing a wonderful job with them."

"Thank you," he said softly. "They've made me very happy."

Then she asked gently, "Hear anything?

"Not a word. I always thought she'd try to contact them, at least at the holidays. But we don't talk about it anymore, and they seem to be okay with it, at least outwardly."

"They certainly look secure," she said.

"And you look content," Frankie said.

She smiled. "I'm thankful for what I have."

Then she changed the subject. "How are you feeling?"

"The doctor says I'm doing good. I'm watching what I eat when I'm not here and I go to the gym three days a week. My test numbers are getting better."

"Wonderful," she said.

"By the way," he said. "Nick and Jimmy send their regards."

She laughed. "I got a nice card from them. I wish they would accept my invitation for dinner."

"You know how awkward they are. They're having a quiet dinner with Angelo and Donna. Donna's a little down with Johnny still in Iraq. The army just extended his stay."

"I pray for his safety every day," she said. "Those explosions. Why don't we have the proper armor on those vehicles? And why do I read that some families are sending their boys flak jackets or bullet-proof vests for Christmas? Why don't they have them already?"

Frankie shook his head.

"Never mind," she said, forcing a smile. "It's Christmas. Why don't you relax, and I'll finish up with dinner before Sissy and Tom come."

Frankie didn't feel like sitting, so he decided to look around. He admired the tree, especially the two hollow Christmas balls that held photos of Sissy and Johnny. Sissy looked to be about ten and was sitting on a new bicycle. Johnny was eight and was wearing his midget football uniform without his helmet. Above the number were the words Bristol Moose. Frankie smiled. He remembered that year. Frankie played for the Hibernians in the same league. It was the only time he could remember that they were opponents.

He noticed a floral arrangement on the coffee table from Ralph and Judy and chuckled. In high school they used to tell people that Ralph sent his girlfriends day-old flowers from the funeral home. Poor Ralph, they used to bust on him unmercifully. Frankie loved the guy, but he still couldn't help but wonder about the flowers.

He moved to the shelf where Anna displayed her favorite Christmas cards. He picked up the first one and looked inside. A note read, "We'll be over again in the spring to wash your windows and clean out your rain spouts. Merry Christmas."

It was signed "Nick and Jimmy."

The next card was one of those preprinted business types with a tasteful holly wreath on the outside. The inside featured a photo of a smiling black couple. The caption above the photo read, "May your home be filled with warmth and peace this holiday season. Below the photo the inscription read:

Johnson Real Estate

Samuel "Mo" Johnson and Yolanda Johnson

Serving the South Oakland Area for 24 years

Frankie read the hand written note. "Yolanda and I hope this card finds you in good health. Remember, if you ever decide to visit sunny California, you'll have a place to stay for as long as you like. Love, Sam and Yolanda."

A card from Angelo read, "I'd love to include 'Anna's Famous Stuffed Olives' as one of my menu offerings. It's a chance for you to make some good money. Best wishes for a wonderful Christmas. Love, Angelo, Donna and Johnny."

Next was a spiritual card from Father Creeden. He wrote:

"Dearest Anna,

I hope you've been well since we last spoke. Sometimes I'm busier in my priestly retirement than I was at St. Therese's. I say daily Mass at two nursing homes and minister to the sick. It's a sobering environment, but I find it rewarding. I hope to be in town for a day during Christmas week and will be sure to visit. You are in my thoughts and prayers every day. Please give my love to everyone.

Fondly,

Father Creeden."

Frankie smiled. He thought of Father Creeden a lot and hoped to see him when he visited.

The last card set him back a little. It was from Allison and included a photo of her family. Frankie hadn't seen her in years. Her hair was ash blond now, and was cut stylishly short. It was a dramatic change from her younger days, but she looked great. A guy who must have been her husband was standing next to her. Their adult children and their spouses were in the photo too, and Allison held an infant dressed in a Santa suit.

Allison's note read, "Mrs. Francelli, I so enjoyed your last letter. I'll write as soon as the Christmas rush is over. This will be our first Christmas with our new grandchild. You can imagine our excitement. Best wishes for a wonderful and healthy Christmas.

All my love,

Allison."

Frankie didn't hear Anna walk up behind him. "That's the card that touched me the most," she said softly. He turned to face her and saw that her eyes were filling up. "The thought that it could be my Johnny standing there, surrounded by his family." She shook her head. "Sometimes it hurts too much."

Frankie held her tightly and gently rocked her.

"You're the strongest person I now," he whispered.

"That's funny," Anna said as they parted. "I was thinking that about you."

"Maybe we're both a couple of fakers," he said.

"Then good for us. We've done a pretty good job of it." She found a tissue and wiped her eyes. "I loved him so much," she said, still fighting the tears. "It was such a loss. I hate sending these boys off to war. " Then she forced another smile. "I know it doesn't look it, but I'm truly happy." She gestured to the shelf. The people who sent these cards make me happy. Knowing Sam Johnson is alive because of Johnny makes me happy. And seeing you with Joey and Erin makes me especially happy. Thanks for being here all of these years."

Frankie nodded. "I have something interesting for you."

"Not another gift," she said. "The kitchen…"

"Nothing like that," Frankie said.

"Nick wanted me to show you this. He said it's his gift to you." He handed her an envelope. The return address read Washington, D.C.

78- The Next Pilgrimage

February 2005

The gang met at the deli at five in the morning and Pete the Mailman and Donna were there to see them off. "I have to admit, you guys could pose for GQ today," Donna said as she finished tying the knot on Nick's tie. "Jimmy, your trim body was made to wear suits. You look great!"

Jimmy blushed.

"Hey, what about my body?" Frankie joked.

"You're living proof of what a good tailor can do," she said smiling. "That suit looks good on you, the tie too."

"You picked it out," Frankie said.

"She picked everything out," Angelo said, squeezing her waist and giving her a kiss.

"What time are you guys leaving?" Pete asked, checking his watch.

"Ralph should be here at 5:15," Frankie said.

Jimmy was excited. "I feel like we're in the locker room before a big game. Remember when Coach Lukins used to say, 'suit up? Well, we're suited up!" Jimmy said. "Except only one person's playing." It got quiet for a minute. Then Donna looked at Nick and asked him if he was nervous.

"No," Nick said

"No?" Donna seemed surprised. "A one word answer from Nick? Is that it?"

"That's it."

Donna wanted to see some of the smiling, wisecracking Nick. "It's okay to be nervous," she said. "Is that why you're so quiet?"

Angelo laughed. "You don't understand, Donna. That's his game face. He never talked in the locker room before a game. He just sat there and thought about his job, but when the game started he took charge. Trust me, Nick's fine. Right, Nick?"

Nick nodded.

Ralph pulled up with the limo right on time, and Donna and Pete the Mailman walked them to the curb. It was still dark, but the limo glistened in the reflection from the deli's lights. "We should have taken these wheels to Washington in '63," Jimmy gushed. "Does this thing have a bar?"

Frankie punched him on the arm. "Kidding!" Jimmy said.

Nick handed Pete the Mailman another letter. "Can you take care of this for me?"

"I've done it a thousand times," Pete said proudly.

Frankie looked surprised. "Another letter? You've done enough, Nick."

"This one's different. It's for Trish."

When they were in the limo Frankie said, "Don't forget, we've got a stop to make before we leave town."

"I'm on it," Ralph said.

They found Anna waiting on the porch, sitting in the darkness, bundled against the cold January morning. Sissy had driven in from Langhorne to see them off too.

"You guys wait here," Nick said.

Anna, Sissy, and Nick met briefly, and Anna did most of the talking, while Nick nodded. Then they embraced and Nick limped-trotted back to the limo.

"What a lady," Nick said when he got back in.

"This is important to her," Frankie said.

As they pulled away from the curb, Frankie saw the Grundy clock in the distance. It's illuminated clock face looked even more imposing in the morning darkness. Ralph must have seen it too. "It's five-thirty," he said. "I'll have you guys in DC by half past eight."

"Hope we don't get lost like the last time," Jimmy said.

"Damn, Jimmy!" Angelo said. "That was over forty years ago!"

"Well it seems like yesterday," Jimmy said sheepishly. "And I don't want to get lost."

"We're not getting lost," Ralph said. "This baby has GPS."

"That's nice," Jimmy said. "Does it have a bar?"

Frankie punched him on the arm again.

Ralph put on a Sinatra CD and lowered the volume. Soon Frankie and Angelo were asleep. As dawn began to break, Jimmy said, "Hey, Nick, I'm curious. What did you say to Trish in the letter?"

"I told her what we were doing today and thanked her for everything."

"You liked those long talks you used to have with her. I could tell."

"She helped me a lot."

Jimmy thought for a while. "What's the most important thing she ever told you?"

Nick didn't have to think. "She said that some day I 'd have to stop hiding behind whatever it was I was hiding behind and find some purpose in life."

"Think it helps to find a purpose?"

"I think so," Nick said.

"It helps," Frankie interjected without opening his eyes. "Trust me. It really helps."

79- To Have Laid Such a Sacrifice...

Security was tight in post 9-11 Washington, with concrete barriers restricting the flow of traffic to the Capitol area. The limo was funneled into a checkpoint, where it was stopped by police officers that questioned Ralph, studied his passengers and searched the trunk and underbody. Angelo understood the procedures, but quietly cursed the terrorists who had made them necessary.

The hearings were scheduled for 10:00 at the Cannon House Office Building, across the street from the Capitol, and Nick served as tour guide. "The building is named for 'Uncle Joe' Cannon, Speaker of the House during the Teddy Roosevelt days," he said. "He was a tough son of a gun, but he knew how to get things done." Jimmy soaked up the information.

Debbie had arranged for their parking, and they got to the building easily. They entered the lobby and found Debbie waiting for them.

"Sergeant Hardings?" she said, reaching out to shake hands.

"Nick," he said, surprised to be recognized.

"How did you know?"

She smiled and tapped the folder under her arm. "Military records. Your photo."

Nick nodded. This woman was obviously important.

"Besides," she added, "after one thousand letters I feel as though I know you."

Nick thought back to the day Anna had suggested that Nick write to Debbie. In her correspondence with Allison over the years, Anna had learned that Allison's college roommate had a big job in Washington with the Veterans Affairs Committee. One thing led to another, and Nick started writing. Now, the letters had gotten him to Washington. Nick introduced the rest of the guys and Frankie asked, "How's Allison? Hear from her?"

"Heavens yes," Debbie said. "We talk all the time and do a girls' weekend twice a year. She just became a grandmother, a young grandmother I should add. She's very happy."

Frankie gave half a smile and Debbie could see that it was painful.

"I can tell you that in spite of her happiness, there is still a very large part in her heart reserved for Johnny, and there always will be," she added.

No one responded. She looked at each of them and added, "As for me, I never met Johnny, but what happened to him and Allison had a personal effect on me. He represents a period of my past that shaped who I am and my beliefs. That's why we're here today."

"Thanks for doing this," Nick said.

She laughed. "Thanks for asking a thousand times!" She checked her watch. "Let's go. The Under Secretary of the Veterans Benefits Administration is testifying later and the hearing room will be packed. Plus there are kids here on a class trip."

She walked like a person accustomed to a busy schedule, until she noticed Nick struggling to keep up. "I'm sorry," she said, slowing her pace. "People in Washington are always in a rush. Actually, we have plenty of time."

"I told you guys I'd get you here early," Ralph said.

"Speaking of time," Debbie said to Nick. "Once the congressman finishes his introduction, you will have exactly ten minutes. Congress operates under strict rules when it comes to time, so be sure to make your most important points first."

Ralph asked Nick if he had his speech with him.

"He doesn't have to," Angelo said. "It's in his head."

"No it's not," Jimmy said. "It's in his heart. Right, Nick? It's in your heart. That's what you said."

Nick nodded. He had his game face on.

When they entered the hearing room Frankie was taken back by what he saw. It was larger than expected. Visitor passes ensured everyone a seat, but the room was packed. A cloth covered witness table with microphones faced the elevated desks where the congressmen would sit. Between them were reporters, photographers, and cameramen.

"Like I said," Debbie whispered, "This will be a busy day. You're first on the agenda, kind of a fluffy warm-up for the undersecretary, who will speak later. Don't be offended if some of the congressmen seem preoccupied. They have a full day ahead of them."

"Thanks," Nick said.

She turned to Frankie and the guys. "Your seats are here. I'll be taking Nick to his place down in front."

They looked at Nick. It was still hard to believe that he would soon be offering testimony before the Veterans' Affairs Committee of the United States House of Representatives.

"Go get 'em," Frankie said.

"Good luck," Ralph added, patting him on the back.

Angelo shook his hand without saying anything.

Jimmy was last. He tapped Nick's heart with his fingertips and said, "You tell 'em real good."

"I'll try," Nick said. Then he gave him a bear hug. When they broke, Debbie led him away.

Frankie and the others found their seats in the back. Frankie entered the row first and ended up next to the school kids. They looked like they were in junior high, seventh or eighth grade maybe. The kid next to him was at the far end from his teacher, so he decided to make Frankie his source of information.

"Are you a congressman?"

Frankie laughed. "No," he said. "I'm just a visitor."

"Me too," the kid said. "We're on a class trip."

"Great," Frankie said. He hoped the kid wouldn't talk the whole time. The committee entered the room and the congressmen took their seats.

Frankie noticed that Nick was already seated at the witness table with Debbie next to him.

The chairman called the hearing to order and stated its purpose was to take testimony relative to funding for the next round of Veterans' benefits. Then he yielded to Debbie's boss for comments.

"Thank you, Mr. Chairman. I would first like to offer my appreciation to the committee for allocating the time for my guest, former Sergeant Nick Hardings, to speak. He is an exceptional American."

Most of the media representatives remained idle as the congressman spoke. They knew Nick's testimony was just a courtesy thing, a warm up for the testimony of the undersecretary. The congressman continued.

"In 1967, Sergeant Hardings was part of a four-man Green Beret team that took part in a covert mission in North Vietnam. Army intelligence had reported that a recently downed pilot was being held in a village just above the DMZ. Sergeant Hardings and his team were sent to confirm the reports and, if possible, rescue the pilot from his captors before they could transport him to a secure POW camp. The dangers of such a mission were obvious, and all members of the team had volunteered. To avoid detection, they traveled over ten miles on foot until they came upon the village. Of course their plan was based upon total surprise. While two Green Berets set off diversionary explosions from the far side of the village, Sergeant Hardings and the fourth team member, a Corporal Mitchell, infiltrated the camp and executed the rescue. However, the rescued pilot's injuries left him unable to walk, and it was necessary for Sergeant Hardings to carry him from the camp while Corporal Mitchell provided additional cover fire. They reached the rendezvous point and waited. The two men who had provided the initial cover returned, but Corporal Mitchell did not.

"Sergeant Hardings ordered the other team members to proceed south with the pilot while he returned to the village area alone in search of Mitchell. Hardings hid for two days, surveying the village, during which time he

observed that Mitchell was alive, although wounded and now a captive himself. He also noted that their earlier raid had inflicted heavy causalities on the enemy. Incredibly, on the third night, Sergeant Nick Hardings reentered the village, killing two guards without firing a shot, and carried his fellow Green Beret south toward safety. They found a cave and hid there while Sergeant Hardings scavenged for food and treated Corporal Mitchell's leg wound. On the fourth day, an enemy patrol found them. Sergeant Hardings engaged them in a firefight and recorded four more kills before suffering a serious neck wound that left him unconscious. He and Mitchell were captured and eventually ended up in a POW camp in Hanoi, where Hardings spent the duration of the war."

By now the press had decided this was no typical fluff story. Reporters had flipped open their notebooks and cameras were rolling.

"Mitchell died in captivity, but not before sharing Hardings' story with his fellow POWs. Hardings was released with the other POWs and spent more than a year at Walter Reed, recuperating from injuries and ailments sustained while he was held captive.

"For his actions Sergeant Hardings was awarded the Army Distinguished Service Cross, for extraordinary valor in the face of the enemy. I quote, 'For actions so extraordinary so as to distinguish him from other men.'

"After his recuperation, he dedicated his time to serving as an unofficial advocate for veterans, first from Vietnam, then from Desert Storm and I suspect he will continue for those engaged in Operation Enduring Freedom. It is my honor to introduce to you an extraordinary American of uncommon valor and dedication, former Special Forces Sergeant, Nick Hardings."

The room erupted with applause, and the chairman allowed it. The boy next to Frankie stopped fiddling with his jacket zipper long enough to join in.

Frankie thought about Nick's old weather report days and wondered how he would react with the C-Span cameras pointed directly at him. He didn't have to wonder long.

"*Thank you, Congressman,*" he said in a booming voice. "*And thank you for mentioning Corporal Mitchell, who was the real hero in that story. I want to thank the committee for the privilege of speaking with you today on such an important topic.*

"*Let me begin by apologizing, because I have nothing new to offer. Everything I will say today, you have already heard. In fact, many of you have said it yourselves. They are sentiments that all good Americans share. But sadly, our actions don't always match our good intentions and we fail our veterans. We sometimes fail them in the field, and we frequently fail them at home. In fact, our veterans often fight two wars, the war they fight in their country's behalf and the war they fight at home to receive the assistance they deserve.*"

He reached for the binder in front of Debbie. "*This book contains the handwritten stories of one thousand veterans. Over the years I've sat across a table from them and listened to their problems one by one. These are men who couldn't handle the bureaucracy, men who fell through the cracks, men who never recovered emotionally from what they had to endure, who lacked a support system to help see them through.*

"*Let me tell you about the women I've sat across from. War widows, who were unable to work because their children were too young, families that were destitute because their soldier husband's life insurance policies were so pitifully small. I've sat across from mothers who were facing eviction from their apartments just months after their soldier husbands had died. I know we've made strides in these areas recently, but it took shamefully long and the aid is still shamefully small.*"

The reporters had to write feverishly once they realized there were no advance press copies of Nick's speech because he wasn't speaking from prepared notes.

"…*I know in your hearts you want to help them. I know the citizens of this great country would want to help them if they clearly understood what was happening. I know you would like to quote me statistics about your annual increases in allocations for veterans. I know they have improved. But I'm here to tell you that it's not enough. Not nearly enough.*

"*We live in an age of political divisions. Democrats, Republicans, liberals, conservatives, it seems we attempt to turn each issue into winning and losing sides, to take credit for successes and ascribe blame for failures. I'm here to say that there should be no distinctions, no party positions when it comes to aiding our veterans. There can be only one position and that is that we will do whatever it takes, regardless of the cost, to care for those who defend our freedom, in both popular and unpopular wars.*

"*I submit to you that each time we send troops into battle, the entire country should feel it. Not just the men and women who are going, not just the children and spouses they leave behind, not just their parents, but the entire country. It is repulsive to me that we continue to live our lives undisturbed, while our young people are in battle and then we "consider," and I stress the word "consider," the manner in which we will care for them upon their return. I find it repulsive that we have to search for funding later to address their needs. That the Veterans' Benefits committee has to hope, and I stress hope, that this committee will support their requests and then this committee has to hope, and again I stress hope, that the full Congress will support it if it asks for more. I consider the adequate caring for veterans as a moral imperative that is not optional.*"

Again the room applauded.

"In fact, I'd like to ask for a commitment from this Congress that any declaration or resolution that sends troops into battle, must be accompanied by a requirement that a corresponding veterans' allocation accompany it. Let me be clear. I'm not only speaking of funding for the equipment and materials they will need to fight. I'm speaking of the funding they will need to heal."

There was another round of applause, and the young boy, long since distracted, turned to Frankie and said, "What war was he a hero in?"
"Vietnam," Frankie said.
"Did you fight in the Vietnam war too?"
"No, son," Frankie said softly. "I missed it."
Hearing the exchange, Angelo leaned in to Frankie and said, "Like hell you did."

The End.

About the Author

Bill Pezza was born in Manhattan and has lived in Bristol, Pennsylvania, most of his life. He has taught American History and developed curriculum in the Lower Moreland Township School District for almost four decades, specializing in interdisciplinary studies and incorporating oral, grass roots history into his work. Beyond the classroom he has enjoyed extensive experience on all levels of government. He and his wife Karen have three adult children, Leighann, Bill, and Greg. Bill can be contacted at bpezza@comcast.net

Printed in the United States
89349LV00004B/1-63/A